FIRST TIME
WITH A
HIGHLANDER

GWYN
CREADY

Published by Sourcebooks Casablanca, an imprint of Sourcebooks,
Inc.
P.O. Box 4410, Naperville, Illinois 60567–4410
(630) 961–3900
Fax: (630) 961–2168
www.sourcebooks.com

Printed and bound in Canada.
MBP 10 9 8 7 6 5 4 3 2 1

*For Teri. Thank you for a lifetime of laughter
and support. Your father said it best: "Now
that's what I call a friendship."*

One

The Hollow Crown Inn, Edinburgh, 1706

"WHAT IF ONE COULD PIECE TOGETHER A PERFECT MAN the way Abby's dressmaker has pieced together the perfect gown?" mused Serafina Fallon, gazing appreciatively on the neatly pinned amethyst silk with soon-to-be-beaded sleeves her friend Abby Kerr modeled before the mirror. Serafina remembered a time when she had not regarded the possibilities of the masculine sex with quite so much cynicism. If her former fiancé, Edward, had been a gown, he would have been a cheap printed cotton, finished to look like Oriental satin—very much like the gowns Serafina's reduced circumstances forced her wear—but betraying its inferiority within the first few wearings.

Undine appraised the half-completed dress with her knowing fortune-teller's gaze and took a generous sip of the Kerr whiskey. "If we could, my friends, what sort of man would we piece together?"

Abby, who wore a veneer of solemnity in public to earn the respect of the clansmen she led, could not subdue her natural vivacity in private. "Start with strong arms," she said, quirking her brow.

Undine smiled. "And a mind nurtured by experience and curiosity."

"Add a sense of humor that makes his eyes twinkle," Abby said, "and a pair of calves that do the same for mine."

Undine laughed and filled Serafina's glass.

"You two are scandalous," Serafina said, trying without success to stifle her own smile. In truth, she was quite glad to have been invited to share in the wonderful friendship these two women had. She had grown up on a ship, with no sisters or brothers, and as an adult had only a few friends, most of who had cut her from their circle when she'd begun her ill-fated liaison. But even at the best of times, her friends had never drunk whiskey and discussed the relative merits of male attributes. This was eye-opening.

"Ooh, and fields of copper hair!" Abby cried. "'Tis rather like wrapping your arms around a flesh-and-blood bonfire."

Clan Kerr's steward, Duncan MacHarg, the dashing and devoted man who had recently won Abby's heart, had hair the color of newly minted pennies, and the women dissolved into peals of laughter.

The owner of the bonfire in question opened the door. A silence so complete crashed down on the room, Serafina could hear the words of the song the brewer sang as he stacked kegs on his wagon in the busy Edinburgh street a block away.

Duncan narrowed his eyes. He was as canny as he was handsome, so it did not take much observation of the bitten lips, downcast gazes, and pink faces to deduce the general nature of the conversation he'd interrupted.

Patches of bright rose climbed up his neck—the curse of being a redhead, a state for which Serafina had much sympathy, being possessed of similarly colored hair herself.

"*Mmphf.*" He backed out, re-closing the door with a disapproving *click*.

The women broke out in renewed giggles.

Abby said, "There is at least one benefit to falling in love with one's steward. One never minds the long hours spent reviewing the balance sheet."

Serafina gazed in admiration at the gleaming fabric that fell from Abby's waist, held together with pins and tacking thread. "Is that to be your wedding dress?" she asked.

Abby's face lost a bit of its joviality. "The clansmen have just begun to accept me as their chieftess. 'Twould be unwise to introduce such a change now, I think."

Serafina knew Abby put the needs of her people above all else, but she also thought it must hurt Duncan's pride to have to keep the relationship secret.

Undine met Serafina's eye. "What about you? You've contributed nothing to our ideal man. What would you desire?"

"*Och,*" she said, flushing, "dinna ask me. I've proven to be quite unwise in my choices."

Abby laid her hand on Serafina's shoulder. "Making mistakes is the only way to learn, ye ken? Look at me. I'm the wisest woman in Scotland."

Serafina smiled.

"Come now," Abby said. "Where would we begin in a man for Serafina? A Scotsman, of course—no proper Scotswoman could want anything else."

Undine, an Englishwoman, rolled her eyes.

"A Scotsman would be good," Serafina said, nodding. Edward had been English, and long before she'd begun to feel like she'd betrayed herself by falling in love with him, she'd felt a bit like she'd betrayed her country.

"*And…?*"

Serafina thought of Edward's lean waist, golden hair, and finely cut features. When she'd met him, she'd thought him a perfect Adonis. Had she only remembered then that the Adonis of mythology had two sides to him—the attentive lover for whom the goddesses pined and the narcissistic man whose happiness depended upon capturing the attention of every woman he met.

"Shoulders," Serafina said boldly, naming the feature of Edward's that had most disappointed her.

"Shoulders, is it?" Abby said. "How do you like them?"

"Large and labyrinthine. All hollows and girders—as if a warm coat of flesh had been laid over the most carefully sculpted bones. Shoulders upon which I could rest my head as easily as be tossed, whole body, like a keg of gunpowder. And with the scent of surf on them."

Abby ducked her chin in approval. "I'm glad we didn't ask about eyes."

Undine swirled the whiskey in her glass. "And his chest?"

"Two planes of burnished gold."

"Mouth?"

"Generous when it needs to be," Serafina said, "demanding when it doesn't."

Abby looked at Undine. "I don't have the courage to ask any more."

Undine said, "Wisps of smoke are rising from my drink. I think you may be in need of my special marigold tisane, Serafina. I usually recommend it for women whose husbands have lost the spark of virility, but in this case…"

"Does it restore their marital happiness?"

"Certainly the wife's. Once the tisane has been steeped in alcohol—I recommend Abby's fine Kerr whiskey—it brings on what one might call a prolonged fever dream."

Abby said, "This is the reason why we never let Undine pour the whiskey."

Undine put down her glass and leaned forward, frivolity gone. "Serafina, I'm sorry my business in the borderlands and again here in Edinburgh has kept me from addressing your issue. I know we've reached the point where we can delay no further."

Serafina's eyes widened. She had told no one of the possibility of the ship's arrival. She had only heard about it herself yesterday, when their traveling party had arrived in Edinburgh after a two-day ride from Kerr Castle.

"You seek a man," Undine said. "I can tell that from your face. But what sort of man do you seek?"

"'Tis not the man of shoulders and burnished gold," Serafina said, firmly pushing such whimsy aside. "The only man I seek now is the one who will help ensure my small inheritance is returned to me."

"And what sort of a man is that?"

"To begin with, a man both brave and true."

Undine stretched her feet toward the fire and sighed. "A rare creature, don't you think?"

"Will Duncan do?" Abby said.

Serafina flushed. "Oh, Abby, I need him for a night—"

"Duncan will *not* do."

"—and he must resemble Edward."

Her friends' eyes narrowed.

"Why?" Undine asked carefully.

Serafina bit her lip. "I'd rather not say. 'Tis only to protect you," she added quickly, seeing their faces.

"Keeping part of your mission from me is a risk," Undine said. "I can help, but my help is apt to be less than perfect."

"'Tis a risk I accept."

Undine dug in her pocket and withdrew two twists of the distinctive orange paper in which she dispensed her herbs. "I have crafted a concoction I believe will bring you what you seek—a man brave and true, aye, but also capable of deceit, susceptible to a woman's charms, and willing to hold his tongue."

Abby's eyes widened. "Is that true?" she said to Serafina.

Serafina shifted, shocked at the accuracy of Undine's description. "Well…aye."

"I have to leave now for an appointment in Argyle Square," Undine said, putting the herbs on the table, "but when I return, we'll figure out the best way to help you."

"But dinner is on the way," Abby said. "And you didn't eat this morning."

Undine held up an allaying hand. "I will eat, I

promise. Serafina, while I'm away, pray consider whether secrecy is the best route and whether the man I described is truly the sort of man with whom you wish to consort."

The heavy silence that followed was broken by Abby, who announced her intention of tracking down the seamstress. Serafina followed her friends from the room, feeling as if she must have betrayed them.

From down the hall, Duncan caught her eye and gestured for her to remain behind. Abby and Undine descended the stairs into the inn's public rooms, and Serafina approached him.

"I did as you wished," he said in a low voice. "And the dockmaster confirmed the ship is arriving, though it's sooner than you were expecting."

"When?"

"Tonight."

"Tonight!" Had Undine left? She needed her help right away. "Thank you, Duncan. I…well, you can imagine the likelihood of a woman's inquiries being answered."

"I should never think of allowing a woman to walk the docks of Leith, no matter how strong the likelihood was." He bowed chivalrously. "What do you intend to do with the information, if I may ask?"

"The cargo the ship contains belongs to me—well, some of it in any case."

"That's not what the dockmaster said. Nor is it an answer to my question."

Her cheeks warmed. Why had she thought he would limit his inquiries to the single question she had asked him to answer? "The cargo's not in my name," she admitted. "But 'tis mine, nonetheless. My father was a sea merchant and before that a sea captain. As his only child, I inherited his business when he died. As you know, I fell in love and behaved foolishly. And part of my foolishness was allowing my fiancé to gain control over the business. He bankrupted it, or nearly so, the blackguard. That cargo is all that remains, and I intend to have it."

Her words had been more passionate than she'd intended, and Duncan led her farther away from the staircase. He was an imposing man, over six feet tall, and not one to suffer fools with patience.

"I'm not without sympathy," he whispered. "But stealing, however moral, is incontrovertibly illegal, and Abby will have me flogged if she thinks I contributed in some way to you ending up in prison. Frankly, though, I'm far more concerned about Edward and whoever his partners might be. Investors are an uncompromising bunch, as are the men who work for them, especially in Edinburgh. If you cheat them out of what they consider to be theirs, they'll nae go easy on ye because you're a woman. The docks are nae place for mischief."

She stood straighter. "I'm not that much of a fool. I'll have the help of a man who can—"

"What man?" His eyes narrowed into slits.

"He's a friend of the family," she said, lying, "and well versed in the ways of the sea trade." She had no wish to implicate Abby and Undine in her scheme. If they wished to tell Duncan about the help they were giving her, they could.

"A friend of the family?"

"Aye," she said, attempting not to wilt under the heat of the gaze. "You know I'm from Edinburgh. I have a considerable number of friends here."

"I have nae doubt. Well, I'd like to meet him. Will you be bringing him here?"

"I-I…can do that."

"Do."

"Duncan, my money is nearly gone. Abby is kind, but I dinna wish to be dependent upon her to live. I dinna have your skills or Undine's powers or Abby's position. That cargo is my last hope."

"You will never be penniless. Abby needs a secretary, but if you somehow felt work was beneath you—"

"I'm penniless, Duncan, and pragmatic. No work is beneath me. But if there's a chance I can get back the money that was mine, I insist on the right to try."

He chewed the side of his cheek but seemed to recognize he faced an immovable force. "You will bring the man to me though, aye? Abby and I are dining with the bankers this evening, but we should be back before eleven."

"I will." She hated to lie, but she had barely enough time to carry out her plan as it was, let alone give Duncan the right to approve the players. She hoped she could still catch Undine's carriage. She waited a beat longer, then turned.

"One more thing," he said.

She turned back, hiding her impatience.

He looked down his long nose at her. "Use your head, aye?"

Using her head was not as easy as she might have wished. Undine and the carriage were gone. The ostler in the inn's stables knew nothing concerning her destination. Without Undine's spell, Serafina would have to hire someone on her own. She much preferred a man who had been summoned out of the Edinburgh crowds specifically to meet her needs. She had no idea how Undine's magic worked, but work it did. Duncan was sterling proof of that.

The cobbles of the Royal Mile stretched southward toward Leith and the sea, and she could smell the briny scent even if she couldn't see the water. Employing someone to pretend to be Edward offered risk enough without the added uncertainty of using a person of questionable skills and trustworthiness, but what choice did she have?

She sighed. *If I'm going to hire someone*, she thought, *I'd better hurry*. With a fortifying shake, she pelted into the inn, up the stairs, and into the sitting room the traveling party shared. She'd need to change her clothes and gather what little money she had—

A flash of orange caught her eye.

The herbs lay on the table, abandoned. Serafina's foot tapped involuntarily. What had Undine said? Mix it with alcohol? But these were Undine's herbs, not hers. It was one thing to steal cargo, quite another to take advantage of a friend's kindness.

She wandered to a chair and sat down, gazing at the twists of paper. Undine had said quite clearly the herbs were for her. She'd mixed them *for her*. Serafina shifted. The onion-shaped Kerr whiskey decanter sat uncorked on the table.

With a sigh, she reached for the papers and slowly undid the ends. She would have to add this to her ever-growing list of sins.

Two

HIS SINS, IN NO PARTICULAR ORDER:

Drunkenness. Would that be classified under Gluttony or Sloth? Gerard Innes was not a religious man, but he felt the amount of twenty-five-year-old Macallan single malt he'd consumed in the last hour probably qualified him for both.

Pride. No question. He had given a killer presentation today, which was not in itself out of the ordinary, but it had won Piper Cornish the Highland Distilleries account, their largest client ever.

Greed. He considered this thoughtfully and rejected it. He would accept his sins without complaint, but love of money was not one of them. What drove him to succeed was the work, the look in his clients' eyes when they recognized his unadorned brilliance, and the power to move people to act.

A partygoer dressed as Cinderella brushed by him, her blue skirts brushing suggestively over his feet.

He had come straight from the client's boardroom, which meant he was dressed only as himself. Though the room's darkness made it hard to see specifics, she gave off an altogether satisfying sense of being plump, blond, and agreeable.

"Who are you supposed to be?" she asked, the beauty mark she had drawn on her cheek disappearing into a bottomless dimple. "Adonis?"

Lust. He had forgotten Lust.

"I would have to be considerably more undressed for that, would I not?" He sipped the Macallan. Above their heads, the swimmers in the hotel's see-through pool made their way across the glittering turquoise water. Half the women were topless, and two of those were bedmates of Gerard's from previous parties. He hoped neither of them spotted him. He was, as always, in search of new adventures.

A lovely pale brow lifted. "Maybe you just need a little help getting into costume?"

"Do you work for Piper Cornish?" he asked, leaning closer. She smelled faintly of licorice and he wondered if she would taste of it as well. "I don't think I've seen you around."

"No. Hunter, Hammond, and Hayes. I'm the manager of training there."

Not a colleague and not a client. *Just the way I like it.*

"You're Gerard Innes, aren't you?" she said.

"I am."

"This pool is like something out of a science-fiction fantasy. Do people even realize how amazing it is to be watching people swim over your head?"

Gerard laughed. "Probably not."

A waiter passed and she squealed. On his platter stood an army of tiny pink confections.

"Look!" she cried, snagging two and dropping one into his hand. "It's a little gift box! And yours is a tiny rose!"

The pleasure on her face made him smile. "*Tiny* being the key word, I guess." He popped his in his mouth. "A bit sparing though, don't you think?"

"It's like eating joy." She swallowed and touched the thumb holding the Macallan. "May I?"

He wasn't sure what he was giving permission for, but it didn't really matter. He was not the sort of man who said no. She took the whiskey and drank.

"Whoa!" She coughed a few charming coughs. "That's a *big* drink."

"Aye," he said in his grandmother's Highland burr. "And a wee bit rough."

Message received, she gave him a loopy smile. "Now you taste mine."

Her cup was filled with something green. He took a long sip. Absinthe. "Now that's a dangerous drink."

"I like dangerous."

He thought of the bottle upstairs. What was the point of waiting? It seemed the perfect start to an enchanting night.

"Would you care to adjourn to my suite?" he said. "I have something there I think you might enjoy."

"Oh, do you now?"

When they reached the bright lights of the lobby, it was clear Cinderella was not at all ready for the ball. She had evidently begun her drinking many hours earlier and could barely stay upright as the elevator made its ascent. When she began to slip down the wall, Gerard picked her up and tucked her over his shoulder.

He laid her in his bed, turned out the light, and heaved a long sigh. Willing she might be, but the rules of the game required her to possess the ability to move and assent.

Ah, well. Needn't detract from the glory of the day. And there are far worse things than sleeping next to a pretty woman.

The ancient, squat bottle on the nightstand seemed to call his name. It had come from the personal collection of the chairman of Piper Cornish. A bottle of whiskey from one of the oldest crates ever sold at auction. Over three hundred years old and worth thousands of dollars, it was a thank-you for his work that day. If it lived up to its reputation, it would make the twenty-five-year-old Macallan seem like a tepid glass of lemonade in comparison.

He grabbed a glass hanging upside down over the top of the water pitcher and plunked it down on the nightstand. Then he grabbed the whiskey. The aged cork slid out with a satisfying, soft *pop*. Three centuries of slow evaporation had reduced the contents to little more than half. He closed his eyes and brought the bottle to his nose, taking in the smell of green, loamy hills as well as the grittier scents of smoke and sea air. He'd been to Scotland once with his grandmother, as a child, and the experience had never left him. The bottle's label, if there had ever been one, was long gone, but even in the glow of light from outside his window, he could make out the word stamped into the glass: Kerr.

He poured himself an amount worthy of the work he had done, lifted the glass in a private toast, and drank.

Three

DUNCAN HAD RETURNED TO THE INN CONSIDERABLY later and drunker than he had wished the night before. Their banker's port had been watered down with cheap wine, and the man had not only refused to discuss more favorable terms on the loan for the canal, but he had also taken it upon himself to lecture Duncan on the ways he might pinch pennies on it, including the replacement of concrete with cheap stone and the use of a lock construction business owned by the banker's brother-in-law. All in all, the evening had left Duncan with a throbbing head, a roiling gut, and the certainty of having wasted four hours. He called for a pot of hot coffee, and as he settled into a chair, the reflection of the doors of Undine's and Serafina's bedchambers in the long cheval mirror in the corner reminded him he still had Serafina's cargo mess to untangle. *Och.* There were times he missed the twenty-first century more than others, and this was one of them.

He'd been yanked out of his own time like an unwilling rabbit out of a magician's hat. Espresso

machines, smartphones, V-8 engines, his job on
Wall Street—all of them lost to him when Abby
had decided she needed a strong arm and scattered
Undine's powerful herbs across the field of a battle.
Of course, there were *some* benefits, he admitted,
thinking of Abby's warm body tucked against him
this morning and the scent of gardenias that rose
from her hair. But it had taken him a long time and
a lot of hard work to get over the ego-crushing blow
of waking up in a world where the only things that
counted were the size of your sword and the fortune
of your father.

The hardest thing for him now was not having a
single person with whom he could reminisce—no
rehashes of the latest Manchester United game, no
head shaking about the prime minister or the president.
Only Abby and Undine knew of his past—discretion
was important in a world where they wouldn't stop
burning witches for another half century—and they
talked to him about the life he'd left. But talking
didn't mean they'd laugh when he did his imitation
of Obi-Wan Kenobi or hiss when he pretended Lance
Armstrong had gotten a raw deal.

He opened his sporran and pulled out the broadsheet that had been stuffed in his hand last night as
he and Abby made their way home along the Mile.
Broadsheets would never take the place of online
access to the *Times* as far as he was concerned, but he
was counting on the inevitable attacks on the English
and Queen Anne to enliven his morning. Some
things, at least, were timeless.

☙❧

Gerard opened his eyes and immediately shut them. He explored his psyche tenuously. He was not hungover—surprising given the amount he'd drunk. Instead, he felt as if he'd slept a deep and boundless sleep that had lasted not just the night but the day, the week, and quite possibly the rest of the fiscal year. In his head, he heard the voice of his first boss, a Frenchman named Brisbois, who had introduced Gerard to the pleasures of old single malts. "*Gerard,*" he'd said, giving the name its Gallic due, "*you cannot rush the moment. Good whiskey is like a woman of the world. She opens her robe slowly.*" Even with his eyes closed, he could tell Cinderella was still there, breathing heavily beside him. He was naked, however, and how he got that way gave him a moment of concern.

Had she returned from the land of Nod clearheaded enough to make love?

Maybe. It would certainly explain the liquidity of his legs and the vague but undeniable sense of self-congratulation bubbling through him. Though if they had made love, why didn't he remember? The bits of the night he could capture, like a boy gamboling after lightning bugs, seemed rather to involve a different sort of woman—fiery and imperious rather than blond and accommodating—Catwoman, not Cinderella.

Still half-asleep, he brought the back of his hand to his nose, and there she was, the woman he remembered. Not licorice, nor anything remotely sweet. Instead, he smelled juniper and rosemary and the peat of the Kerr whiskey. His cock thickened in Pavlovian accord. What exactly had transpired?

He slitted his eyes, which didn't help. He must have taken out his contacts before they'd started—or perhaps after they finished. The room was a pastiche of soft, mutable blurs.

I need coffee.

He reached for his glasses, which he couldn't find. He had a faint memory of leaving them in the other room but couldn't summon the wherewithal to abandon this blissful fog.

"Why is the room moving?" the woman moaned. "Am I on a bloody, goddamned ship?"

He summoned a few sympathetic blinks. Absinthe was not a drink for amateurs.

She rolled away, pulled the pillow tightly over her head, and moaned again.

Glasses. Coffee. Email. Gerard's hierarchy of needs. He threw his legs over the side of the bed and sat up. *Whoa.* Apparently three-hundred-year-old whiskey wasn't something to be toyed with either.

He stood and nearly toppled. His legs felt like slowly melting rubber. He steadied himself.

Glasses. Coffee. Email.

❧

Duncan flipped the broadsheet over. He was enjoying the writer's delightfully full-bodied allusion to Her Majesty as a "prickle-backed badger" when Serafina's door opened.

A naked man stumbled out.

The broadsheet dropped from Duncan's hand.

The man rubbed his eyes vigorously, patted down the console table, and mumbled, "Well, she may open her robe slowly, but she goes down like a thousand-dollar whore."

In three strides, Duncan had the man by the shoulders.

"You have five seconds," Duncan said, breathing fire. "What would you like to say before you can't say anything ever again?"

The man blinked. "Who the fuck are you?"

"Bad choice." Duncan flung the man against the wall.

"Are you out of your mind?" the man cried.

"Aye. Where's Serafina?"

"Who the fuck is Serafina?"

Duncan head-butted him. "Next one, and your nose is going to look like a relief map of New Jersey."

❦

Gerard had spent fifteen years dealing with clients who'd done everything from threatening his mother (already dead) and demanding sex (Gerard kept an open mind, but the guy hadn't brushed his teeth since the advent of cable), to rear-ending his car over a commercial shoot that ran over budget (the client lost two teeth, Gerard won a Palme d'Or, and the bill was paid in full). He didn't know if this kilted Highlander on steroids was a jealous husband, jilted boyfriend, or overprotective cube-mate, but in Gerard's mind, what Cinderella did before the clock struck midnight, or after, was nobody's business but her own.

He considered a knee to the man's balls, but the move would just supercharge his attacker, and Gerard decided, as he often did, that finesse made more sense.

Holding up his hands, he said, "I have something

you're going to want to hear, and you're going to want to hear it because it involves you."

The magic line. The words that turned grown men to putty.

The hold on his shoulders loosened.

"Look, I'm as eager to find her as you are," Gerard said, summoning his finely tuned bullshit machine, "maybe more. Serafina's great—sorry, she introduced herself to me as Sera; I didn't make the connection. She and I talked half the night. I had no idea she was a stargazer. All this Perseids this and Leonids that. I tell you, it was fascinating. Unfortunately, she caught me yawning around one, and I think I might have offended her because all of a sudden she said she had to go. No excuses, of course, but I'd had this absolutely exhausting day, and I doubt even duct tape would have kept my lids up, if you know what I mean. Anyhow, I'd love it if you could convince her to at least consider our offer. That kind of curiosity and ease with people is something you just don't see anymore. We'd be thrilled to have her on board at Piper Cornish."

The idiot cocked his head, entirely flummoxed. "Did you say 'duct tape'?"

Totally not the question Gerard had been expecting, but then again, nothing that morning had been what he was expecting. "I did, yes. I was beat."

The man's eyes glazed over and his arms dropped to his side. Gerard got the sense he could knock him over with a sharp poke.

"*Undine*," the man said mysteriously, apparently to himself, the word choked out as if a vision of some terrifying Pict god had just appeared in his head. And then: "*Shite.*" He flew to a door Gerard didn't remember being there.

Gerard ducked back into the bedroom, threw the lock, and bounded to the bed. "Your ship came in," he said, shaking the arm clutching the pillow. "Unfortunately, it's the *Titanic*. You have about five seconds to get your lifeboat in the bathroom and lock the door."

"*Mmphf*," came the voice, muzzy with sleep.

"Serafina, are you in there?" the Scot demanded, rattling the knob.

"*Och.*" The arm twitched. "Who is making all that bloody noise?"

"Don't tell me you haven't been introduced to Paul MacBunyon?" Gerard yanked the covers off the bed.

He froze. The woman was not plump, blond, or Cinderella. She was a flaming redhead with pale legs that, in his foggy eyes, stretched out like two glorious lengths of beach beneath the azure blue of his Ermenegildo Zegna shirt, which, via some inexplicable dark magic, she was now wearing.

And he had never seen her before.

The woman swallowed a screech, banked herself against the headboard, and whispered fiercely, "Who the hell are you?"

"I could ask you the same thing," he said. "This is *my* bed."

Her chin dropped. "It is *not!*"

"Serafina!" The knob jiggled harder.

"You may keep the shirt," Gerard said, "but if you could assist in the return of the rest of my clothes before Sasquatch breaks down the door, I'd be very grateful." He tossed the covers aside.

She flung her hands across her eyes. "Mother naked, ye are!"

"Pot, kettle: black, black." He scrabbled across the bed and peered over the side, catching another inspiring whiff of that juniper-rosemary combo. A heap of gray wool filled his heart with joy and he fished his trousers off the floor.

"Get out!" she demanded.

"That's a fine thank-you." He jumped up and jerked the trousers on.

The door rattled harder. The man was using his shoulder now.

"What exactly would I be thanking ye for?"

"Last night." He gave her a look that would translate even into her overwrought Robert Burns Scottish.

She braced her shoulders. "I did *not*!"

He brought his hand before her nose. "That's your perfume, is it not?"

She gasped.

He shrugged. "I'm rarely wrong when it comes to that kind of thing."

"What a repellent quality."

"Look, I don't know what brand of crazy you and your boyfriend have going on, but you probably should keep the weird cosplay to yourselves." The next crash nearly brought the door off its hinges. "Do what you like, but I'm adjourning to the bathroom to hop on the phone to the concierge. I'll tell you what else: they are *not* going to like the TripAdvisor review coming out of this."

She drew herself even farther into the headboard. "Are you *mad*?"

"Mad. Blind. Shirtless. You name it. And definitely off whiskey." He reached for the bathroom door but found only wall. "What the…?"

A splintering explosion of wood, and MacBunyon burst into the room. "*You*," he said, pointing to the woman, an eerie calmness about him. "Out here."

Gerard heaved a heavy sigh and moved between MacBunyon and the bed. The time for finesse was over. He lifted his fists. "Why don't you start with me, big guy?"

The Scot regarded Gerard with a look of amusement and disgust. "Chivalry? Now? Seriously, man, do ye have *any* idea what she's done to ye?"

"Duncan!" the woman said, aghast.

"There's no reason to be ungentlemanly about it," Gerard said. "We're adults."

"I didn't mean *that*," Duncan said. "Though if she did, which I doubt, and ye still felt the need to make that comment about her robe, perhaps you and I will have a little tête-à-tête when I finish with her, aye?" He added to the redhead, "I'll wait out there while ye dress."

Gerard shifted but didn't lower his fists.

Duncan rolled his eyes. "*Och.* If you're so worried about protecting her, why don't you join us while we chat? I have a sneaking suspicion ye'll be no' too happy with her when we're done."

Four

THE SUN WAS BRIGHTER AND HIS HEAD WAS CLEARER, and as he entered the suite's living room, Gerard, despite his preternaturally bad nearsightedness, saw that the suite's living room was someone else's living room—someone with his grandmother's taste in decorating. He felt as if he'd walked into a Dickens' novel—bed warmers by the fire, sconces on the wall, rough-hewn wood floors. Panicked, he spun in a circle, searching for something he would recognize.

Duncan caught him by the shoulder. "Relax, mate. It'll all make sense soon. Well," he added, reconsidering, "that's a bit of an overpromise. Let's say it will all be *explained* soon. But you're in no immediate danger, comments regarding Serafina's robe notwithstanding."

"That wasn't about her robe," Gerard said, irritated and increasingly disoriented. "Or her. That's what an old boss used to say about expensive whiskey. 'You cannot rush the moment. Good whiskey is like a woman of the world. She opens her robe slowly.'"

Duncan's lip curled. "Was that supposed to be a French accent? It's god-awful, ye ken?"

"Pardon me. My powers of mimicry have been overwhelmed by your hospitality. Would you mind telling me where we are?"

Duncan pointed to a spindly legged settee next to Gerard.

"I'll stand, thank you."

Duncan shrugged. "Your call. We're in Edinburgh."

Gerard sank into the settee, speechless. "Pennsylvania?"

"Seriously? That's the one that popped into your head?"

The night had obviously been filled with activity Gerard didn't recall, as the random shards of memory and bare-legged woman seemed to attest, but travel?

"I…um… We shot an ad in a college stadium there once," Gerard said, trying to process this information. "The marching band wears kilts."

"Let's hope for your sake you don't find that odd. And, no, not Pennsylvania."

The woman emerged. His shirt was gone, replaced—to his way of thinking at least—by a much less interesting gown. The mass of orange-blond curls had been pinned up. Without his glasses, her face was still elusive, but he could sense a simmering and attractive energy there. He could also sense she had no desire to speak to Sasqua-Scot.

Gerard rose instinctively, ready to insert himself into a fight.

"Relax, Romeo," Duncan said. "We're all friends here. Have a seat."

The woman remained standing, so Gerard did as well.

Duncan heaved a heavy sigh and sat down himself. "I can tell this is going to be a long morning."

"I dinna know this man," Serafina said to Duncan, "or what he was doing in my bed."

Duncan templed his fingers and cocked his head in Gerard's direction. "Do you know her?"

Gerard shifted. The level of threat appeared to have subsided a bit, but he also didn't have his shoes, his shirt, his glasses, his cell phone, or a clear idea of where he was or how to get out. "It depends what you mean by 'know.'"

Serafina reared back. "How would you like to get to know the toe of my boot?"

"He has ground to stand on," Duncan said flatly. "You were practically naked. I'd say he knows *something* about you, if only your shirt size."

She made an irritated sniff.

Duncan went on to Gerard, "Apart from whatever may have been exchanged in the transaction involving the shirt—and *please* dinna feel the need to tell me—do you know her? Her name? Her family? Where she comes from? Anything?"

Anything? *Well, the scent that wafts off her skin is the olfactory equivalent of cocaine. Her legs are the color of vanilla gelato and look just as rich. She brims with a smoky incandescence that makes me want to buy her a drink, tell her a dirty joke, and vaporize in the detonation that follows. I'd like to grab a handful of those curls and feel the spring of postcoital perspiration in them. More than that, I'd like her to pull a curl loose right now, just for me. But do I know anything?*

He shook his head. "She has red hair."

The woman snorted. "Deft observer of mankind, are ye?"

"A thousand pardons. If I had my glasses, I have

no doubt I would bowl you over with my powers of detection."

At once he was seized with a perfectly clear vision of him dropping her on a bed in slow motion, her flame-colored curls fanning out across the linen like rays of a setting sun. What had gone on between them?

He looked at her, shocked, and she, for the first time in their brief acquaintance, lowered her eyes. *She sees it too!*

"What do you remember about last night?" Duncan asked.

Gerard froze. Then he realized Duncan wasn't asking about the vision but the final moments in his hotel room.

"Not much," Gerard said. "I had a drink. Whiskey."

"The robe, aye. Nothing else? Just you, a glass of whiskey, and a bed?"

With a coy smile, Gerard, unable to help himself, lifted his shoulders. "Well…"

Serafina made a noise of disgust he hadn't heard since his gran caught him spreading Marshmallow Fluff on his toast.

"And it wasn't a glass," Gerard added. "It was a bottle, a very old bottle. With the name…" He squeezed his eyes shut to summon the image of that embossed word. It appeared, but so did another vision, this one far less enchanting than the one of Serafina on a bed. It was three men on a dock beside a huge, dark sea, and he and Serafina scrambling in terror when the men began to chase them.

"Kerr?" Duncan said.

"Pardon?" The vision disappeared but the rapid firing of his heart did not.

"The bottle. Was it Kerr whiskey?"

Gerard stared at Duncan in amazement. "How did you know?"

"Lucky guess."

A subtle change came over Serafina with the name of the whiskey. A look of uneasiness replaced the general irritation on her face, and one hand quested nervously for its mate.

She inhaled sharply, then immediately hid her surprise in a mask of unconcern.

Duncan hadn't been watching and swiveled when he heard the gasp. But Gerard had, and the image of what he'd seen almost made him dizzy.

There, on the fourth finger of Serafina's left hand, sat a slim gold band.

Five

Nearly deafened by the blood roaring in her ears, Serafina stilled the hand in her pocket and fought to remain calm.

"What is it?" Duncan eyed her suspiciously.

"I bit my tongue."

He cocked his head farther.

"It's fine now."

The other man had seen something, though what, she wasn't sure. He looked at her as if she were a Highland ox whose horns had sprouted thistles. All she remembered clearly about the night before was that he'd appeared to her sometime after she'd first sipped the adulterated whiskey, though he'd been no more than a shade, his translucent image waxing and waning like mist on a loch. Wide jaw, the shoulders of a smith, hair as gold as a wagtail's breast—the man was no trouble on the eyes. The more she drank, the clearer his image had become— though the foggier her apprehension of it—until at last she'd slipped into a thick, hibernating sleep, like a child after a summer fair, floating through hazy, happy dreams filled with random glints of remembered pleasure.

But the waking glints, beginning to arrive with increased regularity, were stirring an emotion closer to concern. The man's hand, running lightly down her back. A hurried run down a dark dock. Tugging the waist of a man's breeks—beautiful wool breeks, whose rich, gray fabric caressed her fingers, as soft as the fur of a baby rabbit.

She couldn't stop herself. Her eyes flew to the man's breeks. *Oh, God! Gray wool!*

When she looked up, he was looking right at her. Her cheeks exploded in flames.

How could any of this have happened without her remembering it? *The answer*, she told herself, *is because it didn't.*

But the ring…

She wriggled her fingers in her pocket, desperately hoping the solid, immutable gold was gone. But it wasn't.

Unbuttoning a man's breeks was one thing—and she prayed it was the last in the series of unorthodox activities she appeared to have engaged in the night before—but marrying him? How far out of her senses had she been?

She felt dizzy, as if she might faint, and she too lowered herself onto the settee.

"Well, look at this," Duncan said. "A pair of woebegone twins."

"I have reason to be woebegone," Gerard said, straightening.

"Do you?" Duncan said. "Let me guess. You have no idea where you are or how you got here, and you have something important to do tomorrow?"

Gerard visibly plumped, like a frigate bird trying to

attract a mate. "Monday, actually," he said. "I'm about to be voted a partner in my firm."

Duncan regarded the man with renewed interest. "What sort of firm?"

"Advertising. Piper Cornish."

Duncan laughed a short laugh. "Blimey. At least I had bookkeeping to fall back on." He held up his hands. "Sorry. I shouldn't laugh."

"Did you just say 'blimey'?" Serafina had noticed a subtle change in Duncan from the moment he'd burst into her room. She couldn't quite describe it, but it was as if he had thrown off a too-small frock coat and was enjoying a freedom of movement he hadn't had in a long, long time. He talked differently. He sat differently. He even moved differently.

Duncan coughed and reddened. "Aye, well, it was something my ma used to say. It means 'oh, dear' or '*och*.'"

Gerard stared at Serafina, frowning. "You've never heard 'blimey' before? You're a Brit, aren't you? Or am I right? That accent's really a fake?"

Serafina couldn't have been more surprised—or insulted—if he'd called her a whore, though considering the relationship she appeared to have developed with his breeks, the accusation in that case might have been deserved.

Duncan laid a calming finger on her hand, which had balled itself into a fist.

"I am nae a 'Brit,'" she whispered, hot with fury. "Nor is my accent false. Though yours might be. I've nae heard such an ear-churning mix of bleats and barks in all my life. Where, might I ask, does such cacophony originate?"

"No reason to answer that," Duncan put in quickly. "We have other fish to fry here."

"Look," Gerard said, anger rising, "I don't understand the weird performance art you two have running here, but enough is enough. Either tell me what's going on, or pantomime a death scene for me and let me get the hell out of here."

"You've never seen her before, then?" Duncan said.

A knock sounded at the door. Before Duncan could rise to answer, the door opened. The inn's housekeeper stepped in with an urn of fragrant coffee. "Oh, there the two of ye are," she said to Serafina and Gerard. "You asked me last night to be on the lookout for unsavories from the docks. There are three of 'em downstairs, and they dinna look like they are looking for a game of push-the-hoop."

Six

GERARD'S STOMACH TIGHTENED. WHATEVER UNPLEAS-
antness the Scot offered, it was nothing compared
to the men he remembered from last night. "This
is bad."

The men's voices grew louder as they tromped up
the inn's stairs. "I'll go any damned place I please,"
one of them said in a voice instantly identifiable to
Gerard. The hair on his arms stood on end.

Duncan strode to the door and closed it. "Go," he
said, pointing to Serafina's bedroom. "I'll handle them."

And it was then that Gerard saw the same sort
of ancient pistol on Duncan's belt he'd seen on the
belts of the men in the visions. The contents of his
gut curdled.

"We need to get out of here."

He pulled Serafina from the settee and hurried her
through the bedroom door and locked it.

"Were we at a dock?" he whispered.

The men's knock rattled the hallway door.

"We need Undine's magic to undo this," she said.

Gerard didn't know this deity who answered human

entreaties, but he was beginning to feel a distinct need to fall to his knees and beg for help himself.

Serafina ran to a door on the adjoining wall and threw it open.

"She's not here," she said, crestfallen. As best as he could tell, the room beyond was a bedroom much like the one in which they stood.

Either the deity made earthly visits, or Undine was a mortal with more interesting things to do than hang around waiting for her friends' lives to implode.

"We need to get out of here." She ran to the window and looked out.

"I'm not leaving Thor to the bad guys." The guy might have been a pain in the ass, but you never left a man behind.

"Thor, as you call him, is perfectly capable of taking care of himself. And he has a pistol."

"Come in, come in." Duncan's voice carried through the closed bedroom door, full of relief and bonhomie. "You have the hands of a surgeon, I'm pleased to see. Did ye bring your cauterizer? My piles are as hot as a blacksmith's coals."

Gerard was impressed. Now, there's a man who could sell dish soap.

Serafina had already grabbed a handful of clothes and opened the shutters. "C'mon!"

He snagged his shirt from the floor and ran after her. She was descending a ladder, whose presence triggered another memory flash.

"We used this last night," he said, astounded. "I remember."

"Did we?" Serafina said evasively.

"God, man, put yer kilt down!" one of the dock men cried. "I'm nae a surgeon, and I have no wish to look at your bloody arsehole!"

Serafina grabbed Gerard's hand when he reached the bottom and tried to pull him toward the street.

But his legs were frozen.

There, before him, was a screeching, bustling, stinking scene from an Elizabethan commercial gone wild. He couldn't see much, but what he could make out astounded him. Horses pulled wagons through the streets, kicking up clouds of red dust. Barking dogs circled a man carrying something feathery. Women in all manner of long dresses hurried from storefront to storefront. Somewhere, a tin whistle played, and the notes were pure and clear. The scent of garlic cooking filled his head as well as the more pungent smells of burning wood and human waste. And the men—the men!—in dingy shirts and gigantic plaid wraps—red, green, blue. He saw more colors here than he saw on women most days in Manhattan. And there, rising above the tops of the houses across the street, stood the blurred but familiar outline of a castle.

He collapsed against the ladder and nearly slid to the ground. "He meant Edinburgh, Scotland, didn't he?"

"Of course he meant Edinburgh, Scotland. Are ye daft?"

The last syllable of her "Edinburgh," so different from his, had been swallowed in that deep well of reverberation found in the throat of every Scot.

"What year is this?" he asked, on the verge of terror.

"Oh, God, not again." She yanked his arm harder. "I canna go through this *again*!"

"What do you mean 'again'?" he said, barely avoiding a speeding carriage as he shrugged on his shirt.

She hesitated long enough for Gerard to know she knew something.

"What happened last night?" he demanded. "What do you know?"

She pulled him down a close, one of those remarkable Edinburgh artifacts that were part darkened alley, part apartment hallway, and part barely navigable crawl space.

"I don't *know* everything," she whispered. "But I remember some things—and I definitely answered that question for you. You were bawling like a wee baby."

"I was *not*."

"You were practically bawling like a wee baby out there," she said, pointing to the street. "It's 1706, and stop buttoning. You canna wear those clothes."

1706?

"Take them off," she commanded.

"Wait. What?" Gerard searched his head for what he knew about the turn of the eighteenth century. The answer, it seemed, was remarkably little. It was the start of the Age of Enlightenment, after Plymouth Rock and before the Continental Congress, both of which had happened half a globe away. He dug in the storage closet of his memory and shook the dust off the threadbare remnants of his secondary education for something of British history. Two queens—cousins, he recalled—and a beheading. Shakespeare. And something about corn.

A door opened, and a woman with a boy at her feet and what looked like a musket resting in her arms came into view behind Serafina.

"Take off your clothes," Serafina repeated.

"Is he bothering ye?" the woman asked Serafina.

"Am I bothering *her*?" Gerard held up his palms. "You *are* hearing this, aren't you?"

"Nae," Serafina replied. "Just a wee skirmish about his breeks."

The woman lifted the stock to her shoulder, and something made a small, metallic *click*. "I've not known a man to refuse a lady's proper request regarding his breeks. In my experience, your sex usually can't get them off fast enough."

"Oh, we-ll," Gerard said theatrically. "As long as the lady has made a *proper* request." He unzipped his fly, looked at the women, and made a prim about-face. "And what, pray tell," he said, kicking his finely tailored trousers to the cobbles, "would you have me wear instead, or do the folks in 1706 prefer bare asses?"

One of the women giggled, and he was willing to lay odds it was Serafina.

He felt something being guided around his waist.

"Hold that," she commanded.

The wool was far less polished than his trousers, and yet the weave had a lovely hand, neither too thick nor too thin, with a pleasant worn-in smoothness.

She removed the belt from his trousers and tightened it around his waist. The ministrations, performed in the alley, with her bending before him, brought sparks of heat to his cheeks. Or perhaps it was the prickle of cool air on his thighs. Whatever it was, it certainly added to the sense of being well and truly alive that this world seemed to offer.

Could he really be more than three hundred years in the past? When he tried to consider the idea, his thoughts veered away, as if it were a bottomless pit his mind wouldn't let him disappear into.

Serafina finished the adjustments she was making to the fabric, and when she straightened, he found himself looking directly at her.

"This is the first time we've seen eye to eye," he said with a laugh, trying to hide the awkwardness.

She *mmphf*ed. "Take off your sark."

"My *huh*?"

She shook her head, impatient with his stupidity. He noticed her eyes got bluer when she was angry.

She took the first button under his collar and undid it.

Oh, my shirt!

He wanted to tell her he got it now, that he was not the imbecile she imagined, but nothing short of death would persuade him to interfere with her precise and beguilingly short-tempered unbuttoning. He wished the shirtfront ran to his ankles.

She tugged the fabric off his shoulders as if he were a recalcitrant child and pulled a length of snowy fabric from the things she had stuffed under her arm.

"Goodness," he said. "You come prepared."

She glanced behind her and replied sotto voce, "I told you last night to keep this on."

"Perhaps," he said just as quietly, "we found a pressing need to remove it."

He took the linen from her hand and slipped it

over his head. The shirt—or sark as she called it—was exceptionally long. When he tucked it in, the tails fell nearly to his knees.

Serafina tightened the laces at the split neck.

"Mama, are they going to kiss?" the boy asked.

Gerard realized his mooning must be obvious and cleared his face.

"Or clash, I expect," the woman said, repositioning the musket. "Either way, he hasn't a prayer of defending himself. Do ye need an escort to St. Giles, by any chance?" she asked Serafina. "Your man has the look of an errant bridegroom, and I have had enough of those to last a lifetime."

"*Och*, he's not *my* man." Serafina reached for the loose ends of the plaid wool and lifted them to his shoulder. "Though I seem to have been tasked with his care."

Gerard thought of the ring. He turned to look at her hand and saw the gold band was gone. "Wait, are you married?"

Serafina paused in the middle of knotting the corners. "What a question! No."

The other woman raised a disapproving brow. "*Och*, now ye ask?"

But there was something in the way Serafina had answered and in the odd frisson he'd gotten at the mention of St. Giles that made him certain his gut was onto something.

Serafina held out a pair of thick knee-high socks.

"Ah, that's a girl's pair," he said.

"Would ye rather wear yer skin to blisters?"

He took the socks from her arms as well as a pair

of rough leather shoes. "What the hell is this?" He held up two narrow straps of leather that he found inside the shoes. "I know what we'd use them for where I come from, but I somehow doubt that's your intent."

"They're garters," she said, rolling her eyes. "For your stockings."

He donned the accessories grudgingly. He also grabbed his trousers from the cobbles and was thrilled to discover his contact case in the pocket with the contacts still inside.

"Well, I'm dressed to your exacting standards now," he said, putting the first contact in while the women stared in fascination, "and I think with the thorough search you've just concluded, you've established I represent no risk." He put in the second, and the world transformed from a blurred panorama of strangeness to a clearly delineated one. "Might we take the rest of this discussion to the closest dining establishment? I'm starving, and I have some *very* pressing questions to ask *you*."

Serafina turned to the woman and curtsied prettily. "Thank you for your help."

The woman made a noncommittal noise and lowered the musket. "He has nae weapon, aye. But if I were ye, I wouldn't assume he represents nae risk."

Seven

SERAFINA SCANNED THE FACES OF THE ROYAL MILE crowd, not only to ensure the men at the Hollow Crown hadn't followed them but also that Gerard was passing for a Scot. It was with the greatest surprise that she saw he seemed to be, though she could barely look at him without seeing the dissonance of clashing culture in every detail. His hair was too short, his pace too swift, and he walked as if he were at all times sharply aware of the balls between his legs. She had to admit if she put aside her worry, he did look rather dashing in the plaid. It was one of Duncan's. She hoped Duncan didn't mind.

She felt the weight of the ring in her pocket. She needed time to sort this out. And she desperately needed to get to the docks. She cut her gaze to Gerard and realized he'd been watching her.

"What am I doing here? How am I going to get home? And who was the guy cross-examining us in the inn?"

"Keep your voice down," she said. People's heads were turning, and the men from the docks could be anywhere. "He's the steward of a clan chieftess named Abby Kerr. She's my friend, and he's her sweetheart, but ye canna tell anyone." She dragged him into a tavern called the Squeak and Blade.

Gerard's eyes bulged. "Did I really just see a pig with his throat being cut on the sign over the door?"

"The establishment is well-known for its pork."

Even putting aside the sign, it was not quite as fine a place as the Hollow Crown, but it was clean, the proprietor greeted them effusively, and a variety of sausages sizzled on the brazier over the hearth. She hoped the presence of the other diners would keep Gerard in check. She ordered a pot of coffee.

"Why am I here?" he asked. "Why am I in this getup? You haven't answered my questions."

She shifted. There was no easy way to begin. "You, it seems, are the answer to my…well, my…"

"Prayers?"

The brown in his eyes lightened to a honey glow. He really could have been related to Edward, she thought, amazed at Undine's magic. They shared the same tousled waves, elegant cheekbones, and deep-set eyes, though Gerard had that fascinating hole in the middle of his chin. It reminded her of a whirlpool she'd seen off the coast of Norway with her father, the strong currents tumbling wildly into the unknown below.

"What?" He saw her looking at his chin and his hand went to it.

"Nothing. And, no, you did not answer my *prayers*. 'Twas my invocation."

"Your invocation, eh?"

She swore she saw his chest puff.

"And how exactly am I the answer to your invocation?" It was clear he'd decided the answer involved a secluded bridal bower and a jug of wine.

"'Tis not what you're thinking."

"I wasn't thinking anything." He waved the innkeeper over and selected half a dozen sausages from a platter. "I worked on a spot—er, ad—advertisement—for a bandage company once with a Sleeping Beauty theme. You know, spells, pricks, the handsome prince who must awaken the heroine with his kiss."

"Indeed?"

"I'm just saying I know the general idea."

Both he and Edward radiated a dangerous charm, she thought. But Edward's danger was that of a sharp-toothed sea monster, ready to swallow you whole, while Gerard's reminded her of a young tiger rolling a ball toward you. You realized you might be in danger at some point, but all you wanted to do was play.

The man dug into the first sausage with the precision of a stone mason engraving marble. She wondered how he could eat. Her wame was still feeling the effects of the whiskey and herbs.

"I am not familiar with the story," she said, "though I am relieved to say there are no princes, no bandages, and certainly no pricks in this tale."

He swallowed and raised the corner of his mouth. "Not a one?"

"No. And, if I may say, what a dreadful idea for an advertisement. Who would want to look at bloody fingers?"

"We got half a million views," he said, spearing another coin of sausage, "but I'm sure you're the expert. So, this invocation, what did it involve?"

"Whiskey and some fairly repugnant herbs."

"That's not what I meant."

The tip of her nose tingled with heat. "Oh. I see. Well, I needed a man—"

He snickered.

"—to help me secure something important."

"A line of credit? A loose rope on your tent? Fifty-yard-line tickets to the Giants?"

She stared at him. "Giants?"

"Serafina."

It was the first time he'd said her name, and she was taken aback. When a Scot said it, it was like a growl that started with a hiss and ended with a bark. Edward's precise pronunciation rendered it empty, the husk of a thought. But this man, with his odd, seductive *S* and lyrical vowels, made it into a tiny and effortlessly enchanting musical phrase.

"My future," she said. "I need your help to secure my future."

❧

Her future? Gerard couldn't begin to think what that might mean. Behind him, the tavern door opened as it had half a dozen times since they'd sat down, but this time Serafina stiffened.

"Oh, God."

Gerard turned. The man, in trousers and a long gray coat, who swept his gaze around the room, looked entirely unassuming. "What?" Gerard demanded.

Serafina stared hard at the tabletop. "I think that's the man whose ship we stole."

"What?"

His near-shriek turned heads. Fortunately the man had returned his attention to his friend outside, who was considerably better dressed, with a finer coat, walking stick, and copious ruffles at his neck. He spoke energetically, and the other man let go of the door and it fell shut.

When Gerard turned back, Serafina was gone. This was problematic on several levels, not the least of which was he had no money to pay for his meal. He waited for several minutes as he finished his sausages, then signaled the innkeeper.

"Where's the ladies' room?"

"Ladies are welcome in this room so long as they don't attempt to procure business or insist on a chair for their parcels."

"No, I mean where do they go to the bathroom?"

The man's brows shot up. "I couldna say. I would never discuss bathing with a lady."

"A *piss*," Gerard said sharply. "Where do they go for that?"

"Oh, that." The man jerked his thumb toward the back. "There's a pot in the alley."

"Thank you," Gerard said, rising. "Did you see the men at the door a moment ago?"

The man shook his head.

"Thanks." Gerard was already feeling guilty about having to run out on the bill. "The sausages were great, by the way."

"Pig's face. That's the secret ingredient."

"I can see why you keep it a secret."

Gerard laid his fork across his plate, an attempt to suggest he would be returning shortly, but before he could turn, someone tapped his shoulder. He found himself face-to-face with the well-dressed man from the street.

Once or twice a year, Gerard would spot a fellow out of the corner of his eye on the streets of New York who he thought resembled him. That tingle of surprise and fascination would diminish as a better angle revealed the face was different or the coloring hadn't been quite what he'd first thought. Such was the case with the man before him, who, while by no means an identical twin, sported the coloring, the build, the deep-set eyes—even the wavy hair.

The man scanned Gerard's face, evidently noting the resemblance himself. He made a smug *hm*. "That woman you were with, where is she?"

Gerard was not in the habit of being questioned, not by a man who seemed to regard Gerard as a clod of excrement he'd accidentally trod in, and certainly not by an Englishman who said "woman" as if he'd meant something much worse.

"Why?"

The man stiffened. "That's not your concern."

"And her whereabouts aren't yours."

Red-cheeked, the man took a closer read of Gerard and his clothing. "You're not even a Scot."

Gerard wasn't sure what he meant, though it was clearly not a compliment. "Not a Scot, no. But I do take some comfort in the fact I'm not an Englishman either."

The man's face turned to ice and he gripped his

walking stick. "She is not what you think. Do not be taken in."

"Being outsmarted doesn't always mean you were taken in. It may just mean you're not very smart."

The grip on the walking stick tightened, and Gerard half expected the man to strike him with it.

Sensing an imminent fight, a few of the patrons had risen from their chairs, and the man mastered his anger. "If you see her, tell her—"

"Your message is immaterial. I may not see her again, but if I do, I won't pass it along."

The man looked left and right, assessing the number of people who had witnessed his humiliation. He made the tiniest bow. "I see I shall have to give her the message myself," he said and left.

Good luck with that. Serafina didn't seem the type to waste a lot of time on assholes—as Gerard himself had so recently discovered.

He caught the eye of the innkeeper, and leaned in the direction the man had gone.

The innkeeper shook his head. "Can't help ye on that one, laddie. Not the sort of customer we usually get in here."

Gerard sidled up and stuck out his hand. "I'm Gerard Innes, by the way. You didn't, by any chance, happen to see where the woman I was with went, did you? Hair like wildfire. Tongue like it too, come to think of it—"

"Oh, I know the lass. Verra striking. Did she abandon you?"

"So it seems. I'm just going to check the alley." He coughed guiltily. "May I add that my impolite behavior in your establishment—just now or even in the future were I to do something to annoy you—is in no way reflective of the delight I took in your sausages."

"'Tis verra kind of you to say, sir."

"And might I suggest… Well, perhaps it's not my place—"

"Let it never be said John Dawes is not open to suggestions."

"Well, Mr. Dawes, might I suggest that you would be well served—very well served—by changing the sign in front to that of a plate piled high with sausages, and that you might consider—when weather permits, of course—doing your grilling outside. The scents and sounds of sausages cooking over a fire are among the most alluring in life. I have no doubt you could triple your income."

Dawes looked stunned. Gerard wondered if he'd overstepped his bounds. But then Dawes broke into an expansive smile. "I like your ideas, sir! I like them verra much."

"And you might—well, this may be too much even for an open-minded man like yourself—but you might consider changing the name of your establishment to the Squeak and Sizzle—you know, like the sound of sausages on the grill?"

The man whooped. "*Och*, what an idea!"

It wasn't much, but Gerard prayed the wisdom of an award-winning creative director might offset the unrecompensed breakfast. He headed toward the alley, hoping to find Serafina. He'd had about all of the Scottish hospitality he could take—especially hers, which seemed to consist of jerking him out of his present, denying she knew him, forcing him into this ridiculous getup and ditching him. And if he'd actually had a hand in stealing a ship, the sooner he got back to French-press coffee, garments with legs, restaurants with ladies' rooms, and that one-thousand-dollar-a-night suite, the sooner he could put the past behind him.

After adjusting the shifting and unwieldy fabric at his waist for the dozenth time, he headed for the exit the innkeeper had indicated, which sat at the end of a long hallway. He was nearly there when a door behind him opened and he heard one of the room's occupants, a man with a basso profundo voice, say breathlessly, "Undine, do you have time for another? I'm happy to pay for a second."

Undine, the woman whose "magic" had done this to him, was a whore?

"I'm exhausted, gentlemen," she said.

And a hardworking one at that.

Gerard doubled back as half a dozen men quit the room.

The James Brown of promiscuity.

Then he looked inside. The den of iniquity was, well, just a den, though a rather large one, with an energetic fire burning at a hearth at one end and a long desk in the center. Undine, a slim, cool blond, sat enthroned there, surrounded by a dozen men and women. They sat in chairs or milled around the desk, and their attention was focused on her.

"One more," someone begged.

"You know perfectly well I am available for consulting at my home in Drumburgh," she said. "Come to me there. I will lay out your fortune in rich detail for you to digest at an agreeable pace and with no one to hear but you and your conscience." The audience chuckled. "This"—she gestured to the cards laid out in neat rows on the desktop—"is mere showmanship."

"I have a shilling—two, if you make it entertaining," said a man in a dark coat.

"Keep your coins, sir," she said, eyes flashing. "I'm not a dancing bear."

"Perhaps," Gerard said loudly, "you'd consider telling the fortune of the man who has been forced to travel a considerable distance because of you." He made his way through the crowd to the table.

"Because of me?" she said, surprised.

"You sent your invitation with a bottle of Kerr whiskey—if that helps you remember."

She didn't register shock, though his words made her lean back in her chair and regard him with something closer to interest.

"I dinna consider the person who provides the directions to be responsible for the destination the carriage reaches," she said. "You, sir, will have to take up your complaint with the driver."

He put his palms on the table and leaned forward until his face was a foot from hers. "I don't know where she is. I'm taking it up with you."

The circle of onlookers had gathered closer. Disgruntled customers were evidently a rarity in Undine's business. He was okay being the exception to the rule.

"Sit down, then," she said, gathering the cards. "And shuffle these while I think." Grimacing, she moved a bottle of ink and a quill aside to clear the space. Then she pushed the deck toward him.

The cards were tattered and worn, with a faded print of a lake on their backs. He shuffled twice, feeling, as always, the skepticism with which he regarded carnival tricks. But he reminded himself he appeared to be sitting in a kilt in a tavern in Edinburgh in 1706. Perhaps he needed to keep a more open mind. He picked up the cards and turned them over in his hand.

"They're blank," he said, surprised.

Undine's brow arched. "Surely that can't make a difference. You dinna believe this works anyhow."

Had she seen his skepticism? He'd been told he had a poker face. "I'd be happy to be proven wrong."

"I dinna think happy is what you're going to be."

She had the palest green eyes he'd ever seen and a dangerous grace of movement that made him think of manta rays—or rattlers. Her eyes tightened for an instant when she retrieved the deck. "You are a man with a house but no home. You are a man of accomplishment but not substance. You are surrounded by admirers but have hardly a friend."

He felt like he'd been sucker punched. "That's ridiculous."

"Is it? You've shared the beds of two women in the last twelve hours."

The crowd inhaled, and heat rushed up Gerard's neck. In New York that would barely raise an eyebrow, not that he would have announced it in a room full of people—or even mentioned it at all. But how had Undine known? He longed to point out he had made love to, at most, one of the two women—the redhead—and that assumption was based on fragmentary and, at this point, far from reliable evidence. But he said nothing, just screwed himself deeper into the chair. None of what Undine had said was completely fair, but taken as a whole, it did have an uncomfortable ring of truth to it.

"I see you're not quite so quick to make a denial now," she said. "Come, come. The audience is curious. Are these women pretty? Highborn? Risk seekers? Abandoned? Are they cursed with scoundrels for husbands? Tell us so that we may revel in their disgrace."

Gerard was horrified. "I most certainly will not."

Undine's face relaxed. "Good people of Edinburgh, he has demonstrated his true worth by refusing to turn the women into objects of public scrutiny. We can overlook much in a man of chivalry." She pushed one of the blank cards toward him, along with the quill. "I can see you home this hour if you do but one small thing. Write the names of the women you have bedded on the card and put it in the fire. No one will see the names but you. By the time the card has turned to ashes, the bonds that have held you here will be erased."

Gerard looked at the card and licked his lips, which had turned uncomfortably dry. He knew Serafina's first name, of course, but not her last. And he didn't know Cinderella's name at all.

The crowd turned cooler.

"Perhaps there's a reason you find yourself in the sophisticated city of Edinburgh," the fortune-teller said. "Perhaps there is a lesson or two you need to learn."

"Sophisticated? Gimme a break. There's not enough in this place to engage a turd-throwing chimp, let alone a man of more worldly tastes."

"You best take care, sir." She bit off the "sir" with a hiss of pain.

Her lids began to flutter, and Gerard realized she was going to faint. He leaped from the chair and caught her before her head hit the desk. He lifted her into his arms and saw a red stain near her ribs.

"Don't say anything about the blood," she whispered in his ear.

"She's fainted," he said to the crowd. "Let me through."

Someone cried, "Call for brandy!"

Gerard pushed his way into the hall, wondering from whom Undine wanted the truth to be hidden. He especially wished for Serafina now. She'd know what to do.

He dashed into the alley and backtracked to the Hollow Crown, intensely aware of Undine's small moans as he moved. When he reached the inn, he hurried up the stairs. The door to their rooms was locked and no one answered his knock. He took a quick look up and down the hall, then kicked the door open.

Serafina emerged from her bedroom and gasped.

"She's bleeding," he said.

"What?!"

"Close the door." He carried his charge into her room and laid her on the bed. "It's her side."

"I'm bruised," Undine said as Serafina examined her. "I dropped from an upper window. I cut myself landing, but it's not serious."

Gerard looked at Serafina, confused. Why would a fortune-teller need to drop out of a window? Serafina shook her head. She began to loosen Undine's gown. "Wait outside."

After an excruciating few minutes, Serafina emerged.

"She'll be all right. I think she may have cracked a rib. She hasna slept or eaten in almost two days. The cut is relatively minor. I dressed it. The bruising though…"

Gerard made a long exhale. He was relieved she'd be okay. And he was relieved for Serafina too. She seemed quite attached to the woman.

"I, ah, never asked your name—your last name, that is."

Serafina looked at him, surprised. "Fallon. My name is Fallon."

"Ah. Very nice to meet you, Serafina Fallon. I'm Gerard Innes."

She curtsied, and he surprised himself by attempting a bow.

It dawned on him that there were no emergency rooms in 1706—or penicillin or Vicodin. Even a moderate wound would probably be fatal. People here must lose friends and family members as often as he lost paper clips. He regarded the world around him with renewed concern. He barely made it through blood donations.

"Why would Undine be jumping from buildings?" he asked.

A curl loosened itself from Serafina's pins and fell nearly to the neckline of her gown. She tucked it absently behind an ear. He wished she'd left it dangling.

"I dinna know for certain," she said, keeping her voice low, "but I think she may be involved in things she doesna talk about—political things. I walked in once on her and Abby—you haven't met Abby. As I said, she and Duncan are set to marry. You'll recall Duncan."

"Oh, I doubt I'll forget him anytime soon."

"And she and Abby were talking about something that was going to happen when one of the Queen's advisors was visiting Edinburgh. They stopped when they saw me, of course. But 'twas the way they acted…"

"Is she a spy?" Gerard did not have a great grasp on Scottish history, but one of the campaigns he'd worked on for Highlander Whiskey had begun with a montage of key events in Scotland's tumultuous relationship with England. The spots ended with the modern drive for Scottish independence. Scotland always won or held their ground—cue "Scotland the Brave"—but Gerard knew five hundred years of tragic, deadly losses had been glossed over rather egregiously.

"It wouldna surprise me," Serafina said. "She's nae a supporter of war."

And therefore an enemy of both sides. "She's not a Scot though, is she? Her accent—"

"She's English, aye. From Cumbria, though she recognizes no borders. She has a house near Drumburgh."

"Yes, she mentioned that, right before she gave me my performance review. Let me tell you, for personality summaries, Myers-Briggs has nothing on her."

"She told your fortune?"

"Yes. I had some spare time after I'd been ditched."

Serafina flushed. "I didna mean to leave you, but I had nae desire to speak to the man in the doorway."

"The ship's owner…or the other man?" He wanted to see her reaction.

"Either of them."

"The second man said he had a message for you."

Her face tightened. "What was it?"

"I don't know. I told him I wouldn't deliver it, so he didn't tell me."

She relaxed. "Good for you."

"You say you didn't mean to leave me, yet when I came in here you didn't really look like you were rallying a rescue party. In fact"—he pointed to a bag on the floor of the sitting room that appeared to be filled with her clothes—"it sort of looks like you were planning to disappear."

"I-I…"

"Look, I don't much care what you do after you reverse this process. We drank, we met, we…did *something* all night long, then we did the whiskey a-go-go. Fine. Whatever. But I need to get back. I've got a partnership coming, and I have no plans to die of an infected hangnail."

"Doesn't having a hangnail imply you've actually done something?"

"Ooh, good one. I guess getting roughed up by your sidekick and helping Elphaba in there doesn't count as doing something in your world. Is she awake?"

"Do you need to do it now?"

"I realize the Great and Powerful Oz is a very busy personage. But unless you'd like to escort me back to the land of club chairs and heated toilet seats on your own, then, yes, now is when it needs to happen."

Serafina sighed. She called for some soup and coffee for Undine, then led Gerard back into her friend's room.

Undine leaned against several pillows, her hair loose around her shoulders, writing on a portable desk. Her room looked like a cross between a military campsite and the apothecary's shop in *Romeo and*

Juliet, neither of which gave him a very good feeling. There were dozens of bottles and twists of orange paper lined neatly on the room's chest of drawers, and unless one counted the half-drunk glass of water on the table by the bed, not a single item of a personal nature was visible.

"Aren't you supposed to be resting?" he said.

"I took some tincture of willow bark and am feeling a bit better. Would you have preferred to interrupt my sleep?"

"You didn't seem to mind interrupting mine. I need to get back. I need you to reverse whatever you've done."

She sighed and laid down her quill. "I am not in the habit of responding to demands. However, I do owe you a debt of kindness." She ducked her head in what appeared to be an unpracticed display of gratitude.

"You're welcome," he said.

"Perhaps the substance I said you lack is merely a deficiency, not an absence."

He bowed. "You are too kind."

"Serafina?"

Serafina, who'd been fidgeting behind him, squirmed by. "I'm sorry. I told him he shouldna—"

Undine waved away her concern. "I am assuming you ignored what you knew to be my wishes and mixed your own potion."

Serafina lowered her head. "I did, aye."

Undine made a short, unhappy noise. "Bring me the herbs. I need to see what you've done."

Serafina slowly lifted her head. "What do ye mean?"

"You used the herbs, did ye not? Bring me the

whiskey and what's left of the herbs, so I can estimate the potency."

A tiny muscle under Serafina's eye began to twitch. "I used them all."

The desk overbalanced and the inkwell crashed to the floor. "You did *what*?"

"All of it. The whole packet."

"Gods in heaven. How did you eat so much?"

"I didn't eat it. I drank it. In whiskey."

"In whiskey!"

"You said to."

"I said I recommended putting my marigold tisane in whiskey. I said nothing about the mixture I gave you. Well, I hope you two enjoyed your little liaison. I'm surprised either of you can walk...or talk...or"—she looked at Gerard's midlands with such naked curiosity he took a step backward, tripping over the threshold and only barely catching himself with the back of the settee—"or anything, frankly. Did you drink it too?"

Gerard hesitated. "I drank whiskey, yes. In the twenty-first century though. Not here."

Serafina, who'd swept the pieces of broken inkwell onto a sheet of writing paper, dropped them with another crash. "You're from the *twenty-first century*?!"

Undine collapsed back on her pillows. "Oh, this is recuperative."

"That's three hundred years from now!"

"There's no slipping anything past you."

"Why didn't you say something?"

"Why didn't you say you summoned me with magic?"

"Stop!" Undine cried. "Both of you. Fortunately for us, 'tis very little trouble to reverse a love potion."

"It wasn't a love potion!" they said simultaneously.

Undine rolled her eyes. "Call it what you like. The mixture of invocation and fornication you gave form to could have powered Paris and his kinsmen throughout the entire Trojan War."

Gerard grinned. "Trojan. Heh."

Undine pointed to large jar on the chest, which Serafina retrieved instantly. Undine shook the gray, powdery substance into her palm. "To summarize, we have a man from the future summoned to the past for a single night of passion. You didn't leave these rooms except to find me, and you didn't talk to anyone else. Is that the sum of it?"

Gerard looked at Serafina; Serafina looked at the floor.

"We didn't make love," Serafina said, busying herself with the glass.

"Except we did," Gerard said. "And I think a lot else happened too." He cleared his throat. "Quite a lot."

Undine flung the powder back into the jar and brushed off her hands. "What exactly? I have to know everything."

Serafina said, "I want to tell you. I do. But the problem is I can't."

Undine gave her a fiery eye. "Have you taken an oath?"

Gerard said, "She can't tell you because she doesn't know. Neither do I. It's as simple as that."

Undine closed her eyes and took a deep breath. Gerard could almost feel her counting to ten.

"'Tis not simple at all," she said, opening her eyes. "Nor do I have time to explain why. I have an urgent task that must be done. But I cannot undo anything the two of you have done until I have a full and detailed accounting of the things that need to be undone. Where is Abby?"

"I dinna know," Serafina said. "She and Duncan were here this morning when this all began, though she was sleeping—"

"Sleeping. What a notion. I shall need you to deliver this note, then. I was supposed to do it myself, but I don't think I can. It's to a tailor on Canongate, who is apparently a friend of the cause. There's a coach rented in my name in the stables. If you can do this and put together your list of activities while I rest, I'll be much better situated to help you later. I promise."

Serafina nodded. "Of course."

"But don't tell anyone else I'm here. After last night, I need to stay as invisible as possible."

"We'll be back with our list before you awaken." Serafina gestured to the door, and Gerard followed.

"Oh, and try not to imbibe any more herbs until the current ones wear off," Undine said to her friend. "You may find yourself running naked through the streets."

Eight

NAKED THROUGH THE STREETS. NOW THERE WAS AN image Gerard was unlikely to get out of his head soon. Nor, to be fair, did he want to. The carriage was waiting, and Serafina bristled as he tried to lead her onto it. This was a woman who didn't like to be told what she had to do. There was only one thing to be done for that.

"Sit down," he commanded.

The flash of her eyes had the approximate radiant flux of a small volcanic eruption. He felt like Vulcan, the all-powerful god of fire.

The driver appeared in the open door. "You're sure you want to take your lady to this place, sir? 'Tis not the most salubrious part of Edinburgh."

Several spurts of lava blasted into the air.

"Aye," Serafina said through gritted teeth. "I thought I made that clear when I told you the address."

The driver bowed politely at her before catching Gerard's eye for the official answer.

He nodded. "I can look out for her."

"As you wish." The driver shut the door and disappeared.

Serafina arched a brow. "You can look out for me?"

"I can."

The carriage burst into motion, jostling her hard enough to knock another curl loose. She was sitting across from him, and with the sun on her face, he could see a spray of very fine freckles across the bridge of her nose, like caramel stars in a vanilla sky. He had a sudden desire to kiss them.

"And how might you do that?" she asked. "You dinna have a sword or a pistol or even a knife."

"I'm actually pretty smart. I can finesse just about anything I put my mind to."

She made a small snort. But her amusement fell away when his gaze didn't waver.

"I hope for your sake we dinna have to test it," she said, cutting her attention to the street beyond the window.

Or for yours. The horses clopped crisply down the Royal Mile and turned into a neighborhood considerably less cheerful than the one they had left. "At some point, we need to hammer out the events of the last twelve hours, do we not?"

"Aye, we do," she said, lips tight as she kept her attention fixed on the road.

"That is, unless you're dragging your feet to keep me here longer? In that case—"

"Eleven o'clock," she said, "you're in bed, not alone, drinking Kerr whiskey, counting the shillings that come with your partnership. You have not offered your bedmate whiskey. How do I know this? She is not here. Why have you not? Because you're cheap? Because you're selfish? Let's call it a misunderstanding and let it pass."

"Did you even consider the fact she might not drink whiskey?"

"Doesn't she?"

He thought of the woman's slow descent to the floor of the elevator and hesitated.

Serafina rolled her eyes. "Eleven o'clock. I am drunk and, unfortunately, getting drunker. You arrive. I am hard asleep. What happened?"

"*Whoa.* Why do you presume you're asleep?"

"Because I canna remember a thing after closing my eyes."

"You cannot remember anything after drinking your third glass of whiskey. That, my friend, is entirely different."

Her lips, full and round, compressed into a pink line.

"And in any case," he went on, "you do remember something because you said I was surprised when you told me it was 1706."

"'Surprised' was not the word I used. You—"

"There's no need to lower ourselves to character attacks," he said. "Suffice it to say, I was surprised and you remembered that fact."

"Just as you remembered the men from the docks."

"I think we need to be honest here. We need a complete list. Some of the things we did may be of a somewhat personal nature," he said, thinking of her hair splayed across that pillow, "but in the interest of expediency, we need to simply say them and be done with it."

"I agree."

"Good. So, on three, okay. One. Two. Three…"

Neither said a word.

"Oh, for God's sake. I took you to bed. There. Was that so hard? I dropped you on the bed and your curls scattered over the pillow. I remember it clearly."

Her cheeks blossomed red. "Mr. Innes, I am not familiar with the mores of your time, but here, in Scotland, we dinna make reference to the things that transpire behind the doors of one's bedchamber. 'Tis both churlish and indecent. Such a statement would get you barred from the homes of upstanding people, and if I were to be named…" She shook her head, overcome, and returned her gaze to the street.

Gerard was stunned. "I would never knowingly… I mean, things are different in my time, I guess. I'm sorry."

She accepted his apology with a rigid nod. "What," she asked, fiddling with a fingernail, "happened after that?"

Did she want to know? He wished he could remember more of the details. Had he loosened her gown, kissed the beating hollow of her throat? Had the rest of her smelled as intoxicating as the whiffs he'd gotten earlier? Had her belly been soft and round, the sign of fecundity and abundance, or hard and unforgiving, like so many of the women he knew. Had she come to him tentatively? Or given herself with unfettered desire. *God, had she been a virgin?*

He sat straighter, internally speechless. Women in the eighteenth century could hardly enjoy the sexual freedom they did in his time. Wasn't it likely—or almost certain—that last night had been her first experience? He hadn't bedded a virgin since his teens—if you could call that awkward mix of pin the tail on the donkey and carnal sack racing bedding. He was so used to being on equal footing, experience-wise, with the women he saw—or even at a disadvantage—that the idea of being confronted with a virgin was a bit like being confronted with a pterodactyl or woolly mammoth—and only slightly less alarming. But what must it have been like from her point of view? He felt like a heel.

"I don't know what your particular situation was," he said, uncomfortable, "but if I… I mean, if it turned out that this was a new experience for you, I just want to say that I hope it was—"

"Oh, good Lord, Mr. Innes. I'm not…well, what you're thinking. Nor," she added with more bite, "did we make love."

"Far be it from me to contradict a lady, but given that we have been tasked with describing with precision the events of the last few hours, I think we need to accept what happened."

She leaned back and crossed her arms. "Describe again what you saw, please."

"The pillow was white. You fell upon it with a certain eager bounce." He adjusted his cuffs, admiring the sound of the copy as it flowed from his tongue. "And your hair fell free—of pins or your hands or mine, I don't know—but the curls flung themselves in every direction. And you giggled. Your cheeks were flush. There was an air of decidedness between us—"

"Good God. Is this what you write? In the advertisements?"

"*No*. But it is well written, isn't it? And, more important, it's what happened."

She sighed. "Go on. You and I and our 'air of decidedness.' Go on, go on."

"That's it."

"That's *it*? Pillow, curls, cheeks?"

"Yes."

She let out a long sigh of relief. "An air of decidedness is not a deed done."

"We were undressed…"

"That, as someone once told me, is entirely different. First, I wore a shirt. Second, for all we know, you…took a bath after I fell asleep."

"In a room with no bathroom? Serafina, be reasonable. I am hardly going to put you on the bed and not follow through. I mean"—he shrugged, helpless—"it's me we're talking about."

"I dinna doubt you *intended* to bed me. 'Tis very clear your relationships with women are tryingly single-minded. However, all you've described so far is placing me there. There are many a slip twixt the cup and the lip."

"Oh, there was a lip—two of them, in fact. But I can assure you there was no slip. I am congenitally incapable of not…er"—he caught the warning in her eyes—"closing the deal."

She made a noise of disgust. "The truth of the matter is," she said, "we know very little. And what we know may be misleading. The bounce of curls on a pillow doesna mean ye bedded me. The caress of fingers across gray wool doesn't mean I—" She clapped her hand over her mouth.

His gaze bounced from the plaid covering his legs to her face.

The slim fingers parted. "'Twas very fine wool," she said. "My compliments to your tailor."

The carriage filled quickly with an intriguing sense of possibility. The random bumping of the road had deposited his leg beside hers, and the electric charge that leaped between them raised the hair on his flesh.

The carriage shifted, and his knee lurched between hers. The fabric of her dress caressed his calf. In his head, he raised the silk and inserted himself between those thighs. He could hear her quickening breaths and feel the jut of her breasts as he took her—quickly, expertly, thoroughly.

"I think," he said, "we need to test our memories."

"*Test* them?"

He saw a spark of something in her half-lidded eyes—or did he? She hadn't moved her knee and it was clearly touching his. The air of the eighteenth century seemed to unlock a dangerous disregard for propriety, as if being at all times several steps closer to death also put one several steps closer to living.

"Yes," he said. "One of the memories, surely, if repeated, will unlock more."

"There is no pillow or bed," she said, and this time he was certain there was something in her voice.

He wished he'd remained in the gray wool she'd liked so much. He would gladly have her hands on him again, fumbling with his button, unzipping his fly.

He leaned forward, rustling her gown, and met her eyes. Heart thumping, he waited. She bent forward too, as if by the pull of a magnet. Her breath tickled his chin and that inebriating rosemary filled his head. Her right hand lay across her lap, and he took it in his, a diagonal brace, in case her courage was slipping. Her hand was warm, and he could feel the racing beat of her pulse. Curiosity shone in her eyes.

He grazed her cheek with his, stubble brushing her flesh, before stopping at her ear. "Take off your gown."

She inhaled sharply. He found the delicate bumps of her spine, certain he'd felt their outline before.

"We've done this," he whispered into the intoxicating mass of curls. "Do you feel it?"

"Aye."

"Take it off."

"Mr. Innes."

"Off."

"Without a kiss?"

He kissed the lobe of her ear. She arched her neck, and he kissed her there too.

"Before we stop?" she said, amused. "We've no more than a moment or two."

"Perhaps a shout of a revised destination then? How far is Edinburgh Castle?"

"Now? Ten minutes." Her thumb pressed the base of his.

"London, then."

The vibrations of her throaty laugh passed under his lips, and he brought his mouth to hers. There was something in her kiss that stirred him as no other—self-possession and strength, sadness and determination. And desire—smoldering and controlled.

"You are a blackguard, sir."

"And you are intoxicating."

"But I shan't undress."

"No?" He wasn't surprised. And it made him want

her all the more. "Ah, well, a man can only try. But you won't deny me completely. I can hear it in your breath. Loosen a curl."

"'Tis not a thing a lady does for a gentleman."

"You kissed me."

"A kiss." She shrugged her shoulders in a way that flamed his desire. "Even a lady might spare a kiss. But a curl suggests something more prurient."

"I know. Loosen one. For me. I want to twist it around my finger."

She let go of him, and he wondered if he'd gone too far.

Eyes bright, she lifted her hand to the back of her head. A single curl fell. He reached for it, belly hot, and pulled the silky end all the way down to the hollow of her throat, then lower, until it reached no farther. She inhaled, and he let it go. With a bounce, it returned to the base of her neck. She lowered her hands and the entire mass of orange and gold fell. He caught it in his hands, delighting in the silken weight, and spread it on the back of the seat. Then he brought her mouth to his.

When the dizzying fire receded, the vision was there—the pillow's white linen, the bed, the joy on her face, and the slow sowing of pleasure.

He gasped, the sense of her hips under him as clear in his head as the scent of her was now.

He looked in her eyes, which sparked a bright cerulean blue. She laid a hand on his cheek as the carriage came to a stop, and the tip of her fine, pink tongue found the hole in his chin and pressed itself inside. A second later, the door opened, and she hopped down the stairs, waving off the driver's offer of a hand.

She walked away, arms up, repinning her hair into a roll.

"Sir?"

The driver was staring, and Gerard realized he'd been sitting there half a minute, jaw hanging open. He shrugged off his daze and lumbered out of the carriage. He'd seen amusement, pleasure, and even hunger in those eyes, all of which had moved him. But the one thing he hadn't observed was the slightest suggestion that the vision that had returned to him had also come to her.

Nine

SERAFINA UPBRAIDED HERSELF SILENTLY, BITING HER tongue to quiet the tingle.

Another man in another carriage? You are as predictable as you are incautious.

Charming, he was, but the man made no pretense of wanting more than a quarter hour between your legs. At least Edward had plied her with the words of love.

Gerard appeared beside her, looking quite stupid with desire. "That was nice."

"Foolish as well."

Their entry to the small shop ended the debate.

Undine had explained the tailor handled only the least dangerous communications. Nonetheless, Serafina knew caution would be necessary.

A slight, aged man sat at long table, unrolling a bolt of fawn-colored fabric for a woman and her husband. He looked at Serafina expectantly.

"I've come for a tippet," she said, the words Undine had instructed her to use.

Wordlessly, she slipped the note under a small shelf on the counter, again, as she'd been instructed. The

man excused himself from the couple, gathered a
frilled satin stole—far too frivolous, Serafina knew, to
ever be something Undine would wear—and wrapped
it in paper.

When the parcel was tied, he dug through a stack of
receipts, found Undine's, and handed it to her, folded.
The receipt on top read "Edward Turnbull."

The man noticed her interest. "Do you know
the man?"

"I do. He's having a gown made?"

"'Tis for a woman named Hiscock, I believe."

Her cheeks warmed. Elizabeth Hiscock was the
daughter of Lord Hiscock. She was neither pretty nor
charming, but she was wealthy, which would be of far
more interest to Edward.

"I don't know her," Serafina said.

"They live in Dean Village, I believe."

"How nice."

"The dress is for Lord Hiscock's party on Monday."

"Ah, of course." She hoped the tailor exercised
more discretion with Undine's communications.
"Thank you."

Gerard took her elbow and, with a bow to the
tailor, led her from the shop.

❧

Harrow peered around the corner of the shop. "Do ye
think that's them?"

"Her, aye," said his colleague, Cambers. "I'd recognize that red hair anywhere—and the pips. Him, I'm
not so sure."

"You can't tell if that's the man?"

"'Twas dark," Cambers said, "or didn't you notice?"

"We're paid to be sure."

"*Och*, I dinna hear you proclaiming your certainty. Bill!"

Bill turned his head, the stream of urine still splashing against the brick wall. "Aye?"

"Is this the man?"

Bill managed two more spurts, then jogged to the corner, adjusting his flies. "Perhaps," he said, unconvinced, peering down the street, "but whoever he is, he bears more than a little resemblance to Mr. Turnbull. Maybe Lord Bridgewater would like a pair of bookends?"

He laughed, and Harrow elbowed him hard in the wame.

"What was that for?" Bill demanded, coughing.

"You're not to mention his name, idiot. Oh, there they go. Cambers, run after them. Bill and I will follow."

"Why am I always the one who has to run?"

"Would ye rather be the one with my fist in yer face?"

Cambers heaved a sigh and pelted up the street.

Ten

THE CARRIAGE SEEMED CONSIDERABLY MORE CONFINING to Serafina than it had ten minutes earlier. She kept her attention on the world beyond her window.

"What's a tippet?" Gerard said, breaking the silence. He gestured to the parcel on her lap.

"A stole." When he shook his head, she added, "A shoulder coat."

"And Edward Turnbull? Is he someone you know?"

"He is—was—my fiancé."

"Ah." Gerard dropped his gaze. "Was this a recent turn of events?"

"It happened six months ago."

Gerard's face softened. "I'm sorry."

"Don't be. He's a blackguard and I was a fool."

"I'm glad to hear you say 'was.'"

Edward would never again enjoy her attention, but given the way the man sitting across from her was make her blood bubble in her veins, she could offer herself no guarantee that she'd never be foolish again.

"Edward is the reason I summoned you."

"Is he? I'd be happy to break his nose for you."

He gave her a crooked smile, and she remembered him inserting himself, fists up, between her and Duncan.

"I have something better planned," she said.

The smile turned full curve.

"Not *that*."

The man was uncomfortably persuasive. She pulled her attention away from that dimple, which, like the whirlpool it resembled, seemed to want to draw her into its swirling depths.

"Pity," he said. "There's nothing like a little sauce for the goose to really make the gander squawk."

"*Hm.* I'll take your offer under advisement."

"Just sayin', I'm here if you need me."

"What I need involves something rather more important."

His expression turned more attentive. "Securing your future. I haven't forgotten."

She bowed. It touched her that he remembered. "My father was a merchant…well, stepfather. He left me a small inheritance. Edward and I… Well, I had something he needed after he exhausted his inheritance and his family's patience. I was a fool to lend him the money, but you know love. Soon my money was nearly exhausted too. He wanted the last bit I had to invest in some cargo. I refused. He took it anyhow. Now the ship has come in, and I intend to collect whatever is there."

"Using me."

"Aye."

"How?"

She picked a loose thread from her gown, avoiding his gaze. "You must sign for it as Edward."

He leaned against the seat, and she could see the calculation in his eyes regarding risk and reward.

"Is that why we were at the docks last night?" he asked.

"Aye."

"What else did we do?"

She shook her head. "I dinna know. I wish I did."

"Are we on our way to the docks? I don't mind helping you, but Undine was rather insistent we make a list of what we've done. Perhaps if we start there…"

"We are on our way to the docks, but by way of the inn. I need to get this to Undine," she said, rattling the parcel. "I imagine there's a message in here somewhere."

"Is that the state of spycraft in the eighteenth century? Messages hidden inside women's clothes and names like Lord Hiscock?"

She frowned. "'Tis not a fake name."

"'Lord his cock' isn't fake?"

He looked at her in such surprise, she nearly laughed. "No, it's not. Crispin Hiscock is one of the wealthiest men in Edinburgh—and a baron as well."

"*Crispin* Hiscock? My God, it just keeps getting better. Crispin Hiscock and his sons, Aaron and Holden."

Serafina snorted.

"And the daughter? Sharon, perhaps?"

"I have no doubt," Serafina said, trying to hold back the laughter. "I believe it's a prerequisite when you're being courted by Edward."

"Though perhaps the gown is for the lord's wife, Preston."

Serafina laughed—long, gasping peals that filled the coach box and drew looks from the people walking the Royal Mile. "If you only knew what Lady

Hiscock looked like," she said between paroxysms. "Pressed *on* at the start. Pressed flat to finish."

Gerard fell back against the back of the bench, clutching his belly. A moment later, he bolted upright, still gasping. "Oh my *God*!"

"What?"

"His name... The man's title is...Baron Hiscock."

The carriage was nearly to St. Giles again before decorum settled over them.

"Oh my God," Gerard said, wiping his eyes. "That is a name I will put in an ad campaign someday. It would have to be something for teen boys—a body spray, maybe, or an energy drink. It's a treasure chest, that one. I had no idea you were the sort of woman who spent her time in the company of noblemen— even if they are named after body parts." His brows shot up. "You aren't a noblewoman yourself, are you? I never thought to ask."

"Nae." She shook her head, wondering if he was making a jest at her expense.

He smiled. "Not Lady MacDonald or the Duchess of Danforth or the long lost Princess of Poldavia?"

He looked at her as if he actually believed it to be possible, which only made her wonder grow. Could he not see the disreputable state of her boots or the wear in her silk? The right shoulder had been mended so many times that a patch could barely hold it together. "I am not, sir. I assure you."

"You live in a castle. The coachman at the inn told me so."

She pointed out the window to a sooty, narrow structure of red bricks and seedy shutters. "Do you see that house? No, not the one with the window boxes and gables. The one beside it. I live there, in a room I let on the top floor. 'Tis about the size of this carriage. For the last month, Lady Kerr has kindly permitted me to stay with her at her castle near Langholm while I waited for Undine's help, but I do not live there. And 'tis very unlikely I shall ever return."

He regarded her with interest. "Why?"

"Well, 'tis a good distance from Edinburgh for one. It took me two days to get there." And nearly all her remaining funds, though she preferred not to share that part with him. "And my life is here."

"Friends and family, I suppose. Anyone else?"

She gazed at the floor, hiding a smile. He certainly didn't hesitate to pursue the things he wanted. In that, at least, they were similar.

"No family. No sweetheart. A few friends. But Edinburgh offers more than the pleasures of company. Lady Kerr's castle is stunning, but a hundred miles from the sea is too far for me. I need to be able to smell the salt, hear the gulls, feel my curls beaten back by the breeze."

The mention of curls cast a singular silence over them. The pins in her hair seemed suddenly to make her itch, but she dared not touch them.

"Speaking of curls," he began, but he did not finish his thought. The carriage came to a sudden stop, throwing Gerard nearly into Serafina's lap, the furious driver shouting, "*Get your foucking hands off my horse!*"

"Dinna fash yerself," said a voice. "I'll just need a quick peek in the carriage."

Gerard looked at Serafina. He recognized it too. The voice of one of the men from the docks.

She slid the lock closed just as the door handle turned. Gerard pulled her out the opposite side and into the street.

"Where?" he demanded.

She looked around. "There. St. Giles."

They ran across the cobbles into the shadow of its massive edifice and odd, open, crown-like metal steeple. For a split second, Gerard was amused by the notion of him running *to* a church with a woman. He hadn't forgotten Serafina's alarm at finding a ring on her finger, nor the start she'd given when the woman with the musket in the close had mentioned St. Giles earlier. Perhaps in the end, the joke would be on him.

For now though, he did his best not to lose his footing as he pulled her past the tents full of jewelry and merchandise banked along the church's outside wall, and followed her shouted instructions to turn left and then right, into the darkened nave.

The place was enormous, with vaulted ceilings and arched buttresses and—

"Jesus, it that a wagon?" he said.

"'Tis the fire brigade," she said, unfazed. "There's a guillotine here too, as well as the case that held St. Giles's arm, though I canna recommend stopping to look."

She directed him into the space farthest from the entrance. The building looked like a single church on the outside, but inside it had been carved into several large spaces. Six or seven supplicants were sprinkled throughout the pews, bent in silent prayer, while dozens of Edinburgh denizens roamed the circumference, looking at the architecture or engaging in heavy whispers. A strange frisson went through Gerard. He'd been here before as well.

They slipped into a middle pew and sank side by side onto the kneeler. She began to pray—he hoped for the possibility that they had not been followed. Gerard cast careful glances behind them. In the true Presbyterian tradition, the nave was aggressively unadorned, as if the merest brass candlestick would be an abomination in the eyes of God—or perhaps more importantly, John Knox. He shifted on the unpadded bench.

"We've been here before," he whispered.

The ring was gone from her finger, but that didn't stop her thumb from questing for it. She frowned and he waited for her to dismiss his statement, but then something above the altar caught her eye.

"Aye," she said, nodding. "I suspect we have."

Gerard hadn't had much use for churches, having grown up in a world where more attention had been given to the nearness of the family's pew to the minister than to the nearness of the family to his teachings.

She'd tucked her telltale hair into a sort of cap she'd pulled from a pocket, but he saw the orange gleam through the linen when she bowed her head. The light from the windows danced along the porcelain curve of her neck and disappeared around her shoulders. Her eyes were closed and her face intent. She wasn't just hiding. She was praying.

Her devotion, authentic and uninhibited, struck him. He shifted, and she smiled.

"Will ye pray?" she asked.

"Is that what you're doing?"

The peace on her face receded, and he kicked himself for asking.

"Nae," she said carefully. "Confessing, I guess. In my own way."

A movement in the aisle caught his attention, and when he turned, he saw a bearded, black-haired man scanning the pews.

"Is it them?" she asked.

"Yes. Stay down. He's with two companions. I saw swords, and Lord only knows what I couldn't see. Are you allowed to bring swords in a church?"

"Jesus said to put your swords away, that those who live by the sword will die by it. But on the matter of swords before the altar, he was silent."

"Well, Jesus had his father's twelve legions of angels to back him up. For the rest of us, I think a 'check your sword at the door' policy might be in order." The men were walking down the farthest aisle, peering at the face of each worshipper. "We need to get out of here."

"No, we need to part."

"What?"

"They might catch one of us. They won't catch us both. And one of us needs to get the parcel and receipt to Undine."

"And here I thought you were going to say one of us needs to call the cavalry."

"Cavalry?"

"Like a legion of angels. It doesn't matter. I'm not leaving you alone."

"Listen to me. I know this church as well I know my own name. Even if they do recognize me, they'll never find me here. Every Scottish church has secret hiding places. You need to get away. Here." She pressed the receipt into his palm. "Please. Trust me. I'll be safe."

"You're asking a lot."

"I know. You haven't disappointed me yet though."

He brushed off his plaid reluctantly and started toward the exit. Halfway there, the men, who had just finished their search of the first aisle, turned and headed toward the center one. Serafina was making her way toward the altar. Gerard hurried toward the men, catching them before they saw her.

"It's him," one of them said.

"Gentlemen," Gerard said, "could I have your attention? I have something you're going to want to hear, and you're going to want to hear it because it involves you."

The men swiveled slowly toward him.

"I am on a bit of a felonious quest here, aye?" he said, bursting into full Scots. "And you'll nae mind, I hope, that you look like men who might help."

The bearded man, clearly the leader of his idiot-faced companions, cocked his head, half his attention still on the pews beyond.

"That fount there," Gerard said, watching Serafina reach the altar and cross it, "is an original Henry Dowling. I'm sure you can tell by the artistic lines."

The fount, possibly the plainest Gerard had ever seen, seemed to swell in the glow of attention. He hoped he would live to amuse Henry Dowling, his college roommate, with the tale.

"Anyone knows," Gerard continued, "you can turn

a Dowling into"—what was an appropriate amount of shillings in this backward time?—"enough to buy us each a bull, er, a sword—*a horse*. A rare white one with a braided tail. But I canna lift the thing on my own. I'll split the sale four ways if you can only help me get it into my carriage."

One of the bearded man's colleagues leaned over, hands on his knees, to examine the bowl. "I've never noticed the lines before," he said. "They are quite fetching. Look, Cambers, ye can see the artist's hand."

The second man was more of a skeptic, but after a quick look, he was a goner too. Gerard grinned. How he loved advertising! Now, if he could just get old Beardy to buy in long enough for Serafina to get away, he'd be set. She had almost disappeared behind the altar. But Beardy was having none of it.

"Fools, the both of ye. There are no 'lines.' That fount's as plain as yesterday's groats."

"Not true," Gerard said. "Not true at all. Sir," he called to a well-dressed passerby. "How much will ye give me for an early Dowling fount. Henry, that is, not the father—in my opinion, a much lesser artist." Serafina passed the back of the altar and slipped out of sight behind a tiered row of benches.

The man frowned. "I didna realize the fount was made by an artist."

"Oh, aye," Gerard said. "'Tis not a fount, you see."

"It's not?"

"Oh, no. 'Tis a *statue* of a fount. Those are very different things, as I'm sure you know, and this man has offered me two shillings for it."

"I did not," Cambers said.

The man looked at his wife.

"I can sell it for ten in two snaps of my fingers once I take it outside."

"I'll give you three," the man said.

"Three? Sir, ten is robbing me. But I need the money. I'll take five."

"Four," Cambers said.

"Five," the man said.

"Sold to the man with an aficionado's eye." Gerard shook the man's hand and took the coins. "You'll never tire of it. I promise. Sorry, gentleman," he said to the three men.

"Wait a second—"

"Perhaps next time." Serafina had disappeared, and now so would he. He dashed toward a large group of older women approaching the doorway and made it through the exit just before they entirely blocked it. He ran to the front of the church, ducked inside. When he saw the men had left, he began to circle the nave. He needed to be sure she was safe.

❧

She gazed at him through the oculus in the steeple, directly over the nave. *Och, foolish man! I told you I'd be safe.* But the remonstration was halfhearted. She watched the care with which he looked for her, searching casually enough not to arouse suspicion if he was being watched, but carefully enough to spot her if she was there. He circled the entire nave, not once but twice, and when he reached the altar, he scanned the pews before slipping up the steps and following the path she'd taken.

Good God, he's going to search the entire place for me!

His determination sent a swirl of confusing emotions through her—irritation, gratitude, amusement, and something more troubling that seemed to squirm and stretch uncomfortably in the hollow of her chest. She pushed the feelings aside. She'd been motherless since childhood, fatherless since she was nineteen, a woman bereft of her standing in society since that fateful coach ride two years ago, and entirely alone since Edward's departure. She had learned that one could depend on no one but oneself, as well as the harder lesson that went with it—that believing otherwise only led to pain and disappointment.

Eleven

GERARD'S SHOULDERS RELAXED. HE HAD COVERED every conceivable inch of this place, upstairs and down, rattling doorknobs and poking around in rooms he had not been invited to enter. If she was here—and he had the sense she was—she was well hidden. Good. And the men following them had not reappeared.

Gerard was scanning the church's cheerless underground level, trying to remember which hallway led him to the stairs, when a voice said, "Oh, *there* you are."

He turned. He saw a young, low-level cleric in a frayed shirt with rolled-up sleeves. If he'd been wearing a cell phone on his belt, he could have passed for Gerard's accountant.

"Did she convert you?" he asked, giving Gerard's kilt the once-over. "*Och*, nothing to be ashamed of, aye? I'd wear just about anything for a chance to look at *her* over my morning bannock."

Gerard hoped a bannock was some sort of breakfast food. "I…guess."

The man looked both ways and lowered his voice. "Aye, well, the document is done."

"Document?"

"Gah, you really were oot your heid, weren't ye, lad. You don't remember?"

Gerard shook his head slowly.

"Last night? Stamping yer foot and wringing yer hands? 'What sort of a man do ye take me for? I willna be had without the benefit of a ring,'" he said, imitating Gerard's consonant American accent. "Let me tell ye, lad, I'd have gladly been had without the benefit of a ring, a nod, or even a 'good day to ye, sir.' She's a bonny lass, that one. Is it true the red curls burn when ye run yer fingers through them?"

Gerard stared, stunned. "I wouldn't be had without the benefit of a ring? *I* said that?"

"All of it—and more."

"Then…did we?"

"'Tis between you and the lady, sir. I am but a lowly cleric. I dinna presume to judge."

"No, I mean get married. Did we get married?"

"I canna say. I was on my way out when you found me. The lady had come in to purchase an entry in the marriage register. But you got wind of it and that's when the stramash began."

"Wait. 'Purchase an entry'? What does that mean?"

A man and a very pregnant woman approached, and the cleric took Gerard by the elbow and led him into an office and closed the door.

"She wanted to register a marriage that didn't happen," the man said.

"Jesus, you're selling indulgences?"

"A marriage isn't an indulgence, aye? Indulgences remit a sin. Marriage is a sacrament."

Gerard threw up his hands. "A thousand pardons—unless that would cost me too much, of course."

"Are you having a fling at me? Perhaps you'd like to take your wee deception to Tron Kirk and see if they'll make a copy of the record as pretty as this." He scooped up a sheet from the desk and waved it at Gerard.

Gerard snatched it from his fingers and scanned the florid hand. But it wasn't the rococo flourishes that made him stop. It was the sight of his scribbled signature at the bottom. "I signed this," he said, looking up.

"Aye, ye did. That's how it works, ye ken? You sign; she signs. I sign as the bishop. The seal goes on, and kiss your auntie, you're man and wife. The harder part is sneaking it into the register book. I did that too. But just look at the record copy. It's beautiful."

Gerard went back to the document, and the man read aloud, "On this day, in the year of our Lord One Thousand Seven Hundred and Six, Miss Serafina Seonag Fallon and Edward John Turnbull—"

"What? *No.*"

The curate raised a brow. "Nae what? You are Edward Turnbull, are ye not?"

Gerard looked again at the signature. That was definitely his scrawl—"virtually unreadable," his admin Bev had said, which Gerard always took as a compliment. Only people who needed to be known through their signatures worried about readability. But if Serafina wanted a fake marriage, why wasn't it a fake marriage to *him*?

The curate's eyes were narrowing.

"Aye, of course I'm Edward," Gerard said.

"Good," the man said, relieved. "I can hardly falsify a marriage between people who havena agreed to it."

"I can see where that would cross a moral line."

"Then what did you say nae to?"

Gerard shifted. "Er, it's just that…you spelled her name wrong. There's an *a* at the end."

"At the end of what?" The curate took back the copy. "Fallon?"

"No, no, no. Her middle name."

"Oh, so it's not—?" The curate made a noise like he was clearing a wad of phlegm from his throat, and Gerard realized with a start that he was saying the name.

Gerard shook his head. "No."

"Verra interesting. How *do* you pronounce it then?"

Gerard looked at the mishmash of letters in Seonag. Ever since he'd tried to bed a Shiobhàn, he'd known that in Gaelic, the letters on the page had very little to do with the way to say a name. She'd made him take a shot of tequila each time he'd mispronounced it. He'd ended that night stretched out in the backseat of a cab, singing "Single Ladies" to a terrified Eritrean driver on his second day on the job, who decided by the end of his time with Gerard to return to his homeland and join his brother's dry-cleaning business.

Gerard shrugged. "Like you said it, really, only with a bit of an 'uh' at the end."

The man frowned at the paper, unconvinced.

"Think of the *a* as silent."

"I can fix it, I suppose," the man said, reaching for the paper, "but 'twill be another two pence though."

"Never mind. It's fine. No one will notice."

The man handed him the copy. "Well, if that was

all you were seeking last night, I might have finished it then and there, but you began your bawling—'If ye want to bed me, ye must marry me proper!'—and the lady dragged you out, yelling she would come back later to fetch the thing."

"And did she? How will I find out?"

"Of course, she didn't. That's why I still have it."

"No," Gerard said, impatient, "I mean did she marry me proper?"

"Oh." The man looked disappointed. "I could ask my colleagues, I suppose. Come to think of it, Colm mentioned that Archie said a couple who came in before dawn to be married were like none he'd ever seen—drunk as baronets and barely able to stand. He sent a boy to follow them when they left."

"For safety reasons?"

"More financial ones. The drunk ones and smitten ones are the easiest to separate from their purses. And these two, Archie said, were both."

"You *rob* your patrons?" Gerard supposed he should be glad for his lack of pockets.

"'Rob' is a harsh word, sir. I like to think of it as freeing them from their worldly goods at a time when they should be focused on the spiritual. You know this church doesn't run on goodwill. The curates can't eat gratitude. We also let the spire tower if you ever have a need."

Gerard slapped his forehead, realizing the omission in his search. "You can get to the spire?"

"Oh, aye. 'Tis a lovely little space up there—so long as you get out before the bells peal. Verra private, with a view for ten miles in every direction—not that many are there for the view. And Colm and I have outfitted it to a discerning gentleman's standards. There's a crossbar on the door, a blanket, a candlestick, and a nice, thick stack of rugs."

"Prayer mats, I suppose?"

"Devotionals come in many forms, sir."

"Do you rent it by the hour?"

"And by the quarter and half too," said the man, pleased with himself. "Some needs are met more quickly than others."

"I'd like to take a look."

"Many have said that, sir. Sadly," the cleric added, the word heavy with meaning, "the door is locked."

"I see." Gerard considered his options. He could pay to have the door opened, but he was beginning to enjoy this one-on-one selling. "Last night notwithstanding, I am a man who would find the use of such a tower a very pleasing luxury. The men with whom I do business would also appreciate having a place to shed their worldly cares for an hour or two. Have you ever heard of word of mouth?"

The cleric shook his head, rapt.

"Aye, well, 'tis a very powerful motivator," Gerard said. "If I have a good experience—that is to say, a *very* good experience—I am likely to tell my friends about it. 'Tis the fastest and most inexpensive way for a brand—a business like yours, I mean—to grow. The men I'll be seeing at Lord Hiscock's party on Monday have money in their pockets and time on their hands. What could please them more than a spiritual sojourn in their own private tower?"

"At one with their salvation?"

"The very picture I had in my head! I would certainly spread the good word if I was given a chance to sample the wares."

The cleric was practically drooling. "Oh, *aye*. The door is at the end of a long hall at the top of the stairs. The key hangs behind the cracked headstone of one Donal Urqhardt. Shall I send a note for your lady?" His voice lowered. "Or would you prefer to sample one of MacGregor's girls across the street? I heartily recommend Peg—not that she or anyone could compare to Mrs. Turnbull, of course."

Gerard accepted this very questionable compliment with a bow. "Thank you—er, what is your name?"

"Kincaid, sir. Father Kincaid."

"Thank you for your verra generous offer, Father Kincaid, but today I am feeling quite self-sufficient. I believe I'll be able to satisfy my present desires on my own."

The man had the sangfroid to make it in the business world. He didn't even blink an eye.

"As you wish, sir. The next bell ringing ain't till vespers."

Gerard folded the register copy and slipped it carefully in his shirt pocket. He had a reasonable guess at what Serafina was playing at here, but he intended to be sure. "And I would be appreciative—*most* appreciative—if you could find out from Archie if the couple last night happened to be Mrs. Turnbull and I, and if we actually married."

"'Twould be my pleasure."

Twelve

Serafina inhaled deeply and lowered the spyglass. Here, above the bustle of the dirty streets, with the salt-soaked air in her lungs and the freshening midday breeze twirling her skirts and blowing tendrils of hair across her cheeks, she could think clearly. She had come here often as a child, when her da conducted his business with the merchants in the streets below. They had not been often in town, but when they were, this was the church they'd attended. She gazed at the people below her, as small as ants, scurrying to attend to their errands. But it wasn't the teeming humanity of the city below that captured her attention, nor mile upon mile of gentle green hills to the west and south. It was the vast blue expanse of the Firth of Forth and the tiny moving dots of white beyond the Leith shore that held her riveted. She would know the ship instantly—a fat little barque with a red stripe.

That much she did remember. The ship Duncan had told her was arriving had not reached port last night, contrary to his report, and her questions to the dockmaster regarding the new arrival time had eventually led to the wild chase through Leith.

Perhaps it had been a mistake to confront Edward about the cargo, she thought. She'd gone to him weeks ago because she'd wanted him to admit he'd stolen the money, and his denial pushed her to the boiling point. She'd told him she intended to steal the cargo away from him, that it belonged to her.

Had *he* hired the cutpurses and instructed them lay in wait, knowing she'd come? Edward was not one for unnecessary expenses. And in any case, he'd laughed when she'd made her threat. Spurred on by his derision, she'd formulated her plan, made her way to Kerr Castle to find Undine, and accompanied Undine and her friends back to Edinburgh.

The door at the bottom of the stairs made a noise, and her heart stilled.

Gerard ascended slowly, holding the key up as if to show he came unarmed. A bottle sat snugly beneath his arm. She met him at the top of the stairs.

"I wondered if you'd find me here." And she had wondered. She'd found herself unable to think about almost anything else since she'd climbed the narrow stairs.

"Did you wonder if I'd look or if I'd find? The men appear to have gone, or in any case, they didn't follow me here."

"I told you I'd be safe."

He shrugged and placed the key in her hand, which sent a shiver to her toes.

He said, "I was told if the crossbar had been thrown, I was to return again in a quarter hour and knock. I was told quite a number of interesting things about this place, actually."

She knew the rumors well enough, and her cheeks warmed. "Oh, aye. I suppose there are people whose enjoyment would require the insurance of a crossbar. I, however, came for the view, and, as such, am happy to share the space with others."

"Well, I locked the door when I came in. There's no point in inviting unhappiness, right? I must say, it was certainly a challenge to find you—" He stopped mid-sentence when he noticed the view. "My *God*."

"Do you like it?" Foolishly, she felt the view to be a gift she was giving him, and she wanted very much for him to be enamored with it.

"I live in a city," he said, clearly struck, "in a very tall building. Higher than this even. And I have a beautiful view—of fifty other buildings equally as high—"

"No! It's not possible." The thought made her dizzy.

"Oh, it is. The building I was in when you summoned me is as high as this and has a pool in it."

"'Tis something out of a story."

He chuckled. "I suppose it is. But the people in my time don't even think about how lucky we are. The woman I was with said—" He stopped and cleared his throat. "Not important. But this…" He gestured to the castle and the verdant hills beyond. "This is… I mean, it's just…"

"Aye," she said, beaming. "I know."

He looked at the soaring structure over their heads, a steeple atop a dome of iron ribs twenty feet high, beyond which a vista of several hundred square miles was visible.

"This is…amazing," he said.

"Isn't it?"

"This is your church, then? Where your family attended services, I mean?"

"When we were on land, aye. My father captained ships before he was a merchant. Most of the time, we sat for services on the deck of the ship, with the terns and kittiwakes looking on."

He turned a quarter turn to the west and grinned. "The castle."

"Oh, aye. Never been breeched."

He turned a quarter turn again, and she waited, hoping, hoping…

A small, thrilled sound rose in his throat. "*Wow.*"

"'Tis the Firth of Forth," she said, the flush of pleasure running deep. "It empties into the North Sea—sometimes called the German Sea, though not by Scots, of course. We believe the sea to be ours. The Celts called it *Morimaru*—the dead sea."

"Because of dangerous navigation?"

"*Och*, no. 'Tis not dangerous, not when you've done it enough. 'Tis a beautiful stretch of sailing water, though she demands attention and respect."

"As any good woman does."

"Any good Scotswoman," she said, laughing. "But she can hide her currents under patches of water that are still—what a sailor calls 'dead.'"

"The parallel to a good woman continues."

Serafina grinned. "She brought us the Saxons and the Vikings, who gave us our warriors and the will to fight. Then she brought us textiles from France and grain from Germany and timber from Scandinavia, so that towns like Edinburgh and Glasgow could rise like oases in the beautiful hills. And now Scots fill their bellies and their pockets with the riches from her waters. Is she not the most giving of mothers, the most glorious of gods?"

"You should write copy."

"For your advertisements?"

"Yes."

"Would anyone care for a woman's thoughts?"

"Good copy has no gender."

He took a step backward, and she caught his arm. "Careful." She pointed to the hole in the floor. "'Tis a long way down."

He peered into the nave. "I knew falling was going to be a risk around you, but I wasn't thinking this."

His eyes were like two tiny capstans, pulling her closer, turn by turn. She made a skeptical noise and looked away.

"What's over there?" He pointed to the east. "I mean, if one sailed as far as one could go?"

"It depends. By latitude, Denmark. By proximity, Sweden. But by current alone, you would reach Bruges long before you reached anything else."

"Really?"

"Oh, aye. A good sailor could have you in Bruges in four days—three with the wind at your back. Have you sailed?"

He smiled. "In my time, ships sail above the ground on the wind—miles above the ground. They can sail from New York to Bruges in eight hours."

"*No!*" She thought of her father's ship, the *Starling*, beating through invisible currents high over their heads. It was too fantastical. "Can you sail over a city? Have you seen Bruges's belfry from above?"

He shook his head, sheepish. "I've been to Bruges twice. I'm ashamed to say I've never even seen the belfry from the ground."

"Oh, *Gerard.*"

He laughed. "You sound so sad for me. No one feels sad for me. You also called me by my first name. I like that."

She handed him the glass and he put it to his eye. As he swept the sparkling ocean, she observed the strength of his profile. He did resemble Edward from a top-of-the-mast point of view, but in more specific ways—the strong set of his jaw, the lightness always at the corner of his mouth, the dimple, of course—he was so different. And the way he carried himself, like a man used to having his way, not by dint of his family's position but by force of natural intelligence and charm—that was different too.

"Do you see the ship there? At the very edge of the horizon?" She took his sleeve and pointed him in the direction she wanted him to look.

"That's not a ship. It's a speck of white—a wave, maybe, or a flash of sunlight."

She laughed. "'Tis a ship. With a square sail. Which means it's probably a barque."

He pulled the glass away and shook his head. "Honestly, it's a dot, and a round dot at that. How can you see anything in it?"

"Ah, when you've looked at enough dots on the horizon, you begin to recognize the difference. We cannot see the whole ship because the earth curves— they still know that in your time, aye?"

"Ha ha."

"And the curve hides the rest of the ship from view—and it will for the next few minutes."

"It's like a sunrise."

"Exactly. And soon it will be hull up—er, the front will be visible but nae the back. And a few minutes after that, we will be able to tell the ship's color *and* its colors."

He gave her an inquiring look.

"Its color is the color the sides have been painted. Its *colors*," she said, emphasizing the *s*, "are its flag, or at least the flag it's sailing under. A ship may carry a Saltire—Scotland's flag—or a Jack—England's—or even the French white ensign. Of course, that doesn't mean it's a Scottish ship or an English ship or a French ship. Ship's captains can be verra unscrupulous. Sometimes it's safer or wiser to sail under another country's colors."

"You seem to know a lot."

"I've been watching that one for the last few minutes. I thought I saw a speck of green at the mast top, replaced quickly by a speck of blue. I have an idea the captain is weighing his options."

"I must admit," he said, returning the glass to his eye, "I prefer sea gazing up here to trying to keep ahead of the bad guys. That was one hot mess down there."

She tapped her chin. "With 'bad guys' I can deduce the meaning. But 'hot mess'?"

"Just exactly the way it sounds."

She laughed. "Plain and simple. We Scots like it that way."

"I'll have you know I'm a Scot too."

"Och, *you*?" The idea intrigued her.

"My grandmother was born in Aviemore."

"A Highlander no less! What was her clan?"

"Macintosh," he said absently, picking up a stag-shaped candleholder from a broken barrel and examining it. "Inghean Macintosh of Clan Macintosh."

He had pronounced the name *knee-ayn*, exactly as a Scot would, softly and in the back of his throat. For an instant, draped in his plaid, with the ramparts of the castle on the hill behind him, he had transformed into a real Scot. And without any of Undine's magic in sight.

"'Tis a good name," she said.

"It is." He returned the candleholder to its place. "My grandfather called her Jean though. He didn't care for 'the whiff of old country' in the name. Used to tease her about it." The lightness left his face. "My male role models are not exactly heroes. My dad cheated on my mother. My grandfather treated my grandmother unkindly. They were both sort of pricks, actually. Oh, um, prick. Let's see—"

She held up her hand. "Oh, aye. Just like it sounds. We have plenty of those here—pricks and bad guys. And they all seem to be intent on finding me."

He laughed. "Why is that? I mean, apart from the fact I'd expect all men to want to find you?"

His compliment warmed her cheeks. "You *are* a practiced wooer, aren't you?"

He pursed his lips. "Somehow, I don't think you mean that as a compliment."

"'Tis neither a compliment nor a fling. 'Tis an observation. Is it... Well, I mean to say, is it quite easy to seduce a woman? You seem a deft hand." She thought of Edward and how easily she'd fallen.

"Well…"

"I dinna mean against her will, of course."

"Thank you for the distinction." He turned and rested against one of the dome's ribs. "I'll tell you what. I'll make you a deal. I'll answer your question if you answer mine: What does a woman like you have to confess?"

She flinched internally, but the look on his face was one of gentle concern, not censure. "Everyone has something to confess, don't you think?"

"No."

She made a skeptical noise but could see he was wasn't jesting.

"I think there are a few people who have a lot to confess," he said, "and a whole lot of people who need to be nicer to their spouses or lovers, more attentive to their kids, more patient with the people in their lives, but in general, no, I don't think everyone has something to confess, and I certainly doubt you do."

She scraped the metal of one of the steeple's intricate ribs with her thumbnail, afraid to meet his eye. "You were no' raised in my church."

"I *was* raised in your church. That doesn't mean I believe everything I was told. Did you kill someone or do them irreparable harm?"

She shook her head.

"And if you harmed someone in a reparable way, did you apologize and mean it?"

She thought of her father and the look of despair

on his face when she told him she was placing herself under Edward's protection. "Aye. Many times."

"Then forgive yourself, Sera. God, I think, wants us concentrating on the good—in ourselves and others—not fixating on the bad."

"Do you think?"

He touched her cheek. "Believe it."

She wanted to. The soft light in his eyes made it seem so easy. And where had he gotten "Sera"? No one had called her that since her father died. Edward had used it once or twice, but he'd done it when chiding her. She found she very much liked the sound of "Sera" when Gerard said it.

"Now ye must answer my question," she said.

"You *do* realize you didn't answer mine."

Now the light danced. She fumbled for a response. He laughed.

"Seduction implies undue influence," he said, rescuing her. "It's like pushing someone off the side of a ship when she doesn't know how to swim. It can be done, I suppose, though I have a pretty low opinion of the men who do it."

"Not an arrow in your quiver, then."

"No, but I wouldn't make me out to be a hero for it. I like to think of myself as the sparkling blue into which a woman is unafraid to fall—safe, warm, buoyant. But the best experiences—the absolute best—are when a woman knows what she wants and dives in to get it."

He took the bottle from under his arm and uncorked it. The scents of smoke and malted barley wafted through the air. "One of the perks of letting this space." He wiped the mouth of the bottle with his sleeve and handed it to her.

She was thirsty and the whiskey was good. When she handed it back, he drank deeply too, his mouth firm and pink across the opening, and for an instant, she wondered what it would be like to feel that mouth on her bud.

He pulled the bottle away and gazed at the swirling liquid. "Given what's already gone on, I should probably be more cautious when it comes to whiskey, but honestly, what more could happen?"

She took his face in her hands and kissed him.

"Whoa," he said with a breathless exhale when she released him. "I wasn't expecting *that*."

She buried her hands in the thick silk of his hair. "Could you seduce me?"

"I'm wondering if I could even stop you."

She kissed him again, just as intently. This time, he reached for her and opened his mouth. Her blood in her ears roared.

"What if I said no?" she asked.

"I'm getting some very mixed signals here," he said. "I'd stop, of course. Are you going to say no?"

Everything about him felt solid under her touch— his shoulders, his chest, the long muscles in his thighs—fixed, dependable, unchanging. He had stayed at St. Giles to watch over her. She hadn't thought such concern was possible in a man. The act would have never crossed Edward's mind. He would have reprimanded her for her recklessness. Gerard was different. But Gerard was also leaving. *Don't be a fool!*

"Why would I make love to you?" she demanded. "Why would I risk such a thing?"

Gerard looked behind him. "Am I part of this debate?"

"You canna deny it would be foolish indeed to involve myself with a man whom I need but for one act and who, by our mutual desires, will return to his own time as quickly as he is able."

"One act?" His eyes burned bright.

"'Tis not the act you imagine."

"What act do *you* imagine?" he said in a low voice. "Command me."

"I want your mouth," she said.

He kissed her.

"Not there."

He swept her into his arms, and in a moment she was on her back, on his unbelted plaid on the rugs. She wanted him badly, to sweep away the worry, to reassure herself she could feel something again, to experience desire in the arms of a man whose goal was not to strip her away piece by piece until she barely recognized the woman she'd become.

Gerard lifted her skirts and stroked her thighs. The long-hidden flesh tingled.

"I'm so afraid I'll regret this," she said.

"Don't be." His face disappeared between her legs. She gasped, the familiar warmth flooding her limbs, and she bit her wrist to keep from moaning. The plaid, still warm from his body, caressed her. The end came violently, her boot on his shoulder, and the wrist flung away.

"You taste like mango." He crawled over her and brought his mouth to hers. She tasted it—and his tang too.

The act he had performed was not entirely new

to her. Edward had performed it once, when he was quite drunk. Despite his clumsiness, she'd arched and cried out, discovering for the first time the rumored end she had never experienced during his more prosaic acts of lovemaking. But when she'd asked him to repeat it the next morning, he'd told her with disgust only whores took pleasure in riding a man's tongue. She wondered what you called a man who took pleasure quite regularly in riding a woman's.

Gerard eyed her hungrily. "More?"

"Oh, aye." She rolled him onto his back and crawled on top of him.

The sark covered him and she pulled the linen free. A light dusting of gold hair ran from his chest to his mons, where it thickened and darkened around his cock. She liked the contrast between the creamy skin of his thighs and the burnished, hard brown of his belly, where Edward had been pale and soft.

"Take it off, aye?"

He put on the sark and drew the fabric over his head. "How is it I'm naked," he asked, "and you're fully clothed?"

"It feels safer this way."

He gave her a gentle smile. "Safe it is."

She adjusted her skirts and drew him inside her. He closed his eyes, allowing her to find her pleasure in peace. And she did. She hadn't forgotten any of it—the dark hunger or the shared joy. Edward had not destroyed her ability to find succor in this, and the relief stung her eyes. She wiped away the wetness and took in Gerard's face as she moved. The long, imperial nose, the hint of whiskers, the beating in the hollow of his throat. He opened his eyes, and she touched his cheek, signaling her approbation. When the end drew near, he threaded his fingers into hers and held her as she arched.

A moment later, she found herself tucked against him, his plaid over both of them, while he stroked her hair.

"Safe?" he asked.

"Safe enough."

She traced the bones of his shoulder, as intricate as fretwork, feeling both light as air and rattled as a cart full of stones. "You call yourself a seducer?" she said. "You didna even take care enough to serve yourself."

A rumble passed through his chest. "What can I say? I'm not a very good one."

Ha! He was an excellent one—though she'd cut out her tongue before she said it. The man's self-importance could fill a carriage on its own. Her transformation into a boneless heap of jelly at his hands would have to be assurance enough.

He stirred, something else on his mind. "Did our liaison, by any chance, remind you at all of something else we may have done?"

She lifted her head and looked at him. "Do you think I'd forget something like that?"

"I don't know what you'd forget." He leaned down, dug in his sark, and pulled out a piece of paper.

"What is it?" She didn't like the look of it nor the look on his face.

"You told me you need me to sign for the cargo as Edward."

"Aye."

"And that's it?"

"Yes." The warmth between them was receding. She sat up, pulling the plaid more tightly around her.

He gave her the paper, and she unfolded it.

She saw what it was—could read the words clearly—but her mind couldn't quite bring itself to believe what she saw. "*No.*"

"Oh, yes."

This marriage record was exactly what she needed, though how it got created or ended up in Gerard's hands, she could only begin to guess. She realized he was watching her.

"We're not actually married," she said.

"Are you sure?"

The words were a challenge, not a question.

"Aye, of course. Did this come from the men downstairs?"

"Yes," he said. "I take it it's something you commissioned?"

She flushed. "Aye. It's…a bit complicated."

"Which must explain why you chose not to share anything about it with me."

"To be fair, I hardly know you." She regretted the words the instant they left her mouth.

"Ouch." He sat up and began coolly buttoning his cuffs. "Let's see if I can summarize the parts that have been shared with me. First, you would like me to claim cargo as Edward, your fiancé—"

"Edward is not my fiancé. He's the Englishman to whom I used to be engaged."

Gerard paused. "Englishman?"

"I say it with no pride."

"But claiming to be Edward is not enough. You also need a wedding record that shows that you and Edward are married."

"Aye."

Gerard pulled the sark over his head. "If you needed his name on the record, is there any particular reason why you didn't simply marry him?"

"I told you why," she said, standing. "He's a blackguard."

"You also told me you wanted the cargo."

"I hope you dinna think I'd marry him in order to get the cargo."

"I don't know what you'd do. As you pointed out, we hardly know one another."

"Gerard—"

"Just tell me the truth, would you?"

"I wanted the marriage certificate in case you failed," she said, squirming. "Then I could try again as his wife."

He reached for his shoes. "I appreciate the vote of confidence."

She had taken him to her bed out of desire, plain and simple, but if she had had any thoughts in the moments after their joining that the act might have softened his irritation with her over being summoned to Edinburgh against his will, she had been mistaken. And why should his irritation be softened?

She looked at the spread of blue water and the little barque caught her eye. A wee bit closer and she'd be able to see the color of the flag.

"I'm sorry," she said. "I'm determined to succeed one way or another. I act as if I'm the only person involved, and I shouldn't. I should be more considerate of your feelings."

Gerard bowed stiffly. "Tell me the truth then. Are we stealing the cargo?"

She made a long sigh. "According to the law, aye, but—"

"Oh, Christ."

"The money he used was *mine*. He'd lost his own sizable fortune before he even met me. The man searched me out, chose me for a purpose, and used me ill."

Gerard met her eyes. "I imagine that would make someone pretty angry."

"I-I—" *Damn him.* "I said I was sorry. Shall I apologize again?"

"Let's just get to the docks. I want to get home."

The message was clear. Whatever had transpired here, high above Edinburgh, was done.

This time at least you can say you got as much as he did out of it. But why didn't it feel like it was enough?

The ship they'd been watching glided into a brilliant tack, and its side came into full view. Red. The color she knew it would be. And under a Scottish flag. This was the ship with her cargo. She'd have half an hour before it reached the docks, then an hour after that before Edward swooped upon it, no more. She had the paper. She could do it without Gerard.

"Why don't you get dressed," she said, "and wait for me here. I'll talk to the men below and ensure the record represents everything we did here last night. Undine will want to be sure." She stuffed the paper into her pocket. "It should, but we canna know."

Gerard lifted two corners of the plaid, now draped over the rugs, a look of alarm on his face. "How in the hell am I supposed to...?"

"Lay out your belt. Lay the plaid on top. Fold it lengthwise, like a fan. Buckle the belt around you. Knot the top corners. Thread your arm and head through. You watched me do it."

"That's like saying I watched you perform open-heart surgery."

She descended the stairs amidst the noises of complaint.

"Belt, plaid, fan, buckle, knot," she called. "You said you're a Highlander, after all. 'Tis time to show it."

Thirteen

GERARD TUGGED MOROSELY AT THE HEM OF THE WOOL, now belted into a reasonably acceptable facsimile of a kilt, and looked at his nonexistent watch.

No phone, no watch, no pockets, no underwear. It's like Gilligan's Island *with whiskey and horseshit.*

And Serafina.

That was something New York didn't have. He could do without underwear for a long time if it meant Serafina might climb onto his lap again and warm herself on him. He thought of those fiery curls and looked at his hands. *Nope, no burns there.* His ego had taken a singeing though. He'd never been one to argue that making love opened the window of your soul to another person, blah, blah, blah. But for her to say she hardly knew him...

Had she used him as Edward had used her? What if she had? He could hardly argue the moral high ground here.

It dawned on him that he'd never felt used before—at least not in this way—and that it was a wretched feeling.

Ugh.

Where was she? It had been ten minutes at least.

There was no point in waiting. He could intercept her on her way up. He trotted down the stairs, opened the door, returned the key to the hook behind Donal Urqhardt's headstone, and made his way to the office of petty larceny in the basement.

"I'm looking for Father Kincaid," he said to a beefy-looking bald man gnawing the flesh off a chicken drumstick.

"Gone." The man belched.

"Are you Archie, by any chance?"

The man shook his head. "Colm," he managed to get out through the mouthful of food.

"Did you happen to see a woman with red hair? Quite pretty?"

At this, the man swallowed and straightened. "Are you the man in the spire?"

There's a title with a lot of baggage, Gerard thought. Nonetheless, he nodded.

"You liked it, I hope?" the man said eagerly. "Did ye see the candlestick? I found it at May Fair."

"I did. Brass, shaped like a stag. It definitely caught my eye."

"And you liked it? The candlestick, I mean," he added hurriedly, face reddening, "nae the rest. We don't usually get men going up there on their own."

Gerard sighed. "Getting back to the red-haired woman—I'm hoping you might have seen her."

"Last night? No, but I heard the stramash all the way in—" The man stopped, embarrassed. "It was, er, rather loud."

"Not last night," Gerard said, reddening himself. "Just now. Did you see her just now?"

Colm shook his head. "No one's been about," he said. "I've been here half an hour or more."

"Dammit! She was *supposed* to be here."

Colm's eyes darted back and forth. "Oh, God, it's happening again."

"She lured me up there with the promise of—"

A pock-cheeked cleric stepped out of an attached room. "Are ye talking about the ginger-haired lass?"

Colm quieted the cleric and said to Gerard, "You're saying she was in the steeple with you?"

"Yes," Gerard said.

"And you two…?"

"Of course!"

"And then she left you?"

"She was supposed to be here. She made it very clear she would be *here*, and I was to wait and then we would go back to the inn and…" Gerard noticed the men were observing him with the sort of sympathetic faces one reserves for lost children.

"Deserted at the altar," the pock-cheeked man said to Colm.

Colm nodded sadly. "And ruined in the process, it sounds."

"I wasn't *ruined*."

"Was it not what you expected? Not every man can pace himself in such a way that—"

"*I wasn't ruined!*" Gerard realized he was starting to sound like a lunatic. "I've done it before. Trust me."

Colm shook his head sadly. "No, no. A man's palm dinna count. 'Tis quite different with a lass—"

"No, I've done it with *lasses*! Lots of them!"

The pock-cheeked man took a step back. "Maybe the lass didn't care for such debauchery."

"A lot of them don't," Colm said. "Did ye mebbe give her the pox?"

"*No.* Nor ague, nor the grippe, nor an apoplexy, nor any of the crazy-ass stuff you people have here—though I wouldn't bet against a bad case of boot-to-the-backside when I catch her. And by the way, is your name Archie?"

"Alan," the pock-cheeked cleric said, "and she passed me at the main door. Heading north, if I'm not mistaken."

"Of course, she did. All right, I'm done here."

"You should have held out for the vows, laddie," Colm called as Gerard raced up the stairs. "Now ye have no leverage."

Fourteen

GERARD STORMED PAST THE ROWS OF TENTS, ANGER rising. Jerked from the past, showered with lies, mounted, and *abandoned*!

He ran into Father Kincaid in front of a shop filled with men's clothing and caps.

"There you are," the cleric said. "I was ducking into the tavern across the street for a wee dram a bit ago when I looked up and noticed your lady friend in the spire. May I assume you found the place, *ahem*, to your liking?"

Gerard raised his hand for a high five. "Oh, yes, I did."

Hesitantly, Father Kincaid lifted his hand too.

Gerard struck it hard. "Nailed it, baby! Like Martin Luther and his theses." Gerard wheeled around and ran directly into a wall of Duncan.

"What did you say?" His ears appeared to be emitting smoke.

Gerard held up a finger. "There's something you're going to want to hear, and you're going to want to hear it—"

The rest of the words and a sizable chunk of the

next five minutes were lost in the miasma of pain that followed his balls being kneed into the upper quadrant of his abdomen.

When the cobbles under his palms swam into focus, he said, "I take it you're not a Martin Luther fan."

Duncan pulled Gerard to his feet. Father Kincaid had taken his leave.

"Look, I don't dislike you," Duncan said. "In fact, in another time and place, I might even—" He frowned. "Is that *my* plaid?"

"Um." Gerard instinctively covered his face. "Maybe."

"Here's the thing, mate. I've been where you're standing. Trust me on this. Between Undine and her magical potions, swords, oaths, quests, some really potent whiskey, and a bunch of bloody-minded clansmen who'd just as soon kill ye as shake your hand, you don't stand a chance. The deck is stacked against ye, and Serafina will have ye if she wants. So, I'm probably not going to hit you again."

Gerard dropped his fists an inch or two. "Really?"

"But keep a gentlemanly tongue in your heid, aye? Where is she?"

"Dunno. She ditched me. Told me she was coming back to get me. Never came. I think she's headed north."

Duncan groaned and started scanning the heads of the shoppers.

"When you said you've been where I'm standing," Gerard said hesitantly, "were you suggesting that you… I mean…"

"Come from another time?"

"Yes."

Duncan gave him a wry smile. "Not exactly how you thought you'd be spending your Saturday, is it?"

Gerard was stunned. "Then you... You too..."

"Oh, aye."

Gerard slapped his forehead. "Duct tape! That's how you knew about me!"

"God, I miss it. Here, if hammer and nails dinna fix it, you're done."

Gerard tried to sort out a new worldview in which he was no longer the only person in the wrong time. "Did Serafina summon you too?"

"Nae. Abby. She needed a strong arm."

He sized up Duncan's triceps, which looked about like his. "Are you a black belt or something?"

"Bond trader."

"Oh."

"Exactly. I'm a steward here."

"Wow." Duncan pondered this as they walked. "Are you bored?"

Duncan laughed. "Clearly you haven't met Abby."

"But you must miss our world."

"Abby," he said, shaking his head. "You need to meet her."

The crowds had thinned a bit, and he and Duncan passed easily into the next lane of shops.

"Are there a lot of us?" Gerard asked.

"Like a race of men they've kidnapped to serve their dastardly desires?"

Gerard's jaw fell. "Oh my God."

"Nae. You might think that though, after you've fallen in love with one."

"I doubt that's going to be happening. So it's just us?"

Duncan clapped him on the shoulder. "So far, mate. But the day's young."

They walked by a bake shop, or what passed for one in 1706. The table held loaves of mud-colored bread, knots of something that looked like fruitcake, which Gerard knew in theory was supposed to be wonderful but in practice tasted like a box of decade-old Jujubes, cardboard and all, and a square cake onto which the baker was pouring icing.

Duncan walked a few steps and slowed. "You have no feelings for Serafina?"

Gerard instinctively lifted his fists again till he saw Duncan was still wearing his more domesticated countenance.

"She's pretty focused on what she wants. I don't think that includes me. Which is fine. I mean, nothing against Serafina, but she'll have her shipping thing going on and I'd just as soon return to New York. I've got a job I love, and an apartment and some really good leftover pad see ew still in the fridge."

"Pad see ew?" Duncan groaned hungrily. "Who do you work for?"

"Piper Cornish."

"Nice. My friend used to work at an agency. He said it's like Omaha Beach with status meetings."

"No. Seriously?" Gerard was shocked. "It's like the greatest job ever. I can change lives. I can fix the world. I can take anything and make it better—make people want it like they never wanted it before."

"Anything?"

"Anything."

"C'mon."

Gerard marched back to the baker. "Excuse me, sir. I have an idea I think you're going to want to hear."

The man didn't look up. "I doubt that."

"How much is that cake?"

"A shilling."

"Can you make the icing pink?"

The man looked in his bowl, then up at Gerard. "If you pay me. I can do most anything if you pay."

"How?" The possibilities were churning in Gerard's head. He needed some inspiration.

"With raspberries." He pointed to a basket of them behind him.

"Oh, excellent!"

"So glad you approve." The baker returned to the icing, clearly unmoved by Gerard's enthusiasm.

"And can you cut it into cubes, maybe"—Gerard held up his finger and his thumb, trying to remember the little cakes—"an inch and a half by an inch and a half?"

The baker put the bowl on the table. "No, why would I do that?"

"How much does that cake sell for?"

"A shilling."

"How about if I told you that you could sell each little cake for—" Gerard leaned in confidentially to Duncan, who was observing this interaction with fascination. "How many pennies in a shilling?"

"Pence. And twelve."

"Six pence," he said to the baker.

The man's eyes bulged. "Are ye out of your heid? For a bite of cake and pink icing?"

"Try it."

"Listen, laddie, if you want me to try it, you buy the cake. One shilling."

"I have a better idea. You give me the cake, and you and I will split the proceeds. If I can't get you your shilling back, I'll wash every pan here."

"For the next three days."

Three days. He'd miss the day he'd be made partner. He looked at Duncan, who held up his hands.

"Don't look at me. I think the baker's right."

But he wasn't, and Gerard's certainty went bone deep. He stuck out his hand. "Agreed."

Five minutes later, the baker was pouring pink icing over a dozen little cakes.

"Now I want you to put a raspberry on each cake, right on top, right in the center."

The baker had given up questioning Gerard's requests. Gerard didn't know if it was learned helplessness or the shilling sitting in his pocket, though he suspected the latter.

Gerard admired the baker's work. "And now…"

"Diamonds for sparkle? A coat for the cold? Upside down teacups for cake stands?"

"No, but I like the way you think. Nuts. What do you have?"

"A couple wee chestnuts and a basket of hazelnuts."

"Hazelnuts," Gerard said. "Sliced thin and chopped in two."

The baker returned with the prepared nuts. "And now?"

"I need you to put them around the raspberries like little leaves. Maybe five or six each."

The baker looked at him.

"What?" Gerard said.

"If you want leaves, you'll have to do it yourself."

Gerard was not afraid of a little pastry work. He started poking the nut slices under the raspberry.

"Oooh!" a voice squealed. "What is *that*?"

Gerard turned. A well-dressed young woman stood with an older man.

"These are…" *God, what had Cinderella called them?* "Pinafores. No, petit fours."

"They're little posies!" She clapped her hands. "May I have one, Papa?"

"Two for a shilling," Gerard said, quickly decorating the second and a third.

"We should get a couple for your mother as well," the gentleman said, digging into his purse.

Astonished, the baker wrapped the cakes.

"Blimey," Duncan said when they'd walked away.

"This is where you're going to be sorry you didn't underwrite me," Gerard said, tossing the shilling to the baker.

By the time the next woman walked up, the remaining eight petit fours, each with hazelnuts and raspberry, stood on a platter atop a ceramic stand borrowed from the jeweler next door.

The woman gasped. "*Och*, look at the wee sweets!"

"A shilling each." Gerard winked at the baker.

"Oh, I shouldn't."

"It's like eating joy."

She dug a coin out of an embroidered pouch and ate the treat while she stood there.

Ten minutes later, Gerard was seven shillings richer than he was when he'd walked up. There was one petit four left, and he gave it to a little girl in a threadbare dress who'd looked on, openmouthed, as he'd conducted the last two transactions.

"The key," Gerard said to Duncan, "is to remember the attraction of even the tiniest moments of true happiness."

"And the magic of a strong margin."

"There you go, friend," Gerard said to the baker. "Boxes with bows, baby zoo animals, anything with flowers." Gerard combed through the list of the things that pleased women that could also adorn pastry. "Jewelry things—maybe a ring. Whatever princesses wear or do—I have no idea. A wedding cake. Lace. Figure out what makes your wife squeal—within reason of course—and execute it in pink."

They left the baker staring into his bowl, murmuring, "I canna believe it."

"Well done," Duncan said.

"Twelve shillings," Gerard said, jingling the coins in his shirt pocket. "I'm on my way."

"I have nae doubt you'll do well here."

"If I were staying. I'm not." A pair of earrings on the table of the jeweler who'd lent him the stand caught his eye and he stopped. "Hey, how much would a nice pair of earrings be here?" he said to Duncan. "Emerald, I should think, for that hair."

"And you still think you're going?"

"I know I'm going," Gerard said.

"Well, we'd better find Serafina first," Duncan said, pulling him on. "Undine isn't going to do anything about you without her agreement."

Gerard stopped. "Are you effing kidding me?"

"Welcome to life in Clan Kerr, my friend."

Duncan began weaving his way through the crowd, with Gerard on his heels.

"Speaking of Undine," Gerard said, "I have a receipt for her from the tailor here and the stole is in the carriage."

"Oh, good."

"What is she doing anyway? Is she a spy?"

Duncan pulled him instantly into a deserted stall. "You canna be saying things like that here. She's working to keep Scotland from being swallowed whole by England in the treaty they're trying to pass."

Gerard looked both ways then back at Duncan. "You and I both know she fails."

Duncan fell silent. "No one knows whether it's possible to change what happens. Not you, not I, not Undine. Abby and I are helping the cause. I can't not help. Too many lives are at risk."

"But aren't you afraid if the treaty is stopped that you'll suddenly be a citizen of the United States of Canada, or Belgians will rule the world, or your mother will marry Hitler or something—you know, that step-on-a-butterfly sort of thing?"

"I can only worry about what's happening now, and now a union would be a verra bad thing for Scotland, which means it would be a verra bad thing for the woman I love. There's an English major, Lord Bridgewater, who leads England's northern armies—a nasty bastard if there ever was one. If Scotland falls to England, he won't rest until he destroys the clans."

"Jesus."

"And there's a party Monday night—"

"At Lord Hiscock's."

Duncan lifted a brow, impressed. "How did you know?"

"The tailor."

"Aye, well, Abby will be going—and I will too. As her advisor," he said with a hint of unhappiness.

Poor guy. Gerard had never seen a man as in love with a woman as Duncan seemed to be with Abby Kerr.

"All the big players will be there," Duncan added, "and I have a sense the party is where the final deal on the treaty will be made."

"So, if the party's Monday, why the fancy duds today?"

Duncan looked down, embarrassed, at the gleaming breeches, polished boots, frilled shirt, and knee-length frock coat. "*Och*, we're calling on the bishop tonight. He's one of the biggest buyers of Kerr whiskey. But I'll be wearing this to the party as well. Abby says wearing a plaid would be a sign of disrespect given Lord Hiscock's staunch pro-treaty views. I say, fouck 'im, but you know how women are."

"I hear ya, friend. I have to say, while getting a plaid on is a challenge on the level of solving a Rubik's Cube, wearing one is actually pretty damned comfortable." He gave Duncan a jocular poke of the elbow. "And you gotta admit, pants-less ain't a bad place to be when you're ready to"—the words died under Duncan's gaze—"take a piss. Say, how long have you been here, anyway? You seem to know a lot."

"A few weeks, no more. Like you, I was determined to go back too…until I wasn't."

"Abby?"

"Aye. Then I found myself sent back when I wasn't

ready. Fortunately, my grand-da had traveled back here before me and knew how to help me get back."

"Really?"

"Apparently, he'd fallen in love with a golden-haired lass from Dingwall while he was here many years ago."

"Dingwall?"

"Aye. It's up north. Apparently, the lass had been sold off in marriage to a merchant. She and my grand-da met at an inn. She was supposed to take a carriage to Edinburgh to meet her husband-to-be, but it didn't arrive. They took a tinker's wagon instead and the banging of the pots kept them from sleeping. They fell in love at once, and, well, pretty soon the pots weren't the only things banging. But then he was whisked back to the present day as quickly and with just about as much warning as he'd been whisked away." Duncan gave Gerard a look of embarrassed pride. "Sixty, the man was."

"Whoa! I take it your grandmother never found out."

"Long dead—which was lucky for him, as she would have kicked his arse to Inverness and back." A pleased, faraway expression came over Duncan's face. "Actually, Abby rather reminds me of her."

They had reached the street and found the carriage waiting but no sign of Serafina. "Do you think she went back to the inn on foot?" Gerard asked. "I'm a little concerned because the men at the inn followed us to St. Giles. We managed to ditch them, but they could have come back."

"Let's hope she's there. She's been mulling over some sort of plan, and I know it involves the arrival of a red barque, but—"

"Oh, *shit*. I know where she is."

❧

When the carriage started down the Royal Mile, Serafina stepped from behind the tent of a shop, her purchases under her arms.

Nailed it, did he? She'd never heard the phrase before, though it hardly needed translating. Idiots boasting of their exploits with women were identifiable in any language they spoke. She only wished it had been her knee in his stones, not Duncan's.

Given Gerard's unenthusiastic support for her plan, she'd decided in the steeple to disentangle him from it. Now she was doubly glad she had. She didn't need a man. Not anymore. She tucked her purchases under her arm.

"Did you buy your sweetheart a new sark?" a jeweler in the next tent asked, ducking his head toward the shop she'd just exited. "If so, he'll need a new brooch for his plaid to go with it." He held out a beautiful hand-worked circlet of silver bisected by a pin as sharp as a blade. "You could surprise him."

"Oh, I could definitely surprise him with that," she said. "But I'm afraid I'm the only one who would enjoy it."

Fifteen

René Duchamps gazed at the line of landsmen before him, all who were hoping for a job on his ship, *La Trahison*. Drunken, poxed buggerers, all—he had no high opinion of Scotsmen as sailors—and yet he, as acting lieutenant, would be required not only to teach them to make sail, keep a watch, and fight but to feed and clothe the brutes as well. In truth, the landsmen should pay him, not the other way around.

"Take this to the purser," Duchamps said to the gap-toothed Scot before him. "He'll provide you with breeks and a shirt."

"I dinna wear breeks."

"You do on this ship, *oui*?" He stamped the man's papers. "We'll have passengers on our next voyage. We cannot have them searching the sky for Polaris or Ursa Major and finding an orchard's worth of Scottish plums instead. *Next*."

"Harris, sir—Struan Harris."

"*Bonjour*. I'm Lieutenant Duchamps. What are you here for, Harris?" The young man was nearly as tall as Duchamps but much slimmer, with features except for his thick, black brows that were as delicate as a girl's, and the rosy cheeks and beatific smile of an angel.

"I want a job and I'm willing to work hard." The lad lowered his head and swept off his cap, revealing ginger hair braided into a tight plait.

When the boy looked up again, Duchamps tried to find a place to look other than his blue eyes and long, lacy lashes. He cleared his throat uncomfortably. "Can you make sail, climb, and work a gun crew?"

The boy nodded. "Aye, sir. All verra well."

"Then sign here. We have a ship full of cargo and could use your help."

The boy leaned down to sign, and Duchamps leaned forward without thinking and drew in a lungful of the boy's alluring scent. When he realized what he was doing, he jerked back hard enough to make his chair squeak.

"Is everything all right, sir?" the young man said.

"*Oui*. You can pick up your uniform from the purser."

"Thank you. You won't regret it." The lad made a formal bow, then hesitated.

"What is it, Harris?"

"About the cargo—will ye be moving it into a warehouse or directly onto wagons?"

Duchamps frowned. "That's an odd question."

"Is it? I have a brother who works at one of the warehouses. I just wondered if I'd be seeing him."

"Move along, Harris."

The boy bent to pick up his bag from the floor and the opulent curves of his arse took Duchamps's breath away. Horrified, Duchamps slapped a hand to his forehead, wondering if he was succumbing to a fever.

"You, there!" he called to a passing cook's mate. "Get me some coffee and make it strong, *oui*?"

Sixteen

SERAFINA'S BLOOD THRUMMED WITH THE HAPPINESS OF being on a freshly scrubbed deck in the middle of a briny breeze as she looked out over the docks of Leith. Once she knew which cargo was Edward's and where it was going, she'd be off the ship and on the way to collecting it.

A man in a blue coat with coal-black eyes stepped between her and the rail. It was the captain. She could tell by the lace at his shoulder. "We don't pay men to stand around and stare. Who are you, sailor?"

"Struan Harris, sir. I'm new."

"New is no excuse. Find your company and get to work. Next time it'll be the cat for you."

Serafina sniffed. *A pleasure to meet you, Struan. Welcome aboard. So glad you chose* La Trahison. Her father had been a disciplined captain, but discipline didn't preclude civility. And a ship's company worked together far better under a captain they admired than under one they hated. So, a French lieutenant and an English captain. She expected she'd hear a number of tongues aboard. Merchantmen traveled the world to gather and deliver their precious cargoes, and they picked up sailors anywhere they could get them.

Serafina followed a stream of sailors heading for the narrow companionway. What she wanted would be below. The ship had just arrived in port, and the wagons were only beginning to gather on the docks to collect the cargo.

"Are you here for the cutlasses and knifes?" asked the man at the bottom of the steps. The men before her nodded and she did too. "Dinna know how he expects the armorer to sharpen all these and fix the grates in a single afternoon, but I ain't the captain, am I?"

When the men disappeared into the weapons room, she threaded her way to the next set of stairs and descended again. The lowest decks were dedicated to cargo, which would be packed in crates and barrels marked with the owner's name.

The hemp of ropes as thick as her leg, the pine of spars, the sweat of men working the pump—the smells reminded her of the carefree happiness of her youth. She'd had a hundred hiding places in her father's ship and could play from dawn to dusk without ever getting bored.

She turned the corner and found the cargo. The crates were stacked three high and ran for the length of the ship. Sailors were just beginning to secure the first ones for removal. She padded down the center walkway, reading the names on the containers.

Piggott-Jones
Macniece
Carlton

FitzGerard
Nixon
Foster & Blair
MacAfee
Cockburn
Frazier
MacNulty

No *Turnbull*. She walked the length again with no more success. Her contact had assured her the ship with Edward's cargo was coming in this week, and Duncan's questions at the dock the afternoon before had unearthed the fact that the Turnbull cargo would be on *La Trahison*, a red barque under a French flag. She stopped a man examining one of the ship's ribs, angle in hand, a man she guessed to be the ship's carpenter. "Is this all the cargo?"

"Why, lad? Not enough to keep you busy?"

"Lieutenant Duchamps asked for a status on the Turnbull cargo."

The man laughed. "The captain will be handling that on his own, I expect."

This was the right ship!

"Perhaps he's already removed it to his cabin, then?" Serafina searched the man's face for confirmation.

He returned to his rib. "You're new, ain't ye? Take my advice and let it go. The captain will handle it."

Unfortunately, "let it go" was not in Serafina's nature. She headed down the next companionway into the lowest level of the ship.

Here the ballast—usually iron pig or, as on this ship, rocks—sat to balance the vessel, and there were a dozen sailors redistributing the weight. The balls and shot for the great guns were stored here as well, in small rooms, and covered with grease to ward off rust. The foul-smelling bilge water lapped beneath the walkways, and she edged past two sailors knee-deep in the stuff. There appeared to be little enough of interest on this deck, but she wanted to be sure. A padlocked door stood at the far end of the deck. It could be the arms, but it would be unusual to store them in so damp an atmosphere. She made her way over to investigate. She was almost there when nearby men's voices brought her to a halt.

"...you're sure no one knows? You're the only man on board I can trust. No one must know, aye?"

She recognized the voice of the captain. He was directly behind her in the walled-off carpenter's walkway, the narrow space running the circumference of each deck used to inspect the timbers for leaks and damage.

She took a step to hide and the floor squeaked. The voice stopped. She hurried back toward the ballast and got in the long line down which men were transferring the rocks. A dozen rocks in, a hand came down on her shoulder.

"Monsieur Harris, what are you doing here?"

Had Lieutenant Duchamps been the man to whom the captain was talking? She hadn't seen from what direction Duchamps had come. The captain was nowhere in sight.

"I was looking for you," Serafina said.

"Were you?" The man frowned and took a step back. "The carpenter said you might be."

"I couldna find the purser. Someone said he might

be on the orlop deck, but I must have gone one deck too far. I am used to my last ship. Forgive me, sir."

"The purser is on the quarterdeck. Hurry along. The captain will be calling all hands soon."

Serafina raced up the companionway to the top deck. She wanted no parts of the purser *or* the all hands. She was ready to leave and slipped, head down, into the group of sailors splicing rope and waited until Duchamps passed. Then she ran past the opening to the gangplank and jerked to a stop. An armed guard stood at the top, blocking anyone from exiting.

She sidled up to a sailor who was adjusting some rigging. "Why is the gangway blocked?" she asked under her breath.

"The captain says we're sailing out."

"*Tonight?*" The ship had barely arrived.

"Now."

She felt a prickle on her neck and looked up. The masts, previously bare, were beginning to open their sails like butterflies emerging from their chrysalises, and men ran barefoot over the yards, working in beautiful unison to secure the canvas. Serafina had no wish to be borne away to God knows where on a ship with a captain doing something questionable enough to want to hide it from his crew.

Panicked, she peered over the side in search of the metal footholds used like a ladder to descend into a boat. She spotted a set to her right. She swung herself over the railing and felt for the first rung.

Her toes had just found a purchase when a fist grabbed her collar.

"Harris, we do not take kindly to deserters."

Seventeen

GERARD PEERED OUT THE CARRIAGE WINDOW, DUNCAN next to him. The ship was a hive of activity, and wagons lined the dock, waiting to carry away the treasure within.

"Are you sure that's the one?" Duncan asked.

Gerard nodded. "The ship she was watching was red with square sails."

"And red with square sails was the description of the ship the dockmaster gave me when I asked him how Edward Turnbull's cargo would be arriving."

Gerard gave him a look. "You're after his cargo too?"

"I asked on Serafina's behalf yesterday. She sent me to the docks."

"Our Serafina has had a busy twenty-four hours, hasn't she? Well," Gerard said, hopping out, "it's the only red ship in port. She's got to be around here."

Duncan followed, but his attention was immediately caught by a young, well-dressed woman with dark hair standing in front of a chandler's shop. He ran to her side, chatted with her briefly as she gazed at Gerard over her shoulder, and led her back to the carriage.

She carried herself with the bearing of a queen, and Gerard found himself bowing automatically.

Without ado, she said, "Did you find Serafina?"

"Possibly," Gerard said.

Duncan said, "Lady Kerr, may I ask you to make the acquaintance of Mr. Gerard Innes."

This was Abby, then, the chieftess with whom Duncan had fallen in love. Lady Kerr extended her hand, palm down, and Gerard, with a nod from Duncan, bent to kiss it.

"I'm Lady Kerr's steward," Duncan added.

Sure you are.

"And the man I am to marry—though you are not to say a word to anyone," she added in a voice that expected to be obeyed.

"No, ma'am."

"I am Abby to you, please—in private. Lady Kerr, otherwise, of course."

Gerard nodded briskly.

Abby smiled. "I hear you are to marry Serafina."

Gerard sputtered. "Is that what Duncan says?"

"No, that's what Undine says. Duncan says you bedded her and made light of it to one of the curates at St. Giles."

Gerard flushed. "It was a moment of annoyance, and I have come to see the error of my ways."

"He has also come to see his breakfast again," Duncan added helpfully, "when he cacked it up on the cobbles of the Royal Mile after an urgent meeting with my knee."

"I'm glad to hear of it. Serafina is a most treasured friend. We are quite glad she had the opportunity to attempt to dismiss her odious fiancé from her thoughts with your, well, assistance. However, if you have any hope of being permitted to marry her, you will behave in a manner more befitting a gentleman, aye?"

"*Permitted* to marry her? Who are you, the pope?"

"I am the chieftess of Clan Kerr, and as a guest of mine, Serafina is under my protection. Until such time as she decides to remove herself from it, you require my assent to marry her."

"You'll require mine too," Duncan added, amused, "but only because she's my friend."

Gerard looked from one face to the other. "Oh, this is rich. I'm dragged from my bed against my will, and now you're saying somehow I have to *earn* the right to marry her? Listen, I have no intention of marrying Serafina, but if I did, the only person's assent I'd need is hers."

He didn't know how Abby could look down her nose at him given that he was easily four inches taller than she was, but she managed to. "Good news, sir. With that sort of regard for her feelings, you're on your way to earning my approval."

Maddening! The women here were pushy, willful, and utterly full of themselves. Why would any man want to stay? Then he remembered the feel of Serafina's hand in his before they kissed and the way her legs enveloped him on that stack of rugs in the spire.

Duncan saw the sudden change on his face and laughed. "You'll get used to it."

"Well, all of this marriage talk is well and good, but until we actually find Serafina, we're wasting our breath. There are three idiots with pistols following us—the worst kind of idiots, in my opinion—who are probably looking for her too, and I'd prefer they didn't find her first. If that's the ship, then the cargo of Edward the Odious is sitting there, waiting for someone to collect it. Oh, *shit*." Gerard pointed to the ship, where, high above them, a sailor hung half over the railing, searching for an external rung with a questing foot.

"He won't fall," Abby said, unconcerned. "Sailors do that all the time. They're absolute monkeys when it comes to climbing."

"That's not a sailor," Gerard said. "At least not a career one. It's Serafina. I'd recognize that ass anywhere."

An officer in a tricorne—clearly the captain—grabbed Serafina by the collar and jerked her back onto the deck.

"*Christ*, now what?"

Abby tapped Gerard's arm and pointed to the top of the main mast. "We have bigger problems. That flag means the ship is about to leave port."

Gerard grabbed Duncan's arm and pulled him toward the carriage. "C'mon! I need your clothes!"

"Again?"

Eighteen

SERAFINA WAS DEPOSITED INSIDE THE CAPTAIN'S QUAR-
ters with a shove by a burly sailor by the name of
Rondo, whose only words of collegial support were
"Stand there until the captain comes" and "Take yer
hands out of yer pockets."

She was well versed in the ways of shipboard
justice. She had heard her father mete out whip-
pings and floggings, though she'd been confined to
her small quarters when the actual punishment took
place. Once, when she was nine, she'd shimmied up
to the barrel at the top of the mast in order to see a
sailor of whom she had been quite fond receive his
twenty lashes. The spray of the blood and the jerk of
the man's body had horrified her to such an extent
that she'd cried herself to sleep that night and nursed
a silent grudge against her father for weeks. After that,
she'd always taken care to curtsy deeply to the sailor.
It seemed to her a campaign of dutiful respect was the
only cure for the abject humiliation he'd suffered.

She had no wish to suffer twenty lashes, nor ten,
nor even one. But the punishment for desertion was

death, and if this captain had reason to believe she'd overheard his duplicitous plans, lashes might be the best she could hope for.

The captain's quarters held a gleaming mahogany dining table that ran the length of one side. His desk stood against the opposite wall, covered in stacks of the usual lists, logs, and reports necessary to the running of a ship. A latched glass-doored case holding a few books, a shaving cup and brush, and a silver elephant hung on the wall beside the desk, and beside that, on hooks, was an ancient ebony-handled pistol and the whorled tusk of a narwhal. Everything on a ship had to be secured in place, except the lanterns that swung from the ceiling, to ensure they didn't fall off a table, and decanters of wine, which were round-bottomed, to roll with the swells during dinners. If Edward's shipment was in here, it was a rather small one. Gems, perhaps, or gold. The only place to hide anything was the curving row of floor lockers topped by cushions that formed a bench under the stern windows. She briefly considered trying the desk drawers and lockers but decided surviving might be a better objective for the moment and turned her attention to that. An armed guard stood outside the door, standard in a working ship where the threat of mutiny was ever present. Her best option was the tiny balcony beyond the stern windows. She could swim—many sailors couldn't—and if she could reach it to jump into the water...

The captain strode in, head ducked for the low ceiling, dashing her hopes. He closed the door behind him and sunk into a chair at the dining table.

"Where is your salute, seaman?"

She did as he asked.

"You were rated an able seaman."

"Aye, sir."

"In my experience, able seaman do not have trouble finding the purser, they do not find themselves accidentally in the hold, and they don't help themselves to shore leave without permission."

"No, sir."

"Take off your cap when you speak to me."

Reluctantly, she grabbed the cap and pulled it free. A thick pigtail, so popular with sailors, uncurled and slipped down her back.

She had bound her breasts, inked in brows and whiskers, and carefully chosen a loose sark and trousers. Despite her best efforts, however, she knew from the plays she'd seen that projecting a reasonably believable version of the opposite gender was hard.

The captain's eyes narrowed. He circled his finger in the air.

Serafina turned slowly.

"What were you doing in the hold?" he asked.

"I was looking for a girl."

"A girl?"

Girls were occasionally smuggled on board ships by lovelorn sailors and hidden in one of a ship's many out-of-the-way places. "Molly was my girl," she said defiantly, "at least I thought she were. A sailor on your ship convinced her to come aboard with him. Said he would hide her in the cable deck. Which is why I signed on. I came here to find her."

The captain considered this story, fingers templed.

"Are you aware your signature binds you to us for

the next year? And that the punishment for desertion can be death?"

The hairs on her neck stood on end. "Aye, sir. I am dreadfully sorry. I am here to serve. For the duration."

"'Tis very good to hear. However..." He shifted oddly in his seat. "I should not like to start this trip with a hanging. It sets a pall over the men."

A wave of relief washed over her. "Thank you, sir."

"I shall paddle you instead. Twenty strikes. Lower your trousers."

She froze. "I beg your pardon?" Paddling was not a punishment at sea—at least not that she had ever heard of.

"I said lower your trousers. If you think you'll have any trouble with it, I'll have the guard in to help us."

"No, no. I won't." Shaking, Serafina unbuttoned her breeks but held the fabric tightly. "W-where do you want me?" She started reluctantly toward the table but had only taken a step or two when she spotted the tight script of an unsigned note peeking from a stack of notebooks on the desk. She dropped her palms on the wood. "Here?"

"That'll do."

He stood and she heard the click of the door's lock behind her.

"Wait." He scurried to the desk and moved the papers and ink pot from the side over which she'd be leaning and stacked them just beyond her reach.

She gazed straight down, hoping the captain didn't take note of what he in his hurry had overlooked. She kept her thighs tucked tightly together.

She could feel his indecision.

"No," he said. "I think perhaps the table instead..."

She dropped her breeks.

For a long moment, the captain said nothing—for such a long moment, in fact, Serafina had begun to hope he'd suffered an apoplexy. Then he exhaled.

He situated himself behind her, which was bad enough, but the rustling of his own clothing sent a thunderbolt of fear through her.

Focus on the papers. The note was upside down. The first words were—

She felt a stinging crack and lurched forward.

The man's breathing quickened. The ceiling wasn't tall enough for him to stand straight, and she knew he must be hunched over awkwardly.

Though, perhaps not as awkwardly as you.

He seemed to be positioning himself for a better swing, though what constituted a better swing, she was reluctant to imagine.

The second smack stung more than the first.

"Too much?"

She wasn't sure what answer would satisfy him, so she said nothing.

He regarded her arse with the interest of a surgeon. "We want to redden the skin but not draw blood."

Is that what we want?

"You will have a very hard time sitting for the next week, I'm afraid." The warning had a disconcerting note of pleasure to it.

She heard more rustling followed by a succession of rubbery tugs. His breathing came in short puffs.

She screwed her face in disgust.

"What is it, sailor?"

She froze. "Sir?"

"You made a face. Do you have an issue with this punishment?"

"No, sir."

"I intend to lengthen the break between strikes. I find anticipation of the lash does as much to improve a sailor's behavior as the lash itself."

"I'm certain you're correct."

The rubbery noises resumed. She waited until the rhythm quickened. She had no idea where he was looking, or if his eyes were open at all. She slid her fists slowly across the desk and had nearly reached the stack when the captain mumbled, "Oh, God."

She froze, waiting for an accusation, another strike, or something worse.

But nothing happened and the noises continued.

She reached the final few inches, gently pulled the note from the stack. The communication concerned a meeting at certain coordinates that night. She tried hard to memorize the numbers.

"Are you a virgin?"

Serafina felt ill. "Sir?"

"That girl you mentioned. Have you bedded her?"

"I–I–"

"No reason to be shy. I haven't met a sailor yet who hadn't tried his hand at a whore."

"No, sir."

"You're a liar." He smacked her hard—the hardest yet. "Tell me the truth and I shall reduce the strikes to fifteen."

The heat of the blows was building. "I canna."

"Do you prefer boys then, Harris?" He laid a hand on her buttock, and she gasped. "Some sailors do."

"No, sir. Sodomy is a crime."

The other hand came to rest on the other buttock.

"I was her first," Serafina said quickly.

"Oh?" The hands slid away.

"But you're wrong. She wasn't a whore. She's the daughter of a lieutenant. I picked her up in a carriage. She said she wanted to be driven around the park like a fine lady. The ride cost me half a shilling."

"And did you get your money's worth?" The noises had begun again.

"She was reluctant, of course." Serafina gritted her teeth, thinking of Edward and that afternoon in the carriage. "Any proper lass is. But once she'd let me loosen her bodice, I knew there'd be little stramash for the rest."

"Did she like it?"

Serafina nodded sadly. "Verra much."

"And did you?"

"I told her I loved her."

"Did you?"

"I did that day."

The man made a husky laugh, like the puff of the gunpowder in that interminable instant before a great gun fires. Serafina braced herself.

A knock at the door shattered the suspense.

"Later," the captain cried hoarsely.

"Sir, Mr. Edward Turnbull desires to see you."

Serafina jerked so hard she nearly knocked the ink pot to the floor.

"Not *now*! Tell the man I will call on him tomorrow."

"Sir," the voice said, distraught. "He is beside me."

The captain swore under his breath. "Don't move," he said savagely to Serafina.

She heard him struggle to close his breeks and sink into the chair. "Come."

The door opened behind her, and Serafina died a thousand deaths. There was no possibility Edward would not recognize her face—that is if he didn't recognize other parts of her sooner. But at least she would live unbuggered if not unshamed.

"I beg your pardon, sir." The captain rose to make a protracted bow. "I was punishing a seaman. I am Captain Peter Thistlebrook. I'm very pleased to make your acquaintance at last. We have done very well for you on this voyage, and I had every intention of sending a—"

"What is his crime?"

Serafina's eyes flew open. The voice was Gerard's, not Edward's, and he was doing a wretched imitation of an English accent.

"Desertion," the captain said.

Another crack across her cheeks, and she yelped.

"*Stop*," Gerard ordered. "The ship hasn't even left port, and while I can imagine the lad being a deserter—he looks the type to promise a friend he'll be one place and then be somewhere else entirely—I do not think paddling is the appropriate response."

"These young boys need a firm hand. They don't forget it either. I've rarely had to paddle a boy twice."

No, because they stay the hell away from you, you brute.

"Here, try it yourself," Thistlebrook said. "You won't soon forget the feeling of shaping their character. It's as if you hold their future right in your very palm."

Gerard stepped into view, stroking his chin,

apparently considering the particular shape of the character before him. "Well…"

Serafina gave him a murderous look. He lifted an intrigued brow.

"No," he declared. "It's inappropriate. Please instruct the man to cover himself."

The captain lifted his arm to strike her again instead, and Gerard seized it on the downswing.

"Did you hear me, Thistlebrook?"

Gerard and Thistlebrook appeared evenly matched, but Gerard had a look in his eye that suggested he'd snap the man's arm in two as easy as letting it go. Serafina lifted her breeks. The balance of power in the room was shifting.

"'Tis the captain's right to maintain discipline in any way he sees fit," Thistlebrook said, furious, "not the owner's." He shook himself free.

Owner? Edward was the owner of the ship? Serafina's fortune, at least the part that had remained, would not have been enough to purchase a ship. Edward must have partners.

Gerard had caught the implication too. "Not the *owner's*, you say? Not me…the *owner*?"

"No, and if wish me to continue on captaining this ship for you, then I suggest you let me do the job you pay me to do."

"I do not. You're relieved of duty. I'll take the helm."

She nearly dropped her breeks again. "You, sir?"

"Are you mad?" Thistlebrook said. "What experience do you have captaining a ship? The men will never rally around a landsman. What if a storm came? What if the enemy fires on you? What if the ship founders upon rocks? How long do you think men will be loyal to a man who they know will get them killed?"

"Longer than to a man who will get them buggered. I wonder what the other men who hire you might say if they heard that?"

The captain's eyes flashed. "You're a fool."

"Perhaps I am," Gerard said. "But I own the boat, so I can be any goddamned thing I choose. And if you don't care for that fact, perhaps a little time in the brig will help you come to peace with it."

The fire in Thistlebrook's eyes was eventually doused. He paced to his desk, dejected, and sank into the chair.

Too late, Serafina remembered the note.

But it wasn't the note Thistlebrook was after. It was the pistol.

He grabbed it from the wall and pointed it at Gerard. "We're going to put you in the hold until this is over. No one is going to get between me and what's owed me." He edged closer to the door, keeping the two of them in his sights. "When I open this, you will walk quietly before me to the companionway." He put his hand on the door latch and unlocked it, which was exactly what Serafina had been awaiting.

"The captain!" she screamed. "He's bleeding!"

The guard threw open the door, knocking Thistlebrook to the ground, and ran in.

Gerard scooped the pistol off the floor. "He had this pointed at us. I'm Edward Turnbull, the owner of the ship. He's out of his head. I've relieved him of his duty. Watch him while I gather his things."

Shocked, the guard looked to his captain.

"Don't be a fool, Murren. This man pulled my gun on me. I took it from him."

Serafina held her breath. The guard weighed the calmness of the ship's owner dangling the pistol by two fingers against the disheveled, spittle-mouthed man on the floor. His eyes went to Serafina and then to the desk, half-cleared of its papers.

He turned his bayonet toward the captain. "Get up, sir, and follow me."

The captain climbed to his feet with a look of cold fury. Serafina saw the astonishment on the sailors' faces as he walked through them at the bayonet-point of his guard.

"Jesus, Sera," Gerard said under his breath, "is there anything about you and this goddamned plan that's going to be easy?"

"I don't know. Perhaps you'll want to ask Martin Luther."

His face fell. "I can explain that."

"Dinna bother. We have bigger problems."

"The only problem we have is figuring out how fast we can get to the gangplank and get the hell off this boat."

"Ship," she said. "And we cannot." She directed his attention to the windows behind him, where the distance between the stern and Leith was rapidly being filled by a carpet of blue.

Nineteen

"'Brig,' 'helm,' 'relieving you of your duty'?" Serafina said, bristling at the sight of Gerard in the chair at the captain's desk. "Who gave you such a thorough grounding in nautical terms?"

He turned the page in the notebook he was examining. "Oh, just a couple of my captain friends—James Kirk and Han Solo."

"Well, I hope they taught you more than just words. We'll be running the place now."

"I'm not worried."

"Nae?" Uncaptain-like he might be, but he was particularly handsome in that frock coat.

"I don't know anything about ships," he said. "That's true. But I do know how to lead people."

"Your advertising concern, it employs more than just you?"

"It's not an advertising 'concern.' It's an agency. And I'm the head creative and soon-to-be partner."

"And a creative is what?"

"Someone who creates."

"Oh, like the hunchback who whittles three-headed

snakes in front of the Blinded Maiden? I bought one for one of Abby's servant boys. He loved it."

"Yes, only with multimillion-dollar products instead of three-headed snakes and the Chrysler Building instead of the Blinded Maiden—and, by the way, the entire tavern brand experience here could use a major relaunch."

"Speaking of snakes," she said. "Look at this."

He perused the note. "So?"

"So he's meeting someone tonight at those coordinates."

"Maybe it's his lady friend?"

"Well, I hope she can swim. 'Tis in the middle of the North Sea. And perhaps Captain Solo might have mentioned that stopping in port for a mere hour is rather odd."

"Is it?" Gerard tapped his fingers. "I suppose you're right."

"Why did he stop?"

"To drop off the cargo."

"Did you see any cargo unloaded?" she said. "I didn't."

"Well, I wasn't watching the whole time, but there were wagons waiting outside."

"How many?"

"A dozen easily."

She said, "So it seemed the *plan* was to unload the cargo. But we left—very suddenly. By the way, before I was dragged in here, I overhead Thistlebrook asking someone for his silence on something."

"Who was it?"

"I dinna know. And the captain may know I overheard him."

"Certainly didn't seem to quash any feelings he had for you." Gerard looked up, eyes twinkling.

She sniffed. "What can I say? I am verra likable."

"Indeed, you are. And Edward is the owner of this ship?"

"Aye." She shook her head. "It doesn't make sense. My fortune would not have been enough... I don't know what to think about that. He must have partners."

Gerard leaned back and put his feet on the desk. "Where are we heading, by the way?"

"Duchamps has us on a course to Haarlem. I overheard him say it to the master as I was being walked in. But before long, he'll knock on that door and ask if you wish to take the shore route or the more traveled path that crosses the Dutch road."

"That's a trick question," Gerard said, "and since the ship doesn't have wheels, I am comfortable that the answer is the shore route."

"With the rocks off Iron Craig and the sandbars of the Isle of May?"

He licked his lips. "Yes."

"I see this is going to be a verra short voyage."

"And remind me if you would why we can't just return to Leith? Seems to me a nice turnaround would be in order. Dinner at the Squeak and Blade, maybe another glass of whiskey—"

"The trouble is—"

"Did I ask about trouble?" He shook his head. "No, I did not."

"The trouble is I have no wish at present to return to Leith."

"Oh, please don't say you want to go to the rendezvous. What if the ship Thistlebrook is supposed to meet has a particularly large cannon on board?"

"I have no wish to meet the ship, but I'd like more time to look for the cargo. Let's keep *La Trahison* out till the morning. Tell Duchamps to sail us toward fifty-six longitude, eighteen latitude."

Gerard regarded her with a look of awe mixed with curiosity. "You're a navigator too?"

"If you mean can I read a map, then, aye, I can. I lived on a ship until I was sixteen. The sea here is like my village green."

"Shouldn't we question Thistlebrook too? Maybe using some of that nice flogging this century is known for? I wouldn't mind seeing the guy worked over a bit."

"What a barbarous streak you have," she said, though it pleased her to hear the hints of his anger. Her hands were still shaking and she held herself tightly to cover it. "I dinna think we should show our hand at this point. Not until we've finished searching the ship. Even if done in the deepest hold, there's nothing of a cross-examination by whip—or even without—that willna be known immediately by every sailor on the ship. 'Tis the nature of ship life."

"I suppose. The nature of ship life in my time involves desserts in the shape of dolphins, drinks with umbrellas, and Garth Brooks tribute bands."

She pinched her face. "You paint a picture of a verra strange place."

"Says the woman who bought a three-headed snake from the hunchback in front of the Blinded Maiden." He gazed at her contemplatively. "May I say the stubble and thick brows are not my favorite part of your look."

"*Och*. Nor the awkward, tight breeks," she said, digging at her waist.

"Funny," he said, "I'm having no trouble with that feature. What do you think Edward's cargo is?"

"I don't know. But it's odd it wasn't in the hold, at least not marked as such. If it's small enough to be put somewhere else, then it would have to have a more concentrated value, like gold or jewels."

"What if it was gold? What would he be doing with gold?"

She rolled her eyes. "What do Englishman usually do with gold?"

"That's a bit slanderous."

"You're not English."

"I'm half-English."

"Are ye?" Her face fell. "Ah, but you're half-Highlander," she said, brightening. "That drowns out everything else. It's like dropping a bit of spoiled mutton into a bubbling kettle of bilberry custard. You might know it's there, but it's simply not going to make a difference."

He leaned back. "Bilberry custard, eh?"

"Dinna get too lost in the praise. Bilberries make me costive."

He pushed the notebook aside, suddenly sober. "You're certain the captain didn't harm you?"

She flushed. He had a maddening propensity to annoy and attract simultaneously, and she was having trouble choosing which emotion to respond to first. "'Tis kind of you to worry. A bruised ego was the worst of it." She waited for a jest about other bruised parts.

Gerard watched her, chin on his fist. "I didn't know what I was going to do when you were climbing over the rail and I saw you being hauled back," he said.

"There was an implicit threat of violence in the man. And the gangplank was being pulled up." His voice grew husky. "I can honestly say, I've never been quite so worried. And when I walked in here…"

He seemed to search the top of Thistlebrook's desk for the words that would explain the extent of his horror but found none. A weighty guilt came to rest on Serafina. She had not expected to become entangled in the life of the man she'd called with Undine's magic, nor he in hers. The spell was to have produced a bland, nameless replica of Edward to do her bidding, not this flesh-and-blood man with wry asides and complicated shoulders and expectations about her well-being that she would have to wrestle with. The realization made her uncomfortable and a bit resentful.

"Why did you leave me in the spire?" he asked.

Her face grew warm. "The ship came into sight. You had once again expressed your frustration with my calling you here. I chose to allow you to avoid further entanglements."

He traced the edge of the ink pot. "Yet here I am."

She swallowed hard. "Thank you."

"Did you enjoy our lovemaking?"

She gritted her teeth. A fool she might be to have given in to her desire, but if he made a jest about it, he would wear the contents of that ink pot. "You know I did."

"Enough to do it again?"

"Mr. Innes, I realize you are not of this time, but that is not something a gentleman asks a lady."

"I make no claim to 'gentleman.'"

"And I make no claim to 'lady,' but you must see

being asked such a question serves only to remind me of my status."

"What status? You're over twenty-one, aren't you? In my time, men and women don't worry about the thing we did. It was lovely. There's no shame."

"Mr. Innes, how many women have you taken to your bed? A dozen? Two?"

In his eyes was the sizable distance between her guess and the truth.

"More?" she said, incredulous. "Fifty? *A hundred?*"

When he didn't reply, she sat back, stunned. "Was there any chance—any chance at all—when you mounted those stairs that you were nae going to bed me?"

The muscle in his jaw flexed, and he summoned a weak smile. "There was no chance after you first called me out of my hotel room that I wasn't going to at least try."

Her thoughts went to the awkward coupling on that carriage seat and the anger she'd felt when she discovered Edward's outpourings of love to be but the tools of a practiced seducer.

"If you're honest," she said, "which I know you to be, for you have answered every question I've ever asked you, what are the chances, based on your experience, that you would have failed in your attempt?"

His gaze, sad but steady, did not falter. "Zero—or near to it."

She inhaled, refashioning the moments in the spire, his joy upon seeing the great expanse of blue, his awe at her knowledge of sailing, that unrepentant kiss. How different they seemed in another, harsher light.

"I'm not like Edward," he said. "I don't want to take anything from you. I like you very much."

"You have been verra kind to help me as much as ye have. And I take responsibility for the things I do. I just didna know until now exactly what I was doing. Friends?" She extended her hand.

"Yes." He clasped it reluctantly.

Duchamps's call of *"Stuns'ls aloft"* echoed in the captain's quarters as a line of demarcation settled permanently between the brief past they'd shared as lovers and the present they'd share as something else.

"Well then," Gerard said, trying to manage the ungainly silence, "I suppose we best get back to our work. Time is money, aye?" he added, slipping back into his dreadful accent.

She shook her head, confused. "Your Scots accent is so lovely. How can your English accent be so poor?"

"I'll have you know I was the finest King Arthur in the history of the Hotchkiss School."

She smiled. "Oh, I'll bet you were."

"'Gerry Innes brings a childlike charm as well as decidedly masculine sense of intrigue to a role he makes his own.'" He began to sing a song of Camelot in a voice that carried halfway to Leith.

She laughed. "I had no idea King Arthur sang. And you are quite right. Your singing accent *is* far less jarring. Perhaps if you were to sing instead of speak?"

"Ha ha." His face filled with a faraway grin. "The 'decidedly masculine sense of intrigue' got me through a lot of lean years, let me tell you."

Odd, she thought. *I would have guessed it was the childlike charm.*

A knock made her jump.

"Duchamps, sir."

"You're not ready," she whispered furiously to Gerard. "Send him away."

"I'm ready."

"Send him away. You don't have the faintest idea what the men do who work this ship. And we might not like Thistlebrook, but he was right when he said that men will not live under the command of a man they think will get them killed."

"I don't need to know how to run the ship because I know how to do something far more important."

"Do ye? And what might that be?"

"Watch and learn. *Enter!*"

Duchamps opened the door, hat in hand, and saluted. "The captain is in the spare cabin with guards at the door." He gave Serafina a nervous smile.

"Thank you," Gerard said. "What's your name?"

"Lieutenant Duchamps, sir."

"Thank you, Duchamps. Unfortunate business. I was just questioning young Harris here about it for the report. By the way, I have decided to make him my man Friday."

"Your what, sir?"

"Um, aide-de-camp?"

"On a ship?"

Duchamps shook his head, evident anxiety growing, and a fleeting image of them being dropped over the side of the ship in chains went through Serafina's head.

"Batman? Admin? Secretary?"

At "secretary," Duchamps relaxed. "A secretary.

Aye, sir. If I can be of any assistance to you, Mr. Harris, please let me know. I'm assuming you would like him to be placed in the cabin next to yours."

Gerard blinked. "Yes."

"*Nae,*" said Serafina.

Duchamps said to Serafina, "You can of course sleep in the wardroom with the warrant officers."

Gerard gave her a look that suggested he had only been trying to save her from a fate worse than death but that if she chose to expose herself to half the seafaring barbarians in Europe as she dressed for dinner that it was certainly her choice, not his.

She sighed. "The cabin will be verra nice. Thank you, Lieutenant."

"I am glad to be of service. I came to see you about our course, sir. Shall I continue it? I thought I should ask in light of the, er, unpleasantness."

"No," Gerard said. "We need to set sail for a location that is eighteen degrees latitude, fifty-six degrees longitude. If you please."

Duchamps frowned. "Brazil, sir?"

Serafina, whose back was to the lieutenant, realized Gerard's mistake and cleared her throat loudly.

"On second thought," Gerard amended, "make that eighteen degrees longitude and fifty-six degrees latitude. I was just testing you, Lieutenant. Brazil would be ridiculous, of course. Well done."

"Thank you, sir. By the shore route? Or Dutch road?"

"Oh, I think we both know which way makes more sense." Gerard caught Serafina's eye and waggled his brows.

"I don't, sir," Duchamps said, stone-faced. "The

shore allows us to avoid privateers, but the Dutch road is faster."

"Lieutenant, my management style has always been to empower my team to make decisions on their own. I'm here to advise, coach, and help you build on ideas. If you need me, I'm here. Otherwise, you may conduct the business of running this ship as you see fit."

Duchamps shifted. "So, the path that goes by the Dutch road?"

Serafina tapped the desk theatrically, waiting for Gerard to make his decision.

He templed his fingers and gazed at a spot just beyond his lieutenant's head.

Duchamps fingered his brim. "Sir? The Dutch road path?"

Exasperated, Serafina opened her lips and formed the word "aye."

"No," Gerard said with an imperious wave of his hand. "The shore route."

"The shore route?" Duchamps's eyes widened.

"That was one of the choices, was it not?"

"Oh, aye, sir. It just surprised me to hear you say it. I will make it so." Duchamps bowed and left.

Serafina said, "*Och*, that was a verra poor idea."

Gerard crossed his arms and turned, captain-like, to gaze out the stern windows. "I'll live with my decision."

"Let's hope the rest of us will be as lucky."

Twenty

"I TOLD YOU," SHE WHISPERED, "THE DUTCH ROAD IS not the place to be doing something you dinna want anyone to see."

Gerard wished the "something" she referred to was more like the effort they'd collaborated on that morning at the top of St. Giles, rather than sailing a ship through waves like bucking broncos while sixty pairs of eyes watched him rake the sail-filled horizon with a spyglass.

His stomach was in his throat, the quarterdeck was anywhere but under his feet, and his new secretary stood so close to him, he didn't know where to look or what to say without betraying his feelings.

He abandoned the glass for an instant to steal a glance at her. Even wrapped in the guise of a man, her salt water–fueled joy made his heart ache for her. His grandmother, who had adamantly refused to board his father's thirty-nine-foot Philip Rhoades sailboat, used to say Scots were not made to have water under their feet. But his grandmother had never met Serafina. Nor was there much chance she would either. Besides living three centuries away, Serafina had made it very clear her relationship with Gerard was no longer the sort that had even the slightest chance of leading to gin and tonics on the Innes family terrace.

It was funny how sad losing an option could seem even though one had never seriously considered it while it was at hand.

You have her friendship, at least, which is probably more than you deserve.

He believed—truly—that he esteemed women and treated them with respect. He had close friends who were women and had developed and promoted a number of women at the agency. But he had never been forced to step back and consider what his extended series of one-night stands might look like to a woman like Serafina.

Is it possible to be a man who respects women and *one who collects them?*

He had always chosen to look at his behavior as his way of ensuring no obstacle stood between him and the unencumbered life he wanted to lead. But now, for the very first time, he saw his behavior itself as the obstacle—a fifty-foot-tall curtain wall keeping him from a prize he very dearly wanted.

"Are you keeping watch?" asked Serafina, who had caught him looking at her. "The men expect their captain to be focused on identifying potential adversaries." She wrote something in the notebook she'd brought along to look the part of a secretary.

He returned to the glass. "I don't even know what I'm looking for. Are the triangle sails the good ones or the bad ones?"

"For the love of Saint Margaret," she murmured.

"We don't need you to *actually* identify them, Mr. Innes. The barrel man will spot them long before even a capable captain could. We just need you to look as if you might. Think of yourself as a symbol, like the mermaid carved onto the ship's prow. The more believable the execution, the more luck it augurs."

Gerard made a wounded noise. "I think I have more to offer than a carving."

"More than a carving? Oh, my dear captain, that carving is the first thing other sailors see on a ship. 'Tis the ship's envoy to the world—the shining signal that communicates friend or foe, French or Prussian, marine or merchant. What could be more important?"

"Wow," he said, "you really should write copy."

"I think I'm beginning to understand what you do. It has a strong relationship to lying, doesn't it?"

"What's a barrel man?"

She pointed up, and Gerard leaned back as far as his neck would allow. An enormous barrel hung lashed to a point not far from the top of the mast. It had to be thirty feet above them.

"A crow's nest." His cocked hat fell and he caught it the instant before it reached the deck. "That's what they call it in my time."

She nodded appreciatively. "I suppose it does look like one hanging in the tallest branches of the ship. Uh-oh, sailors. Time to be a symbol again."

He returned the glass to his eye as a crew of men carrying ropes passed by. The ships he could see, which numbered close to a dozen, did not seem to be doing anything worthy of notice.

"Oh, dear," she said. "This is why I didn't want us

to take the Dutch road. Can you see the yellow sloop? The one that is fore-and-aft rigged?"

Yellow he could work with. He drew the glass from ship to ship. None were exactly yellow. "Do you mean the one with the skinny blue flag at the top?"

She tapped his arm, and he realized she was looking in the opposite direction.

"Ah." The ship was tiny compared to the one they were on—closer to the sea and with only a single mast. It was a bit smaller than his grandfather's sailboat. "What about it?"

"I don't like the look of it."

He looked again. "Yellow not your color?"

"I look dreadful in yellow, but that's not the reason. It's been exactly the same distance behind us since it first appeared half an hour ago."

"Seems like a good safety rule."

"But that rig can outsail this one as easily as I snap my fingers," she said. "So, why isn't it?"

"Because it's following us?"

"It's a possibility."

Gerard snapped the glass closed. "But is it following you or the cargo?"

"Don't forget Thistlebrook. He's an option. He seems to have a problem or two of his own."

"To say the least."

"'Twould be best, I think, not to confide in Duchamps."

Gerard started. "You suspect *Duchamps*?"

Several sailors turned, and he added stentoriously, "I'll have to thank him in that case. The jam was excellent."

Serafina coughed. "Such cunning. Why didn't you tell me you've worked in intelligence before? Aye,

Duchamps is on my list. Anyone on this ship could be part of whatever the captain is doing and, therefore, none too glad to see us—well, you, specifically. We need to be verra cautious. Oh, tell the master to move the ship two points closer to the wind."

"Huh?" He turned to find himself looking directly at Ginty, the ship's master.

"Orders, sir?"

"Oh, aye. Move her two points closer to the wind."

Ginty raised an impressed brow. "I will."

Gerard leaned back on his elbows on the railing and watched the master pass Gerard's order on to Duchamps as well as the master's thoughts on how best to set the sails. Duchamps shouted the orders to the men on the yardarms overhead.

"So the master is essentially Scotty," Gerard said, working it out in his head. "'I'm tryin', Captain. But she's not respondin'.'"

"Scotty?"

"He works for my friend, Captain Kirk. You'd like him. He's a Scot. He's the guy who keeps the wheels turning on the ship."

Serafina looked stricken. "You are jesting, aye? You ken there are no wheels on a ship. You said it to me earlier."

"Yes, I know there are no wheels. What I mean is the master's the guy who keeps the gears turning, the engine running, the balls in the air. It's a metaphor."

"Oh, a metaphor. I suppose, aye. The master's responsible for navigating, knowing the ship's position, managing the hold, setting the sails, and overseeing various parts of the ship—the fittings, the pulleys, the anchors, etc."

"Sir," said Duchamps, who had stepped over to join them, "the purser wishes to speak to you."

"Oh, *shite*."

Both men looked at Serafina, who shook her head. "Bit my tongue."

"Send him over," Gerard said.

The moment Duchamps descended the quarterdeck stairs, Serafina said, "The purser is Edward's cousin, Tom. I completely forgot. Stay calm."

"*What!?*—a great pleasure." Gerard extended his hand to the frock-coated man ascending the stairs as Serafina melted into the rigging. If the purser knew Edward, Gerard and Serafina were sunk.

The purser hesitated when he saw Gerard. Gerard broke out in a sweat.

"Eddie?"

Gerard nodded, afraid to speak.

"Lieutenant," the purser called. "This is most peculiar."

Duchamps turned, alert. The sweat was running freely down Gerard's temples now and into his hair.

The purser frowned. "How can this man not be throwing his arms around his beloved cousin, Tom?"

Gerard put his arms around the man, never so grateful to hug anyone.

"How long has it been?" Tom asked.

"Too long!" *Thank God!*

"The things we did in that barn…" He thumped Gerard on the back, grinning.

"Boys will be boys," Gerard said confidentially, giving him an elbow.

"I meant when we built the stone wall for my father. My back still aches, I think."

Strike one. "Mine too. Thank you for all your hard work here. It's clear the ship has been, er, well pursered. Sad business with Thistlebrook. The men are uneasy. I can tell."

"I have to admit I was surprised."

"Were you?"

"Well, I had thought you were partners in this."

"In this?" Gerard made a vague gesture that could have suggested anything from the buckles on his shoes to the North Sea.

"Not the ship, of course. That other business—but perhaps 'tis best not to tongue wag."

"Indeed. Thank you."

"We'll sit down later."

"I can't wait."

Tom smiled but there was something in his eyes. "You sound…so different than I remember."

"'Tis the time in Edinburgh, I expect. Nothing flattens a vowel like the boots of a Scotsman, isn't that what they say?"

"Is it? I admit I am rarely in Scotland or the North Sea. My work is mostly in the West Indies. Would you like to join us for dinner later in the wardroom?"

"I am engaged."

"Aye, I'm certain your first day is quite full. Shall we plan to meet on the morrow? How's your mother, by the way?"

"That is a story for tomorrow."

Tom bowed and headed down the stairs.

Gerard exhaled and Serafina reappeared. "He hasn't seen Edward since they were children," she said.

"Gosh, that would have been a good fact to know."

"I'm sorry. He's the reason I needed you. I could have bribed another purser for the cargo, but not Edward's beloved cousin."

Gerard hesitated. "He says Edward is in league with Thistlebrook."

"How? On the cargo or something else?"

"He didn't say."

"I'm going to look through the cargo again. There was also a locked room down there. I want to take a look."

"Are you sure you should go by yourself?"

She gave him a devilish look. "Are ye worried for me or for you?"

"You. You have me thinking everyone is a danger."

"Good. 'Twill encourage you to be cautious."

"Is there anything that might encourage you to do the same?"

She lifted her shirt far enough for him to see the sheath of a knife tucked in her waist. "I don't need caution. I have something more effective."

"Jesus."

"'Twould be helpful if ye would call the men to their stations for a long review—at least a quarter of an hour. And when you're done, ask the cook for an omelet."

"What's that for?"

"Me, ye gawk. I'm starving."

He didn't like the idea of her doing this on her own, but there didn't seem to be much hope of stopping her. "Fine. A review of the men, and then I'll just crawl up in the barrel and hide for the rest of the trip."

"Ha. That's something I would pay dearly to see."

"You don't think I could make it up there?"

"I dinna think you could make it up *that* barrel." She pointed to a water butt on the deck below. "I dinna doubt your strength. But scaling anything on a moving ship is a perilous experience. It takes even the bravest man several attempts, and that's with a man above and below to place his hands and feet."

Gerard crossed his arms. "That sounds like a challenge."

"You need more of a challenge than pretending to be a captain on a moving ship three hundred years before ye were born?"

"I'm close to being offended. You do realize I won the harness challenge on the climbing wall at my gym?"

She stared, blank faced. "No matter what order I put those words in, I canna squeeze a bit o' sense from them."

"Trust me. I can do it."

"As you wish. I accept the challenge, and ye can name your price. But if you lose, you will do everything I say from now on. Now, dinna forget—review, then omelet."

He growled. "I don't like it. Every man here is a potential bad guy."

"Remember, Captain," she said, giving him a crisp salute, "you have at least one person on board who ye can depend on not to be a danger to ye."

But danger, he thought, *comes in many forms*, and he laid his hand over the new ache in his heart as he watched her disappear.

Twenty-one

WHAT HAD CAUSED THISTLEBROOK TO RAISE ANCHOR so soon? Had he planned to stay longer but received news that caused him to change his mind, or had the plan been to leave all along? Serafina considered this as she jogged lightly past the crates.

She reread the names:

Piggott-Jones
Macniece
Carlton
FitzGerard
Nixon
Foster & Blair
MacAfee
Cockburn
Frazier
MacNulty

None missing. Nothing delivered. *Och*.

The locked space at the end, however, continued to hold her interest. She looked around. There were no men in sight. Gerard had managed his assignment well. She'd smiled when she heard the roaring call to stations followed by the rumble of feet. He was turning out to be far more helpful than she'd first expected when she'd found him in her bed—a whining, worthless voluptuary.

She felt a stab of regret.

She'd misjudged him. His abilities strictly in relation to her objective might be more limited than she had hoped, but his ability to learn, his courage, and his desire to help her had been more than she probably deserved. She wondered if she'd misjudged him on anything else.

She considered the long parade of women through his bed. He had an appetite that rivaled a sultan. Had his time with her been the mere sampling of a man addicted to carnal pleasure or the beginning of a cherished connection? She had mistaken one for the other once and had no wish to endure that pain again. But she couldn't deny he looked at her, then and now, in a way few men ever had—as a woman worthy of conversation, friendship, and partnership.

The door's lock hung on a chain threaded around the latch. The space was quite large—large enough to hold two or three of the crates that stood behind her. She could break the lock with a hammer or a crowbar, but she didn't have either with her. Walls in a ship were ephemeral objects, set up to designate space and removed in a matter of moments to address changing needs or to prepare for battle. She found the space between the structure of the ship and the hanging wall and peered inside.

In the darkness, she could make out what looked like enormous bundles wrapped in waxed paper—the

sort one would see covering a captain's most important papers as protection against the damp and water
of a ship—tied with rope.

What cargo merits such fastidiousness?

She slipped into the carpenter's walkway, where
she had overheard Thistlebrook talking earlier, to
see if anything there caught her eye. But the walkway looked the same as any other walkway—dank,
exceedingly narrow, and full of tiny pairs of glowing
red eyes that turned when she entered. "Shoo," she
said. "I'm hungrier than you."

The lack of a set of crates clearly marked "Turnbull"
seemed to mean there would be no easy redistribu-
tion of wealth for her. If the locked room didn't yield
something of value, the trajectory of her life, which had
been on a slow but inexorable decline both in status and
happiness since her decision to give herself to Edward
in that carriage, would reach its inevitable conclusion.

She thought of Mary MacAvoy, the kindly spinster
in Niddry Street who did Serafina's mending, and the
threadbare clothes she wore. That is what Serafina's
life would become, and she would be lucky to live as
well as Mary.

*Are ye too proud to mend, then? A woman who throws
away her future should not be too proud to do anything.*

And she wasn't. She would mend or wash or tat—
whatever it took to eat and live—but finally acknowl-
edging the full extent of the change that was to come
was a blow even if the change had been sitting there,
beyond the edge of her hopes, for the last few months.

She took a deep breath. "What will happen will
happen," she said. "And you will survive."

She set out for the smithy, where she knew she'd find something to break the lock.

Twenty-two

EVEN BEFORE SHE KNOCKED ON THE DOOR OF THE captain's quarters, the smells of bacon and toasted bread filled the hall and made her dizzy with hunger.

"Harris, sir."

The door opened. A look of such heartfelt relief washed over Gerard's face, she had to smile. He closed the door behind her.

"You're safe," he said.

"As are you."

"I don't know what sort of inspection the sailors are used to, but they definitely found being asked to tell everyone their hometown and talk a little bit about what they hoped to accomplish this voyage a little odd."

"Oh, dear."

"Good news. Nobody said 'Mutiny.' I consider that a big win. Next up: brainstorming ideas for more effective 'make and mend' nights. Did I give you enough time?"

"Oh, aye. Thank you. Is that a *basket* of bacon?"

"I wasn't sure how much you wanted. There's also a basket of rolls, an entire soused cock—I refrain from comment—a wedge of very hard cheese, a jug of beer, and something the cook's assistant referred to as ratafia sweets, which appear to be cement in the shape of a cookie."

He made a grand gesture toward the cloth-covered table, and she slipped gratefully into a chair.

"This is marvelous," she said, chomping on a slice of bacon, which she'd pulled, still hot, from under the basket's cloth cover.

"I told you you should've eaten breakfast. It's the most important meal of the day, you know."

She realized it was probably impolite to eat with her fingers, but the greasy, smoked meat melted on her tongue, and in any case, Gerard, who watched her with the unblinking interest of a man watching an illicit tableau, didn't appear to be offended.

His eyes twinkled. "I don't know what it is about seeing a woman eat, but I find it rather enchanting."

"Prepare yourself to be spellbound." She popped the morsel into her mouth and sucked each finger to savor the last traces.

"All right, now I might have to look away—either that or find a bucket of icy water to douse myself with."

She laughed. "You're incorrigible."

"So I'm told."

A warm, inebriating pleasure began to fill her belly. Bacon mixed with Gerard's unmasked desire was a very dangerous combination. She decided on a more puritanical choice. "Pass me the cheese, if ye would."

He complied, pushing the plate exactly half the distance between them, as if it were a tiny snip of red wool and feathers, meant to lure her like a salmon from a waterweed blind. The man could make moving tableware into an act of seduction.

Unintimidated, she reached for the plate. He leaned back in his chair, thoroughly satisfied.

She cut the cheese primly and used the knife's wide blade to place the slice on her plate. Then she picked up her fork—

"What? No fingers?"

"I refuse to contribute to your culinary debauchery."

"Too late."

"I can hardly be held accountable for the state of your character, which has been shaped almost entirely by the relentless storms of your rather questionable misadventures."

"'The relentless storms of my rather questionable misadventures.' I like that." He uncorked the jug and poured a cup. Then he rose and carried it down the table's length, placing it at her side with a bow.

"Your service is not a sign of remorse for a life ill-lived. I take nothing from it—that is, nothing but some very dark ale." She lifted the cup in toast and swallowed.

"Ill-lived till now," he corrected. "You are a cold-hearted judge."

"I am honest…and I should think you might like that," she said, suddenly afraid to meet his eyes.

"Aye," he said quietly. "I do."

The cheese seemed to catch in her throat, and she swallowed another draught of ale.

"The bacon is better," she said and collected the basket herself, as well as a roll and one of the ratafia.

He laughed, and she settled back into her chair, pleased with herself.

He gestured to the platter of juicy legs. "I see you're leaving the cock untouched."

He was a wicked, wicked tease.

"That particular dish holds little interest for me," she said, reaching for more bacon. "I find it a little gamy."

"Then you wouldn't mind if I had one?"

"I assumed you already had."

"Not much of an assumption, is it?" He grabbed a piece and took a generous bite. She watched the long muscles of his throat as he swallowed. She realized she'd stopped chewing.

He reached into a bowl on the chest behind him and turned back with a plump golden pear in his hand. "Oh," he said, catching her surprise, "did I forget to mention the cook sent this as well?"

He raised it to his nose and took in the nectary scent, which she could smell even at her end of the table. Saliva filled her mouth.

"Earthy," he said. "And sweet."

He bounced the fruit in his palm. It made a firm smack. "The cook only sent one. Shall I split it in two?"

She shook her head, not trusting herself to speak.

He reached for a stout knife and pierced the flesh. A bead of nectar appeared.

"I need some air," she said and stood.

A moment later, she stood on the captain's small balcony, the sea breeze filling her head. She could feel him standing behind her, watching her as the ship's foamy wake stretched out into the distance before them.

"The ship's still there," she said.

"I know. I've been watching. I wanted you to eat before I told you."

The breeze was cool and gooseflesh appeared on her arms.

Gerard pulled her against his warmth.

"I am quite aware," he said, after a long moment, "that you haven't told me what you found."

The gooseflesh turned to shaking. She had avoided thinking about it for as long as she could. "Nothing for Turnbull," she said.

"And the locked room?"

"I broke the lock and opened the parcels. It's muslin. The stuff of chemises and petticoats," she added, seeing the question in his eye. "Tuppence a yard. The whole of it might be worth fifty pounds."

The arm around her waist tightened. "Not quite a fortune."

"No. We still need to search this room."

"I did, while you were gone." He shook his head.

"Then our only hope is Duchamps's room, though I dinna see how we might get into it."

"What does it mean?" Gerard asked.

"Well, as I said, Duchamps may be in league with—"

"No, Sera," he said, pulling her closer. "I mean for you."

She held him, steadying herself against his sturdy bulk.

"My hopes..." She found she couldn't finish and laid her head on his shoulder.

"I wish I had something to give you," he said, stroking her hair.

The first shame of poverty flooded her cheeks. "Thank ye for your kindness. I've never wished to be *given* anything. I only wished to have what was rightfully mine."

"Let's put our minds to it, then. We can do anything if we decide we can. I'm here to be commanded, Sera. Command me."

She touched his cheek. "Obliterate the worry," she said. "Chase it from my head."

He swept her into his arms and kissed her. She gasped when they broke apart, still tasting the pear on her tongue. "Again," she said. "Do it again."

This time, he pressed her to the railing, his body a wedge between her and her thoughts. And lose herself she did. She wanted nothing but his hands and his mouth.

"You made it clear I was not to tempt you," he said. "And I obeyed. But when I kiss you like this, I think I'll die if I can't have you again."

"You canna die, or I will too."

"*Captain*," a familiar French voice called from beyond the cabin's inner door. "The lookout has spotted a brig that seems to be behaving oddly."

Gerard sighed heavily. "Yellow?" he called.

"Aye, sir."

Gerard led Serafina in and opened the door. "What more can you tell me?" he said to Duchamps.

"She's running parallel to us. She hasn't done anything in particular, but she hasn't asked us for a signal."

"Have we asked for hers?"

"Not yet. That's why I knocked."

"Sit. I'd like to hear what you know of privateers in the region. Harris," Gerard said, and Serafina jumped. In the swirl of emotions, she had forgotten she was a sailor.

"Please give the cook my regards," he said to her. "The meal was wonderful. I should like a pot of coffee and make it hot."

Serafina's face must have shown her strong disinclination to take such an order because he cleared his throat and bent his head toward Duchamps.

Oh. She stood and saluted. "Aye, sir."

"And be sure to gather the most current information about the unknown ship before you return. Duchamps and I will be engaged here for a quarter hour at least."

She gave him a gratitude-laden nod and exited.

Twenty-three

As Serafina had expected, Duchamps's tiny cabin could be explored in full by standing in one place and turning. His cot—the sort of coffin with a bedroll allotted to the officers that was such an improvement over the hammocks of the sailors—was neatly made and rocked quietly on its well-oiled chains. His locker, under the cot, was the only personal item in the space apart from a small, framed portrait of a young woman, probably his sweetheart, which hung on the wall over his small desk and chair. But it was not the portrait that brought her to a stop. Next to the ink pot, stowed away in a tin bowl for a future indulgence, sat a golden pear, the twin of Gerard's.

She picked it up, letting the sweet scent fill her head—and with it the image of Gerard parting the tender flesh with his blade.

She thought of the warrior Paris in the myth and another golden fruit. Paris was required to choose which among Hera, Aphrodite, and Athena would possess a golden apple and with it the title of most beautiful goddess. Hera had offered him a great kingdom to command if he chose her. Athena offered him glory in battle. Serafina remembered from a book her father kept hidden that Paris had not been a principled judge. Even after receiving head-turning bribes, he had demanded the women disrobe so that he might view them in their skin to help him with his decision. But they were powerful goddesses, and their nakedness did not shame them. In fact, the painting in the book—which had made quite an impression on her young mind—made it look as if each one of them found the notion of having Paris see them quite pleasing.

Paris. She had once considered Adonis as her ideal but wondered if the honest, willing, hot-blooded Prince of Troy might be more her match.

Serafina had offered the Paris on the deck above her nothing—no empire, no great victory. Yet he'd chosen her. And she'd turned him down. Despite that, he'd continued to give her his friendship and support. He was a good man, and she wondered what would have happened if Duchamps had not knocked.

Ah, well. Perhaps it was for the best.

She was reminded that the bribe of Aphrodite, who in the end won the apple, had been to offer Paris the chance to marry the most beautiful mortal woman on earth—the already-married Helen of Troy, which drove the Spartans into war with the Trojans and eventually led to Paris's tragic death on the battlefield.

There are good reasons we do not caper about like princes and goddesses, she thought philosophically, returning the pear to its bowl.

Serafina had no prurient interest in Duchamps's belongings, but a search necessitated a certain degree of intrusion, and she slid the desk's single drawer open with minimal reluctance. A few letters, a response started but not finished, and a candle nub were the only things to be seen. She pulled the locker from under the bed and placed it on the table. The lock was open—not a sign of a man with something to hide—and the contents revealed nothing more than two clean sarks, a wool waistcoat, a pair of twice-mended breeks, and a spare cocked hat. Guiltily, she put everything back. If the ship held Edward's hidden cargo, it wasn't hidden here.

She slipped out of Duchamps's cabin and back up to the deck. She glanced toward the stern. *You have time. The captain's door is still—*

She stopped. She was actually beginning to think of Gerard as the captain of this ship, which was completely ridiculous given the fact he couldn't tell the bow from the stern, let alone a hawser from a halyard. But he carried with him a certain sense of expectation that was quite convincing on its own—an expectation that men would accept his orders, that women would climb into his bed, that enemy ships would reveal their hidden secrets. It was effective, she admitted with grudging admiration.

The yellow ship wasn't visible. It might have sped to the west while she was rooting through Duchamps's things, or it might be behind them, blocked from her view. The lookout, looking bored, clung to the overhead rigging just aft.

"What do ye see?" Serafina called.

"A ship," the man said, and his shipmates tittered.

If Gerard or Duchamps were on deck, the men

would never dare to speak so. "Is she west of us or astern?"

"Disappeared—to the west."

"How many men on board?"

"Canna see."

"Maybe if you got yer fat ass up that rigging, ye would."

The men tittered again. This time the lookout scowled. "I'd be happy to offer you a glass for a try—if ye weren't so busy fetching the captain's coffee."

"Oh, is that what they call it?" another said. "He keeps the captain's pen shipshape. I hear the captain likes it spit polished."

"Explains the ink on his fingers."

Serafina said, "I admit I'm surprised the captain didn't pick you for the position. From what I've heard on my short time aboard, you're the uncontested expert at one-handed polishing."

The men roared.

"Now, are you going to get up to that barrel, or am I going to be doing your bloody job for you?"

The lookout made an acrobatic bow and extended the glass.

Serafina scrambled up the underside of the rigging and snatched the glass from the man's hand as she passed.

The glass was long and light, with an ivory case and a lens wider than any she'd ever seen. She tucked it carefully under her arm. She was eager to see what information she could gather with it.

Higher she went, where the breeze grew stiffer and the air cleaner. She was a child again, as at home in the ropes as she was lying on her cot with a toy. She paused just before the barrel to scan the horizon. Here, twenty feet up, she could see thrice the distance the idiot who handed her the glass could. Whitecaps filled the sea. The merchant ships plowed forward ahead of them on the road, but the yellow one eluded her. The ship was neither to the west or astern. She would confirm that with a final look from the bucket before she reported to the captain—er, Gerard.

She swung herself over the barrel's high edge and dropped to the bottom, nearly losing her balance when her foot touched down on a pile of canvas.

The canvas said, "Ouch."

She wheeled around to find Gerard sitting cross-legged on the bottom, barefooted and coatless, the core of the pear dangling from his hand. The gleam in his eye was piratical.

"I told you I could make it up here." He took a last bite and tossing the core out to sea. "I'll give you a choice. You can apologize for your assumptions and acknowledge me as a first-rate captain and a man you have *chronically* underestimated, or I can take you against the mast."

Her eyes went to the rough-hewn wood, draped in loose coils of rope that hung a foot or two above her head. He had her dead to rights, and the hot knot in her belly only confirmed it.

She sniffed. "I choose an apology."

He gave her an "as you wish" sort of shrug.

"But I can't," she said.

"*Oof.* Tough to be so proud." He bent his head toward the mast.

"'First-rate' is coming at it a little high, wouldn't you say?"

He pointed at her buttons. "I believe I'll have you naked this time."

"The sailors will see it." The barrel was the largest she had seen, chest high and four feet across, but even then…

"Not if we're careful. Try not to flail too much."

She snorted.

"Of course," he added amiably, "if you'd prefer, you can stay on your knees, safely out of sight, while I stand…"

"You are too thoughtful."

"Is that shirt coming off or what?"

She took a deep breath and reached for the top button. He put his arms behind his head and stretched his legs.

She summoned Aphrodite, loosened the buttons, and let the shirt drop. Then she untied the knot that held the binding and unwound the canvas she'd used to bind her breasts. They fell free, and his pupils widened.

"It's not too late to apologize, you know," he said.

"Would you prefer that?"

"Truthfully? I'd prefer both."

"No one can say you're not honest."

The next knot was the rope at her waist. When that was undone, the only thing between her and the goddesses' own nakedness was the hand gripping her trousers.

Gerard unfolded himself and reached for her just as an enormous wave lifted the ship. The ship pitched forward and the barrel's additional thirty feet of height sent it into a far larger, accelerating circle.

"Whoa!" He grabbed the barrel's edge like a man grabbing a rescue line.

"Tut-tut, Captain. You can hardly have me at the mast with your hands glued in place. Besides, you need to learn to move *with* the ship, not fight it." She insinuated herself against him, pressing her breasts into his side.

"Oh, Lord." The ship rolled again. He grabbed one of the loops of rope at the mast and swung himself against the other side of the barrel.

"I'm not letting go," he said. "Even for those... those..."

"Those what?"

"Those very good reasons."

Still clutching the waistband of her breeks, she found the end of her braid and lifted it over her head, working the pieces loose one-handed.

He gulped and closed his eyes. "Can you turn the other way when you do that?"

"If ye dinna keep your eyes on the horizon, you're going to get sick."

He slitted an eye.

"Both," she insisted.

He did it, and she turned away from him, shook out her hair, and let go of her trousers.

"Vixen," he moaned.

"Goddess."

After a long moment, he said, "I find myself longing for the other side of you as well."

"Do you?" She bent as the mast made another loop.

"Oh. Oh, Jesus. Don't."

She followed the edge until she was back at his side.

They were shoulder to shoulder now, he facing out, clutching the rope over his head, and she facing in. He flung an arm across her shoulders and tried covering his awkwardness with a caress. She chuckled.

"I can do a lot with one hand," he said.

"So can I."

She slipped the tips of her fingers down the waistband of his breeks, and he gasped.

With two flicks of her thumb, the top buttons popped. His cock, pressed against the wool, was as hard as an iron pipe.

"I wonder..." She edged the wool a bit lower, and it puddled at his feet. "*Och*. My apologies."

"If I could let go," he growled, "you wouldn't be quite so jolly."

"'Tis a big if."

She drew her palm down his length and gripped the chiseled tip. She'd never felt a circumcised cock before and the shape intrigued her.

Standing on tiptoes, she whispered in his ear, "What's it like without a foreskin?"

"Why don't you find out?" He pulled her even closer.

She took his balls, tight and furred, and clasped them gently.

He inhaled. "I hope you don't think this is a punishment for me." He managed to peel his hand from her shoulder and found a place for it on her breast instead.

"'Twill be soon," she said, "if ye canna free your hands." She began to stroke the slippery flesh, feeling it stretch and thicken.

"I can't even take my eyes off the horizon to watch you while you do it," he cried. "You're a godless wench."

The first wet drops of release appeared. "Such a waste it will be, all that seed spent so carelessly."

His eyes turned to brown velvet. "Will you put your mouth on it?"

"Someday, I'm sure of it. But I'm enjoying this, aren't you?" She quickened the movement.

"When I get you in the captain's cabin," he said hoarsely, "I will show you what it means to yield, and in ways you haven't dreamed—on your knees, on your back, bent over the railing of the balcony."

"All you have to do is let go."

"My hands?" he said wickedly. "Or something else?"

"Your hands. The other I forebear to consider."

The cords of his neck tightened. The stroking was taking its toll. She tasted the salty damp of his shoulder and took in his windy, marine scent. His breathing was coming faster. How far would she take him?

"Inside you," he insisted. "Not like this."

"You command like a king, but where is your bargaining power?"

He swung them both in a circle, and she found herself pressed tightly between the barrel and his body. He released the rope, lifted her leg, and entered her.

"You've squandered every bit of restraint I can manage with you," he said, grasping her hips, "and now you'll pay the price."

He hammered her roughly, hardly more than a dozen strokes before crying out and thrusting deeply. The release reverberated through him.

"God, the blood that runs in your veins!" He gazed at her, astonished. "I've never known a woman like you. You're as smart as a fox and determined as a Viking—and *fearless*!"

She'd been told she was a great beauty countless times and found the praise unfulfilling. But smart and determined and fearless? Those were qualities she'd worked hard for.

"You aren't like any man I've known either, Mr. Innes."

"Oh?" He stretched, far too pleased with himself. "How's that?"

"Well, I am hardly an expert at such things, but a dozen strokes? Abby and Undine say a man is hardly performing unless he can reasonably reach at least—"

The rest of her words were swallowed in a dry gasp as his fingers found her bud.

His eyes smoldered. "Oh, I'm quite eager to hear the rest of this."

"He must...he must..." She tried to speak but found her throat unwilling to release the words.

She closed her eyes, letting the slow circle of the ship, repeated between legs, take her away.

When she was close, he got to his knees and finished her with his mouth. She bit back a cry when the enormity of it filled her; then she dropped, liquidly, into his arms. He pulled her onto his lap.

In her hazy happiness, she apprehended only the place where her warmth met his and wondered what it might be like to know this closeness, this dependability, every day, and to live filled with joy instead of anxiety. She became aware of him brushing her cheek with his fingers.

"Why are you crying?" he asked gently. "What have I done now?"

She shook her head. "I dinna know. It's not you. I'm happy, not sad."

He took the tail of his shirt and touched her eyes. "It's one thing to fail to deliver the required number of strokes, but to actually drive a woman to tears—and the first woman I've ever cared quite so much about pleasing... That would be disheartening, to say the least."

She laughed. "You havena displeased me. 'Tis quite the opposite."

He laced his fingers in hers and squeezed.

Somewhere below, the lookout cried, "Brig ahead—two points east of north. She's signaling us to stop!"

Gerard reached for her shirt. "The worst timing."

The lookout added, "She's preparing her guns!"

Gerard slipped on his breeks and leaned over the barrel's edge. "Battle stations!" he yelled, adding to her, "What did you find in Duchamps's cabin?"

"Nothing."

"Good. I need to know who I can trust." He kissed her and swung himself over the edge. "Hurry down. I'm going to need you."

Twenty-four

IT MIGHT HAVE JUST BEEN HIS OVERLY SENSITIVE CON-
science, but Gerard could have sworn Duchamps's
eyes trailed up to the crow's nest more than once after
Gerard had arrived at his side.

"She's not French," Duchamps said, lowering his
glass. "I'm sure of that. The way the sails are set is
not a common practice in my country. Nor do the
men on deck look naval trained. I see beards and
untucked shirts"—Gerard surreptitiously reached for
his shirttails—"an undisciplined crew under an equally
undisciplined captain. A recipe for carnage."

Gerard nodded because he was unable to speak.
I hope Duchamps means their carnage not ours. In truth,
though, the idea of anyone dying in the next quarter
hour made his stomach roil.

"Why are they following us? Any theories?" He
wanted Duchamps's take.

"The cargo, I presume. Insurance aside, though, I
have no intention of losing it."

"When will they be close enough to fire?"

"Ten minutes," Duchamps said. "Maybe less. Of

course, as you know, we won't be able to return fire for several minutes after that. Those nine-pounders reach a good deal farther than our eighteens."

Gerard looked around him. The men were lined up in groups of six, each around one of the cannons running the length of the deck. He had seen every episode of *Horatio Hornblower,* not to mention *Star Trek, Star Wars,* and *Battlestar Galactica,* and could pull off an imperious, cocksure captain until the cows came home, but actually commanding a crew in a life-or-death situation was seriously beyond his capabilities. His palms were so slippery, he nearly dropped his spyglass.

"What did you see up there?"

Gerard said, "Nothing but the ship ahead."

"Should I send a man up?"

"Um…" Gerard raised his gaze long enough to see Serafina swinging through the rigging like a monkey. "Aye."

Duchamps gave the orders, and one of the sailors scrabbled up the same ropes Gerard had just come down. He saw an exchange between Serafina and the man that ended in a gesture recognizable across countries and centuries.

He turned back to find Duchamps's gaze on Serafina as well.

"Sir," Duchamps began, "may I speak freely?"

Gerard hesitated. "Aye."

"You have, perhaps, a special relationship with Struan Harris? As a man you wish to guide in his career—or in other endeavors?"

Danger, Will Robinson. Danger, danger. "He's the cousin of a man to whom I owe a great favor."

"If I may, you would be less likely to stir the talk of the crew if your association with Mr. Harris retained the unbreachable shellac of impartiality."

The poor man was putting his career on the line.

"I thank you for your wise advice, Lieutenant. I have been remiss."

"Oh, no, sir. Not really." The man's voice grew even quieter and he looked as if he wished he could crawl into his boots and disappear—a feeling at this instant Gerard shared quite fully. "I…I have no objection to any man's preference. My most beloved brother is a…a…"

"Secretary?" Gerard offered.

"Aye," Duchamps said, slumping with relief, "and I would wish on no man the misery he has endured."

Gerard bowed. "Thank you, Lieutenant. You are most kind to speak so. 'Tis not a popular opinion to hold."

He nodded and inclined his head toward Gerard's breeks, which, Gerard saw, were misbuttoned.

Gerard flushed and made the necessary adjustments.

Serafina glided in beside them, notebook at the ready, and Duchamps lifted the glass. "Oh! They're sending a signal. 'Captain…to come across.'"

Gerard, who had expected "Surrender, Dorothy," looked to his colleagues. Serafina shook her head firmly. Duchamps was more circumspect.

"Are they offering a negotiation, do you think?" Gerard asked.

"What do we have that they want?" Duchamps said.

Serafina said nothing. Her face made it clear what she thought of the idea.

"I don't know," Gerard said, "but it would be a hell of an opportunity to find out."

"A captain's place is with his ship," Serafina said.

Gerard offered about as much value here as a screen door on a submarine—with probably the same outcome. On the other hand, he had no desire to make his way across the expanse of sea to a ship Duchamps read as an undisciplined recipe for carnage, but the fact remained Gerard was the most expendable man on board.

He didn't need to debate the issue long. A warning shot split the afternoon's quiet, and the speck of black that flew out of the smoke whistled across the water through the sternmost yard, sending splinters raining down on the deck. He figured he had two choices: he could fight—and the men certainly gave the appearance of being ready—or he could attempt to save the men without a fight.

"Ready my boat."

"Ready the captain's barge!" Duchamps hollered.

Serafina's eyes wore a gloss of wetness. "Will ye need a secretary?"

"No."

"Sir, I think—"

"*No.*"

"Don't be ridiculous. I can *help.*"

"Insubordination. Duchamps, write the man up. If he opens his mouth again, put him in the hold for the duration of the battle."

Her eyes were daggers, and Gerard prayed with every fiber of his being she would speak one more time. As far as he was concerned, there wasn't a place deep enough on earth to put her if cannonballs started to fly.

"I understand." Duchamps gave him a sad but knowing smile. "I'll do exactly as you wish."

Twenty-five

GERARD GAZED AHEAD, LISTENING TO THE LAP OF OARS in the water. The sailors rowed in a practiced unison. None of them met his eye. He wondered if that was standard when one rowed for a captain or if he was encircled by an aura of doom and their innate sense of it made it hard to look him in the face.

He'd only looked behind him once. And there she'd been, her gray cap visible at the farthest corner of the stern. Would she be safe? Would he return? How had a party in Manhattan turned into a choppy boat ride to a forbidding, undisciplined ship in the middle of the North Sea in less than twenty-four hours?

He closed his eyes and remembered the sparks of sunshine in her tumbling hair, smelled the tang of salt water on her skin, and felt her fingers laced in his.

"Why are ye smiling?"

Gerard opened his eyes and looked at Thistlebrook. "None of your bloody goddamned business."

One of the sailors snickered.

"Quiet," Gerard said.

"They're going to kill you."

"And why would they do that?" Gerard remembered Serafina's proscription against beating information out of Thistlebrook. He wondered if the same proscription applied when the only witnesses would be the captain's loyal team of bargemen.

"Because you've taken something they want," Thistlebrook said. "Don't be a fool. Turn around."

"They said to send the captain across. I'm giving them two. Like cuff links. Personally, I think they'll be thrilled."

The sailor laughed again.

"Sailor! What's your name?"

"MacIlroy, sir."

"Button it."

"Aye, sir."

There was something about being the most powerful man in a six-foot radius that made Gerard feel like anything was possible.

They were nearly to the other ship. A bosun's chair had been rigged to bring him up. He saw it hanging off the side like a body hanging from a gallows. The boat made a *thunk* as it hit the ship's side. One of the sailors began to secure it.

"Don't tie up," a voice from overhead called. "The captain stays. The boat will go back. We'll signal when you need to return."

"'*When* you need to return,'" Gerard said. "Not if. Did you hear that, Thistlebrook?"

The man chuckled. "Do ye think they'd bury your body themselves?"

Twenty-six

GERARD DRUMMED HIS FINGERS ON THE CHAIR'S ARM. The armed men at the sides of the cabin door watched him with evident disdain. All in all, he preferred being ignored.

He'd been split from Thistlebrook the moment they'd come over the rail. Either the men on this ship were far more interested in Thistlebrook, or Thistlebrook was awaiting his fate, just like Gerard.

The door opened, and Gerard could not have been more surprised. The man he'd met in the Squeak and Blade, the man who resembled him and had been looking for Serafina, entered.

Then it hit him. *Jesus Christ, this is Edward!*

He didn't know why it surprised him as much as it did. He'd been given every clue: Sera wanted a man to help her claim some cargo; the cargo belonged to Edward; a man looking for Sera in the tavern shared Gerard's height and coloring.

And yet, Serafina had not thought to tell him this fact.

He hadn't liked Edward when he'd met him. Now he found he liked him even less.

Edward signaled the men to exit. He took one of the chairs.

"Where is she?" he demanded in a hoarse whisper. "What have you done with her? I need to know right now."

That was not the question Gerard was expecting, and it was clear the man didn't want anyone else to know of his interest. Gerard was tempted to tell him exactly what he *had* done with Sera, but there was something about the worry in the man's eyes that required a straightforward answer.

"She's safe," Gerard said.

Edward's face filled with relief. "Where? She's not in her rooms in town. I checked."

Gerard had no intention of answering this question or any others.

"She's on that ship, isn't she? She told me she would take the cargo if she could." Edward's worry had turned to something else, something more like hunger—a hunger Gerard suspected would very soon turn to anger.

"She's not on the ship," Gerard said. "She wanted to be on it. I stopped her. She's safely tucked away, awaiting word from me."

Edward's eyes widened. Gerard could see what was going through his head. *The man before me has the power to control Serafina Fallon?*

"Who are you?" Edward said.

"You can't guess?"

"She hired you. She hired you to pretend you were me."

Gerard didn't reply. He had found in business, the

less one spoke, the more the balance of power shifted in one's favor.

But Edward didn't know this truth, and the silence incited him. "Where did she find you? You're not a Scot." He'd said "Scot" with the same tone he would have used for "a bag of human excrement."

Gerard had realized, of course, the moment he'd put Thistlebrook on the boat that his stint as erstwhile captain of *La Trahison* was over. Nonetheless, it had seemed an action with a reasonable chance of appeasing the men here, whoever they might be. The fact that Edward had not asked him how he had taken possession of the ship seemed to indicate, just as Duchamps had suggested, that Edward and Thistlebrook were in league, and that Thistlebrook had told Edward everything that had happened on *La Trahison* as soon as he'd been separated from Gerard. Though whether "in league" meant the two were partners in an innocent trading venture or something more sinister, Gerard didn't know.

Gerard's nonresponsiveness was taking Edward, a very poor negotiator indeed, to a rapid boil. Even Gerard, whose knowledge of prisoner interrogation came primarily from several dozen viewings of *The Great Escape*, knew better than to let his emotions show.

"Thistlebrook says you know nothing about sailing, that you're nothing more than a preening popinjay... an empty frock coat."

Gerard looked at him. "Well, I *was* imitating you."

The water burst from the pan. "You don't see it, do you?"

The dark dot of *La Trahison* on the water outside the porthole had begun to shift. The ship was turning.

"She didn't need you to collect the cargo," Edward said. "She could do that with her eyes closed. She hired you for a different reason."

Gerard fought the temptation but lost. He searched Edward's face.

"Ah, cracks in the bulwark," Edward observed. "Do you want to know?"

"No."

"You lie. Let us see how sharp you are. Why would a woman hire a man who looks like the fiancé with whom she is still desperately in love?"

Gerard heard nothing but the roar of blood in his ears.

"That's right," Edward said. "To fuck him from her head."

Gerard flew shoulder first into Edward's gut, knocking them both over with a crash.

The door burst open, and the armed men dragged Gerard to his feet.

Edward lay in a ball, wheezing. "Let him go."

The men shoved Gerard away from his prey and released him.

"Go," Edward said to the men.

The door closed. Gerard let out a long sigh and reluctantly extended his hand. Even more reluctantly, Edward took it.

"I'm sorry. I had to know." Edward wiped the blood from his lip, which had been split in the skirmish. He drew a lace-edged handkerchief from his pocket and daubed his mouth. "I don't blame her, you know. I was boorish and unkind."

Was? Gerard contemplated adding a bleeding nose to the bleeding lip.

"But the fact remains, she is under my protection and, as a gentleman, I know I have treated her abominably."

"Under your protection?" Gerard had no clear idea what Edward mean, but the sound of the words made his anger rise.

"Aye. For the last year."

"And how is bankrupting and abandoning her considered 'under your protection'?"

"Mister…" Edward waited for a last name. When Gerard didn't offer one, he gave up and proceeded without it. "You are in love with her then? Or intend to extend an offer of marriage? I believe your relationship is of no more than a day's length, perhaps two, but 'tis possible I've misunderstood."

Had Serafina spoken to him? Gerard found the idea impossible to believe.

"I am here to do the lady's bidding," Gerard said, "whatever that might entail, for as long as she desires my support."

"What an agreeable assignment this has turned out to be for you then. I don't deny I behaved in an ungentlemanly manner in regard to Serafina. My family was opposed to the union, and I was a fool to listen to them." Edward straightened his coat and cravat. "My feelings for her are unchanged. I need to tell her that we may marry immediately."

"Once you claim the cargo."

A flash of anger appeared in Edward's eyes and was quickly extinguished. "Serafina has never had much of a mind for business. She's fearless, aye, and for a woman, surprisingly intelligent. But her exposure to the real business of trading has been narrow—only enough to give her false confidence and make her a danger to herself. Did she tell you her fortune is gone? She blames me, I suppose. And perhaps I should have stopped her. But I wanted her to have her way if she could. It was never much money, to be sure, but the choices she made…" He shook his head sadly. "Such folly. If you have any regard for her, please try to see that her future will be best preserved if the disposition of the cargo is overseen by me."

If he had any regard for her? *Pompous prick.*

"Let me tell you what I think," Gerard said with exquisite precision. "The best course of action for a gentleman who in his own words has acted abominably would be to hand the cargo over to Miss Fallon without delay and let her throw the income from it one coin at a time into the North Sea if she so chooses."

Edward pulled at a cuff. "I might say the best course of action for a gentleman who professes to be led solely by the wishes of a lady would be to do everything in his power to put a man from the upper reaches of society with an offer of marriage he believes would be welcome in front of her and let her decide for herself."

La Trahison was drawing closer.

"Where are we going?" Gerard demanded. "What do these men intend to do?"

"I believe they intend to take what they believe is theirs."

"They won't succeed. Duchamps will fight. I've given him orders."

"Duchamps would fight even if you hadn't given him orders," Edward said. "That's his job. I can't make any promises about what will happen. 'Tis for that very reason I am relieved Serafina isn't on board."

Gerard thought of the men on the ship. He thought of Duchamps. But most of all, he thought of Serafina—in harm's way.

"I'll take you to her," Gerard said. "But you must guarantee the safety of my men. You can have the cargo, but the men must remain unharmed."

Edward chuckled. "Your men? They are my men. But I have no more wish than you do to see them slaughtered. Let me talk to the men in charge here. I'll see what I can negotiate. But I want your promise that in addition to taking me to her, you will present my proposal as an advantageous opportunity and one you endorse."

Gerard shook his head. "I owe her loyalty and that includes my honesty."

Edward shifted. "What will you advise her to do?"

"To run. As far and as fast as she can."

"I'm sorry to say her current situation won't allow for such a thing. And while her current misfortune will be the means to my good luck, I take comfort in knowing that, in a very short time, 'twill be the means to her good luck as well. I accept your offer." He extended his hand.

Gerard struggled to overcome his distaste for what he was doing, but nothing at the moment could be more important than saving the lives of Serafina and the other men. He took Edward's hand.

"You're doing the best thing for her," Edward said, rising.

Gerard wished he could be certain it was true.

Twenty-seven

TECHNICALLY, HE WAS FREE AND BACK ON *LA TRAHISON*, but realistically, it felt almost no different to be held at pistol-point on one's own ship than it did to be held at pistol-point in the enemy's. Gerard's sailors were locked in the hold below while the men from Edward's ship gathered whatever it was they were looking for and completed the arduous process of raising it by winch over the side, lowering it onto boats, and transporting it to the other ship.

They seemed to be keeping their word about leaving the sailors of *La Trahison* unharmed, though until the other ship was gone, Gerard wouldn't breathe easy. The look of disappointment on Duchamps's face was not one he'd soon forget, and he hadn't seen Serafina since he'd returned.

It was hard to believe his biggest problem a day ago had been deciding whether to go for the sixteen- or twenty-five-year-old Macallan at the hotel.

The door opened. It was Thistlebrook.

Gerard gave him a weak smile. "We meet again."

"We do. Might I impose upon you to take a short

stroll around the quarterdeck? There are a few matters I need to take care of in here."

Gerard shrugged. "The cabin is yours, after all."

"My thoughts exactly."

"Will the armed men come with me or stay with you?"

"I say we split the difference, aye? Hartnell," he called, "stay with our guest. Tolan can stay outside."

Gerard rose and made his way into the sea air. His eyes went automatically to the crow's nest, which held one of the other ship's sailors, then to the crates being lifted over the side. He tried to read the names scrawled on the sides, but Hartnell stepped into his line of vision.

"The better view is to the south."

Gerard turned with a growl. Thistlebrook and the men from the other ship were stealing the cargo, that much was clear, probably so that Edward, the ship's owner, could collect insurance on what had been stolen, and Edward and Thistlebrook could share in the proceeds from the sale of the stolen merchandise. The insurance would be used to cover the investors' losses, and Edward and Thistlebrook would be rich. A good plan if you weren't too fastidious about thievery.

Edward and Thistlebrook were in league in the heist, of course. But according to the conversation Serafina had overheard in the carpenter's walkway, Thistlebrook begged his confidante, whoever the confidante was, to keep something secret. Was the person who was not to be told Edward, Duchamps, or someone else? If it was Edward, Thistlebrook was not as trustworthy a partner as Edward may think.

The last of the cargo was being loaded into the boats. Gerard was desperate to see Serafina.

Edward's voice rose above the hum of activity. He and Thistlebrook were arguing. Edward grabbed Thistlebrook's shirt. Gerard took a step toward them and changed his mind.

Hartnell said, "Wise choice." He chuckled. "The ship is well named."

"How's that?"

"*La Trahison* means 'the betrayal,' and we're the ones who have the gold now."

The next thing Gerard knew, Edward, swearing and kicking, was being lashed to the rigging.

Thistlebrook gave him a wave and disappeared over the side. The men from the other ship followed. When the last man disappeared, Hartnell returned the pistol to his belt and joined his companions.

Gerard ran to Edward. "What's the fuck is going on?"

"How should I know? They're stealing my cargo!"

Gerard grabbed Edward's pistol and ran toward the companionway.

"Unlock me," Edward shouted.

"In a minute." Gerard flew down to the hold. The door was chained shut and a keyed lock held it closed.

"Get away from the door," he shouted.

He aimed the pistol at the lock, lifted the lever, and pulled the trigger. When the smoke cleared, the lock was broken. Men poured out.

When Duchamps appeared, Gerard grabbed him. "They're rowing away with the cargo. Should we shoot them? Chase them? You're in charge. Where's Harris?"

Duchamps pointed ahead in the crowd. In the

press of the crowd, Gerard had missed her. Duchamps yelled, "Battle stations!" Gerard elbowed his way through the chaos, desperate to reach Serafina before she reached the stairs.

But he was too late.

She reached the top, and a hand flew to her mouth. "Edward!" she cried, having forgotten her disguised voice.

By the time Gerard crested the stairs, she was beside her former fiancé, listening as he spoke.

She called to Gerard. "Is he tied up for a reason?"

Gerard shook his head.

She went to work on the ropes, and though nothing in her attention suggested special care, Gerard found it impossible to watch the ministrations without feeling a deep sense of jealousy.

Duchamps, in the midst of shouting instructions to the various gun crews and sailors overhead, spotted the vignette. His gaze went from Edward to Gerard and back again. Gerard made his way to the lieutenant.

"Struan Harris is a woman named Serafina Fallon," Gerard said. "I'm not Edward Turnbull, only a man pretending to be. And the man beside Serafina? That's Edward Turnbull and the ship belongs to him."

Duchamps face turned somber. "Does the woman belong to him too?"

I wish I knew.

Twenty-eight

THE SUN HAD BEGUN ITS SLOW DESCENT THROUGH THE bruised clouds in the west. The ship was quiet at last, and Gerard stood at the railing of *La Trahison* with Duchamps, intently aware of the closed door behind them. The sea was an inky void.

"Are you sure you should be standing?" Gerard asked.

Duchamps, draped in an impressive crown of wrapped linen bandages, gave him a weak smile. "I am not. But it's a captain's job." *La Trahison* had chased the other ship for tens of miles, falling farther and farther behind until she'd had to let it go. Only one shot had been fired, and that by the other ship. The shot had been wide of the mark, dinging a spar, which had exploded in a hundred pieces, including one large enough to knock Duchamps out for several moments. No one else had been hurt.

Lost in the evening's serenity, one of the master's mates awoke from his reverie, turned over the hour-glass marking the quarter hour, and noted the time in the log. Gerard stole a glance at the door of the captain's cabin.

"The length of the discussion means nothing," Duchamps said. "Do not lose heart, *mon ami*."

Gerard sighed. The moment he could, Edward had asked Serafina for a private audience. She refused twice, but his pleas had begun to draw looks from the crew, and she'd relented. Edward had claimed the captain's cabin and led her into it. That had been half an hour ago.

"She's not promised to you?"

"No," Gerard said quickly. "I have no claim on her at all."

Duchamps eyed him skeptically. "Claims exist before hard promises."

"I've known her for a day. Turnbull was once her fiancé. He wants her back. It's likely that would be a very good decision for her."

The Frenchman smiled. "Would it?"

"Yes. He comes from a wealthy family. And he's shown his ability to admit when he's made a mistake."

"I'm sure you're right. I can think of very few women who aren't immediately drawn to a fool with money."

"Laugh if you will. It would make me happy to see her happy."

"Oh, yes, I could tell by the look on your face when he closed the door."

Gerard really didn't have a claim on her. And who was he to judge Edward's sins? People made mistakes, and if Edward acknowledged his and Serafina forgave him...

Duchamps thumped Gerard on the back. "Shall I call for some wine?"

Gerard reminded himself that Serafina insisted Duchamps was still a very likely candidate for the person Thistlebrook had been talking to in the carpenter's walkway. Gerard didn't want to suspect the Frenchman. He rather liked him. But he knew he had to accept it as a reasonable possibility.

"Yes. Thank you. That would be good."

Duchamps gave instructions, and Gerard insisted a chair be brought for the lieutenant as well.

When the wine was poured, Gerard said, "Do you have any idea what the men on the other ship wanted—I mean specifically within the cargo?" Hartnell had mentioned gold. Complicit or not, Duchamps would have to provide a guess, and Gerard was quite adept at reading the faces of his clients, especially if they were lying.

"I don't know if it's anything specific. The cargo as a whole is worth many thousands of pounds. Though the men didn't seem to be mere pirates."

"No. Nor did they seem especially fond of Turnbull."

"*Non.*"

"Do you think he helped plan it?"

Duchamps shifted. "As you know, I had not met Monsieur Turnbull—the real Monsieur Turnbull," he added with a small bow, "until last night. If I had, of course, I would certainly have recognized that you were not he. Thistlebrook's communication with Turnbull was through letters. *La Trahison* was hired to deliver goods to Portugal and Marseilles and pick up other goods from Istanbul, Venice, Barcelona, and St. Petersburg. That is what this ship does."

"And Turnbull owns it?"

"Yes. He bought it six months ago, though rumor has it he plans to sell it again soon."

The breeze died away, and for a moment Serafina's voice, calm but indistinct, was audible on deck.

Gerard had no desire to hear the conversation and was summoning a reason to prowl the far deck when the wind picked up again.

"Edward has an investor—in the ship, I mean, not the cargo," Duchamps said. "He came to the ship yesterday, before Harris—er, Miss Fallon arrived. He's not a sailor, on that I would be willing to wager. One learns to recognize those things—the stance, the way one looks at a ship. Yet there was an air of the military about him. Land though, not sea. But I'm only guessing…"

"Name?"

"He didn't give one. He's English, about your height, and blond too, though his hair is slightly darker."

Gerard felt a further observation coming and held his tongue.

"To say more would be mere conjecture," Duchamps said at last.

"Your conjecture would be valuable to me."

Duchamps resettled in his chair. "I believe Mr. Turnbull owes him money. There was a certain… heatedness to their discussion."

"And you said the ship and its contents were insured?"

"They are. Monsieur Turnbull will lose nothing."

The door of the captain's cabin opened and Edward emerged. He slammed the door hard enough to rattle the panes in the lantern swaying beside it and looked at Duchamps.

"How long to Leith?"

Duchamps, who had leaped to his feet at the first

sound, said, "At least several hours, sir. Though if the wind dies as it appears it might, it could be longer."

"Bloody, goddamned, arse-buggering wind."

"Aye, sir."

Edward stomped down the companionway and disappeared.

Serafina opened the door, and suddenly Gerard felt in need of a chair as well. She remained in the shirt and trousers of a sailor, but she'd loosened her hair, and her face had been scrubbed of ink. The certainty in her eyes spoke of an ending, not a beginning.

Gerard looked to see if Duchamps saw it as well, but Duchamps had retreated to the farthest end of the stern, leaving Gerard and Serafina as much privacy as they could hope to enjoy on a fifty-man ship.

She drew a strand from her cheek and made her way to the railing. As a man, she'd been striking. As a woman, with hair the color of the blazing western sun, full lips, and a figure apparent even in the most shapeless of clothes, she was the focus of every eye on board. Gerard was afraid the sailors might begin to topple from the yards.

"I'm glad we finally get to talk alone," he said.

She laughed. "Aye."

"As I believe a number of the men here know how to read lips, I suggest we replace 'Thistlebrook' with 'unicorn,' 'cargo' with 'dirk,' and 'Edward' with 'boysenberry tart.'"

She laughed again, more lightly, but the mention of her former fiancé had changed something on her face.

"I'm afraid boysenberries are nae tart enough to replace Edward," she said without joy, staring into the water.

Gerard let the silence fill in the space around them. There was no point in rushing her. She would say what she had to say in her own time. A dozen humps of gray appeared in the sea to the south and one rose high enough to reveal a fin.

"Sharks?" he asked.

"Whales."

The rise and fall continued as the hills moved across the water.

"Beautiful."

"You are easily pleased," she said, but a little of the old Serafina had returned.

"You know," he said at last, "I've enjoyed every moment I've spent with you, and nothing you can tell me will change that."

"Are ye expecting me to tell ye something now ye won't enjoy?"

"Well, I…I mean, you and Edward had time to talk…"

She narrowed her eyes. "Aye?"

"And I know he intended to renew his offer of marriage."

"You *knew* that?"

His spine prickled. "Well, yes. He told me on the other ship."

"Did the two of ye come to an agreement on it?"

Oh, he had definitely stepped in something he shouldn't have. "No agreement, no. I did promise I would bring him to you. I had to in order to get him to convince the men running the ship to do the men on *La Trahison* no harm. I told him you were in Edinburgh, that I had forbidden you from boarding."

On "forbidden," her brows rose almost to her

hairline. "I see. So your assumption then is I will accept Edward's renewed attentions?"

He swallowed. "It's not my hope, that is certain."

"What *is* your hope?"

Gerard's tongue felt like a wad of cotton.

"Come, Gerard. You hear Edward declare his love for me. To save the ship, ye agree to bring us together. You say ye dinna wish to see me marry him. What do ye wish, then?"

He was not a man prone to wishing. He lived in the now. There were a few things Gerard did *not* wish for—unhappiness, finding the Yankees in the World Series, Seràfina with a man like Edward—but his pyramid of needs did not extend beyond bedtime.

"I…" He searched for a response.

"Dinna forget that the moment we can provide a complete list of our deeds to Undine, you will return to the land of advertisements and airships. What is it you wish?"

He had lost heart for this game. "I wish to know if you're promised to him."

Her eyes, dark and blue, met his. "I'm not."

He exhaled, unaware he'd been holding his breath. "Why?"

"Do ye think I should've said aye? I canna marry a man I dinna love. Even a man from New York should know that."

Her face, always so open, seemed free of regret, but he wanted her to be sure. "I do think he cares for you. He was honestly concerned for your safety."

The corner of her mouth rose. "Are you his advocate?"

Gerard shook his head. "Not me."

She tucked her hair behind her ear, and he found himself quite deeply in love with her.

"Edward seemed angry," he said.

"Aye, well, he's nae had much practice at accepting no for an answer. 'Twill improve his character. It might improve yours as well."

"I wish I could take your hand."

She drew a spyglass from her pocket and handed it to him. Their fingers touched, and a charge went through him. "A poor substitute, I know."

"Nothing about it was poor. I have other wishes."

"Oh, do ye now? Speak."

"To hold you in my arms and sleep next to you in a real bed. To count the colors in that silky mass of curls. To feel your ribs swell when you breathe. To smell the night on your skin."

"These are all good wishes—and ones I share. But none of them last past dawn. I dinna want what ye canna give, but I'm a Scot. We are constant and unchanging. The man at my side must be more than the dust that disappears in a puff when ye pick up a handful of earth." She leaned closer. "Find yourself a cabin tonight, and we'll see what sort of earth ye have to offer."

Twenty-nine

IT WAS NOT THE LIGHT OF DAWN THAT WOKE GERARD but the rumble of feet over his head. He sat up. She was gone. He dressed in the dark and hurried up to the deck, which was as lively as a skyscraper construction site. The ship was docked and the buildings of Leith harbor lay before him, just dousing their lanterns one by one as the rose in the East.

"Has the lady made her way on deck?" he asked Ginty.

"Come and gone."

"*Gone?*"

Ginty shrugged. "Sailors work while landsmen sleep."

The gangway was in place and men were moving up and down it. One of the men ascending was Duchamps, who looked considerably better than he had the night before.

"Did you sleep well?" Gerard asked, bowing.

Duchamps gave him a Gallic smile. "Not as well as you, it seems."

"Apparently, I slept too well. She's gone. Without a word. Good thing I don't take these things personally."

Edward emerged from the captain's cabin

disheveled and red eyed. He nodded stiffly to Gerard and Duchamps and headed down the gangway.

When he was out of earshot, Gerard said, "I take it he didn't sleep as well as we did."

"Up all night, I believe. Writing letters. Wanted an inventory of what was left in the hold as well."

"Which was?" The Grinch had nothing on the men from the other ship, who had taken everything, including every one of the cook's pots and pans.

"Three barrels of Madeira, nineteen riding crops, and a hundred and sixty-seven bolts of Turkish muslin."

"Now there's a cocktail party you won't soon forget."

Duchamps didn't laugh. "What are the odds," he said, "that you and the lady would ask the same question an hour apart from one another?"

"Pretty high, I guess."

"There is something I have to tell you, and I'm sorry about it. Miss Fallon left this morning in the company of a gentleman. He was waiting for her in a carriage when *La Trahison* arrived in Leith. He sent a note. She joined him in the carriage, and together, they headed up the hill to Edinburgh."

The ramparts of Edinburgh Castle rose above the morning mist, just beyond the steeple of St. Giles.

"To Edinburgh?"

"*Oui.*"

"'Tis a fine morning for a walk," Duchamps said.

"Indeed, it will be."

❧

Duchamps stood at the railing until the forsaken lover disappeared from sight. Reaching deep in his pocket, he crushed the folded note on which a fine, feminine hand had written "Mr. Gerard Innes" and tossed it into the firth.

Thirty

ABBY RELEASED THE CURTAIN. "NO ONE IS FOLLOWING us. Anyone with sense is still abed."

Serafina thought of Gerard's warm chest and his musky scent, still on her skin. She wished she'd had the sense to remain in that pleasure-filled cot.

Abby settled into the carriage bench. "You know," she said to Serafina, "you look like a young Duke of Gloucester in those breeks. If I'm honest, it's a bit off-putting."

Undine said, "I'm less interested in the breeks and more interested in what happened on the ship."

"Oh, aye!" Abby said. "Have your relations with Mr. Innes progressed to the bed stage? Has he decided to stay? He is verra handsome—and also verra taken with you. I could tell by the vast amount of irritation he exhibited."

Undine rolled her eyes. "While Abby would take us down any number of unproductive side streets, my question actually referred to the cargo and Mr. Turnbull."

Abby made a pained sigh. "So dull."

"I will answer your questions," Serafina said, "and

then you must tell me why you have pried me from the ship at so early an hour. As to our adventure, Edward is involved in something nefarious. The cargo on the ship was stolen by another ship last night while we sailed the North Sea, a ship that Edward sailed in on."

Abby jerked upright. "He's a pirate?!"

"Just a scoundrel. He claims the men on the ship double-crossed him, that he had no knowledge the cargo was to be taken."

Undine sniffed. "They may have double-crossed him, but that doesn't mean he had no knowledge of the plan. He could be lying about that part."

"He *is* lying," Serafina said. "Edward canna sit still when he lies. He was worse than a bag of kittens when he told me the story."

Undine ran a finger over her lip. "Interesting. I have heard of a ship like that on the North Sea that—"

Abby gently signaled her to stop. "Let us address the mystery later. We have a more important issue here." She took Serafina's hand. "What does the theft mean to you, my friend? In regard to your fortune?"

Serafina's throat thickened. "'Tis gone."

"All of it?"

"Except three barrels of Madeira, riding crops, and some muslin. They took everything."

"We can fight him," Abby said.

"Of course."

"And ye will have the funds to live until your fortune is restored?"

"Oh, aye." Serafina nodded reassuringly.

"Bastard."

"Aye."

Abby searched her friend's face. "How was Mr. Innes in all this? Was he appropriately supportive? He is all right, is he not?"

"Oh, aye." Serafina thought of the last time she'd seen him awake, the starry night of the porthole a canvas beyond his head, when he had been quite a bit more than all right, as had she. "He acquitted himself quite well on *La Trahison*. He's no sailor, but he is a quick study and showed no lack of courage. He offered himself up to save the ship and ended up saving us all."

"The rebels could use a dozen more like him," Undine said. "And you, for that matter. He knows to join us at the inn?"

"Aye. I left a note," Serafina said. "But I couldna expect him to care much about Scotland's future. 'Tis not his fight. He lives a verra comfortable life back in—" Serafina paused and looked at Abby. Did she know Gerard's origins?

Abby laughed. "You dinna think I can recognize a man wholly out of time and place? The way they gawk and dither? No obvious skills?"

"Did you notice the choice of the word 'obvious'?" Undine said to Serafina. "It used to be 'measurable.' I guess she's found a way to measure the less obvious ones in men who travel across time."

Serafina's head went back and forth between the women. "Are you saying…Duncan?"

"*Och*, aye." Abby grinned.

"But he is such a…a Scot. Does he not want to return?"

"He did once, of course. He has a grand-da there who traveled too, it seems. But then the spark rose between us and there was no turning back." Abby leaned forward conspiratorially. "From everything I've heard about the twenty-first century, it sounds like a horrid place, filled with noise and talking machines and women of verra questionable virtue. I am nae surprised they want to stay once they see the Arcadia we have here."

Serafina bit her lip. Gerard had given her no indication he had any interest in staying. "I'm sure there are many things to love in their time."

"Women of very questionable virtue likely being at the top of that list," Undine said. "You do realize, I hope, you have complicated Mr. Innes's return almost beyond repair. How am I to undo what you have done when you and he continue to leave irreversible events in your wake?"

Serafina hung her head. "I'm sorry, Undine."

"Ignore her," Abby said to Serafina. "Undine doesn't allow for the unexpected. She needs to realize not everyone lives their life according to rules and formulas and potions. Sometimes things just happen."

Undine sniffed. "Sometimes things just happen when one takes ten times the appropriate amount of herbs and mixes them with alcohol. But now that you're done with him, I need the list of deeds so that the return mixture can be properly prepared."

Done with him? How can I be done with him when I've just begun?

Abby leaned forward. "Was Mr. Innes's looking like Edward one of the things that just happened? Or was that part of the plan? Edward was at the railing when I reached the gangplank. At first I said to myself,

'Oh, it's Mr. Innes.' He turned and I waved, but he offered no sign of recognition. In fact, he cut me quite coldly. Then I saw his features were not so much like Mr. Innes's as I had first believed. I asked the sailor at the bottom of the gangplank who the man was. He said, 'Edward Turnbull, the ship's owner,' and I thought, *Oh, Serafina, what are you about?*"

"'Twas part of the plan. I needed a man who could claim the cargo as Edward. Instead, he claimed the ship, but the cargo eluded us."

Undine smiled. "Was Edward surprised to meet this partner in your adventure?"

Abby said, "As usual, our friend is missing the far more interesting point. What was it like going to bed with a less execrable version of your fiancé?"

Serafina's face must have betrayed her surprise because Abby added, "Oh, dear. Mr. Innes *is* less execrable, isn't he?"

Serafina flushed. "No. Yes. I mean of course he's less execrable."

"Did you feel appropriately vengeful? 'Tis a shame the odious Edward could not have seen you riding his twin like the lead horse at Lanark Racecourse. *That* would certainly have given him something to think about."

"You have a verra vivid imagination," Serafina said.

"Duncan says that too. 'Tis one of my better qualities, I think."

Serafina straightened the knee of her breeks. "Let us say the experience was entirely different and that Mr. Innes exceeded my expectations on every count."

Abby sighed happily and gave Undine a thoughtful look. "If you could snap your fingers and have one of your former lovers appear, transformed into a more-deserving version of himself, would you do it?"

"As most of them disappeared *after* a snap, I would find it verra unconstructive. The purpose of our meeting this morning is not, as Abby would have it, to dissect the bedchamber performance of sweethearts past and present—"

"Ooh, I like that."

"—but to dig further into Edward's motives and, in doing so, get us closer to returning Serafina's fortune to her."

Serafina sat up. "What does that mean?"

"It means that ever since you mentioned Edward, I've been doing a little investigating, and I heard something last night. First, he is in debt."

"I knew that. His family cut him off and he's a fool with money."

"Second, every penny of his share of the profit from this last voyage will have to be used to pay his debt. And third, he has an investor—the man who bought the ship. Edward did not finance the voyage on this own."

Serafina worked quickly through the logistics. "Do ye think his investor is part of the scheme to have the cargo appear to be stolen?"

"Either that or Edward is cheating him too. Either way, I think you could learn a lot by talking to him—perhaps even the location of the stolen cargo if the investor is indeed part of the plan to steal the cargo and collect the insurance. This investor wishes to operate in anonymity. He's taken a room at the Bull and the Swan under an assumed name—Francis Weatherall. He's there now."

"How do ye know?"

"My contact works at the Bull and the Swan."

"Take me there!"

"Serafina, wait. This is more dangerous than you think. The man is also involved in trying to buy the outcome of the upcoming vote on the union."

Every Scot was sharply aware of the vote the noblemen in the Scottish Parliament were scheduled to take regarding entering into a permanent union with England. The idea, which would make some of the noblemen extremely wealthy and destroy Scotland's independence forever, sickened her. Undine was working with her network of spies to ensure the effort failed.

"I don't care," Serafina said.

"Well, you should. These are dangerous times. I'd talk to the man myself, but there are things I need to do that require me to keep my distance. I think we may be able to help one another, however."

"How?"

"If you're willing to be careful—very careful—we can arrange for you to talk to him. And while you talk to him, I'm going to search his room."

Serafina's eyes widened. "But I thought you didn't know him."

"I didn't say I didn't know him. I said he wished to operate in anonymity."

"Who is he?"

"Lord Crispin Hiscock."

Thirty-one

FOR ONCE, SERAFINA WAS GRATEFUL SHE WAS AT THE lowest rung of Edinburgh society. Lord Hiscock may have heard that Serafina Fallon was the poor girl Edward Turnbull ruined, but he wouldn't recognize her. No nobleman paid attention to a ruined girl unless he was the one doing the ruining.

She was to keep Hiscock engaged for a quarter of an hour while Undine scoured his room. When the clock chimed nine, Undine would exit via the back door. At that point, Serafina would be free to extricate herself from Hiscock's side and make her escape.

Serafina wore Abby's beautiful, embroidered, pumpkin silk frock. She and Abby had exchanged outfits in the carriage. The rustle of the crisp fabric reminded Serafina she'd left her only gown in a tavern near the dock, expecting to leave *La Trahison* a self-sufficient woman. Instead, she had nothing—unless Hiscock could lead her to the stolen cargo.

"Is Hiscock here?"

Undine's contact, one of the inn's grooms, stood with Serafina in the establishment's entryway.

"Weatherall, remember?" he said. "He's there in the corner of the dining room."

Hiscock had a basket of rolls in front of him and was carving into a chop. Serafina grimaced. The man was thin as a post and cheerless as a hangman.

"Why the need for a different name?" Serafina said. "Is his business that nefarious?"

The groom laughed. "Undoubtedly. But that's not why he uses the name here. He meets the wife of Lord Sanderson on Sunday afternoons. Are you working on the Parliament vote?"

"Oh, no." She shook her head. "I leave that for people more expert than I, though every Scot in Scotland is grateful for your efforts." She made a small curtsy.

"What then?" he asked, curious.

"I am here concerning some cargo."

He frowned. "Cargo? From a ship?"

"Aye. And an investor by the name of Edward Turnbull."

"I havena heard of Hiscock being involved in such dealings. Where did you hear it?"

The clock struck once for a quarter to nine. The agreed start time.

"Just a friend," she said quickly. "Thank you. I must begin." She made her way to the empty table beside Hiscock and called for a plate of eggs.

"Have you seen my husband, Comte de Beaubois?" she asked the maid who delivered the eggs. "He was supposed to take me to the castle today."

The maid disclaimed any knowledge of the comte, and Serafina let out a long, annoyed sigh. "If he has gone for another of his interminable meetings, I shall

never forgive him. Am I never to have any pleasure?"
According to the groom, Hiscock liked to prey on
lusty, bored wives. Serafina had never been a wife, and
she'd rarely been bored, but she'd seen enough lusty,
bored wives to play one in this little drama. She ran
a finger through one of the yolks and sucked it clean.

Aye, that was lusty.

It was tasty too, and she reached for her fork and
speared a large piece.

"Pardon me?"

A shadow fell over the plate. His lordship had
arrived. Serafina swallowed. Before she could respond,
he continued.

"You'll forgive me, I hope. I couldn't help but
hear that you'd like to visit the castle. I'd be happy to
escort you there. 'Tis only open to the army, but as
a close friend of Colonel Bridgewater, I'm sure I can
give you a tour of the inside too, if you'd like. I'm
Lord Hiscock. If your husband has spent much time in
Scotland, he is likely to have heard of me."

"Ah, I believe he has mentioned you once or twice.
I'm the Comtesse de Beaubois, by the way."

"A Scotswoman bearing a French title? How
enchanting."

She bowed. "You are quite a hand at investments,
are ye not?"

Hiscock gave her a satisfied smile. "I like to think
of myself as rather skilled, aye."

"Something to do with shipments?" she asked. "Or
am I thinking of a different nobleman?"

"No, no. 'Tis me. 'Tis an honor to meet you,
Comtesse." He gave her a courtly bow. Serafina had

fuller breasts than Abby, and more of her bosom rose above the neckline in the gown, a fact clearly not lost on his lordship.

"Oh, how kind." She offered her hand and Hiscock kissed it. "I am verra eager to hear about your strategies," she said. "I have a bit of money to invest myself. Perhaps you could tell me more as we walk?"

"I must change my clothes before we go," he said. "There's a dinner for the officers at the home of Lady Blackmoor later. Do you know her? I am vastly unskilled at choosing the right outfits for these sorts of occasions. The fashion changes too quickly for a man like me. You would save me a great amount of embarrassment if you would aid me in choosing the appropriate coat. I keep a room here, for when I have business in the city."

How effortlessly he navigates the situation! A right old Magellan of seduction. Well, he better hope for his sake that he doesn't end up like Magellan, with a spear through his heart.

Serafina leaned closer. "My dear Lord Hiscock, you know verra well a lady canna enter a gentleman's room."

"Well, she can *enter* the room as a lady," he said, signaling an upcoming jest with a large wink, "though how she exits is up to her."

Serafina tittered—that was the only word for it. She whispered confidentially, "It seems to me the job of entering a lady should fall to a gentleman, shouldn't it?"

Laughing heartily, Hiscock picked up his coffee and took up residence at a chair at Serafina's table, gazing at her like a hungry viper.

"Will your husband be returning soon?" He waved to catch the innkeeper's attention and pointed to his cup. "He could accompany us to my room if that would make the visit more acceptable. Perhaps he'd enjoy helping us choose?"

Good God! Was he hinting at a *partouze à trois?* "No. Not for hours."

"A shame." Hiscock moved out of the way as the steaming coffee was poured, and his leg touched hers.

"It *is* a shame," she said. "For while he has few skills in choosing, he does sometimes like to watch me choose for other men."

His lordship's eyes turned as bright as moonstones. Serafina suspected if she let out a strong puff right now, he might topple into the hearth.

"Does he?" the man said.

"Oh, aye. I, on the other hand, prefer to do the choosing on my own."

"Comtesse, you intrigue me. If I wasn't certain I was in need of your services before, I am entirely confident now."

Serafina had been a skilled knot maker in her youth, and in her head, she began to make a monkey's fist, one of her favorites. She looked at the clock. Five more minutes.

"Tell me, Lord Hiscock, what frock coats are you considering?"

"There is a blue one. 'Tis fine but rather plain. Not at all like the blue of your eyes, for example."

"You flatter me."

Wrap the rope three times around your fingers; thread the rope through the middle.

"Then there is the gray one, of course. 'Tis embroidered with black fleurs-de-lis."

"*Och*, verra elegant."

"Aye, but too funereal, I think."

Spread your two center fingers and wrap the rope three times around the existing loops; thread the rope through the middle again.

"There's a green one with embroidery at the cuffs," he said. "Not white. Something warmer. About the color of your skin here." He drew his finger along the inside of her elbow.

She had to hold herself to keep from starting.

Stretch your first and fourth finger away from the middle two fingers and wrap the rope three times again; remove your fingers.

He said, "But the last two are the ones I favor most—a Highland wool the color of your nipples and a French velvet the color of your pelt."

The knot slipped from her hand and skittered across the tavern floor.

"But you dinna know the color of either of those things, sir."

"Not yet, no. Though I should very much like to find out."

"*Here?* In the middle of the dining room?"

"If you wish. No one is watching us. So long as we talk like friends, no one will have any reason to turn in our direction. Just loosen your gown, then rise from your seat to extinguish the candle and sit back down."

"Would it not be easier for me to simply *tell* you the colors?" she said.

"Easier, aye. But not nearly as gratifying."

"There is a hole in your logic. Doing as you suggest will only provide you with the answer to one of the things you wonder about, not the other."

"You are correct, milady. But perhaps with a little help, I can ascertain the answer to that one too." He put the bowl of marmalade in front of him and pushed the cup of dark coffee beside it. Then he waited.

She waggled her finger at him. "You are a verra wicked man."

"And I suspect you are a verra wicked woman. Tell me," he said, "if you dare."

She pursed her lips and let her gaze travel from the cup to the jam. Then she reached for the coffee and lifted it to her mouth. He gasped.

"I've heard it's possible to double one's investment in a single voyage," she said. "That canna be true, can it?"

"Oh, aye. I've done it just recently. Are ye black, then? As black as velvet?"

She chuckled and put down the cup. Then she ran her finger around the rim of the marmalade bowl— once then twice, each time causing Hiscock's pupils to widen. "What sort of cargo can be sold for double in so short a time?" she said. "You must be a *verra* talented investor."

He flushed proudly. "It's a number of things. Tea and tobacco mostly."

"Aren't they notoriously hard to store?"

"'Tis not the humidity of the storage that's a concern in the case but the seclusion. There are a few rules we're bending, you see." He lowered his voice. "Are ye saying marmalade then?"

"Secluded?" she said in a tone heavy with meaning. "Is it nearby? Should we stop there on our tour today?"

"In fact, it's no more than a few hundred—"

A voice said, "Don't say another word, you fool."

Hiscock jerked the table so hard, the cup rattled in the saucer.

Serafina instantly recognized the man peering down at them, though she doubted he knew her. He was the army officer Hiscock had mentioned—Colonel John Bridgewater, the brute who ran England's northern armies. He was the sworn enemy of Undine and her colleagues. He had been a customer of Undine's and had nearly beaten her to death once when he'd not liked the fortune she'd given him.

"Get up," Bridgewater said.

Hiscock rose, flustered. Serafina wanted no part of whatever was coming. She pushed the chair from the table, and Bridgewater's hand came down on her shoulder.

"Give me your room key," Bridgewater said to Hiscock.

"But I—"

"*Give it to me.*"

Bridgewater grabbed the key and pulled Serafina to her feet "Don't say a word," he said to her, adding to Hiscock as he swiped the key from his hand, "Stay down here."

She grabbed Hiscock's cup and flung the steaming contents at Bridgewater. He roared, and she pulled herself from his grip. In two steps, he tripped her. She hit the ground hard, and he jerked her to her feet, saying loudly, "Poor dear, are you all right?" and adding in her ear, "There's a dirk at your back. Don't say a word."

He pulled her toward the stairs.

"She's ill," he said to the innkeeper. "Bring sherry, aye?"

The last thing Serafina saw as they reached the top of the stairs was Hiscock's stunned face, staring up at them from the dining room below. In the distance, the clock struck the first note of nine.

Thirty-two

GERARD CLIMBED THE LONG HILL TOWARD THE CASTLE. The sun was shining, and he could see the lush, verdant hills that stretched beyond the city. He loved New York, and he could feel many of the same things here—the industry, the humanity, the sense that everything can and would change but the core of what made the people who they were would never be altered. And yet so much here was different. The hills, for one, and the vast swaths of green and blue. The quiet drumbeat of a nation on the rise. The Age of Enlightenment had just begun, spilling across the Channel from the salons in Paris, replacing superstition and faith with scientific inquiry. The kilts had something to do with the unbounded energy he felt here. It was very freeing to move about with the wind on your flesh, and he regretted the necessity of the trousers more as each hour passed. Everything about the place hummed with a fundamental and engaging harmonic. Even the grittiness of Edinburgh's streets—horses shitting, babies crying, vendors flogging their wares—made Gerard feel the world was nascent and alive in a way even the always-vibrant Manhattan was not.

Of course, his delight with the place was clearly related to the time he'd passed in the company of one of its most beautiful citizens—beautiful and maddening. He'd always been drawn to women who would give him the freedom to come and go, but being free and being irrelevant are not the same, and he was starting to feel the sting of the difference.

She'd left with a man. That meant nothing to him on its own, though clearly Duchamps thought it did. Gerard did not nurse jealous pique. If a man wanted a woman to choose him above all others, it was up to him to earn it. The trouble was, Gerard had nothing with which to earn a treasure like Serafina—no money, no power, and no promise of either. Not here, at least. He imagined for a moment a life with her in New York. He would buy her a sailboat as big as his grandfather's and a condo towering over the Upper Bay so she could see water all day, and he could see her seeing it. She could run a charter business, drain some money from the pockets of those ridiculously wealthy hedge fund managers. Throw in an onboard chef and berths designed by some edgy designer. Gerard, of course, would create a brand and ad campaign for it. Sailing with Serafina would be the pastime every would-be trendsetter ached for.

He caught himself. All of that relied on convincing Undine to send them both back—if that was even possible—not to mention winning Serafina's hand and convincing her she'd want to accompany him. And given that he didn't even know where she was at the moment…

"Hey!"

He turned and found himself across the street from the Squeak and Blade, which had lost its off-putting sign and now boasted an outdoor grill filled with sizzling sausages. John Dawes, the tavern owner, waved him over.

"Twice the customers," he cried happily, "and three times the sausages!"

Gerard grinned. "And the sign?"

"A new one's being carved as we speak."

"Well, it certainly smells great." His stomach complained loudly of its lack of breakfast.

Dawes grabbed a roll, tore it open, and used it to pull a sausage off a skewer.

"'Tis not pork," he said, handing it to Gerard. "I've been trying out a few things. It's actually—"

"Probably best not to tell me," Gerard said, taking a cautious bite and enjoying the meaty and thankfully unrecognizable taste. "Secret recipe and all."

"*Och*, I like that."

"Do you happen to know the way to the Hollow Crown?"

He pointed up the street. "Turn left at Castle Wynd Close and follow it to Grassmarket. If you reach Ferguson's stables, you've gone too far."

Gone too far. Given the events of the last thirty-six hours, that should probably be written on his headstone.

He had gone no more than a block or two before recognizing the building before him as the one Serafina had identified as the one in which she lived from the carriage.

Since he'd last seen her dressed in the clothes of a sailor, it seemed a reasonable bet she would stop at her lodgings to change before going anywhere else. He immediately scanned the carriages stopped in the area, looking for Serafina or the sort of man who might be waiting for her, though what that sort might entail, he wasn't entirely sure.

He approached the building with caution. It wasn't that it looked dangerous in any way—unless you considered a fat orange cat sunning himself beside the front door dangerous—but trespassing the unspoken boundaries surrounding a lover's abode without first receiving an invitation was a recipe for unhappiness.

The drab wattle and daub structure rose four stories above the street. The door was propped open, and he wasn't sure if he was supposed to knock or simply enter. As he debated, someone said, "What do ye want?"

He turned. The woman behind him scowled and moved a basket of laundry from one hip to the other.

"I'm looking for Miss Fallon."

Her gaze raked him, from his shoes to the cock of his hat. "Are ye her fiancé?"

"No."

"Sent by the judge?"

Judge? "No. I'm a friend."

"Fallen to that then, has she?" The woman scoffed. "Well, she ain't going to be doing such things here. Do ye have money for her?"

"No." Gerard didn't care for the woman's assumptions.

"A shame. She owes me nearly six shillings."

"Is she here?"

"She ain't. And she won't be again. I'll be letting her room to a girl who can help me with laundry. Miss Fallon's belongings are in a sack around back. I may not be rich, but I'm a respectable, churchgoing woman. I was doing what I thought was right by taking her in. 'Let he who is blameless cast the first stone.' But I canna afford to keep her here without payment."

"I'm sure she'll pay you. I can guarantee it."

She laughed a bitter laugh. "Just as ye can guarantee me a pot of gold at the end of the rainbow."

He thrust his hand in his shirt pocket, extracted the coins, and counted out six. He put them in the woman's hand. She stared at them, aghast. "The room is rented. There's nothing I can do about that."

"She has another," Gerard said. "She doesn't need your room."

The woman slipped the money in her pocket and brushed by him to enter the door.

"Wait," he called, and she stopped. "What has Miss Fallon done to require your very generous mercy?"

The woman softened. "I'm not one to judge, sir. Nor gossip. But a woman without a husband, with a known reputation… 'Twas nearly impossible for her to find a room to let, she told me so herself. I dinna agree with those who shout their love for the Bible and live not the words within it, but the world is not mine to change. She's not welcome in any genteel home, ye ken, though I have no complaint with her apart from her debt. She was a quiet tenant and kind. But I canna feed my children on kindness."

"May I?" Gerard took the basket from the woman's hands and followed her to the back of the house, where a cauldron bubbled over a smoky fire.

"You can take her things to her if ye wish," the woman said.

That felt like a far more dangerous trespass than appearing on her doorstep uninvited.

"Keep it, please," he said. "I know she'll be back for it. And please don't tell her it was me who paid her debt."

Thirty-three

Serafina clamped her mouth tightly to keep her teeth from chattering. Bridgewater threw her on the bed in Hiscock's room and took a seat at the desk.

"Let me be clear. This is not going to end well. Though how it ends will be up to you." He took off his frock coat and laid it over his chair. "If you scream, I will throw you from the window. I brought you here to recover, you see, and you revealed yourself to be a rebel spy and attacked me with a dirk."

She sat up, cross-legged, and scanned the room, looking for traces of Undine's search. She found none. That either meant she had gotten away safely or never made it to the room. Serafina hoped it was the former. If she was going to die or be raped, she'd like it to be for something that helped Scotland.

He slipped the wet shirt over his head and tossed it into the corner. "Now open that lovely mouth and start telling me why you were questioning Hiscock or I'll crawl between those pretty thighs and make you wish you had talked. Do you understand?"

Intimidation is not action. Keep your wits about you.

"If it came to that, I'd toss myself from the window on my own."

He laughed. "A spirited lass. I like that. Why were you asking about a ship?"

Serafina realized she must have been betrayed by Undine's contact, the groom. He was the only person other than Undine and Abby who knew Serafina was here and that she'd be asking Hiscock about the cargo. She wondered if Undine was being questioned right now by another officer in another room.

"I'm the daughter of a sea captain," she said. "I'm interested in everything related to the sea."

He slapped her. "Hiscock's a fool. I'm not. What did he tell you?"

The slap had been light, meant to get her attention. It had. "He invests in voyages," she said. "And apparently makes good money at it."

"Did he tell you about the cargo?"

She considered lying, and he saw her thoughts.

"You know I'll ask him when I'm done here," he said.

"Aye," she said, her voice barely above a whisper. "Tea and tobacco."

"What else?"

A knock sounded.

"It's me," came the voice.

Bridgewater opened the door and took a small cask and glass from the innkeeper "Don't come back," he said, and shut the door. He placed the items on the room's small table. "Do you want some sherry? Tell the truth."

Serafina nodded. He filled the glass halfway and handed it to her. She took a sip, not too much.

"Good girl."

He sat down on a chair and pulled off his boots. His arms and shoulders were broad and taut. He was definitely going to be able to outmaneuver her in a struggle.

"What about the warehouse?" He peeled off his stockings.

She didn't care for the direction this was going. "'Tis secluded."

"Location?"

"He didn't say. He was interrupted."

"Fool. Not that it matters now."

Serafina looked up, and Bridgewater caught her curiosity.

"Know about the theft then, do you?" he said, fixing her with cold interest.

"Everyone knows. 'Twas all over Leith a quarter hour after the ship docked."

"Everyone but Hiscock, though he'll know soon enough. He's lost as much as I have, though he can't afford it as well as I can." Bridgewater scratched his cheek and leaned back in the chair. "Are you familiar with a woman by the name of Undine?"

Serafina said nothing, and Bridgewater snorted.

He said, "Tell her I haven't forgotten the insights she shared with me when she read my fortune, and that I intend to revisit that conversation very soon. She's become an annoyance the English army can no longer tolerate."

Serafina wondered what it might be like to read the fortune of a man like John Bridgewater.

He stood again and began to unbutton his breeks. "Was she the one who asked you to question Hiscock?"

"No." Serafina turned her head when he let the breeks drop, but not before seeing the bright red scald marks that reached from his belly to his knees.

He snorted. "Too modest to look, are you?"

She heard his footsteps and clenched. This slap nearly knocked her to the floor.

"That's for the burn. Now, shall I dress? Are we going to have a rich discussion about why you were asking? Or perhaps you'd prefer me to crawl between those pretty thighs right now instead?"

"Dress," she said and hid her face.

"Are those tears?"

"It hurt." Her voice caught. She tucked her knees under her chin and began to sob.

He stepped before her and touched her chin lightly. "Come, let me look."

She reared back and shoved the heel of her boot directly into his stones. He collapsed to the floor, making a noise like a clogged sewer. She flew from the bed and flung open the door. In an instant she was on the stairs and a moment after that she was hurtling into the street.

Every face looked like paradise—a potential savior. The sky was as bright as heaven. The air filled her lungs with life. She would never complain about anything again.

Suddenly, an arm brought her to a hard stop. She screamed and found herself face-to-face with the happiest sight in the world.

She threw her arms around Gerard's neck and kissed him.

"What in the name of God are you running from?" He pulled her into a tight embrace. "Your heart is hammering."

"Have you seen Undine?"

"Funny you should ask. I ran into her a minute ago. She said if I just kept on my path, I'd run into you, and here I am. I seem to be doomed to wander, abandoned and alone, from one bed of yours to another—not the worst fate in the world, mind you, but still a bit disconcerting. Why did you leave me this morning without saying anything?"

"I left you a note."

"You *did*?"

"Aye. With Duchamps. Did you see him?"

Gerard frowned. "Yes. What did it say?"

"Nothing much. I'd awakened before dawn, of course—"

"Sailor, right? Landlubbers sleep."

She smiled. "I wasn't going to say it, but aye. And I saw a carriage on the dock. Abby and Undine had come. They needed me to help them, so I ran back up and dashed off a note. Duchamps promised he would deliver it to you discreetly."

"Well, he certainly accomplished that. It was so discreet, I didn't even notice getting it. So, what did it say?"

"Nothing, really. I'm the one who told *you* to be careful around him, ye ken? I said I was helping our friends, that I wouldna be long, and that when you woke up to go to the inn because I'd stop there before I went to the ship. There's nothing in that to raise anyone's interest."

"No," Gerard said. "Very odd."

"Where was Undine going?"

"The Hollow Crown."

"Shall we?"

He made a courtly flourish. "Lead the way."

Thirty-four

"And that's the story," Serafina said with a sigh, "whole and complete, from the moment I made my way onto the ship until now."

Not quite whole and complete, Gerard mused, thinking of the time in the crow's nest.

"Does anyone have questions?" she asked.

Abby lifted a brow. "Just one. Do the two of ye ever sleep?"

Though Abby had directed the question to him as well as Serafina, he knew better than to weigh in. He sipped Kerr whiskey and examined the buckles on his shoes.

Duncan refilled Gerard's glass, then carried the bottle to Undine and refilled hers. "The question is," Duncan said, "what are Bridgewater and Hiscock hiding? Threatening bodily harm means you stepped on some pretty big toes."

"That's *one* of the questions," Undine said, stepping toward the fire. "I have quite a few more. I'm so sorry I put you in danger, Serafina. Bridgewater has worked tirelessly to identify our agents and use threats to get them to betray other agents."

"I'm just grateful you got out before he arrived. What did you find in Hiscock's room?"

"A few letters, whose information will be helpful to the cause."

Gerard said, "So Edward funds a voyage with the help of investors—Hiscock and Bridgewater—arranges with Thistlebrook to steal the cargo in order to get the insurance money to pay off the investors, and now presumably plans to sell the stolen cargo."

"Aye," Duncan said. "And Hiscock and Bridgewater have just learned the cargo has been stolen."

"And that Serafina is curious enough about it to question Hiscock," Gerard added.

"He doesn't know who Serafina is except an unnamed colleague of Undine," Abby said. "You didn't tell him your name, did you?"

Serafina shook her head. "No. But 'twill be no challenge for him to find out. Especially if he questions Edward about a woman with red hair."

And we can count on Edward not to take the gentlemanly route and deny any knowledge of you, can't we? Gerard watched Serafina, her cheeks still flushed from the danger she'd faced. *How patently unfair that a man like Edward Turnbull would have seduced you. In another time and place, you'd have laughed it off as a drunken mistake. Here, it's your ruin.*

"I don't think Undine should stay at the inn," Gerard said, though what he really meant was Serafina shouldn't. The story of her time in Bridgewater's room had been wrenching to hear, and he could tell by the look in her eyes she'd softened it for his benefit. "It's not safe."

"Bridgewater wouldn't come here," Undine said.

Serafina crossed her arms. "And in any case, Undine is quite capable of taking care of herself."

"No one is capable of taking care of oneself when a man like that is involved," Gerard replied firmly, "not even Undine."

"She's not going to run just because you think she should," Serafina said.

"Duncan and I are entirely capable of carrying her out of here if we have to."

"*Whoa*," Duncan said. "Speak for yourself. I have a verra strong attachment to my balls."

Gerard growled. "Then I can."

"Thank you," Undine said, breaking the locked gaze between him and Serafina, "for your excessive concern. 'Tis comforting to know you keep me uppermost in your hearts. Perhaps we do need to think about a new home—at least until I accomplish what I need to do at Hiscock's dinner tomorrow."

"*You intend to go?*" Gerard was stunned. Bridgewater would certainly be there, and he doubted even the presence of half the grandees in Edinburgh would dissuade such a man from whatever unpleasant act he might consider.

"Is your question addressed to me or Serafina?" Undine said.

Gerard spun in Serafina's direction. "She's not going," he said flatly.

Serafina's eyes flashed. "I beg your pardon?"

"I'd like Serafina to accompany Duncan," Abby said. "I need him to be there, but he can hardly accompany me."

Gerard caught Duncan's flinch, though he covered it instantly.

"Abby, I would help you if I could," Serafina said, pained. "But the truth is I dinna have a gown."

The realization of her misstep washed across Abby's face. "Forgive me," she said quickly. "I have half a dozen here, and with that hair, you'd look wonderful in any of them. The emerald and pink comes to mind, though the azure silk would match your eyes. I thought you'd ordered a gown because of the parcel that arrived today."

"What parcel?"

Abby pointed to a large paper-and-twine package inside.

Serafina gathered the parcel and read the note that was tucked in the twine.

"'Tis samples of muslin," she said. "From Turkey. It's from Edward. He says he knows it's not much, but he's giving me the only part of the cargo that wasn't stolen by Thistlebrook and his colleagues. He says he hopes I can use it to make something lovely. The other hundred and sixty-six bolts are still on the ship, where I can claim them whenever I choose."

While he keeps the money he'll make selling the stolen merchandise, the three barrels of Madeira, and the nineteen riding crops? Generous guy.

"That was a kind gesture," Abby said.

"By the man who stole her fortune?" Undine said, and Gerard cheered silently. "Are you out of your senses?"

Abby opened her mouth to protest, but Serafina shook her head. "Undine's right. It willna make up for what he's done. But," she added with a smile, "'tis verra fine muslin. I can see right through it, and look at the striking stripes and patterns throughout. I've never seen anything quite as delicate. 'Twill make for some scandalous chemises. I should verra much like to give you and Undine as much as you think you might like."

Duncan brightened visibly at this, and Abby said, "It's stunning. I'm certain we can get this made into something lovely in time for tomorrow's dinner, though I forbear to think what Duncan might do with that much encouragement."

The corner of Duncan's mouth rose. "Let's just say, you shouldna count on seeing us much after the last glass of brandy."

"What exactly is happening tomorrow night?" Gerard said. "And other than wearing the finest chemise, is there a plan for navigating a party attended by a man who has threatened bodily harm to Serafina and Undine, another who drained Serafina's fortune, at the home of a third who appears to be trying to ruin Scotland's last hope of holding on to its independence?"

"If you think those three represent the biggest threats at the dinner," Undine said with a smile, "you don't know Edinburgh politics."

"I don't know Edinburgh anything," Gerard said, frustrated. "But I do know I don't want you or Abby or Serafina at such a place. Duncan's tried to kill me twice in the last two days and I think even he should stay home."

Duncan gave him a nudge with his boot. "You're not getting sentimental on me, are you?"

Undine said, "Mr. Innes is right. Dinner tomorrow night will be like a giant powder keg with a lit fuse of indeterminate length. But if something is going to happen, I'd rather we be the ones making it happen. The things I'll be working on are best left unsaid, but I know Abby and Duncan will be looking for support on the canal project, and I assume Serafina will be finding out what she can about the cargo."

Gerard saw he was fighting a losing battle. If he couldn't convince them to stay away, his next best choice was to be there to watch over Serafina. "What can I do to help tomorrow night?"

"Nothing," Undine said.

"Nothing?"

"Your offer is kind, Mr. Innes, but you'll be gone by tomorrow."

"*What?*"

"Serafina has given us a full accounting of your actions together," Undine said, "and you did exactly what you were called to do, which was aid her in attempting to claim the cargo. Your work here is done. And the herbs to take you back"—she pulled a packet from her pocket—"have already begun to warm. You will leave at dawn tomorrow."

"I…well…" Gerard turned to Serafina, who looked equally surprised.

"You did exhort me to ensure the spell could be reversed, did you not?" Undine said to Gerard. "You were quite clear when you found me reading fortunes at the Squeak and Blade that while you had enjoyed your time with Miss Fallon, you had no intention of staying any longer than required."

"I-I did say that, but—"

"Your exact words, if I recall, were 'There's not enough in this place to interest a turd-throwing chimp, let alone a man of more worldly tastes.'"

Gerard felt the room go cold and realized how wrong he'd been. "I was angry. I overreacted. I'd been dragged out of a perfectly comfortable bed—"

"Shared by a perfectly lovely woman," Undine said.

"—and I jumped to a conclusion—a faulty conclusion—and I have since learned—"

"Stop," Serafina said. "Gerard doesn't owe any of us an apology. No one here except Duncan knows what it is to be torn from all ye ken and all ye hold dear. Who wouldn't be angry to lose that? He has a job in his time and a promotion on the way, and a family, and a world in which people sail the sky in air ships. Why wouldn't he want to go back?"

"Aye," Abby said, regarding Gerard closely. "Why wouldn't he?"

Gerard hardly knew what to say. Serafina spoke like his returning was a *fait accompli*. "There are incredible things here—the sausages at the Squeak and Blade, which is now the Squeak and Sizzle, by the way, pop to mind, as does Abby's whiskey, at least when it's unadulterated, and the view from St. Giles's spire. And of course, though we've only known each other a few hours, I would add to the list the friendship each of you has been kind enough to offer me."

Serafina's smile froze, and he kicked himself. *Friendship? You idiot.*

"You're very kind," Undine said. "We will certainly miss your friendship as well."

"Unless he has a reason to stay," Abby put in quickly.

"Aye," Duncan said, "do ye have a reason to stay?"

Gerard looked at Serafina, who fussed self-consciously with the muslin samples in her lap. He could hardly stay if Serafina offered no encouragement. And how could he stay in any case? It was Sunday now. The Brewer boards were on his desk for a final review. The partners meeting was tomorrow. His father was meeting him for dinner on Wednesday. There was a life that existed for him that wasn't here.

"Well, I could certainly stay through the dinner tomorrow—or longer if you needed me."

"Serafina?" Undine said. Abby, Duncan and Gerard turned.

"Aye, I think Gerard should stay to help," she said. "He has proven himself to be quite competent."

No performance review had ever pleased him more.

"I suppose I could try to slow the spell's effects and buy you one more day," Undine said. "Through the party then." She tossed the packet onto the table next to the whiskey.

It's settled then.

Gerard said, "If Sera is to accompany Duncan, and Abby goes alone, it looks as if I will have the honor of serving as your escort tomorrow, Undine."

She chuckled. "I never appear on the arm of an escort. But you'll make a very creditable manservant."

Thirty-five

UNDINE LEFT TO SEE IF HER NETWORK OF CONTACTS had heard any news regarding the missing cargo and declined both Gerard's and Duncan's offers to accompany her. Abby was to use her own network of contacts to try to piece together as many of the names of those invited to the dinner as she could. Duncan was negotiating the terms for the last barrels of Kerr whiskey they were selling that week, which happened to be to Lord Hiscock for his party, and Duncan promised to gather whatever information he could from Hiscock's steward in anticipation of the dinner. Gerard was happy to volunteer to accompany Serafina back to the ship to make arrangements for the muslin.

Gerard pulled Duncan aside in the hallway. "How much is a pair of earrings here?"

"They're called earbobs, my friend, and it depends entirely on what you're looking for."

"Emeralds, I think, with that hair, don't you? Or maybe sapphires."

"*Och*. Out of your league."

"I don't know about that. I have a few shillings. But

I don't know what anything costs." Gerard dug in his pocket and held out what he'd earned. "I want Sera to have something special for the dinner."

Duncan's brows went up, impressed, and he considered the stack of coins. "Pearls, I should think."

Gerard thanked him and ran to catch up with Serafina, who was waiting for him outside.

As they strolled down the street, the dappled rays of the afternoon sun danced in her hair. She was the sort of woman for whom a gown—threadbare or threaded with silver—added little, and the confidence with which she walked hinted she would be just as happy in her skin alone. Even the dimmed light in her eyes, the result of her lost fortune, adding only a small note of melancholy grace to her beauty.

"The muslin," he said, "is a respectable haul."

"Do you think? At six shillings a bolt, it's about fifty pounds."

"How much is a ship?"

She laughed. "A small one? A thousand pounds."

"What would you do with a ship if you owned one?"

"Bring goods to people who want them—olives from Livorno, rum from Barbados, lumber from Bergen—and do what I could to harass Scotland's enemies."

"How do you know what people want?"

"You don't have to know. If you bring enough goods to market, they will sell eventually—most of them in any case."

"What if I told you there's a way to know more precisely what people want? And more important, that there's a way to make them want to buy whatever it is you're trying to sell?"

She looked at him through a stray orange-blond lock. "Is this what your advertisements do? Or are you a conjurer like Undine?"

"Bit of both, actually. People won't buy what they don't want. I don't mean to say that, and anyone who thinks they will is a fool. But if you can present them with something they never realized they wanted, in a way that speaks to a desire deep within them, you can make them want that thing more than they thought they'd ever want anything. That's the power of branding."

"Branding? What we do to cattle?"

"Sort of. That brand establishes ownership, and that's how branding started. But the branding I'm talking about is the value a customer imputes to a product, value that goes beyond the absolute value of the parts. The Stewart estate with their *S* brand raises cattle with a much finer taste than the MacDuffs with their *McD*. And you learn to look for the *S* when you're at auction."

"Aye," she said, "but you make it sound as if I faint with desire for the Stewart roast beef. I can assure you I do not."

"All right, how about this example. Tulips were once the object of great desire in Holland."

"They were and are," she said. "They're quite beautiful."

"And how much would you pay for a tulip bulb—to grow the most beautiful tulip you've ever seen?"

"A penny perhaps, though that would be a lot."

"No, no, the most beautiful, breathtaking tulip you'd ever seen?"

"*Och*, two pence—mebbe. But I'd hate myself for it."

"One summer in the early 1600s, certain tulips with exquisite color patterns began to be highly prized. By the fall of that year, merchants who displayed pictures of the tulips these bulbs would grow into were able to sell the bulbs even before they were in the merchant's possession—just the promise of a future bulb. In a matter of a few months, the price of the most beautiful bulbs rose as high as fifteen thousand pounds."

"*What!* For a shipload?"

"For a single bulb."

Her face twisted in parsimony-fueled horror.

"But the mania ended six months later," he said, "just as abruptly as it had started. The men who'd bought and sold their bulbs at the peak made fortunes. But the men who'd bought and held on...they lost everything. By the time the next summer arrived, tulips were back to their pre-mania price."

"I know how those poor men feel," she said, and Gerard cursed himself for mentioning the loss of fortunes.

"My point," he said, "is that if you can tickle that place of desire in your customers, you can sell almost anything and make a lot of money."

She gazed at him with the same mixture of curiosity and amusement she always did. "Do you have a lot of money, Gerard?"

He made a private groan. Nothing thrust an unscalable wall between people like an unsettling difference in wealth. "Buckets of it," he said sadly.

She laughed. "Oh, dear, it's not catching, is it? You make it sound like a disease."

He laughed too. "No. I think it is sometimes. I

take no pride in it—well, not the part that came from my grandfather's great-grandfather. I *am* proud of the work *I've* done."

"And it has made you wealthy as well."

"It has. Not the sort of wealth my three-times great-grandfather left his descendants. But a much more satisfying wealth, one that's come from hard work and trusting my instincts and fighting people who put obstacles in my path—and frankly, if the money was only enough to buy me a shack and a campfire, I'd be happy with it."

The spire of St. Giles, in view since they'd started out, now pierced the sky directly above them.

"Was there really a woman in your bed?"

Gerard nearly missed his step. He wished he didn't have to answer, but he did. "Yes."

"Is that a common occurrence?"

"More common than it should be."

"Is she waiting for you?"

He rubbed his neck. The sun was hot. "I doubt it. I'd be surprised if she remembered my name. I never asked hers."

He deserved the disappointment he saw in her eyes.

"Who *is* waiting for you?" she asked.

"My dad, I guess. My mom died a few years ago. My grandfather's still alive. My brother, of course, though we hardly speak. It's not so much a 'who' as a 'what,' I guess. My work."

She shook her head. "We do love our work."

"So what can we do to brand your muslin? You said you'd never seen anything quite so delicate. The most important thing about a product is what makes it different from other products like it. 'Serafina's muslin is different...' Why?"

She considered. "Most muslin is plain and a little rough. This muslin is almost like silk. And the designs! Stripes, dots, swirls. If one didn't mind walking down the streets half-naked, one would almost be tempted to wear a chemise made of it by itself."

Gerard stopped and put a hand over his chest. "Hang on. Let me try to start my heart again."

She laughed.

"What if we made it into the most beautiful chemises women had ever seen?" he said. "What if it made them want to lift their skirts to the sky?"

"We would certainly make the gentlemen in Edinburgh happy. The trouble is, women have their seamstresses, and seamstresses have their favored fabric merchants. And women do not raise their skirts, at least in public, so it would require a long run of selling the fabric to merchants, who would sell it to the seamstresses, who would make it for their mistresses, who might—*might*, mind you—mention the fabric to a verra close friend in a verra private setting. Eventually, the muslin might become Edinburgh's favored fabric, but it might take three seasons or more." She met Gerard's eyes sadly. "I don't have that time."

He frowned. "*Hm*. What I wouldn't give to be able to post a picture of you half-naked on Twitter— strictly for business's sake, of course."

"I don't know what that means, but it dinna sound good." She raised a copper brow. "Of course, if it works, perhaps I can pin a sketch of you to the wall of the castle as well. I'm a deft hand at drawing, ye see, and I know which half of ye'd be naked."

His tongue seemed to lose its agency. "I-I…"

"Is that a wee blush on your cheeks? Och, ye canna be so shy, aye? 'Tis Scotland, after all. Surely you've noticed we prefer our men to be unencumbered by breeks whenever possible."

"Serafina!" a child's voice cried. "Serafina!"

Serafina turned and her face burst into the biggest smile Gerard had ever seen her wear. "Charlie! Peter!"

The boys, who looked to be six or seven, flew into her legs, nearly knocking her over, and she bundled them to her like long-lost friends.

"Will you play with us?" the younger of the boys asked. "Do you know Grandmama is getting worse? She's been to see the surgeon. Did you come to see Mama? She and Father are visiting one of Father's friends."

Serafina got to her knees and hugged the boys tightly. "You have grown so in the last two years. Tell me about your grandma. Is she very sick?"

"She coughs all the time," the other boy said. "Father says she will surely die. Will you come to see her? Then you can play army with us."

Serafina looked at Gerard. "Mrs. Turnbull was quite dear to me."

Turnbull? Edward's mother? If so, the boys must be Edward's nephews. He said, "You should go."

"Yes, yes, Serafina! You must come!"

"No, I mustn't," she said, holding her ground. "Especially if she is ill."

"She'd like to see you," the younger boy said. "It'd cheer her."

Each boy took one of Serafina's hands, and they began to drag her down Cockburn, the cross street. Gerard ambled behind. Serafina's laughter, deep and full throated, mixed with the boys' higher-pitched giggles, made him smile.

"Is that your husband?" the older boy asked, stealing a concerned look at Gerard. "He's following us."

"*Och*, no," she said, winking at Gerard. "I'm going to marry you, Peter, remember?"

Peter flushed to the tips of his ears.

"What about me?" demanded Charlie.

"I will have two husbands, of course. One for my country home and one for my city—"

Serafina stopped hard and almost jerked the boys off their feet.

They'd reached the home to which the boys had been leading them, an ornate four-story townhouse with an arched entry over which a balcony decorated in bas-relief leaves and shields stood. An elegantly dressed couple stood before the entry, glaring.

"Unhand my sons," the man said.

Serafina opened her fingers as if she'd been holding burning coals.

Gerard stepped instantly to her side and replaced one of the boys' hands with his own.

"Here," the man said to the boys, and they walked, shoulders slumped, to their mother's side.

"I'm verra sorry," Serafina said, voice trembling.

Gerard squeezed her hand.

The woman ushered the boys inside, and the man stared at Serafina as if she were vermin. Upstairs, a curtain parted, and an elderly woman looked out. She saw Serafina and smiled, but her smile disappeared when her gaze traveled to the boys' father.

"Come on," Gerard whispered, giving Serafina a gentle tug. She turned and Gerard slipped his arm around her waist, holding her tightly as they walked.

He could feel her anguish, and he knew she was crying.

"Who are the boys?" he asked when they had safely reached the Royal Mile and were out of sight.

"They're Edward's nephews," she said, swiping embarrassedly at her eyes. "The man is Edward's older brother."

"Why are they so angry at you? Surely they know Edward's the one responsible for your breakup."

"They're not angry at me," she said, "any more than a man would be angry at dirt under his feet. They are offended by me."

"*Offended?* What could you possibly have done to offend them?"

"I allowed myself to descend from a gentlewoman to a woman no genteel person would consort with. While Edward and I were courting, I was a person most dear to them, and they to me. But the instant I moved in with him, I was cut off from them forever. 'Twas as if day changed to night, or summer to winter."

"They don't blame their brother?"

"A man canna be blamed for his urges. 'Tis the woman who must protect her standing. 'Twas stupid of me to have let the boys lead me there, but I thought I might see Edward's mother one more time, tell her how much her kindness once meant to me. Oh, Gerard, I had thought my heart a stone, but seeing those boys after so long has undone me."

He held her, ignoring the stares of passersby.

"This isna helping my reputation," she said with a small laugh, but did not let go.

"Fuck 'em."

She laughed again, a warm, delicious laugh that stirred his heart.

After a long moment, she released him and swiped at her eyes. "You're a good man."

He wanted to tell her she was better off without Edward and his brother in her life. He wanted to tell her that no one in his world would even blink once let alone twice about what she'd done. He wanted to tell her that the boys would love her even if they never saw her again. But none of those things would make her feel better, so he said simply, "I'm honored to know you, Sera."

She straightened a bit. "Thank you."

They walked quietly toward the docks. Duncan had given Gerard a pistol and shown him how to use it. Nonetheless, Gerard had made Serafina promise they would be cautious. He had no wish to be forced into a confrontation. "Hero" was not his natural state.

Halfway there, Serafina started. "Look. 'Tis Lord Hiscock's daughter. She's going into the tailor shop."

Gerard saw the exquisite carriage stopped just beyond the shop and a golden-haired girl of seventeen or so emerging from it.

Serafina said, "I'll bet she's picking up the dress Edward had made for her."

"That's a rather forward gesture for a man who isn't her fiancé, isn't it?"

"It's a rather forward gesture for a man who *is* her fiancé. But Elizabeth Hiscock is a headstrong girl—"

FIRST TIME WITH A HIGHLANDER 269

"The worst sort."

"—and I'd be willing to bet she'll let her parents think she ordered it herself." Serafina elbowed Gerard. "I heard that, by the way."

The girl entered the shop.

"Talk to her," Serafina said.

"What?"

"Talk to her. You are good with women and she's a flirter. See if you can pry any information out of her regarding her father and the cargo."

"Would she know anything about her father's dealings?"

"You said your father cheated on your mother. Did he *tell* you that?"

"Oh, right. I see your point."

"I'll wait here. It's in your hands."

Gerard smiled grimly. "'They also serve who only stand and wait.'"

"Who said that?"

"You should know him, actually. He's one of yours."

"One of mine? A Scot? An Edinburgher? A sailor?"

"No. Born in an era you'd know. John Milton."

"'Let not England forget her precedence of teaching nations how to live'?" She gave him a gimlet eye. "That John Milton?"

"Oops. Not a fan, I see. Forget I mentioned it. I'm off. Mission calling."

Life was funny, Gerard thought as he crossed the street and rounded the carriage. He had all the money in the world, and the one time he wanted to use it to impress a woman, he couldn't touch a penny of it. How happy it would have made him to dash off a check for ten thousand pounds and hand it to Serafina.

No such luck. He had the twenty-first century equivalent of fifty bucks in his pocket. He had no fighting skills, no spycraft. He couldn't captain a ship—hell, he could barely tie a knot to hold a sail in place. In short, he had nothing to offer Serafina that was of the slightest value to her. Oh, he could please her in bed. But even the world's greatest lover—which Gerard was far from being—became a bore to a woman like Serafina without an equal amount of industry and output. Work made men interesting, after all; sex only made them tolerable. Duncan had the good fortune to know about finance, not to mention being a hell of a fighter. Gerard just wished there was something he could do to help her—

He straightened.

Maybe there was.

He rounded the corner of the carriage and nearly ran into Elizabeth Hiscock. She was pink cheeked with a sparkle of excitement in her eyes. He could smell liquor on her breath—sherry, he thought, and quite a bit of it.

"Are you going to the tailor?" she asked. "There's no point. No one answered my knock."

"That's disappointing."

"I was supposed to have one last fitting," she said. "A gown for my father's party tomorrow."

"Your father's Lord Hiscock?" he asked.

"Aye." She dimpled. "Will you be there? I beg your pardon. I don't know your name."

"Bond. James Bond."

"I'm Miss Elizabeth Hiscock."

She curtsied, and Gerard bowed.

"Your father and I may be doing a bit of shipping business together," he said.

Elizabeth rolled her eyes. "My father and his ships. The way he watches the weather and wrings his hands, you'd think he were sailing the goods across the North Sea himself."

"He must be relieved when they're safely in port."

"You'd think so. But then there's the storing and selling and counting and collecting. It amounts to little bother, I suppose, so long as he doesn't involve me in the details, but just last week he insisted we stop at his newest purchase—a cheerless building in an even more cheerless neighborhood near the castle hill. Shuttered, abandoned—all that was missing were a dozen grimy children playing in front of it. He was supposed to accompany me to the home of the new Lord Beardsley, who has the most enchanting aviary, but I was made to wait in the carriage for nearly an hour."

"Nearly an hour? Insupportable."

"By the time we got to Beardsley's, Amanda Cheswick was already there, absolutely pasted to Beardsley's side, and I was made to walk with the dowager countess." She made a disgusted noise.

Elizabeth's feelings for Edward Turnbull, if she had any, were apparently of a changing and complicated nature.

Gerard shook his head. "I say nothing against Amanda Cheswick, mind you, but Beardsley has lost the plot if he thinks *she* is a better choice than I."

Elizabeth dimpled. "Thank you, Mr. Bond."

"Is the cheerless street Western by any chance?" Gerard asked, making up a name. "I visit a boot maker there and fully expect to find a rain cloud over the neighborhood even when the rest of the city is sunny."

Her eyes narrowed. "I've never heard of a Western Street in Edinburgh. Do you mean West Port?"

"Er, aye. Of course. Silly of me."

"But that's south of the castle, not north."

Gerard was formulating a response that would bring them back on track when she swung back to the shop's door, evidently diverted by more important issues.

"I don't know what I'll do about my gown," she said. "I was supposed to be here earlier, but my friends and I were on a picnic on Calton Hill and were having such a lovely time. And I cannot come here tomorrow. My mother and I are to be in the country, visiting an aunt until late in the afternoon. And I must be wearing a new gown at the dinner, or my mother will positively slay me."

The laughter of young men emanated from the carriage.

Gerard leaned closer and asked collegially, "Where did your mother think you were today?"

It was a guess but evidently a good one. The girl's eyes widened.

"Between us, of course," he added with a smile.

"At church," she said, a mixture of embarrassment and rebellious pride on her face, "and the tailor, of course."

"Ah. And you're supposed to be bringing the gown home?"

"Aye."

"Might not the tailor discover he was one short on buttons and have to hold on to the gown until he could find a replacement set in the morning?"

She grinned. "Aye, he might have at that."

There. That won back a little trust.

"I could deliver it to your home in the morning, first thing?" he said.

"Could you really?"

And a bit more.

"I'd consider it an honor. That would take care of getting it into your hands, but I cannot help you with the fitting."

She waved a hand. "Oh, 'twas just some last minute fuss about the bodice—I don't even know what. The gown looked beautiful the last time I tried it on. I'm sure it will be fine without another fitting. Oh, but you canna let anyone know."

"I'll be very discreet. I'll leave the parcel with your housekeeper. Just a patron of the tailor making a delivery on his behalf." Gerard smiled.

"That would be so very helpful. Thank you, Mr. Bond."

Gerard took her hand and kissed it. "'Twould be my pleasure."

"And if you talk to my father or my mother at the party—God forbid you talk to my mother—you will not say anything?"

"Not a single word. You could trust me with your life." *Just not your father's cargo.*

More laughter floated out of the carriage.

Gerard gave her a narrow look. "You *will* be heading back to your home now though, right?"

"Of course."

"Give me your word."

The green in her eyes turned unexpectedly bright. "I give you my word."

Gerard strode to the carriage and opened the door. Two young men with flushed cheeks and barely hidden flasks sat on the brocade-covered benches. He looked at the more startled of the two. "Whose carriage is this?"

"His, sir." He gestured to his companion, a boy with an irredeemably smug look on his face.

"Excellent." Gerard turned to him. "What's your name?"

"Humphrey. Humphrey Bowman."

"Well, well, Mr. Bowman, I am proud to count myself among your father's many admirers. Tell him James Bond sends his regards, will you?"

The smugness began to evaporate. He nodded.

"Will you have any trouble getting Miss Hiscock to her house in the next quarter hour?" Gerard asked. "She's given me her word."

Humphrey's Adam's apple bobbed. "No, sir."

"Good."

Gerard offered Elizabeth his hand, which she accepted. She took the first step and turned.

"You seem quite intent on getting me home, Mr. Bond."

"Long day tomorrow."

Mischief rose at the corner of her mouth. "I hope so."

Thirty-six

LORD HISCOCK HAS A LOT MORE TO WORRY ABOUT THAN *his cargo*, Gerard thought. *That girl is* trouble.

For a moment he thought Serafina was gone; then she emerged from the shadows of a storefront just as the sight of Humphrey Bowman's carriage faded into the distance.

"Well?"

"She knows where Hiscock's new warehouse is."

"Where?"

"South of the castle wall, but I didn't get the street. She was distracted by the gown she was supposed to be picking up. I can pick up where I left off tomorrow night at the party—I promised I'd personally deliver the dress to her in the morning—but I couldn't ask anything more. She was on the verge of becoming suspicious."

"She was on the verge of becoming something else as well. I saw her face as ye spoke."

Serafina had meant nothing unkind by the comment, but Gerard couldn't forget the look on her face when she'd found out about his prolific past. "She appears to be able to fall in love with anyone—on a moment's notice."

"Don't underestimate yourself." She wove her hand into the crook of his elbow. "'Twas unfair of me to judge ye so harshly. You dinna trick women into your bed, after all. You are charming and good in a way few men can lay claim to. I bedded ye because I wanted ye."

His heart contracted. She made him feel different than he'd ever thought he could. She made him want to be a better man. But what was the point of being a better man if he was doomed to leave her in little more than a day?

He pulled her into the same dark storefront. "I don't want to go, Sera. We've started something here. I don't know what it is, but I want more time."

She laid her palms on his chest, and he felt it all the way to his bones. He caught her hands and held them.

"I canna lie to you," she said. "I want more time too. But it's not to be, and"—her voice caught, and she held herself very still until she'd mastered it—"and I've lost too much to want you and lose you too. So, please dinna make me want you any more than I do."

"We can fight it—"

"We canna."

"We can—"

"*Gerard.*"

He saw the pain in her eyes and fell silent. The hands, warm and alive in his—was he never to feel them again? The cheeks, curving into a majestic mouth; were they, too, lost to him? He traced every feature, every texture with his gaze, committing it to a place in his mind that would taunt him with echoes of it for the rest of his life.

She untangled her hands and let them fall.

"We need to get to the ship."

He held out his arm, heart aching. "I'm at your service, milady."

Thirty-seven

"WHERE DID YOU SEND HIM?" EDWARD LOOKED OUT the porthole window toward the dock, where Gerard was making his way back toward the city.

"I've not *sent* him anywhere," said Serafina, irritated as always at Edward's condescension. "He has things to attend to, and so do I. He'll return in an hour and a half to collect me, which should be more than enough time to transact the business we have here." She gazed at Gerard's broad shoulders, bent slightly forward as he made his way up the long hill, and the measured stride, as if he'd walked seven leagues and would walk seven more. Then, perhaps sensing her prying gaze, he stopped and turned. Her breath caught. Though she knew he couldn't see her, she felt the warmth of a communion with him and unconsciously stretched her arm.

Is that how I found you? Is there a bond between us that time and distance cannot break? Will I still feel it when you're gone? Her heart cramped, a pain as sharp as a blade. *Will I want to feel it?*

Gerard thrust his hands in his pockets, heaved a

visible sigh, and turned back to the hill. A wind blew the porthole shutter closed.

Edward settled into the chair at the captain's desk. How less suited to the seat he seemed than Gerard.

"I knew you'd come," he said.

"'Twas not much of a presumption. I intend to take possession of my muslin."

"That's not what I meant, Serafina. I knew you'd come because, despite everything that's happened, there's a bond between us."

"The only bond between us is that between debtor and debt holder. You owe me the money you took from me. The muslin is but down payment on that sum."

"You are forgetting what we had. We anticipated each other's needs. We spoke a language no one else spoke. And in bed…" He blew out a small puff of air.

"Edward…"

"God," he said, bending to stroke the fabric unrolled across his desk, "that is bloody fine muslin. It's as sheer as a damselfly's wing, and I'm told you can draw it through a wedding band. Just imagine it." He looked at her, eyes gleaming. "The bride in her marriage bed. The wife awaiting for her husband."

"The lover about to be betrayed. I like muslin for its strength."

"Like the owner of this particular sample."

"*Hm*," she said coolly, then with a bit more warmth: "Thank you for giving this to me without a fight."

"Bah! Truth be told, I'm feeling guilty about what happened."

'Tis about time. She wondered disinterestedly if bedding Edward now would be anything like bedding

Gerard, if he could be made to be generous and attentive now that she knew what generous and attentive was. She was certain the answer was no. Most men held on to their character at all cost.

"A little guilt would be good for you," she said.

"I suppose I deserve that. I had every intention of us enjoying the profits of the cargo together when I started this. God, that seems a long time ago, doesn't it, though it has not been a year. But fate—and my foolishness—intervened. I swear the women meant nothing to me—"

"Please," she said, holding up a palm. "We've talked about this so many times."

"Aye, but I have never told you that I... Oh, it doesn't matter."

"No, tell me."

"Well, I spoke to the curate—'twas at my mother's urging, I admit—and I began to pray for God's help to change, to mortify myself of my coarse and selfish desires."

"And did you?"

"Aye, I did," he said, casting his gaze downward, "for all but one woman whose kindness and beauty I can't get out of my head."

"Edward—"

"I've lost the regard of many people. I know I have. But 'tis only yours I want to regain. I can't stand to think you hate me."

"Oh, Edward, I dinna hate ye. You're weak and foolish, but I dinna hate ye."

"Is there any chance," he said, words running faster, "any chance at all, that you would allow us to begin again—as husband and wife—and try to find the happiness again that I cravenly destroyed?"

"No—"

"Don't answer yet! Take some time to think about it. Give me your answer tomorrow night. I shall come to the inn, once I free myself from Hiscock's affair—"

"I shall be there myself."

"At the party?" The surprise in his wounded her more deeply than any uttered insult could have.

"I'm not a fool," he said quietly. "I know I'm the reason you've been cut from society, and nothing would please me more than seeing you welcomed back. Are you certain?"

"I'm in the party of Lady Kerr," she said, defiant, "on the list she provided Lord Hiscock."

"I apologize. When I asked if you were certain, I didn't mean are you certain you'll be admitted. I meant are you certain you wish to endure the scrutiny?"

Edward's concern was valid. Fallen women were invited to attend some of the larger parties, especially if the party was meant to be more of a spectacle than an intimate affair, but the women were almost always included to appeal to the guests' prurient interests or flatter their righteous superiority. She'd known this when she'd accepted Abby's invitation.

"I'll be of service to Lady Kerr. So, aye."

"If you married me," he said huskily, "no one could judge you again. I could right the wrong I've done to you. Promise me you'll think about it."

"Oh, my Lord—"

"Promise me. I'll find you at the party."

"Fine," she said. "I'll think about it. But I dinna wish to excite your hopes. I intend to say no."

"You'll think about it. That's all I ask."

"Might we return to the transfer of the muslin? If you'll take me to the bolts, I can inspect them and sort them. Then I'll oversee the transfer to a wagon, with the help of some of your men. From there I'll see the whole lot delivered to a warehouse." She paused, observing him closely, and asked the question she'd specifically come here to ask. "Do you by any chance have a warehouse you'd recommend?"

"Bah," he said after a short hesitation. "They're all the same. Choose whatever strikes your fancy."

Thirty-eight

Numb, Gerard climbed the Royal Mile, the purple-pink clouds casting Edinburgh's skyline into black relief. He'd been dragged here against his will, and he was about to be thrown back in much the same way. Is this how spells were supposed to work? With no room for negotiation or changed minds? He'd known her for two days, and already he knew, with as much certainty as he'd ever known anything, that his life would never be the same without her.

He was glad at least to be able to provide her some utility before he left. He didn't know how much a relationship with Elizabeth Hiscock, such as it was, would help, but he knew he'd gotten a foot in the door as far as the girl's trust was concerned. And he intended to help Serafina even more if he could.

Gerard was pleased to see the tailor through the open window of his shop, but before he could cross the street, he spotted Undine hurrying past the shops ahead of him, her pale hair gleaming as if viewed through water.

She turned before he could call her name and looked

straight at him, sending an uncomfortable tingle down his spine. How had she known he was there? How did she know anything she knew? She put a surreptitious finger to her lips, hidden in a cough, and immediately he was as aware as a dog on a scent that someone was watching him. She turned again, her turquoise dress undulating like the surface of a lake, and stepped into a shop.

He ducked into the tavern next door to the shop and ran out the back into the alley. No one was there, and he went into the rear door of the shop Undine had just entered.

The shop sold trinkets—belts and hats and handbags—and he found her standing over a small glass case in which half a dozen pairs of pearl earrings lay on velvet.

Of course. Where else would I find her?

"Do you care for any of these?" she asked, finger hovering above the glass.

"Who did you see?"

"I didn't *see* anyone," she said. "But they were there nonetheless."

"I assume it's the three men that were following us before."

"Well, they won't come in here."

"Why?" She inclined her head and he saw the sheer chemises folded like Hermès scarves on the counter. "Great."

"Which do you like?" she repeated, still gazing at the case.

"It doesn't matter if I like them."

"I should think a man would like to see a pair of pearls on a woman's ears that please him as well."

As if I'll be here long enough to see them.

"I wish I could afford more," he said with longing, looking at his options. "I mean, I *can* afford more. Back in New York, I could buy her pearls as fat as your thumbnail, strung as long as your arm."

"She'll be as pleased with your earbobs as she'd be with the rubies of a sultan," Undine said, adding with a faint grin, "Big is not a replacement for heartfelt. If more men learned that, women would be happier."

He frowned, and not knowing quite what response would be appropriate, pointed to a not-quite-perfect pair of creamy, teardrop-shaped pearls hung from a small circle of tiny seed pearls. "I like those."

Undine signaled the shopkeeper, who placed the earrings in his hand. He held them up, the iridescent weight swaying in the light from the shop's window, and imagined the color against Serafina's skin.

"They move," he said. "She'll like them."

"You can be sure of it."

The shopkeeper took them to wrap them up, Gerard moved a step closer to the chemises. "What do women like in these things?"

"Fetching designs, lightness of weight, ease of removal." She laughed at Gerard's face. "It depends where she plans to wear it."

"At a party."

"Ahh. In that case, the most important quality is the ability to make other women covet it."

He shook his head. "But you don't see it—at least at a party, right?"

"Oh, a flash here, a glimpse there."

"Seriously?" Women would always be a locked-room mystery to him.

"Oh, aye."

"Bits and bows?"

Undine nodded. "Aye."

"Colors?"

"*No*. The whiter, the better. Purity, of course, and the display of wealth necessary to keep the fabric spotless."

The owner of the shop returned with a small paper bundle. Gerard counted out the coins, relieved he had enough. "Those chemises there," he said, "which are your biggest sellers?"

"*Sir*." The lady turned a bright shade of pink.

"He's from America," Undine said, apologetic. "No propriety."

"Oh, dear. Well, ladies do seem to like the ones with embroidery—thistles, posies, even sea serpents."

Gerard gave his working mind the parameters and led Undine out in order to turn to a far bigger obstacle. "I don't want to leave," he said.

Undine, who'd been scenting the air like a life-size wolfhound, stopped abruptly. "I beg your pardon?"

"I don't want to leave, and I think you know a way to allow me to stay."

"I am not in the habit of trifling with people. Serafina invoked a powerful spell to which there is no recourse. Now that the steps you two took have been accounted for—and thank the gods none of them were irreversible—we'll be able to restore things to their natural order."

"Then send Sera back with me."

"Is that what Serafina wants?"

His cheeks warmed. Damn, how he hated to be under this woman's gaze. He felt like the frog he'd dissected in high school but with less chance of escape. "I don't know," he admitted.

"Let me know when you do."

"What if one of the steps wasn't irreversible?"

She gave him an arch look. "Ravishment, even by a man as skilled as you, does not mean a woman has been rendered into an irreversible state of love. And many states of love are reversible, if it comes to that. One need only look at the men and women at the party tomorrow to see the truth there."

"Marriage."

"*What?*"

"Serafina and I are married," he said, "or might be."

Her eyes flashed. "'Tis not a thing one is generally unsure about."

"It doesn't matter how certain I am. If we *are* married, what does that do to the spell?"

"Besides rendering it too dangerous to attempt," she said angrily, "marriage is the one complication that renders the spell impotent."

His entire body relaxed. It was as if he'd been wearing a too-tight suit of armor. "I might ask why you didn't bother telling me that."

"I might ask why two people who couldn't name a single reason why the spell shouldn't be cast two hours ago would even think of marrying."

He'd no idea fortune-tellers were so damned frustrating to deal with. He'd faced clients in lawsuits who were easier to work with. "Well, from now on, I'll be at the wheel of my own ship, thank you."

"Are ye married?"

"Aye. It happened the first night."

"Fools."

"Have you never been in love, Undine? That's what it does to people."

She schooled her features. "As you wish. I have to meet a contact here soon, so I must insist you disappear. And you'd better be telling me the truth because you'll be sucked from your boots without as much as a good-bye if you're not."

He'd accept the risk. "I am." He broke her gaze, nodded, and turned for the tailor. Half a dozen steps later she called, "What would you like me to do with the herbs?"

"Whatever you see fit." *Let 'em burn a hole in your pocket. I'm done with them.*

Thirty-nine

WHISTLING HAPPILY, GERARD WAITED FOR THE TRAFFIC on the Royal Mile to clear. Undine had disappeared almost literally before his eyes—from in front of a long brick wall in the time it had taken him to step out of the way of a tinker's cart. But Edinburgh was his now— and more important, so was Serafina—for as long as he wanted, so Undine's shenanigans hardly mattered, and he thumped the tinker happily on the back as he passed.

When the last carriage rattled by, he took a step into the street only to have a hand come down on his shoulder.

"What are ye doing here?" Duncan demanded.

"Jesus! Just how small *is* Edinburgh? How did you know where to find me? I've already run into Undine."

Duncan chuckled. "'Tis nothing magical, I assure you. I've been following you since you left. To ensure your safety. Serafina is quite dear to me. But then I began to wonder why a man tasked with her safety would abandon her at the ship."

"At what point do I earn your trust? Once I've actually given my life for her?"

"'Twould be a good start."

"Well, sorry to disappoint. I have no plans to die or leave, at least for the time being. And, for the record, Serafina did not get abandoned. I was dismissed in no uncertain terms. She said she would handle Edward on her own."

"*Och.*"

"Tell me about it."

"And what do you mean, you have no plans to leave?"

"I mean—" Gerard paused. He wasn't quite sure what Duncan would think of a drunken wedding to Serafina, but he doubted the notion would be warmly embraced. Besides, he wasn't one hundred percent confident it had happened. "There's a glitch. The spell to return isn't working. And I intend to stay for a bit."

The grip on his shoulder tightened. "How?"

"How what?"

"In what manner are ye to stay? Are ye to be Serafina's lover? If so, what would be her motivation to bed ye if you're leaving?"

Gerard could think of several answers but none that wouldn't get him punched in the nose.

"As in all things," he said, "I'll leave it to Sera to choose. She appears to have no trouble knowing her mind."

Duncan grunted. "It's no' a great answer. But I'll accept it." He released his hand.

Gerard straightened his frock coat. He longed for the freedom of a sark and kilt, not to mention the chance to operate with a little less Big Brother and Big Sister looking over his shoulder.

"Let me ask you something," Gerard said. "What do men look for in a chemise?"

"A naked woman."

"I mean while they're wearing them—the women, that is. What do you like to see?"

"I think you're supposed to keep your eyes up here, my friend." Duncan gestured to his face. "'Tis no' gentlemanly to be looking below."

"So you don't care a whit about what Abby looks like in hers. She could be wearing your grandma's nightie, and it would all be the same to you?"

"Well, when ye put it like that…" Duncan ran a hand through his hair. "Let's see. I do rather like them being…" He rubbed his thumb against his fingers, looking for the right word.

"Silky?"

"Aye. But that's not what I'm thinking of."

"See-through?"

"*Och*, no. Mystery is seduction's friend. Floaty. Loose. Not too clingy. I like the fabric to just brush the contours of—" He stopped, horrified, and his neck flooded with color. "You get the idea."

"Yes."

"Oh, and ease of removal." He mimed the tug of a small bow. "A nice well-engineered release, aye?"

"All right. That was helpful. Thank you, I intend to construct the world's sexiest chemise for Serafina. For her to sell," he added quickly, seeing the storm rising on Duncan's face.

"That asshole didn't leave her much, did he?"

"Serafina says the whole thing's worth fifty pounds."

Duncan shrugged. "She could scrape by on that for a good many years."

"I don't want her to scrape by. I want her to own her own ship."

"Well, she won't do that on fifty pounds," Duncan said. "Nor a hundred or even two."

"I know. I just want to do everything I can for her."

Duncan shifted. "Can I give you some advice?"

"Sure," Gerard said. "As long as it doesn't involve your fists."

"If you're going to leave, do it now. It does neither of ye any good to dangle."

Gerard knew he wanted to stay, but did he want to stay forever? "Thanks. You're right. Hey, I've got some advice for you too."

"Oh?"

"If you're going to get married, do it now. It does neither of you any good to dangle."

Duncan chuckled, then the chuckle died away. "Abby's...stubborn."

"She wants you. Any fool can see it. Make her put a ring on it, eh?"

"Thanks. You're right."

The bell of a nearby church rang out the quarter hour.

"Shit. I gotta run," Gerard said, jabbing a thumb toward the tailor.

"Hey, I can buy you a little more time. I'm on my way to the docks to see about shipping some of our whiskey. Can I pick up Serafina for you?"

"Er…"

"It's no' a trick question. You don't lose any points."

"Whew! Then yes. That'd be *great*. I'll catch you back at the inn," he said and began to cross the street.

"Hey," Duncan said, and Gerard turned.

"Yeah?"

"For what it's worth, I'd like to see you stay."

"To be best man?"

Duncan put his fist out. Gerard bumped it.

Forty

"WHERE'S GERARD?" SERAFINA ASKED, HER GUT TIGHT-ening.

"What? You're no' glad to see me?" Duncan offered his arm, and she took it hesitantly.

"Is he all right?" she asked.

"I think he's in some bit o' pain, aye, but nothing that canna be easily fixed."

Serafina stopped, heart clenched. "What happened? What's wrong?"

Duncan nudged her gently into walking. "What's wrong, my friend, is that he has some conflicting ideas about his future."

A future that, for me, ends in a little over twenty-four hours—one night, one day. A thousand nights and days wouldn't be enough, and we have left but one of each. "We're not one of the lucky ones. You and Abby…well, your spell allowed you to be together." She fought the thickness coming to her throat. "I shouldn't have tinkered with Undine's herbs. The things I did made it impossible for him to stay."

"He says there's a glitch, that he will be able to stay, at least for the present."

"In truth?" Her happiness raced a dozen paces ahead of her thoughts.

"Aye, but there's another obstacle."

"What?"

"He doesn't know your feelings."

"Duncan, I don't know how he could be confused...after what we've...what has transpired," she finished primly, aware of the poor model of morality she must represent.

He laughed. "I'm sorry. I shouldna laugh, but women tend to think things are much clearer than men do—when men think about them at all. You're verra different than Abby. She wears her emotions like a spray of diamonds she wants you to notice. There's no mistaking if she likes ye, and God knows, there's no mistaking if she doesn't."

He blew out a puff of air, evidently remembering times when the latter condition might have applied to him.

"You're more like me," Duncan added tenderly. "We keep our feelings to ourselves—at least the kinds that make us feel vulnerable, temper not included."

She laughed. "No, never that. But, Duncan, why, when I have no idea if we can be together, would I cause us both such heartache? Isn't it better for me to just hold my tongue?"

"That dam's crumbled, Serafina. There's no getting the water back. And I'm a firm believer that despite the spell, there's no power stronger than two people in love. It's going to hurt, but you have to do everything you can to fight it. It's the only way you'll be able to live with yourself."

Duncan was right, though she could hardly bear to think about exposing herself to the pain of seeing Gerard at the inn, let alone admitting to herself she loved him.

"When did you become such a strong supporter of Gerard Innes? I thought ye didna like him."

"*Och*, not at all. He's rather interesting to have around." He gave her a sidelong look and raised a ruddy brow. "Would it have mattered if I hadn't liked him?"

"Not a whit."

He laughed. "That's my Serafina."

Forty-one

HAVING DONE WHAT HE NEEDED TO DO AT THE TAILOR shop, Gerard hurried along the thoroughfare, hoping to find Serafina at the inn to share the news about the spell, and though something niggled at him about celebrating a pardon that may in fact be based on an incorrect assumption, he pushed the thought away.

As he crossed Cockburn, something caught his eye, and he turned. The couple who had been so unaccountably cruel to Serafina were stepping into a carriage with their boys. When it pulled away, he saw the same elderly woman at the second-floor window. Her gaze lit upon him for a long moment, and she acknowledged him with a nod before retreating from view.

He couldn't explain what made him head for the arched door except that there had been something in the elderly woman's happiness upon seeing Serafina earlier and her acknowledgement of him just now that made him believe he might be able to help Serafina.

He lifted the enormous acorn-shaped knocker and rapped the door. A frail male servant, not much younger than the woman upstairs, answered the door.

"I have a message for Mrs. Turnbull," Gerard said. "May I see her?"

The man nodded and held out his hand.

"It's not written down. I'd like to give it to her in person."

"She's been ill and is not accepting callers. If you'd like, I can fetch a pencil and paper?"

"No, no. That's not necessary. Please just tell her that a friend of hers, a woman she saw earlier, misses her and sends her love to her and her grandsons."

"Crawford?"

The quavering voice—a woman's—came from the upper floor.

"Will you pardon me?" The man ushered Gerard in and closed the doors before scurrying up the stairs. Thick Oriental rugs muffled the sounds of the carriages outside, ebony and gilt tables lined the hall, and a cascade of previous owners glowered at him from massive portraits lining the staircase wall. Gerard smoothed his ruffled hair and straightened his frock coat. A moment later, the servant returned.

"Mrs. Turnbull will see you," he said. "This is most unusual, and I would ask for her sake you make your stay brief."

Gerard was escorted upstairs to a small sitting room. Despite an abundance of light streaming into the south-facing rooms, Edward's brother had deposited his ailing mother in a room that was both dark and chilly. The evening wasn't cold, but Mrs. Turnbull was wrapped in a wool robe and a tiny fire flickered in the hearth. She wasn't as old as he'd originally thought. Sixty, perhaps, but that probably passed for ancient in the eighteenth century. It was clear she was being ravaged by some disease—her color was gray, and deep lines etched her cheeks. This was a woman counting her remaining time in months or weeks, not years. She clutched a lace handkerchief.

"I should not have invited you in, Mr...?" She gestured to a chair and he sat.

"Innes."

"Innes. My son would not be pleased with your presence." She coughed hard several times and wiped her mouth.

"I won't stay long. I just wanted to give you a message from the woman you saw outside earlier."

"Serafina Fallon." Her milky eyes held his gaze.

"Aye. She heard from your grandsons that you were quite ill, and she wanted to tell you how dear you and the boys are to her, and how much your kindness meant when she was involved with your son."

Mrs. Turnbull did not acknowledge his statement, but the muscles in her jaw moved, and he knew it had touched her.

"That is Miss Fallon's message for you," he said. "I have a different one: I consider your family's treatment of Miss Fallon abominable. I am at least as wealthy as your son, and I was raised to be respectful and polite no matter what a person's status was in relation to mine and, in fact, to be more respectful the larger the disparity. Even if I hadn't been raised that way, I would have learned it by observing others who have been more thoughtfully taught. And for the record," he said as he stood, "Miss Fallon does not know I'm here, and she would be even less pleased with my presence than your son. I'm sorry to have intruded on your evening." He reached for the door.

"Wait."

She gestured him back to the chair. He sat and waited.

She coughed again, so hard Gerard thought he might have to call the servant. When she quieted, she said, "Are you Serafina's fiancé?"

"No, I'm her friend."

"I'm very glad she has one. I'm hoping you will continue your generous service on her behalf and bring her a message from me."

Gerard didn't nod. His willingness to deliver the message would depend entirely on what the message was.

"Serafina has a special place in my heart," the woman continued. "She nursed me through my first illness. Night and day, she was at my side. Of course, that was before the unpleasantness."

"Before she moved into your son's home and bed?"

Mrs. Turnbull pressed her lips into a line. "Aye. Mr. Innes, I know my son is a knave and worse. But whether you or I agree, in this world, a woman bears the responsibility for her actions with a knave. Serafina made her choice—"

Gerard began to rise.

"—but I want to undo the wrong that's been done to her."

"How?"

"Are you aware Edward is still in love with her?"

"I've heard that, yes."

"Are you aware he intends to propose to her?"

And already has. "It doesn't surprise me."

"He's no prize, I admit, and he has squandered his fortune with poor investments."

"His fortune and hers."

"But he does love her in his own way," Mrs. Turnbull said. "I don't have a lot of money, Mr. Innes, but what I have is mine and I can do what I want with it. I've promised Edward he will inherit my money when I die on the condition he marries Serafina. I have arranged for a tenth of that to go directly to her as his wife. Edward will not be able to touch it. I hope this will help her in some small way. As Mrs. Edward Turnbull, she will never have to live in squalor again."

Gerard bristled. He hated that anyone would judge Serafina's situation, whether or not the judgment was true. He also doubted that the ten or twenty pounds this bequest represented would do much to change Serafina's life—and he felt certain Edward would spend the rest in a matter of weeks.

"You are kind to think of her," he said. "I have no doubt she'll be touched."

"Then you'll take the offer to her? Will you let her know I've not forgotten her kindness?"

"I will do that."

"Mr. Innes, tell me honestly. Do you think she'll accept my son's offer?"

Gerard weighed falsely raising the woman's hopes against the possibility that, knowing with certainty a marriage between Serafina and her son would not occur, she might find a better place to leave her money.

"In truth, I do not," he said. "Edward asked Serafina to marry him yesterday. She declined."

Mrs. Turnbull's frail shoulders sagged.

"But she'll be deeply touched to hear of your feelings for her. I know it'll ease her burden considerably. And, as Miss Fallon's friend, I personally thank you for trying to make amends."

The woman did not speak. After a moment, Gerard said, "I know you must be tired. I'll let myself out."

With a deep wheeze, the woman stood and made her way unsteadily to the table beside her bed and returned with something in her hand.

"Take this to her," she said, coughing. "It's a gift from me."

Gerard held out his palm. In it, she placed a stickpin topped by a silver thistle.

"My husband gave me this. Serafina always admired it."

"Would you not prefer it to go to your daughter-in-law or perhaps a future granddaughter?"

The woman made a tart laugh. "My daughter-in-law declared it too old-fashioned for her taste. And as for granddaughters, I will not live to see them. I should prefer it go to someone who might remember me with fondness."

Gerard tucked it into his coat pocket. "She'll wear it with great happiness, I know."

Mrs. Turnbull thanked him and asked if he could let himself out.

Gerard knew the stickpin would thrill Serafina, and he was glad to be the person to deliver it. As he descended the stairs, he debated whether to tell her of Mrs. Turnbull's conditional bequest. Serafina had declined Edward's offer of marriage on the grounds of not loving him—pretty important grounds, he thought—and Gerard doubted the addition of a tenth of Mrs. Turnbull's modest estate would change her mind. But a more overriding consideration, at least to Gerard, was that revealing the existence of Mrs. Turnbull's conditional bequest would render Edward's passionate confession of love for Serafina into an unflattering and manipulative gesture meant only to win him his mother's bequest.

Gerard decided he couldn't hurt Serafina like that, as much as Edward might deserve having his gesture exposed for what it was. Crawford emerged from the dining room, just as Gerard reached the entryway.

"Good news," Gerard said. "You needn't tell your master I've dirtied his halls. I'll be gone before he returns."

The man's brows rose. "Mr. Henry Turnbull, you mean? He's not my master, sir. Nor will he be coming back this evening. He and his family are returning to their home in York."

"Whose home is this?"

"Why, Mrs. Turnbull's, of course. Mr. Henry Turnbull's father left her this and everything in it when he died."

Forty-two

GERARD PUSHED THE SAUSAGES AROUND HIS PLATE, barely aware of the boisterous patrons at the Squeak and Sizzle. The conditional bequest from Mrs. Turnbull wasn't tiny. It's wasn't the financial equivalent of a silver stickpin and handful of crowns. If Serafina agreed to marry Edward, the bequest from Mrs. Turnbull would lift her from the throes of bankruptcy to a place high atop society, where she'd never have to worry about money again.

Gerard knew the money by itself would not buy Serafina happiness. He'd watched his grandfather, a thoroughly repugnant man, spend his old age obsessed with fluctuations in the stock market and furious with decisions made by the boards of companies he no longer controlled, his millions bringing him no perceptible pleasure at all. His father, bland to the point of invisibility, had never had to work, really—only listen to the reports of the men who invested the family fortune. He'd sunk slowly into a wretched pit of half-lidded alcoholism, serial infidelity, and moroseness. It was no wonder Gerard had taken a pass on everything Newport, Rhode Island, had to offer.

But he was equally aware of the soul-grinding problems *not* having enough money caused. His admin, a lovely, smart woman named Bev, had had to resign when her husband was laid off from his bookkeeping job, so they could sell their small Brooklyn apartment, the one asset they had, and move to a less-expensive trailer in South Carolina, where her husband got a job as a part-time manager of a local grocery store. Gerard still used Bev to manage his travel. She'd cried when he'd called to offer her the freelance work.

Doing a job you love—and earning enough money to live from it—was the only recipe for happiness Gerard had ever found. Mrs. Turnbull's money would give Serafina the chance to do that.

"Why the dowie face, lad?"

Gerard lifted his gaze to John Dawes's interrogatory stare.

"Pardon?" Gerard said.

"You look like yer gilpie dropped a puddock in yer groats."

"You know what? I *feel* like my gilpie dropped a puddock in my groats."

"There's only one cure for that."

"What's that?"

Dawes reached under the bar and *plonked* a stout bottle of whiskey in front of him, followed by a glass.

Gerard turned the bottle. Kerr whiskey. Of course. He poured himself a long draw. "You married, Mr. Dawes?"

"For these last twenty years."

"What would you do if your wife had an illness, and

there's a cure, but she'll have to take it every day and it's only available on a faraway island in the Atlantic, an island on which you're not allowed, which means if she takes the cure, you'll never see her again?"

"*Och,* that's a hard one." Dawes frowned. "Will she die without the medicine?"

"No. But she'll be damned uncomfortable."

Dawes threw the rag he held over his shoulder. "Uncomfortable? Like a club foot?"

"Aye. Or wheezing or gout."

Dawes leaned in closer, as if he were telling Gerard a secret. "You ken, I am quite in love with my wife. Not every man in here is, but I am. She nearly died when she had our daughter nine years ago. I prayed and prayed for the fever to go—and I'm no' a praying man. Nothing reminds you of the importance of something like thinking you might lose it. I complain now and then, but my life would be empty without her. If she fell ill, I'd send her to the island. No question."

"Really?"

"Oh, aye. And d'ye want to know the first thing I'd do after that?"

"What?"

"I'd storm the bloody place. They can make the cure as hard to get as they want, but no one's going to keep me from being with her while she takes it."

Dawes is a wise man. Nothing would keep Gerard from Serafina, even if she married Edward.

He swirled his drink. Having come to that certainty, he went a step further. Would it be a good idea for her to marry Edward to take possession of the bequest? Edward wouldn't fight it, since he would come into a chest full of money too. Serafina would receive an independent fortune. There would be no divorce though. Not in this era. She would be Mrs. Turnbull, and to the world, Gerard would be the penniless lover she kept to amuse herself.

He shifted. The vision was not an attractive one. And yet if it brought Serafina a ship and the freedom to do what she wanted, could he bear it? Yes. No question.

Then he remembered what he had nearly forgotten: Serafina was already married. To him, or so he thought. She couldn't marry another. No matter how much Gerard might wish for her to have the money, it couldn't be. Serafina would never commit such a transgression.

He felt the iron band loosen, and he exhaled. He and Serafina would learn how to survive without the Turnbull bequest. He didn't know how, but they would.

Gerard lifted his hand to signal for a refill, but before he could open his mouth, a call of "Edward Turnbull!" rose over the noise of the tavern.

Gerard turned, looking for the man who'd been so much on his mind, but found himself instead looking into the surprised gaze of Father Kincaid from St. Giles.

Kincaid walked over, and Gerard almost asked if he, too, was an acquaintance of the cad until he remembered that Kincaid thought that he, Gerard, *was* Edward Turnbull.

"Ha! Never thought I'd run into you here," Kincaid said. "I've been looking for you since yesterday."

"I've spoken to all my colleagues," Gerard said, remembering his promise about the steeple. "Talked it up to everyone. You should be expecting an absolute run on the place, I promise—"

"Oh, gah," Kincaid said, signaling for an ale. "I wasn't running about looking for you for that. When a man makes a promise, Bruce Kincaid takes him at his word. No, I was looking for you for quite another reason. I have the information you were looking for."

"Information?"

He gave Gerard a gentle elbow and turned to Dawes. "The man doesn't remember asking me to find out if he got married or not."

Dawes laughed. "What? Married and he canna remember?"

"Drunk, he was. Drunk as a puffin."

"And what's the answer?" Gerard said. "What happened?"

"Well, Archie finally made his way in. It seems you did *not* convince the lady to do the deed. I canna say what deeds ye did outside St. Giles, but ye did no' marry."

Gerard shook his head to clear out the cobwebs. "But you said I insisted, that before I'd sign the register copy, I said we had to be married."

"Oh, ye definitely said it, but the couple that came in later, the ones Archie remembered, wasna you. Look at it this way: If it's so important to ye, ye'll now have a chance to do it while you're awake, conscious-like. And there's no rush, of course, as your names are already on the register." Kincaid lifted his mug. "*Slainté.*"

Numb, Gerard reached for his whiskey. He and Serafina had created the fake marriage record, but they had never actually married. They'd apparently even bought a ring, but they'd never married. Undine's spell would take effect exactly as it was supposed to.

Gerard would be whisked away, heartbroken, and Serafina would be alone and penniless unless he convinced her to marry Edward.

He lifted his glass and drank till it was dry. Then he put it down and looked at Dawes. "Another, please, and keep them coming."

Forty-three

GERARD KNOCKED ON THE UPSTAIRS DOOR AT THE Hollow Crown, ignoring the sharp thump of overindulgence behind his eyes, and adjusted the parcels in his arm. He'd been tempted to stop downstairs for a fortifying drink, but he'd been gone all night and half the day, and he'd avoided what needed to be done long enough.

Duncan, looking splendid in a rich green kilt with silver appointments, cracked the door. He looked Gerard over, diagnosed his hangover instantly, and shook his head. "Idiot," he said and swung the door wide.

Abby was at the mirror, adjusting something feathery in her hair. Undine sat by the fire, sipping wine, and Serafina stood by the window, looking breathtaking in a dark blue gown that picked up the sapphire in her eyes.

"There you are." Abby met his gaze in the mirror, but Serafina's attention was focused on something beyond the glass.

"I sent a note," Gerard said, putting his packages on the table. "You got it, I hope."

"We did. Duncan," Abby said pointedly, "could

you help me with my clasp?" She pulled away just as Duncan reached for it, leaving his arms dangling in midair. "In here." She gestured to their bedroom. Duncan shrugged apologetically and followed her in. The door closed.

Undine unfolded herself. "I suppose I should see if—"

"Excuse me." Serafina disappeared into her room and shut the door with a *bang*.

Gerard shoved his hands in his pockets. "Am I going to get the cold shoulder from you too?"

Undine chuckled. "A beautifully descriptive phrase. I didn't realize the denizens of the twenty-first century possessed that much of an imagination. Mr. Innes, you look like a man in need of a fortune reading."

"Thank you, no. I didn't much enjoy the first one. In any case, I know what's going to happen to me."

"False confidence. Such a typically male flaw. You also look like a man in need of a bath. You're still planning to accompany me to the dinner, are you not?"

"Yes. Well, sort of. I've introduced myself to Elizabeth Hiscock as the debonair James Bond, and I promised her I'd look for her there." His gaze went to the closed door. "I think I'd better talk to Serafina."

"Give her some time."

"We don't have time," he said.

"That's rather amusing coming from a man who has been hiding away nearly an entire day. What makes you think you don't have time?"

He lowered his voice. "I was wrong. We're not married. The spell hasn't been altered."

Undine exhaled. "Oh, dear. I'm sorry. What about the ring she's been hiding?"

The ring—another thing Undine knew. He shrugged. "I guess she bought it to make it easier for her to try to claim the cargo if it came to that," he said, keeping his voice low. "I don't remember everything from that first night, but I know for a fact we didn't marry."

Undine pointed to her room. "Come. We'll talk in there."

She led him in and took a seat on a large chest. A copper tub filled with water sat in a corner, and he hesitated.

"I had a bath drawn for me," she explained, "but I find I'm not in the mood. Take it, please."

Gerard longed for the rejuvenating qualities of that hot water. He'd be better able to face Serafina with the foolish excesses of the night before washed from him. He slipped off his jacket and began to undo his shirt buttons.

"I am verra sorry to hear your news," Undine said. "I know you'd set great store by the implications."

"We need to do something to help Sera."

Undine put a finger to her lips and gestured to the wall separating Serafina's bedroom from hers. "Keep your voice down," she said in a whisper. "She can hear us. Why do you think she needs help?"

"Have you seen where she lives?"

Undine shook her head. "Serafina has been one of our party since I met her."

"You and Duncan and Abby have been very good friends to her. The place she lives is"—he shook his head, remembering the low circumstances—"wretched. She has nothing now that the cargo is gone. Not even a gown to wear. She's dead broke—penniless."

"*Nothing?*"

"Not a crumb."

❧

Serafina wrenched herself away from the wall, the throb of shame in her ears as loud as the trumpet blare of fury. How did he know? And why would he tell Undine? She'd become an object of pity and laughter, as if someone had placed her in the town square and nailed her ear to the pillory. And not just anybody. The man she thought loved her. She wanted to run, to hide her face, to never be seen again.

She marched into the empty sitting room, then into the hallway. She grabbed a passing maid and said, "Tell Lady Kerr I need some air."

❧

Undine said, "Abby can help her."

Gerard shook his head. He knew what Serafina's reaction would be. "She won't take it. And I could help her if she came back to New York with me. And I might be able to help her here, but not now. Not yet." He kicked the tub, angry with himself.

"She won't starve. She's too smart. She'll accept Abby's help if it comes to that."

"Don't you see? I don't want it to come to that. And you shouldn't either." His shirt hung open and his hand was on a trouser button. He waited for Undine to step out or at least turn her head. She didn't. He gestured to his pants. "Do you mind?"

"Not in the least." She turned slightly, not enough to block him from her view.

He gave up. With a few quick moves, he was undressed, and with one more, he was sinking into the water. He wondered for an instant what it might have been like to have Serafina climbing in with him, perhaps in her own muslin chemise, the fabric puddling in warm wet curves around her hips. He'd have loosened the ribbon slowly, and the straps would've fallen off her shoulders, freeing those soft, round breasts. But it would be her eyes, simmering with desire and defiance, that would've entranced him, and the press of her palms on his chest as she began to move. *Oh, Sera...*

"Mr. Innes?"

He jerked hard enough to spill water over the tub's side. He wished he had an aluminum foil hat. There was something about the exasperated look on Undine's face that made it seem like she was drawing the thoughts from his head with the strength of an electron magnet. "Yes?"

"Are you ready to focus?"

"Yes."

"Good. We have another problem on our hands tonight."

"What's that?" he said, reaching for the soap.

"My contacts intercepted a note from that miserable Henry Boyle regarding a bribe England is sending to Scotland."

"Henry Boyle?"

"The chancellor of the exchequer. 'Tis a final effort to sway the votes of the men in the Scottish Parliament. If exposed, it would turn the people of Scotland even harder against the union and make it near impossible for Parliament to ignore them."

"So what's the problem? You have the note," he said. "Expose it."

"The note doesn't have Boyle's name or signature on it. We know, but it wouldn't work as cudgel. Our best bet is to try to dry up the source of the bribes. We know they come in a small amount at a time—enough to bribe a single lord—and go through a high-placed man sympathetic to their cause."

"Hiscock."

"Aye."

"Is the money for the bribes part of the stolen cargo?"

"We don't think so. It needs to be gold, and we'd have heard if a cache of gold coins had hit the streets of Edinburgh. But now that we know Hiscock is the man aiding England, we can narrow our efforts. And tonight I'm going to see what I can find out."

"While I press Elizabeth Hiscock for the location of the warehouse. Oh, God," he said with a long sigh. "I wish I could spend my last hours with Sera and not that girl. But I know it's the best thing I can do for her." He realized it was time to get to the heart of the matter with Undine. "There's another option."

"For the gold?"

"No, for Sera. Edward wishes to marry her."

"And Serafina turned him down."

"There's more to it," Gerard said. "I visited Edward's mother. She very much wants to see Edward right his wrong and marry Sera."

Undine snorted. "Good luck."

"It would be a good marriage for her—financially, I mean. Mrs. Turnbull intends to leave Serafina a sizable bequest. I don't know the exact amount, but it's a tenth of her estate and even with a conservative estimate, Serafina would live very well."

"Then why would she marry?"

"Because the bequest is contingent on a marriage to Edward."

Undine groaned. "She'll never say aye."

"But she should."

Undine straightened her gown and coughed. "There is a third option as well, you know."

Gerard knew what the option was. He'd been thinking about it most of the night.

"Are you going to ask what it is?" Undine said.

"No," he said. "I'd rather see her married to Edward. A marriage to me gets her nothing."

"You'd rather see her *married to Edward*? Yesterday, you could barely contain your pleasure when you thought her marriage to you had stopped the spell."

"Yeah, well, that was before I found out about the bequest. Serafina should be at sea. She needs a ship. She could kick the ass of any man afloat. But no matter how many times I go over it, I can't find a way to be able to give her that." Gerard hung his head, defeated.

"Perhaps you misunderstand what she needs. I'm not going to argue with you, Mr. Innes. If your mind is set, there's nothing I can do to change it. What can I do to help?"

"I don't know exactly how marriage works here, especially among the wealthy, but with her own money, mightn't Sera be free to…live as she wished? It's certainly how they live in my time."

"She would," Undine said. "I can think of very few couples who do not hide certain things from one another."

"I don't mean the freedom to take a lover—though I hope Serafina would find someone to make her happy in that way. I mean the freedom to sail."

"She might have that too," Undine agreed. "If that's what she wanted."

"Edward is also to get a bequest, and his, like Sera's, depends on them marrying."

Undine's eyes turned dark. "Bastard. That's why he's proposed, isn't it? He knows that."

"I think so, yes."

Gerard gazed into the copper-tinted depths between his feet. "I want him to love her—truly love her. Do you have a potion for that?"

"Mr. Innes, you are treading on very dangerous ground. Trying to force love when it doesn't exist—or to deny it when it does—is playing with the crux of human emotion. 'Tis nothing to make a man fall in love with a woman for whom he already longs. But to kindle emotion where nothing but cruelty and manipulation exists…"

"I know he longs for her. I saw it in his eyes."

"Longing for control, or a few moments between her legs, is not the longing I mean. Surely you of all people know the difference."

I know the difference now. "Nonetheless, that's what I want. And I'm hoping you'll give me what I need to make Edward fall in love with her."

Undine's eyes held warning, but she was relenting. Gerard could see it.

"You're playing with fire," she said.

"I'll live with the burns."

Abby flung open the door. "Undine—" Her eyes

widened when she saw Gerard in the tub. She looked behind the door for Serafina, and on finding no one asked, "Is everything settled then?"

"Not in the way you'd expect," Undine said. "He needs a clean shirt and frock coat."

"From where I'm standing, it looks like he needs breeks as well." Abby turned for the sitting room.

"Wait," Gerard called, adding to Undine, "Apologies, but would you mind collecting the clothes? I'd like a moment alone with Lady Kerr."

Undine and Abby exchanged significant looks, and Undine left. Abby leaned against the door frame, entirely unperturbed by the scene before her. Gerard made a mental note to email his college history professor when he got back. Everything he'd told the class about the modesty of women prior to the twentieth century was wrong.

"I'm going to tell you something I don't want anyone else to know."

Abby smiled. "Excellent."

"Sera's penniless. She's lost everything. The only thing she has left to her name is the muslin, which I intend to help her sell. However, there's a chance—a good chance—she will make an advantageous marriage"

"I feel certain of it," Abby said with a gentle smile, and Gerard felt a double stab of regret.

"But if for whatever reason she doesn't," he said, "would you be able to employ her? She's very talented, and I know she loves being with you and Undine."

"Mr. Innes, you needn't worry. I'll keep Serafina by my side—forever if necessary."

"But it must be a proper job," he said. "She won't accept your charity."

Abby smiled. "You've gotten to know her well, I see. Aye, I'll do what it takes. You have my word."

"Good. Thank you." He dunked his head under the water and sat up, gathering his courage. "There's one thing more."

She must have heard the change in his voice, for she closed the door and leaned against it.

"Sera and I, well, you probably know we…well…"

"Danced the Paphian jig?"

"I-I—Probably. And we didn't use anything to keep her from getting pregnant—well, I didn't, in any case. And I'm leaving."

"Oh." Abby's face fell. "I'm sorry to hear that."

"So, if there's a child…" The extent of his villainy overwhelmed him.

"My promise extends to any child of Serafina's. Neither of them will ever want for anything. Though I'm surprised you'd leave thinking this a possibility."

"My leaving may help Serafina in ways you don't understand."

"Indeed? I'll have to take your word on that, Mr. Innes."

"Thank you. Please don't mention any of this to her."

The door rattled then opened. Duncan, clean frock coat and shirt folded neatly over his arm, observed the tableau before him. "Are those your balls in here with my fiancée?"

Gerard gulped. "We're done."

"Glad to hear it. Here. Wear them in good health." Duncan tossed the clothes on the floor and exited.

"Don't mind him," Abby said, gathering her skirts. "He's always a bit fashed about other men's balls."

Undine slipped back in, next to Abby. "What happened with Elizabeth Hiscock, Mr. Innes? Serafina told us you struck up a friendship."

Abby ducked her head. "Well done, sir."

Gerard's chest puffed. It was one of the few useful things he'd done since he'd arrived. With any luck, he'd be able to get the location of the warehouse out of her tonight.

"Getting a woman to do what I want is no big deal," he said, and was about to add, "Getting a woman *I care about* to do it—well, that's a whole other story," when he saw Serafina staring at him from the sitting room. He didn't need to be a fortune-teller to know she'd heard him. The look on her face made it quite clear. Nor did it help that Abby and Undine turned to see what Gerard saw and fell instantly silent. The entire picture was one of three friends having thoroughly hashed over the actions of a fourth.

Gerard exhaled. "I think I'd better get dressed."

Forty-four

HOW DARE HE SIT THERE WITH THAT BLAND LOOK ON HIS face, looking damp and irritatingly handsome, as if he hasn't embarrassed me to the bone?

Serafina felt the silent waves of sympathy from the room. *Poor girl. Not a penny to her name. Even Edward Turnbull wouldn't stay with her.*

She didn't want a man. Not then, not now. It had been Edward who'd begged and begged.

"...and that leaves Hiscock. Is that all right, Serafina?" Undine checked for agreement.

She flushed again, this time for having been caught woolgathering. "I beg your pardon?"

"I wonder if she should go at all?" Gerard said, avoiding Serafina's eyes. "Besides the obvious issues with running into Lord Bridgewater, it might do us good to have someone sitting tight with the carriage in case—"

"What Mr. Innes means," Serafina said, "is he's afraid I'll be cut by the partygoers. He doesn't understand that parties are the one place fallen, penniless women *are* permitted. They are part of the evening's entertainment."

Undine let out a sigh. "Mr. Innes, Serafina under-
stands the risks and has accepted them. Let's focus on
what we can change, aye? Serafina, we're reviewing
the plans for the party in Dean Village tonight. I'll
be working in the background. Topham Finch has
asked me to read his fortune, and I intend to flay his
conscience so roughly for his disloyalty to Scotland,
he'll be costive for a fortnight."

Gerard winced. "Why *do* men seek your service?"

"Take care, or you might find groats growing in
your warm places."

Gerard cleared his throat. "If I could take the floor
for a moment, I have a couple of things I'd like to say.
First, I apologize for my absence. It was thoughtless.
I'd gotten some distressing news, but that's not an
acceptable reason."

"What news?" Duncan said, catching Serafina's eye,
and she shrugged, embarrassed. Apparently, Gerard
did not choose to share his secrets with her anymore.

Gerard sighed. "I'd come to believe Serafina and
I were truly married. Our adventure the first night
involved a falsified marriage certificate, and I thought
it might have also involved a true marriage, but it
didn't. I've done the job I was called here for, and
according to the terms of Undine's magic, I'll be
whisked away by morning."

An aching loss sweep through Serafina, as if she'd
been told of the death of a loved one. She wanted to
reach for Gerard's hand but dared not.

"I'm distressed, of course," Gerard said, "by the
thought of leaving all of you. Before I go, though, I
intend to aid Sera as much as I can in the branding

and marketing of her muslin. To that end, I took the liberty of having a chemise made for each of you—"

Duncan made a Scottish noise.

"—not you, of course." Gerard opened the parcels and handed out the delicate items. "They're rather plain on top—just a single ribbon closure"—he nodded to Duncan—"as I had the tailor concentrate on the parts visible near the hem."

Serafina was stunned by the intricacy of the embroidered patterns and the subtle elegance of white thread on white. The embroidery appeared only within a tall band on the wearer's right side, just at the place that might be visible if the wearer were to raise her skirt to accommodate stepping from a carriage, descending a staircase, or even reveling in one's obviously superior finery. Undine's had a mother elephant followed by a line of baby elephants; Abby's had an intricate Persian pear design, and hers, the most beautiful of all, had a tableaux of the myth of Atalanta and Melanion, Atalanta's suitor, in which they run the footrace that will decide whether he can claim her hand in marriage, and in this representation Atalanta had red hair, the only color in the otherwise all-white scene.

"They're beautiful," Undine said.

"The ones we sell will have the embroidery all the way around, but for these, I told the tailor quantity was more important than quality."

"But the quality is excellent," Serafina said. "Is it my muslin?"

"Yes. The tailor has a cousin who works in one of the warehouses, and he assured me the cousin could find your muslin and smuggle enough out to make the chemises." Gerard shrugged apologetically.

"They're absolutely lovely," Abby said.

"There's a fourth that's even nicer," Gerard said proudly. "It's embroidered top to bottom and end to end. But"—he paused triumphantly—"I gave that one to Elizabeth Hiscock last night."

Serafina froze.

"Elizabeth Hiscock?" Abby employed a not at all subtle tone of "please provide a justification for meeting a woman on a night you didn't return to your erstwhile lover's bed," a signal entirely lost on Gerard, who continued to beam at Serafina with pride.

"Yes, and I have every reason to believe she'll wear it tonight," he said.

"Do you?" Serafina said.

"She promised she would. I told her I'd be looking for it. I hope you don't mind."

"Duncan," Abby said pointedly, standing up, "could you help me with my clasp?"

"Jesus. Again? I thought we just did that—*Oh*." He jumped to his feet. "I'm right behind you."

"And I'll put on my chemise," Undine said, rising. "Thank you, Gerard. All in all, though, I think you'll find having your fortune read might have been easier."

"Huh?"

Undine patted him on the shoulder and exited.

Serafina's face must have shown her shock because Gerard said, "What? I thought you'd be happy."

"Why would I be happy about you spending the night with Elizabeth Hiscock?"

"Whoa! I didn't 'spend the night' with her. I

went to her father's house and threw a pebble at her window. It was a very chaste carriage ride—"

"Oh my God."

"She'll be wearing *your* muslin, Sera. That's the only thing that matters."

"Under the dress Edward had commissioned for her?"

Gerard's shoulders fell. "Yes."

"And you can't see how that might hurt me?"

"I-I can, but the word of mouth! Think of it, Sera! It's one thing to have you wear it, but to have—" He realized what he was saying and caught himself.

"The wealthy, respected daughter of a nobleman who hasn't chosen to destroy her reputation with an ill-advised affair wear it."

His color rose. "I didn't say that."

"You didn't have to."

A knock sounded on the door.

"Mr. Innes," a voice called, "there's a delivery for you downstairs."

"The carriage will be here in a quarter hour," Serafina said. "I'll leave ye to do what ye need to do."

Forty-five

SERAFINA SETTLED ONTO THE CARRIAGE'S CUSHION TO
wait for her companions. She'd never been much for
face paint or complicated hair arrangements and could
always count on being ready many minutes before
her female friends. The footman turned up the flame
on the lantern that hung near the carriage window,
bowed, and closed the door.

My sojourn into the world of the wealthy, she thought
with a wry smile. *I might as well be a traveler across time
myself given the distance between where I sit now and where
I shall sit in a few days.*

She tucked her skirts around her—Abby's skirts—
and stared into the darkening sky.

The door opened, and Gerard popped in, another
parcel in hand, this one considerably larger than the
ones that held the chemises. He banged the box with
his fist. "Driver, begin," he called and slammed the
door as the vehicle jerked into motion.

"What about the others?" Serafina said, startled.

"Let them wait. We need to talk."

The locks of his hair, golden in the lantern's glow,

hung like a fringe over the collar of his frock coat. He hadn't bothered to shave, which made her irrationally angry, and he simmered too, like a pot about to boil.

"You should have worn a plaid," she said sharply, though what she really meant was *Why are you dressing in the breeks that will please Elizabeth Hiscock and not in breeks for me?*

"Why?" he said. "What possible difference could it make what I wear?"

"You're a Scot."

"Edinburgh is filled with Scots who don't wear plaids."

"Not the Scots who fight for independence. Not the ones who cherish their country."

"Oh, for God's sake. Breeks worked well enough when you needed me to claim a cargo. And in any case, I'm *not* a Scot—at least not the kind you're talking about."

"Of course you are. 'Tis in your blood. Courage, stubborn determination, loyalty—and ye'd talk the ears off a donkey. Anyone could see it. Why can't you?"

"Courage?" He leaned forward. "If Scots are so goddamned brave, then tell me why you haven't asked if Scotland survives the vote."

He held her gaze until she dropped it.

"Because I already know the answer," she said, baleful. "If we survived it intact, you would have told me long ago."

He touched her arm regretfully, and she knew she'd been right.

"But I dinna accept it," she said.

"And there's that stubborn determination."

"And neither do you," she said. "Admit it. You

believe the future can change, and you'd like to be a part of it."

"Jesus, is that why you think I'd help?" He took her hands and squeezed them between his. "I'd do it, Sera, but it wouldn't be for Scotland. It would be for *you*. I don't give an Englishman's ass about the treaty except in the way it affects you. You told me you needed the cargo; I went for the cargo. You told me you need to sell the muslin; I'll sell the muslin. I'd do anything for you. And, yes, I do want the future to change, but not because of the bloody treaty." He collapsed against the back, the fight in him nearly exhausted. "I want the future to change because changing it might mean I could spend another day with you."

Serafina's throat dried. "The things you say…"

"Are the truth. Why did you call me here, to Edinburgh?"

"You know why. I needed a husband for the night."

"If that's what you called me for, then my time here is truly over."

Serafina's heart thumped. He was right. By all rights, she should be willing to let him go. *Should* be. Time seemed to be going even faster than the streets beyond the carriage window.

"I think that isn't all you needed," Gerard said.

"I'm quite certain what I called you for. 'Twas my wish, after all. I'm the one who should know."

"Maybe you needed something more. Maybe," he said carefully, "you needed saving."

"Saving?"

"Listen to me. I went to see Mrs. Turnbull today."

"*What?*"

"Sera, I know you're in bad straits. I know you're facing some tough decisions. But most of all I know you're…" He averted his gaze, searching for the words, and the heat blazed up her cheeks. "Sera, I was there. I saw the way Edward's brother and his wife treated you. I want to help you forget that. I want to take you where no one can hurt you again. Will you come back with me—to New York—to a place and time where none of it matters?"

He waited for her response and, getting none, added quickly, "I think it can work. Undine led me to believe as much. And if it can, I'm certain we can convince her—"

Serafina felt like she'd been slapped. "No."

"Pardon?"

"No. I willna go back with you."

"Why?"

"Why, Mr. Innes? I don't need to go to a place where it doesn't matter because it doesn't matter *here*. Not to me, and I had thought not to you. That is the most offensive thing you could have said to me. Thank you for your help. You've done everything that needed to be done and more. I apologize for the trouble I've caused you."

It was his turn to look as if he'd been slapped. "And we're done? Just like that?"

"I fail to see what more there is to say. Your service," she said tartly, "is complete."

He rapped smartly on the box. "*Stop.*"

"What are you doing?"

He leaped out before the carriage ground to its unsteady stop. "You can turn around and pick up your friends. I'll walk from here. With any luck, I can get Elizabeth Hiscock to cough up the location of the warehouse during the first dance. Then I can go home and everyone can enjoy the party."

He slammed the door hard enough to rattle her teeth, and she closed her eyes, trying to sort out the tangle of emotions—the red coals of anger that burned behind her eyes; the buzzing shame, like a cloud of bees around her; oh, and we mustn't forget the jealousy, that cold, black stone weighing down her heart. But more than anything, what she felt was the bone-deep sorrow of losing him. He'd seen her for what she was, and he'd been ashamed of it.

She managed to lean out the window to tell the driver to return to the inn before losing herself in tears. When she opened her eyes, she saw it—across from her, still on the bench where he'd been sitting. The parcel was large—it took up half the bench, and tucked under the twine holding it together was a folded piece of paper. "Serafina" had been carefully written on it in a neat script. She picked it up and opened it.

Dear Serafina,

When this idea popped into my head, I didn't know you and I would be saying good-bye. I don't know what I thought exactly. I guess I wasn't thinking at all. (Being around you can do that to a man.)

I've loved every moment I've spent with you— some more than others, and a few a lot more than others—and I can only hope that you felt some of the same joy.

You are a remarkable woman for the eighteenth century—Strike that. You are a remarkable woman for any year, in any century, in any era of the world. And, as you occasionally remark, I am in the position to judge. But nothing in my experience could've prepared me for you, just as nothing in my experience could've made me deserving of the time I've passed in your company.

I have no gift to give you but this. I hope, nonetheless, you will find it a helpful one. I've told you about the value buyers can impute to a product beyond the absolute value of its parts. Tulips, remember? As you are a merchant now, it's incumbent on you to create this additional value. Doing so requires faith. If you understand what intrigues potential customers about you and your product, then the tiniest push can turn intrigue into heartfelt desire (in the way a love potion from Undine can only work if a person is already inclined toward the other.) Note that I said "intrigue" not "like." Dislike can be exceptionally intriguing and can be turned into a strong like with the right push.

Of all the things I thought I might give you (and at one time the list was quite long), this lesson is the last thing I would have imagined. But in this world, it's all that I have. Please know that I give it with gratitude, admiration, and great affection.

> *Your friend across time,*
> *Gerard Innes*

Serafina's hand dropped slowly into her lap. *I give it with gratitude, admiration, and great affection.* She could hear his voice, see the earnestness in his eyes. This was not a man who was worried about her shame. He was a man who cared for her and wanted to give her something useful. She read the letter again, heart tight with regret.

With trembling hands, she loosened the twine and peeled back the paper. Immediately, a tightly packed heap of snowy white burst, wave after wave, from its bindings.

Muslin?

It was her muslin. She recognized the intricate patterns—stripes and dots and crosshatching. Then a tiny satin ribbon in the sea of fabric caught her eye, and another and another. A long line of bows had been sewn into the muslin. She lifted this curious length of tailoring from her lap and a skirt dropped to the floor—not just any skirt, a billowy, tiered marvel of muslin that seemed to fill the floor of the carriage and rise almost to her knee. The tailor must have used thirty yards of fabric. It was an ocean of gleaming muslin, and each pattern caught the candlelight differently, shining as if the threads had been polished by hand.

Speechless, she wrestled the chemise around to look at the front and nearly cried out in joy. Dozens of precise knife pleats ran across the low-cut, fitted bodice, one muslin pattern alternating with another in a pastiche of subtle, monochromatic textures, and this is where she found the bows. Each pleat was anchored under one arm with a tiny, white bow. The close-fitting capped sleeves were entirely sheer and the back nearly so. She couldn't see her fingers when she ran her hand inside the bodice, but the fabric emanated the faintest pink blush of her flesh. The knife pleats pulled the garment, just barely, from the edge of scandal.

It was the most breathtaking, gasp-inducing, attention-grabbing chemise she had ever seen—the chemise of a French princess or the wife of an Indian potentate. She loved it.

But would she dare wear it?

Forty-six

GERARD PACED THE EDGE OF THE DANCE FLOOR, HIS gaze sweeping the lines of men and women. He told himself to just get done what he'd promised to get done so he could get out, but he couldn't keep the memory of Serafina's words from his thoughts. He'd never wanted a woman the way he wanted her, and he'd certainly never put his heart at risk by exposing his feelings. He felt as if he'd exercised a set of muscles he'd never known he'd had, and now he ached from it. Jesus, would he ever recover from Serafina Fallon?

He'd been keeping a close eye on the staircase in the center hall, down which guests made their grand entrances, and as near as he could tell, Elizabeth Hiscock had not arrived, nor had his party, except possibly for Undine, who seemed to be able to materialize and dematerialize at will.

"Good evening, Lord Hiscock," a nearby man said in passing.

Gerard turned to see the man responsible for so much mischief in Edinburgh. Hiscock, who stood with his wife, was a wiry man with a granite face and the sort of calculating eyes he was accustomed to seeing in clients with no appreciation for anything but money. His wife, on the other hand, reminded Gerard of the talking wardrobe in *Beauty and the Beast* and looked entirely affable.

He spotted Undine moving through the crowd. She wore a green gown that shimmered like the scales of a fish. He hurried over and hooked her arm.

"What are you doing?" she said.

"Follow my lead." He led her to the Hiscocks.

"They know me."

"It doesn't matter."

"Lady Hiscock," he said, "so good to see you again. I trust you're in good health. Good evening, my lordship. May I introduce my sister, Undine, er…" He realized he'd never heard her last name, if she even had one. "Undine."

"Quick-witted," Undine said under her breath.

"Have we met?" Lady Hiscock asked, blinking at Gerard owl-like through her lorgnette.

"You wound me. 'Twas at the party last year. You remember, right after the musicians played? I am Bond, James Bond." He bowed. "I admired the tasteful glimpse of white at the hem of your gown, or rather, I did after my sister pointed it out." He nodded apologetically to Lord Hiscock. "But it got me to thinking: Why shouldn't the merest glimpse of a chemise please the eye? Should not even the most minute slice of a lady's life bring her pleasure? Well, my brother knows an excellent tailor—"

"We have a rather large family," Undine said.

"And together we dashed off some patterns,"

Gerard said. "The muslin is the finest I've ever seen, and, thanks to your inspiration, I do think we have created some very winning designs. Just the thing for the most elegant, admired gentlewomen in the city."

He elbowed Undine, and she lifted her gown to her knee, uncovering the elephants.

Lady Hiscock gasped. "They're enchanting!"

"Oh, I'm so glad you think so. We call this—and I do apologize—the Hiscock model. We will, of course, not use that name when we sell them."

"Why *wouldn't* you use it?" Lady Hiscock said, enthralled. "Did you forbid it, George?" she said pointedly.

Her husband shook his head, disavowing such an act. "I was never asked."

"You *must* use my name," she said. "And I insist on being the first customer."

"Oh, dear," Gerard said. "That's a bit tricky. I believe Lady Kerr is set to be my first customer. In fact, I may have to use all the current muslin I have. She's ordered five."

"What? No! I'll give you twice what she's offering."

"My dear!" Lord Hiscock said, shocked.

"I have my *own* money," she said. "'Twasn't *all* yours upon marriage. You seem to have no trouble spending money when it's warehouses in squalid little neighborhoods like—"

"Mama?"

Lady Hiscock started, but not quite as much as Gerard. Elizabeth laid her hand on her mother's sleeve. She wore the gown from Edward Turnbull, which Gerard had dropped off that morning, as well as the chemise the tailor had made out of Serafina's muslin.

Gerard, or rather Mr. Bond, had made her promise she would not tell anyone he'd given her the chemise. Gerard knew enough about seventeen-year-olds to know that meant she would certainly tell all her friends.

"I beg your pardon," she said. "Good evening, Papa." She curtsied and gave Gerard an uncomfortably warm smile.

"Bond, you'll have to excuse me," Hiscock said, obviously eager to extricate himself from the discussion of ladies' undergarments. "I have my guests to attend to."

Gerard nodded, ready to kill the girl.

"Will ye not introduce me?" Elizabeth said.

Hiscock waved his hand. "This is Mr. Bond. He's an acquaintance of your mother's."

Elizabeth curtsied and Gerard bowed. When she straightened, she met his eye and cast a knowing glance at the glimpse of muslin at her feet. Then she lifted the edge of her skirt higher…

"Your daughter is lovely," Gerard said, feeling the sweat break out on his forehead.

She beamed. "Papa, Anne Dillon and Catherine Alistair were in the orangery with Lord Finch and said he brought a sloth. May I go?"

Hiscock's gaze went to the dark sky beyond the windows. "Ladies should not go unescorted."

"Will you take me, Papa? Oh, Mr. Bond, have you seen a sloth?"

"No, I can't say I have."

"Oh, Mr. Bond, you must!" Elizabeth cried. "They're absolutely remarkable. Anne says they are a cross between monkeys and hedgehogs."

"Bond, if you're going," Hiscock said, "would you escort Elizabeth?"

She grinned. Christ, she was terrifying. "Certainly," Gerard said. "I'd be honored."

Hiscock excused himself, taking his wife, and Elizabeth threaded her arm through Gerard's. "I'm not afraid of the dark," she said matter-of-factly when they entered the hall.

"And here I thought you were afraid of everything."

She laughed. "You know me too well, Mr. Bond. Some girls wring their hands and throw a fuss. Not me."

"Fearless, are you?"

"Very."

He led her through the ballroom, past the couples joining in circles and lines, the violins lifting the room in a lively tempo, and into the center hall. He knew the best way to loosen her tongue was to surprise her enough to unbalance her.

"Do you have any interest in dancing, Mr. Bond?"

He said, "The only interest I have, Miss Hiscock, is—" But he was unable to add "pulling you into a dark corner and kissing you" because a collective gasp shook the hall.

Serafina stood at the top of the stairs. He would say she looked like an angel atop a Christmas tree if angels atop Christmas trees wore their undergarments in public. The many-layered skirt, like petals of a upside-down rose, stretched from newel post to newel post, and in the candlelight of the chandelier, the muslin's satiny trim became a sartorial aurora borealis, its flickers and gleams hypnotizing the room's enchanted observers.

Gerard hadn't seen the finished product, but he'd described to the tailor what he wanted and taken it on faith the tailor would meet his objective, which was to ensure Serafina had the most beautiful, eye-catching chemise of any woman in the British Isles. He'd given the man extra time to ensure the work was perfect, and Gerard's faith had been rewarded.

But he'd designed a chemise, *not a gown*.

Serafina met Gerard's eyes, and the corner of her mouth rose. It was a chemise, and dammit, she *knew* it!

The partygoers were both fascinated and aghast. Gerard could feel the mood shifting infinitesimally back and forth across the line dividing the two emotions, and he could see the elbows nudging, the looks being exchanged, the heads bowing in unheard asides as she made her way through the crowd. His heart ached for her vulnerability, and his fists twitched, ready to fight any and all who thought to offend her.

Someone whispered, "That's Serafina Fallon," and he wheeled to look at the sea of faces. The men were transfixed. How often does one see a woman as striking as Serafina striding into a party in a bedroom fabric, after all? The muslin was yin and yang, and Sera had seen that—innocent and knowing, covered and sexy, pure and...quick and dirty. There was nothing untoward to be seen, nothing at all, save the delicate roundness of her shoulders through the sheer white, yet in the men's widened eyes, he saw only collective and palpable fornication.

And he wanted to blacken the eye of every bloody, goddamned one of them.

The fascination on the women's faces was more

intense, and Gerard knew the next few seconds would determine Serafina's fate.

"She shouldn't be in the house of a gentleman," Elizabeth said under her breath.

"Why's that?" he said, unable to take his eyes off Serafina.

"She lived with her lover. 'Tis quite scandalous."

"I don't think this town knows what 'scandalous' means. I must say, she does the dress proud."

"Did you design that *too*?" Elizabeth asked, shocked.

"I did."

An attractive young brunette next to Elizabeth turned to Gerard. "You designed that?"

"Aye. In partnership with a tailor, of course. I sell them."

Elizabeth stamped her foot. "You didn't tell me you made gowns too. Look," she said to the dark-haired woman. "He made this for me." She lifted her skirt.

"Do you take orders?" the brunette said, adding to the woman next to her, "Look at Miss Hiscock's chemise."

"Several ladies have commissioned pieces," Gerard said. "That muslin's in short supply."

"But you can take one more order?"

"Or two?" the woman next to the brunette asked.

"Well, the dresses are rather costly—"

"Cost is no object to me, sir," said the husband of the brunette, stars and something more prurient in his eyes.

"Or to me," said the husband of the second.

Gerard said, "In the end, the garment proves economical, you see, as it can be used both for parties and, shall we say, more private events. And I encourage gentlemen to accompany their ladies to fittings. We offer private fitting rooms and want to ensure all customer requirements are met."

"Exceptional approach," the first husband said.

❧

Serafina had begun her descent, a cloud floating slowly, regally down to earth. Where was Duncan? Gerard wondered. She needed someone to anchor her journey, someone to deflect criticism, someone to keep her safe.

"Would you excuse me?" He shoved his way through the partygoers and met her at the bottom of the stairs.

"Aren't you supposed to be with Elizabeth Hiscock?" Serafina whispered, taking his proffered arm.

"Screw Elizabeth Hiscock."

She laughed. "Is that how all citizens of the twenty-first century solve their problems—with a vulgar dismissal? Or just the unimaginative ones?"

"You want to see imaginative? Get me to an out-of-the-way closet."

"Oh, indeed?"

"You realize that's a chemise, don't you?"

"Is it?" She looked down with mock concern. "Oh, *dear!*"

"I've already sold at least three."

"I figured a gown might attract more interest than a sliver of white at the bottom of a dress. And what better way to leverage my brand. I knew my disgrace would come in handy at some point."

"You definitely bring a fallen angel–sex goddess

aesthetic to it. I'm pretty sure you've blown away the adolescent fantasies of every man in this room."

"'Blown away'?"

"Destroyed," he said. "Replaced their daydreams of Queen Anne in a bikini with Sera Fallon sashaying into a party in her underwear."

"I dinna know what a bikini is, but clearly you've never seen a portrait of Queen Anne. Now, if you can sever your gaze from my muslin for a moment or two, I urge ye to recall we're here for a reason."

"Procreation, isn't it? That's what the Lord says."

"At this party, sir."

"Ah. Let me see... Where did the young Miss Hiscock get to? I'd nearly gotten the location of the warehouse out of Hiscock himself when she arrived and killed the conversation. To be honest, I'd prefer to wring that girl's neck than involve myself with anything lower on her."

Someone behind them cleared her throat. Gerard and Serafina turned to find Abby with a troubled look on her face.

"What is it?" Serafina asked.

Abby said, "I have a rather unorthodox proposal for you."

"No," Gerard said. "I don't care if the guy offers enough money for *two* ships. I refuse to let Serafina be sold to the highest bidder."

Serafina lifted her shoulders. "A quarter of an hour? For two ships? Let's not be too hasty."

"'Tis not quite like that," Abby said, clearing her throat. "Elizabeth Hiscock has offered thirty pounds for your gown."

"Thirty pounds!" Serafina's mouth fell open. "Tell her it's hers!"

"There's a bit more to it. She wants it now."

"Now?"

"Before any more guests arrive. She's willing to offer you another for the evening."

"Oh, she doesn't want me padding naked through the dining room?"

Gerard clutched his chest and closed his eyes. "My heart."

"Gerard—Mr. Bond—is to bring the dress to her—"

"Oh, I don't like the sound of this," Gerard said.

"—and she'll provide another dress at that time for Miss Fallon."

"Did she suggest a place I might change?"

"She did not."

Gerard smiled. "May I suggest the closest closet?"

Forty-seven

GERARD CLOSED THE LINEN CLOSET'S DOOR BY BACKING Serafina into it.

"*Oof*," she said.

"That's the least of what you'll be saying." He tangled his hands in her hair and kissed her hard. God, she smelled great.

"Are you sure the door's locked?"

He reached around and threw the bar. Then he spun her so her palms were on the door. She made a surprised noise that melted into a purr as he found her breasts. Firm and weighty, they filled his hands and then his head.

"Have you been had standing?" he growled.

"No."

"Liar." He took in the dizzying musk of her hair and skin. "I want you, Sera. As hard and as fast as possible."

She gasped, and he tugged her nipples roughly.

"Loosen the ribbons," he commanded.

As she did, he popped the buttons on his breeks, freeing his hardened cock, and watched the sheer fabric slip from her shoulder to her waist.

He lifted her skirts; found the thick carpet nestled at the base of her high, round mounds; and slipped inside.

The first thrust rattled the door.

"Too loud," she warned.

He turned her forcibly into the adjoining bare wall and pressed himself deeper into her.

"Oh, God," she cried, forehead resting on an arm.

He wanted to take the moment and pierce it so it couldn't run away. He wanted to hammer the thought of any other man from her head. He wanted to mark her in a way that the men who came after would instantly recognize. But every thrust mired him more deeply in his own emotions. He was like a man in quicksand, trying to get free and burying himself while doing it.

Damn you, Sera.

Harder he hammered, and she mewled and writhed.

He clasped her breasts and lifted her to her toes with his brutal assault. But she only screwed herself closer.

"You're mine," she whispered. "Serve me."

His knees were jelly. He wanted to end it—plant himself so far in her, she'd never forget him.

Then she slid away and turned, arching her back against the wall. She lifted her skirt and opened a leg.

He fell slowly to his knees, his cock aching, and kissed her. She fretted in the dark, moaning happily, and then she threaded both hands in his hair and stiffened.

Liquid, she slipped down the wall until she was on her knees beside him.

"Poor man." She clasped his sensitive flesh, teasing the tip.

"Have you heard the saying 'Don't stir up a hornet's nest'?"

"No." She stroked from base to tip. "What does it mean?"

He untied the final bows at her waist and the chemise fell to the floor. He tossed it aside, taking in what he could see in the dark of her in nothing but shoes and the bowed stockings that ended at her thighs.

"I'd pay a thousand ships to bed you and still have underpaid."

He pressed her slowly to the floor, lifted her legs nearly to her shoulders, and entered her. He savored each stroke, stretching the moment until the fabric of the universe seemed ready to burst. Then he let himself go and drowned in her arms.

The buzz of pleasure was slowly replaced by the noise of servants passing in the hall. He held her, sad and afraid of the ache of letting go. She brushed his hair from his face, and he could feel her mournful smile. Even without words, they knew they were lost to one another.

"The world awaits," he said.

"Aye."

❧

He left Serafina wrapped in a blanket, and the *click* of the door's bar behind him felt as definitive as the closing of castle portcullis, separating him forever from the woman he loved. When he rounded the first corner, he found Undine waiting for him, arms crossed. She regarded him coolly.

"Is that how you help her fall in love with Edward?"

"We were saying good-bye." He refused to apologize for it. He'd had enough of the white witch.

Undine took his hand, and he realized she was passing him a small glass vial. It had an orange tag loosely tied around its neck with string. On the tag was a hand-drawn heart with an arrow shot through it, angled toward the ground. A regular Cupid's Valentine.

"'Tis the potion you asked for," she said. "It's odorless and tasteless. Take care with it. The person who drinks it will fall in love with the first person they see."

Gerard opened his mouth, but she anticipated him.

"No, Edward won't fall in love with you," she said, "though it would work just fine if he were teetering on the edge of it. The person who drinks this will fall in love with the first person he sees for whom he is already inclined to be in love. For Edward, of course, that would be Serafina. He's a thoughtless fool, but I do think he cares for her in his own inadequate way."

Gerard stared at the viscous liquid. If Undine was right, and he had no reason to doubt her, he had the power at last to give Serafina what she wanted. However distasteful she might find a marriage to Edward, if she accepted his proposal—and Gerard believed he could convince her to—the potion would ensure Edward loved her, and Gerard could be certain she'd be treated with affection and respect, even if she herself was not in love.

And, as usual, it was as if Undine read his thoughts. "No. You cannot have another for Serafina. I'd never use such a thing on a friend, and in any case, she's not predisposed to care for him."

"I wouldn't use it on her either. For Christ's sake, I'd never betray her like that. I have her best interests at heart."

Undine didn't respond.

Gerard said, "She'll have money *and* a measure of independence."

"A measure of independence," Undine said drolly. "Every woman's dream."

The pain of the underlying accusation nearly undid him. "You know I asked her to come back with me. I asked her and she turned me down flat, so if you're thinking there's more I could be doing for her, there's not." He turned, but Undine caught his arm.

"Mr. Innes, you have proven yourself to be a true friend to Serafina. I owe you the courtesy of believing you'd act in no way to cause her harm. You've certainly earned my trust. Come to me when you've finished with Elizabeth and Edward, and I'll help you prepare for your passage."

Gerard took a step and stopped. "Could she have gone with me, I mean if she chose to? Does the magic work that way? Or did she already know from you she couldn't go and turned me down to allow me to leave without feeling guilty?" He was afraid his voice betrayed how eager he was for the answer to be the latter.

For the first time since he'd known her, Undine's cool exterior melted into sincere sorrow. "She didn't ask me, but she could have gone if she'd wanted to."

That's that, then.

With a heavy heart, he slipped the vial into his frock coat pocket.

He reached the door Abby had directed him to, the bundle of gown in his arms. He looked around nervously and knocked. Elizabeth opened the door.

"I have it," he said. "I know you'll be lovely in it."

He held out the bundle, and she pulled him inside.

"I'm not staying," he said firmly. The room was small, just a bed, a wardrobe, and a hearth over which a mass of candles burned, though a pair of French doors led to the estate's enormous gardens, visible in the moonlight.

She lifted herself on tiptoes and kissed him. His stomach roiled.

"You'll have to stay," she said, grinning, "if you want a dress to return to Miss Fallon." She turned and offered him the back of her gown.

"Is there not another dress here?" He gestured to the wardrobe.

She grinned at him over her shoulder. "'Tis not my bedchamber, James. 'Tis a guest room in a rarely used wing of the house."

He sighed and put down the parcel.

"I've never had a man undress me before," she said as he undid the first buttons. "'Tis rather pleasant."

"Don't get too used to it. Your father is a friend, and I respect him too much to take advantage of his daughter."

She laughed. "I don't think you're a friend of my father's at all."

He froze.

"Don't stop."

He returned to the buttons, wondering how he was going to extricate himself and a very naked Serafina from the estate. "Why do you think that?"

"I asked my father about you."

"When?"

"A few minutes ago. After you walked off with Miss Fallon. Are you two lovers?"

He unbent. "That's none of your business."

She reached behind her and undid the last buttons herself. "It doesn't matter. I like you anyway."

She slipped out of the gown, leaving only the thin muslin of the chemise he'd given her between them. "I'm cold," she said.

He slipped off his jacket and put it on her shoulders. Then he picked up the gown she'd abandoned. The fabric was a heavy silk plaid with threads of gold in the pattern of brown and cream.

"Are you in love with Edward Turnbull?"

"Edward *Turnbull*?" She laughed. "Hardly."

"But the dress... He evidently cares for you."

She gazed at him, confused. "I've barely spoken to Edward Turnbull. I know my father works with him, but I hardly know him."

"But he commissioned the dress for you." Serafina had seen the receipt at the tailor.

"No, he didn't. My father did."

Gerard gazed distractedly at the fabric, trying to unravel the implications of what she'd said. When he looked up, Elizabeth was looking at the vial.

"What's this?" she asked.

His heart stopped. "A potion. Give it to me."

She looked at him, a look of happiness spreading across her face. "Are you jealous of Edward Turnbull?"

"Elizabeth, give it to me."

"I will not."

He put his hand out, and she held the bottle out of reach.

"Elizabeth," he said sharply, "I don't have the faintest interest in you. I don't want to sleep with you. I don't want to flirt with you. I don't really even want to be your friend. The potion has nothing to do with you. Give it to me."

Tears filled her eyes. He reached for her, and she jerked away from him, knocking the frock coat to the floor. She grabbed the parcel and ran out the French doors.

He ran after her, but she had the advantage of knowing the garden better than he, and she disappeared through a hedgerow that rose above his head.

Dammit.

He turned to find a likely exit and ran down the first long side. When he turned again, he saw Lord Hiscock, talking with several guests.

Hiscock stepped from the circle when he spotted Gerard and waved his hand. "Mr. Bond, I must insist on a word with you."

Gerard swallowed and dashed in a different direction. He had to find the potion and alert his friends. He didn't know what alarms Elizabeth had set off in her father's head, but it would be best for all of them if he made a quick exit.

He ran toward the house and circled it, peering in each window for his friends, but the rooms were too crowded. He ran up the stairs to the entrance and nearly knocked Abby over.

"What is it?"

"Elizabeth asked her father about James Bond. He disavowed knowing me. I was a fool to have said I was a friend of his. And now Elizabeth is furious with me and he wants to talk—a very bad combination. We have to tell Undine. She may be in danger since Hiscock knows we're together." He shoved the plaid gown into her hands. "And get this to Sera. She's in the linen closet near the servants' quarters."

"You canna be seen," she said. "Hide near the orangery. We'll find you there."

※

Gerard waited in a dense grove of oaks, just beyond the glass building. Serafina climbed the gentle rise toward him.

"I'm afraid the sloth wasn't the only spectacle tonight," he said.

Serafina slipped her hand in his. "Undine says you're not to worry. Abby and Duncan are collecting the carriage. They'll meet us a half mile to the south."

"You look far more beautiful in that gown than Elizabeth Hiscock ever could."

"What happened with her?"

"Not only didn't I want her when she offered herself to me, I insulted her so badly, I suspect she may pick me off with a pistol next time she sees me—and she'd have every right to. I've completely lost my touch with women."

Serafina laughed, and it made his heart sing.

They padded through the trees and past the end of the tall hedgerow.

"Is that a maze?" he whispered. "It looks forbidding."

"You've never been in the center of it. It's a well-known place for liaisons. The scent of the roses fill one's head. The moon shines down. The world and all its problems are far away. Or so I've heard," she added with a smile.

"You've never been there, of course."

"Of course." When they reached the edge of the grove closest to the road, she said, "Wait. There's something here I want you to see." She turned him around.

In the distance stood Edinburgh Castle. Tiny fires around its rampart walls flickered like the halo of an angel.

"It's beautiful."

"Aye," she said with pride. "A striking contrast to what goes on inside. 'Twas never breeched, you know—till we allowed the English inside."

Gerard wondered if perhaps that's how she thought of her heart and Edward. "Why the fires?"

"I'd like to say it was for the soldiers who walk the curtain wall—'tis an English army post now, you see. In truth, though, the fires are rarely lit up. I suppose Lord Hiscock requested it to entertain his guests. 'Tis also his way to show his alliance with those who wish to take Scotland under their control."

The lights of the city, dim and scattered compared to present-day Manhattan or even present-day Edinburgh, still stood out like a twinkling galaxy over the black-purple hills. He looked back at Hiscock's house. Torches flickered around the enormous sculpture in the fountain at the head of the garden.

"Who are the figures?" he asked her. "I never got to see the fountain up close."

"Artemis and Adonis," she said. "Lovers. They're verra provocative."

"I've seen worse." He smiled.

He'd only been here three days, but the land and hills here already felt a bit like his. And he knew the reason why. She was standing beside him.

"Sera, there's something I need to tell you."

Her brows knit. "Aye?"

"I told you I talked to Edward's mother."

The same hurt flared in her eyes.

"I'm not going to ask you to come to my time again," he said quickly. "I-I understand that's not what you want…and I respect your decision even if I don't fully understand it. Mrs. Turnbull gave me a message for you. She loves you, Sera. No matter what her son says. She loves you and misses you."

Serafina's eyes began to glisten. Gerard pulled her into his arms and shared his strength with her. "And she told me how much Edward cares for you. She acknowledged his faults and says he's changed. And her one wish—her only wish," he added, lying most ignobly, "is for you to keep an open mind about him. Can you do that?"

"Oh, Gerard."

"For her?"

"He asked to meet me tonight, you know. In Hiscock's library. He has something to ask me."

Another proposal. A vise closed over Gerard's heart, but he reminded himself she would have a ship and swallowed the pain. "It would please Edward's mother so much if you'd forgive him."

He heard Elizabeth Hiscock's voice in the distance, in conversation with a man. Serafina heard it too. He wanted that vial.

"There's something I have to do," he whispered.

"Now?"

"Go without me. I can see the carriage from here. I'll be there in ten minutes, no more."

"Are you sure?"

"Yes. Go." He retraced his steps until he spotted the girl, a blaze of white in Serafina's chemise gown. She stood in a shelter of vines, beside a path on which party guests traveled in twos and threes. She was talking to a red-coated English soldier—a senior soldier if the gold rope looped around his shoulder was any indication. The soldier faced away from him, but Gerard could see him hand a flask to Elizabeth. She drank deeply.

The soldier said something confidentially to Elizabeth. She laughed again, and the man's hand slid neatly onto her lower back. He pressed her forward, looking over his shoulder as he did it.

They wandered on the path near Gerard, and he pressed himself further behind a tree.

They chose the path that led not toward the house but deeper into the garden. The soldier chatted about the absurd charm of the sloth. Elizabeth shook her head, "You are a wit, Bridgewater."

Bridgewater? The man who'd beaten Undine and threatened Sera?

He followed them, staying off the path to dampen the sound. When they disappeared into the hedges, he stepped from the trees, startling three men ahead of him on the path. He was nearly through them when he stumbled hard. An instant later, he knew he hadn't misstepped. He'd been tripped, and an instant after that, he was flung onto his back and the night went black.

Forty-eight

GERARD AWOKE IN A FOG OF PAIN. HE SMELLED SHIT, which of course could put him in a lot of places in Edinburgh, but this shit was a low note to the smell of straw and the sounds of stamping hooves and whinnying. He was in a barn, and a fire crackled nearby. Men were talking nearby.

"...off the ship and back to the ship. It's a foucking dumb show if ye ask me."

"He didn't ask you. No one asks you. Harrow? Cut me a wedge, aye?"

Harrow, a short, bearded man with a head the approximate shape of a mortar shell, was one of the men who'd followed him and Serafina through St. Giles.

"Get yer own foucking wedge," Harrow said, continuing to chew.

What time was it? Gerard could see the starry night outside a hole in the roof above him. He bet Serafina could tell the time just by noting the position of the constellations. He closed his eyes.

He heard steps draw closer and held himself still.

His stomach exploded, and he jerked into a ball, vomiting onto the cobbles.

Harrow said, "That's for the fount. 'Henry Dowling,' my arse. It's time for us to have a chat."

The man pulled him to a sitting position and thrust him against a wall.

"We're going to ask ye some questions, and if ye know what's wise, ye'll answer. If ye don't, we'll give ye the encouragement ye need."

Gerard could make out an enormous jagged scar across his interrogator's knuckles—as if he'd punched a brick wall. His mouth dried. The fire Gerard had heard crackled in a metal bowl beyond the barn doors. Two men stood beside it—the other two who'd followed them in the church. They were cooking hunks of meat on sticks.

Harrow swallowed and belched. "What interest do ye have in Lord Hiscock?"

"None," Gerard said. "I can't even begin to tell you how little. Wait—yes, I can. Imagine Hiscock is the size of the sun. Now imagine my interest in him is the size of the smallest thing you can imagine—say, your prick. That's my interest in him."

The man's eyes bulged like he were having an apoplectic fit, an effect Gerard enjoyed for the split second it took the man's fist to reach his chin. Gerard managed to turn enough to deflect most of the blow, but what remained was enough to make his ears ring.

Did Harrow and his stooges work for Hiscock, Bridgewater, Turnbull, or some combination? Gerard eliminated Turnbull. The man seemed too fastidious to have goons. They'd been following him and Serafina since before she'd ever mentioned Hiscock. Which left Bridgewater, the unhappiest answer of all. Bridgewater was not known for his mercy.

Harrow waited for Gerard to find his eyes. Then picked up a length of pipe in his gloved hand. "Shall we try again? What's your interest in Hiscock?"

"Hey, the guy's known for making money. I was hoping to partner with him on a venture or two," Gerard said.

The man clucked his tongue. "Known for making money, yet tighter than an otter's arse."

Gerard lifted his head, stunned. "You don't know then?"

"Know what?"

"Listen, boys, I have something you're going to want to hear, and you're going to want to hear it because it involves you."

Harrow cocked his head. The other two slowed their chewing.

"You're underpaid," Gerard said. "You know it. I know it. Your master knows it. Yet you're helping him help himself to more wealth than you could ever dream of. What did you move back onto the ship tonight?" They had to have meant *La Trahison*.

"Fabric, pepper, copper wire, dried fish, cotton, a bit o' wine," said the older of Harrow's companions, a breathtakingly ugly man with ears like chicken drumsticks and a forehead as flat as the cliffs of Dover.

Which sounds exactly like Serafina's missing cargo.

"Shut up, Bill," Harrow growled.

"The wine was blessed by St. Peter," the third man

added solemnly and threw another stick in the fire bowl. "Heavy as a horse's haunch too."

"Okay," Gerard said. "And what do you think he's going to sell all that for?"

Bill shrugged his shoulders. "A hundred pounds?"

"Blessed by St. Peter? At the very *least*. And are you getting ten percent for your troubles?"

"*Ten percent?*" the third man said. "Try ten shillings. And we had to pay for the wagon."

"*I* paid for it," Bill said to Gerard. "Cambers here never has a goddamned ha'penny on 'im, and Harrow dinna pay for nothin'."

Gerard said, "I can get you your ten percent, no problem. Know why? I am very well connected when it comes to that ship's cargo. In fact, I'm having a bit of a flirtation with the ship's owner."

"Jesus God." Camber's face twisted in horror. "Edward Turnbull?"

"No. The *actual* owner. A woman. Silent partner, that sort of thing."

Harrow snorted. "Never known a woman to be silent, myself."

"Ten percent, fellows. C'mon, what do you think?"

Camber and Bill were salivating. Their gazes went to Harrow, whose face betrayed nothing. He jerked a leather glove tighter over his fist. "What you propose is to rob our master."

"No, no, no!" Gerard said. "Nothing like that. The cargo master meets the buyer, tacks on a delivery surcharge. *Boom.* You get your money, I get my money. Nobody's the wiser. Why should your master keep it all? Sure, he provides the capital, but who does the legwork? Doesn't your labor contribute to the end result?"

Harrow rolled his tongue inside his cheek. "You know what it sounds like to me? It sounds like a good way to get killed."

Gerard's heart fell. If he was going to die, he really wished he could have done it after he'd told Serafina he loved her.

"'Killed'?" Bridgewater appeared beside the fire. "Such an ugly word," he said. "I prefer 'meeting one's fate.' Who is he? Did you find out?"

Harrow looked at Gerard thoughtfully, then at Bridgewater.

"Couldna get much out of him," Harrow said, "except that he intended to rob Lady Hiscock."

Gerard was impressed. The man lied nearly as well as he did.

Cambers offered Bridgewater a skewer of meat. Bridgewater waved it away.

"What do you want us to do?" Harrow asked.

Bridgewater looked around the small space. "Tie him up, put him in the cart, then go. I want to talk to him for a bit. Leave the fire."

Gerard's gut turned to sludge. Harrow quickly bound his ankles and wrists. Cambers and Bill carried him out and tossed him between some bales on the back of a wagon. Bridgewater appeared in the doorway.

"No money but a few coins," Bridgewater said, gesturing to Gerard's frock coat, which he'd apparently searched. "Nothing of a personal nature. Very unusual. No snuff. No watch. No papers. No knife. Just a small pair of pearl earrings."

Sera's earrings? Oh, why didn't you give them to her?

"But Miss Hiscock did show me Undine's potion," Bridgewater said.

Gerard's surprise must have shown on his face, for Bridgewater added. "Oh, come. You can't be new to Undine's tricks. You told Hiscock she was your sister, though I know she's not. The orange paper and labels are a bit of a conceit on her part. A trademark, so to speak. And a fornication potion of all things. What does it do? Is that why you wished to befriend Miss Hiscock?"

Gerard shook his head. "Fornication potion? What on earth are you talking about?"

"I'm not a fool. I saw the cockstand on the tag."

Gerard realized with a start that if the tag's heart and arrow were turned upside down, it would very much resemble an erection.

"I've heard of potions to increase a man's length and his ability to perform," Bridgewater said. "How does it work? I assume the man's the one who takes it."

"You disgust me."

"Elizabeth looked so forlorn at the orangery, I couldn't help but talk to her. When she mentioned you, I was intrigued. Hiscock had already told me you pretended to know him in order to befriend his daughter and sell chemises to his wife. What exactly are you and Undine playing at?"

Gerard didn't bother responding. It was his and Serafina's connection to Undine that had caused the men to follow them.

Bridgewater crossed his arms, regarding Gerard with deep curiosity. "Harrow said you were stalking Miss Hiscock and me. Are you a jealous lover? A chivalrous rescuer? A prurient Peeping Tom? You look too dull to be prurient, so I'm going to bet on rescuer. To be honest, I wasn't particularly drawn to the girl. Oh, she's pretty enough, I suppose, but I prefer them more seasoned."

Gerard began to work the knot on his wrists. The fibers had the tiniest amount of give.

"I told her I'd look for you," Bridgewater said. "And here I am. She's waiting in the garden's hedge-row maze. If only she knew you were just a few hundred feet away." He laughed and put the pearl earrings in his pocket. "I think when I return, I'll see if I can convince Miss Hiscock to let me try the potion. I'm not entirely sure what will happen, but I have the oddest feeling I'll enjoy finding out. And if I swallow that, perhaps she'll swallow something else."

Bridgewater had drawn close enough during this disgusting monologue for Gerard to reach him. He shoved his feet, heels first, into Bridgewater's knee, and the man squealed in pain.

Gerard rocked himself to the end of the wagon, but before he could roll out, Bridgewater butted him in the kidney and swung the gate closed, smashing Gerard's foot in the process.

"How far exactly do you think you'd get with your ankles tied?" Bridgewater said, wheezing. "Idiot."

Gerard heard an ominous clank of metal on the fire bowl.

"Do ye know what a malefactor is, Mr. Bond?"

The skin on Gerard's arm rose in goose bumps.

Bridgewater said, "When I was a lad, the men who stole or raped or sodomized were run out of town—well, mostly hanged, but if they had the funds to convince the justice to be merciful, they were run out of town. But before they were carted away, they were marked with an *M* for malefactor."

Bridgewater climbed up the side of the wagon and stepped lightly over the low wall. In his hand was a metal pole, red-hot on one end. He used his boot to press Gerard's shoulder to the wagon. Then he tore open Gerard's shirt and shoved the brand into his flesh.

An electric shock animated Gerard's body, and he screamed. The horses stamped their feet and the iron stench of burnt flesh wafted out on the night air. Then Bridgewater turned the pole around and cracked Gerard on the head.

❧

Gerard awoke groggily with two pictures in his head—Serafina's smile as she fell onto a pillow and Colonel Bridgewater tied to a flogging post. He hoped to God he would get a chance to make both happen.

Am I time traveling? Am I dead?

He closed his eyes and tried summoning Serafina in his mind—eyes, rebellious; curls, tumbling; the gown of transcendent white.

Don't leave me, he whispered.

Never. She shook her head. *I'll never leave ye.*

Will you marry me, Sera?

Marry ye? Why would I marry ye?

Because I love you, he said.

Pshaw. All men love me.

Because I'll fight for you, he said.

You and your advertisements?

Me and everything I am or ever will be.

She drew closer and looked, as if he were an image in a mirror fading into darkness.

It's me. It's me. Oh, Sera. I'm here. Don't leave me. Please, please, please, don't leave me.

Forty-nine

THE RUMBLE OF CONVERSATION MADE SERAFINA TURN, but no one was in sight. She heard it again, this time with bass and contralto parts, and identified it as coming from the hedgerow maze. She'd spent the last quarter hour searching the grounds and house for Gerard. She was terrified Undine's herbs had lifted him away before she'd even had a chance to say... Well, there were so many things she needed to say.

The talking in the maze was too soft for her to recognize the speakers, though the breathy grunts and surprised moans left little question regarding their activity.

Then she heard Elizabeth Hiscock's voice clearly. "Is this the way you like it?" Serafina's heart broke— for herself, for Elizabeth, and for Gerard, whom she had misjudged so completely.

What carried her through the turns of the maze, she couldn't say, for her feet felt like lead. She only knew she had to *see* the betrayal before her mind could accept what would come after.

With a deep breath, she turned the last corner. Poor Elizabeth Hiscock, clad in the infamous chemise, knelt on the ground, directly between a pair of naked booted legs, administering fellatio at an un-tender pace, her suitor's hands on her head.

The man's eyes were closed, and he was lost in his disgusting revelry, but all Serafina could register was relief.

The man wasn't Gerard. It was Colonel Bridgewater, still in his shirt and frock coat. His breeks and gun belt lay on the ground.

"Miss Hiscock!" she said sharply, and the girl must have bitten down in surprise because Bridgewater let out a roar and flung her away. Serafina pounced on the belt and grabbed the pistol.

"Go back to the house," Serafina said to the girl, and her tone brooked no disagreement. The girl burst into tears and stumbled toward the exit. "Wait." Serafina pointed to Bridgewater. "Do ye want to marry him?"

Elizabeth wiped her eyes, shaking. "What?"

"I canna recommend it," Serafina said. "He's a thoroughly despicable man, and ye don't have the experience to know, but a prick that size is going to leave you in a permanent state of unfulfillment. The man's an earl, however. One word to your father, and I can ensure ye you'll be a countess before the night is over."

The girl's bottom lip quivered. She eyed the blackguard, who was holding his shirttails primly over his cock.

"I do not."

"Good girl," Serafina said. "What's happened here goes no further than these hedges. Not from my mouth, not from yours. No matter what happens. The secret stays between us. Do ye understand?"

Elizabeth Hiscock looked from Bridgewater to the pistol. "Aye."

"Then go."

The girl ran off.

"I sincerely doubt you'll kill me," Bridgewater said.

"Why is that?"

"They'll hang you. The English army doesn't care much for the murder of its officers."

"'Tis not murder if I found you raping Miss Hiscock."

"'Twas no rape, Miss Fallon. Ah. You're surprised I know your name. You shouldn't be. After all, you made quite an entrance tonight. However, I knew your name well enough before that. You are involved with some very unsavory women—Undine the witch and Abigail Kerr. The report on their activities is on my desk, and if anything happens to me involving you, I'm afraid your friends will be under suspicion for conspiracy to commit murder. Lady Kerr deserves a comeuppance. But I would be quite sad to see my favorite fortune-teller locked away for the rest of her life. The soldiers tend to be, shall we say, energetic when it comes to handsome blonds."

Serafina cocked the pistol. Every nerve in her body longed to pull the trigger.

"You do realize I haven't primed the weapon," he said.

"Do ye think me a schoolgirl, Colonel? I know a primed weapon when I smell one."

He shrugged off the poor feint. "In truth, the powder may be damp."

"I'll take my chances."

A sheen appeared on his forehead. "Perhaps I'd do better to beg."

"Perhaps you might. Try it. I should enjoy listening."

Undine rushed in. "*Serafina.*"

Bridgewater let out a tiny, heartfelt gasp. "Undine."

"Leave us," Serafina said to Undine.

"Listen to me," Undine said. "Don't waste your time here. You're needed elsewhere."

"Why?"

"He's gone."

A chill went through Serafina.

"Undine the witch," Bridgewater said in a dreamy singsong voice, "the teller of fortunes and the maker of such lovely potions."

"What do you mean 'gone'?" Serafina demanded.

"I thought of you tonight, Undine," Bridgewater said, "when I brought Miss Hiscock here. I rather wish it had been you, not her, in that pretty chemise…"

Undine, who had been looking at Bridgewater, suddenly paled.

"What is it?" Serafina asked.

"Never mind." Undine pulled Serafina to a far corner. "Duncan heard a man scream," she said in a confidential tone, "and ran to the sound. He saw a cart being driven away. He ran after it as long as he could, but it outpaced him. It was heading toward the city."

"I should like to dress you in sapphires and silk." Bridgewater gazed drunkenly at Undine. "Then I should very much like to undress you."

"What did you drink tonight, Colonel?" Undine demanded.

"Drink? Whiskey, of course. A little sherry. Hiscock is too cheap for the finer stuff though. Oh, do you mean the potion? Oh, aye, I drank it. And I liked it so much, I drank it all. Was that pear I tasted? I imagine that's how you taste."

"Is he drunk?" Serafina asked Undine.

"Worse, I'm afraid."

"Where is he, Colonel?" Undine said sharply. "Where is James Bond?"

Serafina's worry turned to panic. "Bridgewater's involved?"

The colonel's face took on the most horrified look. "Oh, Undine, forgive me. I forgot he was your friend."

Undine approached him and laid a hand on his cheek. "John, listen to me. Whatever you've done, you must tell me, aye?"

He dropped his head into his upraised palms, closed his eyes, and began to cry. "He's gone, Undine. He's gone."

Fifty

THE CARRIAGE TOOK THE TURN SO SHARPLY, SERAFINA felt it lift onto two wheels.

"Remember Bridgewater can't recall what happened," Undine said to her. "Gerard could very well be at the Hollow Crown right now. Do not give way to fear."

"'Twill hardly help to kill her on the way," Edward said to Undine, whom he blamed for the carriage's speed, and put his arm protectively around Serafina. Serafina wished Mrs. Turnbull had asked for anything but this.

Undine didn't reply. Abby and Duncan, the other two occupants of the carriage, held their tongues but gazed at Serafina anxiously.

"One more turn," Undine said, looking out the window.

The carriage banged to a stop, and Serafina clattered out.

Fifty-one

GERARD CAME TO AWARENESS WITH A SLAP ON THE cheek followed quickly by another. He opened his eyes. Somewhere in the far reaches of his memory, he recognized the blur of a face.

"Stay with me now," the man said.

"Is he dead?"

"Aye, ye clot-heid. That's why he's blinking and moving his mouth."

"My sister's going to want money for the bedding."

"You may pay your sister from your share."

Gerard coughed and stretched. His shoulder throbbed and his wrists and ankles burned. He was naked and cold despite the warmth of a small fire. His mouth tasted of dirt.

"Where am I?"

The man he knew as Harrow answered. "A safe place—for now at least."

"And it's 1706?"

"*Och*, the man's lost his mind."

"Is it?" Gerard demanded.

"Aye, laddie."

"You rescued me?"

"You could say that. When the colonel finished with ye, we offered to dump you on St. Leonard's Hill."

"Is that where I am?"

"*Och*, no. You're in the house of Bill's sister in the city."

"Thank you for helping me."

"Aye, well, there was a bit o' debate on whether you'd keep your word, but in the end we decided 'twould be worth the risk."

Gerard blinked. Keep his word? Then it came to him. The ten percent. He'd never been so grateful for a service charge.

"Who doubted my word?" Gerard looked at Bill and Cambers, who pointed to Harrow.

Harrow shrugged.

"Well, thank you again." Gerard shivered at a memory of that burning brand.

"We didna do it for thanks. We want our money."

"Can you get it to us?" Bill inquired.

"I can. Can you get me to the Hollow Crown? There's someone I need to see."

Harrow groaned. "Bill, get a clean pair of trews from your sister's husband. I ain't helping a man this dirty through the streets of Edinburgh. I don't care how late it is."

∞

Gerard went up the stairs slowly, feeling a stab of pain with every step. Harrow watched him from the Hollow Crown's dining room below, and Bill and Cambers had taken their places at opposite corners of the building outside, to ensure he didn't escape. Gerard knocked, desperate to see Serafina, but too afraid to open the door.

The woman who opened the door was not Serafina, Abby, or Undine. It was a servant woman he'd seen his first night there.

"*Och*, come in," she said. "I was just getting the fires going. There's to be a small toast tonight—or so the note said."

"A toast?"

"To celebrate an upcoming wedding," she said, sniffing. "In the middle of the night! In my day, brides and grooms married in daylight. I dinna mind cutting up the cold fish pie, but fresh straw for the mattress seems coming at it a bit high—"

"Who's getting married?" Gerard asked.

"I would have thought you. A messenger came. That's all I know."

Gerard collapsed in the chair, undone.

"Will ye be wanting anything else?" she asked.

He waved his hand. "Go."

He wished Harrow and his men had left him on St. Leonard's Hill.

But you wanted her to marry him, he said to himself.

Fuck you. I wanted her to marry me.

He dragged himself to standing and walked slowly into Abby and Duncan's room. He slipped off the shirt and trews—too loose and too ugly. If Serafina were to be married to Edward, he would at least look present-able when they toasted the news.

He pulled off the second boot and stopped. On the table in the sitting room sat the half-empty bottle of

Kerr whiskey, the one Serafina had drunk from to call him here. What if wanting to leave was enough to make it happen? What if he could drink the stuff and end up in New York, drunk, numb, and memory-less. Wouldn't that be better than this?

As he opened Duncan and Abby's wardrobe, he saw himself in the mirror. The brand on his shoulder, a large *M* in a circle, was a pulpy black mess. The brand expert branded. He nearly smiled.

His hand hovered over a pair of breeks, once the most natural choice for his sensibilities, hanging in the wardrobe, but came to rest on a crimson Kerr plaid. He'd never seen himself as a true Scot before, but after the evening he'd just spent with Bridgewater, he'd never see himself any other way. He drew on a sark, wrapped the plaid around his waist as Serafina had shown him, and pinned the fabric over his shoulder.

Those English bastards damn well better prepare for what this malefactor put in their way.

The hallway door opened and the voices of his friends filled the sitting room. He limped to the doorway.

Duncan saw him first. The bottle he was carrying crashed to the floor. "Holy *shite*."

Serafina turned. Her face underwent a transformation akin to the birth of a star and almost as life-giving. Gerard's knees began to give way, and he remained upright only by clamping himself to the door frame.

Edward, whose arm she'd released, said, "Serafina," but she paid no attention to him.

She flew into Gerard's arms, and he pulled her tight.

"Get him out of here," Gerard said to Duncan, who needed no further explanation to usher Edward firmly out of the room. Undine and Abby wore a mixture of shock and happy fascination on their faces.

"Are you to be married?" Gerard demanded.

Serafina looked at him, shocked. "What? No. Why?"

"The woman who works here said there was to be a toast to an upcoming wedding."

Serafina laughed and pointed to Abby, who wore a wide smile.

"Ours," Abby said. "Duncan's and mine."

"Oh, that's wonderful," Gerard said. He pulled Serafina to him and kissed her, her lips more reviving than air. "I love you, Sera. I was so afraid I'd lost you."

When they could bear a small break in their desperate quest for reassurance, she said, "I couldna marry Edward, though he bullied and pleaded. I am meant for you," she said, swallowing, "no other."

"You are." He swung her into the light of the fire, watching the flames dance in her hair. "I know why you told me no when I asked you to go to my time with me."

Her eyes, so blue, turned as transparent as sky. "Why?"

"Because you could never love a man who wanted to save you by carrying you away from the battleground. I should have known better. You'd rather die condemned than live a coward."

Her eyes clouded. "You nearly broke my heart when ye said it. I know it's foolish of me—"

"It's not foolish." Gerard bent his head to hers. "I'm sorry."

"What happened?" she whispered. "With Bridgewater?"

"I was saved by three men who believe in the true worth of labor."

Duncan's brow went up. "Verra progressive."

"And I won't rest until I repay them for their help," Gerard said.

Duncan frowned. "How much?"

"Only ten pounds."

Serafina grinned. "Perhaps I can help. Between you, me, and Abby, we sold nearly seventy pounds' worth of chemises and frocks last night—and we have more ladies coming to the tailor today!"

"Though Lady Hiscock canceled her order," Abby said.

Gerard cleared his throat. "And I'm afraid you're never going to see the thirty pounds from Elizabeth Hiscock. I offended her rather badly."

"In fact," Serafina said, "she paid me before we left the party." Serafina shared a confidential smile with Undine. "It seems she had a change of heart, if not about you, then at least about me and the dress."

"Really?" Gerard asked.

"Oh, aye. I have a wee story to tell you about what happened after you disappeared."

"Well, I have a story to tell you too. I know where your cargo is"—he held up his hand to stop her question—"but before I tell you, the rules of chivalry require me to remind you that if you marry Edward, besides repairing your reputation, Edward will have the ship, which means you'll have it too. And Mrs. Turnbull hinted she may leave a bequest for you." Gerard staunchly refused to mention the bequest stipulation Mrs. Turnbull had in mind for her son so as not to give Serafina any reason to think Edward's affections for her were driven by greed. "But if you marry me—and I mean properly marry—I will have nothing and you will have a half share of that. Your reputation will improve only as much as being married to a penniless but devoted husband may permit."

Her eyes sparked piratically as she considered the two options. "You know what I choose, Gerard Innes. Now where is that cargo?"

He chose to interpret her declaration as one of love, especially given the warmth of her arms around him. "The cargo is on *La Trahison*."

"*Again?*" she cried.

"Yes, but if we take it," he said, "Edward's going to be royally pissed, and you'll destroy any chance you have of sharing in its ownership with him."

An irresistible curve rose at the corner of her mouth. "Screw Edward Turnbull," she said. "Let's steal a ship."

Fifty-two

"LET'S IMAGINE FOR THE MOMENT NO ONE HAD BEEN after us," Gerard said, standing in the ship's bow behind her and holding her arms out to her side like a *T* as the wind blew her hair, "and our walk through Hiscock's garden had taken us to the hedgerow maze. Would you have allowed me to make love to you there? Or even insisted?"

La Trahison cut through the water like a knife, and she smiled blissfully, making him very happy. He didn't even mind she still wore that brown plaid dress they'd thought Edward had had made for Elizabeth. The threads in it sparkled in the midday sun.

"You're asking theoretically?" she said.

"Aye, of course. It's not like I'm planning to take you back there some night after dark and sneak onto the property just to have you in the midst of all that greenery, your stockinged legs wrapped around my back and the moon casting a magical glow over us."

She gave him a narrow look over her shoulder. "It sounds as if this theoretical question has been thought out rather thoroughly."

"*Och*," he said, "you know me. I'm nothing if not thorough."

She pursed her mouth. "I would not have. I am not in the practice of taking gentlemen in the open-air gardens of noblemen I hardly know."

"So, you're saying if you knew Hiscock better…?"

"'Tis not what I'm saying at all."

He kissed her neck. "Not among the rosebushes and their heady scent, with me buried between your thighs?"

"*Och*, I shouldna care for the pricks."

And nibbled her ear. "Not in the spray of the fountain, with me making my offering to your naked Artemis?"

"I should have thought you'd prefer the offering being made to your naked Adonis."

He groaned happily. Many offerings on both sides had been made in the last two days. He'd found each one of them worthy of being enshrined in mythology.

With a pleased sigh, he pressed his hips against her just hard enough for her to notice.

"Is this why you insist on having us stand this way?" she asked, arms still outstretched. "'Tis very odd."

"And surely," he whispered into the warm tangle of her hair, "you would have succumbed to *some* suggestion in the heady scents of that orangery—"

"Oh, Gerard," she said, turning. "I still can't believe Colonel Bridgewater is in love with Undine. How powerful a potion was it?"

"Do ye not find me lovable?" asked Undine, who, as usual, had appeared out of nowhere.

"I find you verra lovable," said Serafina, jumping back to the deck with an agile leap, "and verra foolish. I canna believe you intend to let him woo you."

"There are things I can learn if I have access to his quarters and private correspondence," Undine said, unperturbed. "There's rot in the Scottish Parliament—and the English one as well—rot which needs to be excised. There's no chance I'll succumb to his advances—as we seem to be speaking of succumbing," she added meaningfully to Gerard, who reddened.

Serafina said, "I still don't understand how he came to be in possession of a love potion you made."

Gerard shifted. He'd told Serafina nearly everything, but not that he'd hoped to trick Edward into falling in love with her.

Undine shrugged. "I suppose somebody stole it from me—someone who is probably quite grateful he didn't end up using it himself."

"I don't like it, Undine," Serafina said. "Bridgewater is a brute."

Undine's face softened. "You are good to worry. But you mustn't trouble yourself too much. I'm well trained in the handling of brutes—though I wouldn't mind having someone as quick-witted as me to help."

"I know she's not talking about me," Gerard said to Serafina.

"I'm not talking about either of you. Wits aside, I wouldn't put either of you in such a position again."

"Well, I reserve the right to break a kneecap or two of his when you finish," Gerard said grumpily. "And I want Serafina's earrings back."

Serafina squeezed his hand.

"I assure you, Bridgewater will endure worse than broken kneecaps before this is over," Undine said. "I have my spells, remember. Speaking of which, I'm glad my spells have some limitations." She touched the ring on Serafina's left hand, the same ring that had caused her so much consternation the morning of Gerard's arrival.

The joy on Serafina's face matched the joy he was feeling.

"I am too," Serafina said. "Thank goodness Duchamps was willing to marry us."

"Even after we hijacked his ship," Gerard said. "It's clear the man's in love with you, which is why he threw away the note you'd left for me."

Duncan and Abby climbed the stairs, smiling at the happy couple.

"Duncan, I've been looking for you," Undine said. "Did you find that bottle of Kerr whiskey, the rather infamous one that brought Gerard to us?" She gave Serafina a look.

"You brought it here?" Serafina giggled. "That's playing with fire, isn't it?"

"I *thought* Gerard would be needing it," Undine said. "I left it among the medicine bottles I found in the case in the captain's quarters."

Duncan frowned. "The case stamped 'Inverness'? That wasn't medicine. That was wine, and the case went on the last ship."

Undine blinked. "Oh, dear."

"Where do you suppose it's going?" Serafina said.

"I think I know," Gerard said, "but give me three hundred years or so just to be sure."

"And Harrow and his men have their money?" Sera asked.

"Oh, yes," Gerard said. "Each has a pocketful—with

an extra share for Bill's sister. I think they rather like life at sea. We couldn't have made our way onboard without them."

"They certainly seemed to have outwitted Duchamps easily enough," Duncan said.

"If one considers knocking him on the head with a cudgel outwitting, yes," Gerard said. "I'm just glad he could do the wedding ceremony from his cot."

Sera made a long, happy sigh. "My life is perfect—though I suppose we'll have to return the *La Trahison* at some point."

"It *is* in Edward's name," Undine said.

Serafina gazed at the vast expanse of blue sparkling in the midday sun. "What will happen to him?" she asked meekly.

While her heart belonged to Gerard, he knew she'd never stop caring about her former fiancé—and he found that surprisingly reassuring.

"We may never know who was betraying whom," Undine said, "but here's my theory. Edward needed investors to make his last bet on cargo pay off. Hiscock and Bridgewater were happy to help. Shipping can be a good investment, and in any case, they could use the cargo to sneak in whatever they needed. I believe the three of them decided to have the cargo taken by 'pirates,' so they could pay off their investment with insurance money and still make a profit on the cargo by reselling it."

Serafina heaved a long mock sigh. "'Twas nice for a moment thinking of *La Trahison* as mine."

Gerard smiled. "I warned you. You had a chance to marry Edward and have this ship for your very own."

"Dinna worry," she said pertly. "I intend to buy my own ship. I dinna need Edward for one."

"And how is that?" Gerard asked. "By plying your considerable talents on the—*Oof!*" Duncan elbowed him hard enough to bruise a kidney. "I was going to say 'sea merchants' circuit.' She could hire herself out as a captain. *Sheesh!*"

Duncan grunted apologetically.

"No," Serafina said. "By plying my considerable talents—well, yours too—as dress merchants." She threw her arms around Gerard. "Thank you for your advertising. Between this cargo and the dresses, I'll have enough for a down payment on a small ship of my own soon enough."

"Which I can captain," Gerard said.

"Which you can advertise in your leaflets," she said. "And I can continue to assist my countrymen in their fight for independence."

"Just make sure the ship stays in Serafina's name," Duncan said to Gerard. "One never knows how long relationships are going to last."

"The only problem we didn't solve was the bribes," Serafina said sadly. "Undine said there was nothing in Hiscock's papers about how the gold was being sneaked into Scotland, and we've all looked through the cargo. There's certainly no gold there either."

Undine shook her head. "Don't worry. My colleagues and I won't give up till we know."

"I wish I could trade some of our luck for some for Scotland on the bribes," Serafina said. "With Scots lords willing to take bribes from men like Edward, Bridgewater, and Hiscock, I hate to have the fate of Scotland hanging by a thread—a gold thread, at that."

Almost in unison, an agitated wonder came over the group and their eyes fell slowly onto Serafina's gold-threaded gown. She grabbed a handful of the fabric and scratched at the pattern. She looked up, amazement growing, and scratched even harder. The threads of brown and cream began to fall away, leaving only the crisscross of gold. "It's metal," she said. "Not thread."

"The gold's in the dress."

"But why did Edward have it made for Elizabeth?" Abby asked.

"He didn't," Gerard said. "I asked Elizabeth about it. She said she hardly knew him. Her father had it designed for her."

"Lord Hiscock designed it?" Duncan said. "But he'd hardly bribe himself."

"No, but having the gold in the dress in his daughter's wardrobe meant he could access the gold whenever he needed it," Undine said. "And Elizabeth wouldn't notice a gown or two more or less in her collection. Hiscock has probably already discovered this dress is no longer in his daughter's possession."

Serafina's gaze swung instantly to the horizon. "They'll come after us."

"I doubt it," Undine said. "First, they don't know you know the gold is in the dress. Second, this is just one shipment. They probably have other shipments on other ships coming in. Third, and most important, 'twould be very unlucky for them for it to be known publicly that they're tinkering with Scotland's future. London may want it, but publicly they'll have to censure them. Bridgewater might lose his position in the army. Hiscock will be drummed out of Parliament."

"That," said Gerard, "is what we in the branding business call *bad* word of mouth. I sure hope they have a crisis management team in place."

Duncan took a protective step toward Serafina. "They'll come for the dress. Even if they think Serafina doesn't know what she has, they'll come for it. They might make a threat, trade Serafina's safety for the dress."

"The hell with that," Gerard said. "We'll go to them. If they're looking for a trade, we can offer them silence on the matter in exchange for the ship."

Serafina said, "I'll burn the dress before I'll give it to them."

Undine said, "If you'll give me the gift of your silence on the matter for the time being, I'll work with my allies to come up with a plan that is advantageous for Scotland and for you. We may help Scotland more in the long run by hiding our knowledge and continuing to allow Hiscock and Bridgewater to think they have not been found out."

Serafina met Gerard's eyes. "I can do that."

"If you can, I can."

"Come, Undine," Duncan said, offering his arm. "I require one final chance to talk you out of your Bridgewater plan."

"Jeez," Gerard said, rubbing his side when they were gone. "He's so protective."

Serafina grinned. "Like a brother, aye. I rather like it. The only relative I have is a cousin on my mother's side, up in Dingwall."

Gerard swung around so hard, he nearly hit his head on a spar. Abby was in a similar state of shock.

"Dingwall?" Gerard repeated.

"Aye. It's up north, near Inverness. My mother lived there until her marriage to my stepfather."

Gerard felt a strange prickling sensation on his neck, and he met Abby's eyes. He remembered all too clearly Duncan's story about his time-traveling red-haired grandfather having a liaison with the lass from Dingwall in a tinker's cart. "What color was your mother's hair? I'm curious. Yours is so beautiful."

Serafina's cheeks, always the window to her thoughts, turned pink. "Hers was blond."

"And how did she get to Edinburgh?" Abby asked. "It's quite a distance from Dingwall."

"What an odd question," Serafina said. "I believe a carriage was the arrangement she'd made."

Gerard let out a silent sigh of relief.

"But the carriage never arrived," Serafina said. "She took a tinker's wagon instead."

Gerard blinked. "I'll bet it was hard to sleep. With all the banging, I mean."

Abby covered her mouth to stifle a laugh.

Serafina regarded them both strangely. "That's exactly what she said. You two are acting very odd. Is something wrong?"

"Not at all," Gerard said.

Abby gave Serafina a warm hug. "It seems I shall finally have the sister I've longed for."

"And I will have a wedding gift to give you that fits my budget," Gerard said, "in the form of a bit of surprising news."

"I shall make my exit now."

Abby waved a good-bye and hurried off.

"Tell me," Gerard said, slipping his arm around Serafina's waist, "how much do you know of genetics?"

"Nothing," Serafina said, lifting a tempting brow. "But if the lesson is to be verra long, may I suggest the crow's nest?"

Acknowledgments

I'm especially grateful to the Dr. Rosalind K. Marshall, writer and historian, at St. Giles Church in Edinburgh, who happily answered the questions of a romance writer. Thanks as well to Mary Nell Cummings, who motivates me during wonderful coffee-fueled work-with days, and Madhu B. Wangu, Meredith Mileti, and all my colleagues at Mindful Writers, for the encouragement and friendship. I couldn't do what I do without the expertise of Skye Agnew, Susie Benton, Eliza Smith, Amelia Narigon, and Deb Werksman at Sourcebooks. Claudia Cross is my guide on this adventure and always makes me laugh, even when I occasionally want to cry. Lester, Cameron, Wyatt, and Jean: I love you.

Read on for an excerpt from

Just in Time for a Highlander

by Gwyn Cready

With a shriek of frustrated bloodlust, Duncan jerked to a stop as the crossing signal turned red. The musket-wielding French soldier he'd been chasing sprinted to the safety of the opposite sidewalk, nearly knocking down two young women carrying Macy's bags in the process.

Och, Duncan thought with irritation. *There's only one thing you can count on with Frenchmen: they run better than they fight.*

One of the women looked at Duncan and grinned. At six foot one with flaming red hair and a Scottish burr, he was used to being noticed. However, the kilt—his grand-da's from the Korean War—inevitably turned the looks into something more prurient. A gust of wind blew down Pittsburgh's Grant Street, and he palmed the wool against his thighs. Sometimes he wished he lived in a world where a man's bare legs weren't the object of such fascination.

"Reenactor?" the woman called.

He lifted his carved wooden sword and blank-filled

pistol and gave her a lopsided grin. "Battle of Fort Duquesne."

A roiling gray now edged the blue sky. Duncan hoped the storm they were predicting would hold off until after he was in the air tonight. He hadn't been home to Scotland since Christmas, and by all rights he should have skipped the reenactment since he could only spare a week of holiday time. But there were so few battles in North America in which the Highlanders had fought, he'd hated to say no. His grand-da was his last immediate family member still around, and the old guy was in his eighties. Duncan knew a visit was in order, and he fought off a wave of guilt he knew he deserved for putting the reenactment first.

The walk light turned green just as a band of Seneca warriors, bows drawn, emerged on Fourth Street. In this particular battle, they were allied with the French and therefore his enemy. Not only that, but their leader, a blustery fellow named Dylan, had been a complete arse the night before in a debate over rugby versus gridiron. The Senecas spotted him and Duncan's adrenaline surged. *Time to teach the old boy a lesson.* With a nod to the women, he lifted his sword and flew directly into the hail of rubber-tipped arrows.

God, how he loved a battle.

Two

"NOTHING COULD HAPPEN TO MAKE THIS DAY LESS perfect." Smiling, Abby wiggled her toes in the cool grass, happy that, for once, her clansmen had lost themselves in the joys of a late summer afternoon rather than in the potential it held for a clash with the English.

Undine smiled and shook her head. "That is an invitation to trouble if ever I heard one. Besides, do you not see those clouds? There is a blow coming to be sure."

"Bah. I have no interest in your portents, my friend. This is 1706. We have abandoned the world of superstitions, potions, and charms, or have you not heard?"

"Perhaps *you've* abandoned them. But there are more than enough believers among your clansmen and on England's side of the border to keep my coffers full."

The bodhran's beat echoed, slow and steady, across the field, and the tin whistle's seductive notes hung in the air like summer cherries on a tree.

"You are right, of course," Abby said. "And I would never begrudge you an income, though I cannot help but wish it were different. I tire of fighting their superstitions." She sipped Undine's velvety smooth pear wine. Undine was a renowned fortune-teller and conjurer. Pear wine was the least potent of her elixirs. "This is wonderful," Abby said, "but different than the last. What did you put in it?"

The corner of Undine's mouth lifted. "No more than you can handle."

Abby watched with longing as the young couples made their harvest dance promenades across the freshly cut field, their eyes aglow and hands held fast. That sweet, besotted time held a faraway charm in Abby's mind, like a childhood pleasure one had outgrown. No more than half a dozen years separated her from the dancers, but at times it felt as if it might be a thousand.

"Don't they just look as if they might burst with the pleasure of it all?" she said with a sigh.

"What you need is a dance."

"What I need is a man."

Undine's brows rose. "At last, something I can help you with. I know a lover's spell that will—"

"Not that sort of a man."

"A husband then? Of the two, I can tell you which I'd recommend."

"Ha! If I needed a husband, we both know where I might find one."

As if he'd heard her, Rosston Kerr, Abby's cousin and leader of the family sept that had broken from Clan Kerr in Abby's youth, lifted his gaze from the circle of men at the far edge of the dancing area and met Abby's eyes.

Undine sat up, inserting herself neatly between

Rosston and Abby, though Abby was certain Undine could not have seen him from where she'd been lying.

Undine drew up her knees, wrapping her arms around them. "Help me understand, my friend. You do not want a husband, and you do not want a lover. For anything else, I recommend a dog."

"But I have a dog, don't I, Grendel?" Abby scratched her beloved wolfhound's ears, and he lifted his head briefly and made a wuffle. "What I need is an agent. A strong arm. A fist. A mind possessed of ideas."

"So few parts of a man are truly useful, and you have not mentioned a single one of them yet. There is, of course, Rosston."

Abby grimaced. "And a will that lacks a selfish motive."

"I am intrigued," a voice said, interrupting. "Were such a man to be found, he would be the object of every free-thinking woman between Edinburgh and the Irish Sea."

Abby turned. A woman her age or slightly older with bright red hair, deep blue eyes, and an open smile stood behind them.

"I'm Serafina Fallon. I am here to seek help." She gave them an anxious smile.

Miss Fallon's hair had been pulled into an efficient knot but a few loose tendrils framed her face, and the contrast of the copper against the pale skin was striking. Abby was reminded of a Norse goddess.

"I beg you to rest easy," Undine said, standing to offer her hand. "I'll be able to help you."

Miss Fallon hesitated. "How can you know? You do not even know what I seek."

"I know what you seek, just as I know what finding it will mean to you."

Abby was not surprised to see Miss Fallon's forehead crease. Despite Undine's gentle air and willingness to help, she had a way of making those who sought her counsel uneasy.

Undine, sensing too late the impact of her words, said, "But, here. Join us. The wine is cool, the cheese is sharp, and the grapes, plump and sweet. I am Undine, which you undoubtedly know, and this is my friend, Abby Kerr."

"So you're a part of Clan Kerr then?" Miss Fallon said. "Your musicians are wonderful. I was told I would be well entertained here. Please tell your chief he has exquisite taste."

"I'll be sure to pass along your compliments," Abby said, giving Undine a private smile.

Undine handed their visitor a mug of wine. "Here. Sit down. Relax a bit before we turn to the business that brought you here. We were talking about the sort of men we would choose if describing them were as easy as finding them. I was just about to tell Abby my own requirements."

Abby gave Miss Fallon a smile. "This should prove interesting. Never in life have I heard Undine express the need for a man."

Miss Fallon's gaze went immediately to her boots.

"Ah," Undine said with a wry chuckle. "I knew you had heard of me. One can hardly be the whore of Cumbria without generating some sort of reputation."

"Do not let Undine mislead you," Abby said. "She is no more a whore than I am the queen of France.

Such a reputation is the blind behind which she hides her true profession."

"Which is…spell casting?" Miss Fallon said, with a note of both hope and uncertainty.

"Spell casting, aye." Abby smiled. "And other things."

"Oh, I am glad," Miss Fallon said. "For I, too, am in need of a man."

Undine twirled a lock of her pale hair. "Three lovely women, each in need of a man. If the Kerr clansmen had the slightest inkling, we'd probably be bowled over by the fiercest charge Scotland has seen since the days of William Wallace."

Abby laughed. "Hang on to your mug, Miss Fallon."

"I shall. Oh, but please call me Serafina." She took a quick sip of wine. "I'm afraid my situation might be a bit different than yours. I want a husband, 'tis true, but only for a night."

Undine choked, and Serafina flushed.

"The situation you describe is hardly unique," Abby said, and Undine added, "If we could only find the man uniquely hard for it."

Serafina whooped, then immediately slipped a hand over her mouth when two nearby clansmen turned. "Bah," she said under her breath. "Hard I have had. I cannot recommend it. Give me biddable any day."

Abby snorted, and one of the clansmen lifted a disapproving brow.

"You are a widow, then?" Abby said. But the look of discomfort on Serafina's face made her wish she hadn't asked.

"My fiancé left me," Serafina said flatly. "And the blackguardly bastard left me with a pile of debt so steep I can hardly—" She stopped herself. "But this is not the time. You have been gracious enough to invite me to sit with you. The ride here was long, and the wine and music are wonderful. Please, continue. I should consider it a great kindness to listen to something for a quarter of an hour other than the sound of my own complaints."

Before Abby could respond, she spotted Murgo, one of her clansmen, striding toward her. The way his hand rested on his hilt made her certain the day's pleasantries were over.

"I beg your pardon, milady," he said. "We have received a report of a party of English soldiers on foot two miles south of the Greenlaw Bridge."

Abby groaned inwardly. Colonel Bridgewater of the England's northern armies would not rest until the clans were obliterated. He was a prig, more concerned for his own glory than the safety of England's citizens. Men like that were dangerous—sometimes more dangerous than the most bloodthirsty opponent. She weighed her options. "Tell the men to gather in the field beyond the river. I will give my orders there. Everything here should be ended and the families taken to the castle."

He gave her a pained look. "I dinna think we need to go to such an extreme over a handful of English soldiers."

"Is it a handful or a party?" she demanded, reaching for her boots. "There's a difference. And even a handful of English soldiers can be the harbinger of something more."

"The clansfolk are enjoying your family's hospitality. Why don't we wait until the dancing is over?"

"'Tis *my* hospitality they enjoy, not my family's, and they may continue to do so within the confines of the castle, where they will be safe from attack."

A hint of rebellion rose in Murgo's eyes, but he held his tongue. "As you wish, Chieftess. In the field beyond the river, as soon as possible." With a quick nod to the other women, he hurried off.

The insolence. Abby felt the blood rise in her cheeks. He wouldn't have argued if he'd been talking to her father.

Serafina regarded her with shock. "You are the head of the clan?"

Abby would never get used to the surprise this caused. She felt like the cadaver of the three-eyed pig the surgeon in Coldstream kept on his shelf in a jar. "Aye. For nearly two years now. I want you to follow Undine back to the castle. Undine, will you please tell Bobby to bring me my horse."

Serafina looked at the growing line of men heading in the opposite direction. "Surely you're not planning to join them in battle…"

Undine snapped her fingers. "Grendel, come."

The music had stopped, and the men were dousing the fires. Mothers with babes were hurrying their children toward the castle, which stood to the east, outlined against the darkening sky.

Abby brushed the dirt from her gown. She wished she'd been wearing a riding skirt. She also wished she'd thought to bring a weapon. The soldiers' appearance was likely to be nothing, but no one would take Clan Kerr by surprise. Not while she was in charge.

By the time she reached the river, the men were

standing in informal lines, arranged by family, those
on horses in the back. Rosston and the men from his
family stood closest.

"I did not expect your invitation to include a battle,
Cousin," he said from his mount as she passed. Given
his height and the preternatural size of his steed, it was
like a bit like walking before Apollo.

"Let us hope it does not," she replied. "I shouldna
like to be considered an unwelcoming host. I thank
you and your men for standing with Clan Kerr." She
gave a grave nod to the clansmen at his feet.

"Never let it be said that the Kerrs of Linton do
not support their fellow Kerrs. We have not forgotten the old alliance." He bowed deeply, his blue
eyes sparkling.

The faces of her own men were bright with emotion. In a few, especially the younger ones, she saw
fear. In others she saw suspicion, though she did
not know if it was a response to her or the threat of
Englishmen a few miles from their village. In most,
however, what she saw was desire for direction from
the leader who would drive them into the fight. She
would gladly serve them in this role. Unfortunately,
it was Rosston upon whom their eyes were trained.

"We do not seek battle," she said, raising her voice to
be heard by those at the farthest edges of the gathering.

A few groans rumbled through the crowd, and
Rosston opened his mouth to silence the noise, but a
pointed look from Abby stopped him. *Dammit, where
is my horse?* She felt like a child, standing before the
men on their mounts.

"We do not seek battle," she repeated, "but we will

not tolerate an act of aggression by the English. Not on the Kerr lands. Not ever."

The men cheered.

"We must hope for the best but prepare for the worst. That is the only way. Are you ready?"

The sound of hoofbeats made her turn. It was Undine on Abby's mare, Chastity.

"Bobby had her tied at the gate," Undine said, dismounting.

Abby ground her teeth. Even the groomsmen denied her the respect she deserved. She took a deep breath to arm herself with dispassion, letting it wrap around her chest and limbs like chain mail. From her saddle, only a bow and quiver hung—no pistol. But she'd cut out her tongue before she'd let the men know her groomsmen had failed to prepare her mount properly.

She lifted a boot into the stirrup.

"Wait." Undine reached in her pocket and brought out one of the distinctive twists of orange paper she used for her magic herbs.

"Not this," Abby said. "Not now."

"I know you do not believe in my herbs," Undine said a touch hotly, "just as I do not believe in your war. But I have no doubt my herbs have kept you safe." She loosened the paper and touched a finger to the powder then ran it across Abby's cheek. "In any case, your clansmen *do* believe, and they like to see their chief so anointed. Look at them. They watch *you* now—not Rosston—every last one of them."

Undine was right. Abby could feel their eyes upon her. Perhaps the power of the concoction was not in the spirits it evoked, but in the belief. "Thank you," she said meekly.

"On the other hand, they may simply be imagining you without your gown."

Undine clapped her hands twice, releasing a puff of powder over Abby's head. Then she placed the paper in Abby's hand. "The rest is to be used for your strong arm."

"My what?"

"The man you seek."

"Good Lord, Undine. This is hardly the time."

"Nor is it meant to be used now. Keep it with you. When you're ready, sprinkle a tiny pinch in front of you. Dissolve another pinch in wine, then drink— only a thimbleful."

Abby could feel the odd warmth of the contents. "What's in it?" She began to open the paper.

Undine clapped her hand over Abby's. "Not here! Great skies, not with so many people around. Use it in an enclosed space, when you are undisturbed, with the thought of the strong arm in your head."

A dirty floor and an upset stomach were the only things Abby could imagine being the results of such an exercise. Nonetheless, she dutifully refrained from rolling her eyes and slipped the paper into her pocket. She put her foot back in the stirrup and mounted Chastity, whose large brown eyes shone with anticipation.

Undine said, "Be safe, my friend."

Abby nodded, grateful, and clasped her friend's hand. She might not believe in the power of Undine's herbs, but she did believe in the power of friendship.

With a cluck of her tongue, she geed the horse to

a trot, and the men fell in line behind her. Together they made their way through the forest, toward the rise from where they could view the Greenlaw Bridge.

"Pass the word to spread out," she said in a low voice to the man beside her. "But stay out of sight behind the trees. And let silence reign. So long as the soldiers stay on the road, we will not act. But if they raise their guns or leave the road, we will consider that an act of aggression. No one is to move without an order from me."

She knew what to say—had listened in awe to her father's battle stories a hundred times over—but from her mouth, the words sounded hollow and untrustworthy. How could clansmen used to being led by a man put their faith in her? Aye, she had negotiated a much-needed peace in the borderlands. But her clansmen did not value peace as much as they should, and now she was asking them to follow her, a woman untested by battle, into whatever happened next.

The men spread out as they'd been told. From her perch on Chastity, she could see the bridge, though the road on the farside, the road on which the soldiers were approaching, disappeared quickly into a vale below, hiding them from view.

She could feel the uncertainty of the clansmen behind her as clearly as she could the day's damp heat. A few men shifted. She heard a belch, some whispering. Moisture gathered on her back.

"Quiet," she commanded.

She had three dozen or more clansmen here, if you counted the boys, which she did, and at least as many swords, but they had less than a dozen pistols and even fewer horses. If the English soldiers were out on a harmless but misguided exercise, she would not jeopardize the fragile peace to make an example of them.

Damn you, Bridgewater. Why did you have to choose this of all days?

The muffled sounds of boots hitting the hard-packed dirt grew closer, and the faint scent of gunpowder that always hung in the vicinity of the English army stung her nose. By the noise alone, there were more than a couple dozen men—well more. So much for the reports of her scouts.

Her hands shook. She could almost hear her father's voice. "When ye confront an armed man, take his measure by his hand, not his eyes. Every man with his finger on a trigger has fear in his eyes or he's a bloody fool. But the hand of a man actually willing to pull that trigger is as steady as death. 'Tis the hand that tells the tale."

The first soldiers marched into view, and a palpable, untamed energy rose from the men behind her. This was the most dangerous time. One man could start a war that a thousand could not undo. The nerves in her skin flashed like tiny pistol blasts.

The English soldiers marched carefully, their eyes on their sergeant. Had the men miscalculated their location? To be fair, the Kerr lands sat on the border and the soldiers were only two miles north of it, but it would take a pretty piss-poor soldier to overshoot by two miles. Or was this a trick?

Soldiers continued to crest the hill, their well-shined boots and buckles catching the setting sun. Ten. Twenty. Thirty, she counted.

Her fingers jangled in the reins, dampness turning to raw sweat where flesh met flesh.

Forty. Fifty. Sixty. *Sixty*. Sixty and a few more.

Sixty soldiers. An entire *company*. Each with a musket. Clan Kerr had the advantage of position and surprise, but position and surprise do not prevail in the face of sixty muskets. What was this well-armed company attempting? Should she let them continue? Her mind raced through a dozen possibilities.

A twig snapped.

The sergeant wheeled in a circle and raised his musket, followed instantly by his men.

"Stop!" Abby cried and charged from the shadows.

"I am Kerr of Clan Kerr," she shouted. She stopped halfway between the soldiers and her men. "You have wandered over the border into our lands."

Terror thundered in her veins. Sixty-odd barrels stared her down, the great majority guided by hands as restless as hers, but at least one pair, the sergeant's, was immovable as stone. Her mouth dried.

"You have found yourself in the middle of a day of festivities." She hoped she'd spoken aloud, as the sound seemed to rumble around her head like marbles in a bucket. "My men mean you no harm."

She made a forward gesture with her hand, and the front line of her clansmen emerged just far enough to be spied. It was a Clan Kerr feint of long-standing to suggest many more men stood behind them.

"Attack!" a clansman shouted.

"*No*." Abby turned to her men. "We do not need to fight." Many clansmen had reached for their weapons, and the hands of her men were steadier than those of the English soldiers. Fearing what the next unexpected noise would bring, she pulled the twist of paper from her pocket and held it in the air.

The Kerrs gasped as one. They knew from whom the orange paper had come, and everyone on both sides of the border had heard the stories of Undine and her magic. What power they ascribed to this particular mixture of herbs, Abby did not know, but she hoped it was the power to end this confrontation without the firing of weapons.

She waved the paper again and her men retreated a pace. With her arm still in the air, she turned to the soldiers, and more than a few of them stepped back as well. Undine had earned her reputation.

"I repeat," Abby said, "we mean you no harm."

She did not order the soldiers off her land. She had learned early in her tenure as chief that men did not take kindly to orders from a woman. Instead, she prayed the sergeant would come to this idea on his own, though she damned the world for forcing her to finesse rather than demand action. Even the most plank-headed man would have an easier time of it.

Suddenly, something stung her fingers and she heard a loud *pop*. Someone had shot the paper from her hand.

For an instant, Undine's powder sparkled in the air like a tiny shower of Chinese fireworks. Then the world became a maelstrom of pounding hooves and musket fire.

❧

Duncan cleared the bench and raced through the park. His heart thrummed like an engine and his feet moved like Mercury's. He'd narrowed the distance between him and the band of Senecas to little more than thirty feet. Step after furious step, like a man-machine, he closed the distance. The ancient hunger for devastation squeezed his balls. He could feel it like a magnet, lifting him from his shoes and delivering him to his triumph. And if the Senecas made the mistake of running under the pedestrian bridge, they were done for. A company of English soldiers had disappeared under the same bridge a few moments earlier. In this battle the Highlanders and English were allied against the French and Indians, and as much as it pained him as a Scot to be on the side of his countrymen's ancient enemy, he had to admit there was nothing in his life as a bond trader that equaled the thrill of herding his prey into a wall of waiting redcoats.

Flirting with Forever
by Gwyn Cready

—————————— ❧ ——————————

Campbell Stratford hopes her biography of court painter Anthony van Dyck will give her the credibility she needs to land her dream job as a museum curator. One day, while doing research on Van Dyck and his successor Peter Lely, Cam is abruptly transported to Lely's studio in 1673.

Peter is intrigued by the mysterious newcomer who is definitely more than she makes out to be—but then again, Peter has strange secrets of his own. The uneasy friends become star-crossed lovers when the centuries part them once more, forcing them to choose which they believe in: fate or true love?

—————————— ❧ ——————————

"Entertaining and lively…will leave readers breathless." —*Publishers Weekly* Starred Review

For more Gwyn Cready, visit:
www.sourcebooks.com

A Novel Seduction
by Gwyn Cready

❧

When jaded arts critic Ellery Sharpe is assigned to write a praise piece on the romance genre, her ex-boyfriend and partner on the assignment, Axel MacKenzie, sees it as a second chance at love with Ellery.

Using classic romance novels, Axel gets Ellery to see the best in people, and that people can change—even him. Much to Ellery's to dismay, she finds that she's falling in love with the genre, and with Axel, who's taking his cues from those same books.

Will Ellery risk it all to make the leap from tight-lipped literati to happily-ever-after heroine?

❧

"An ode to the romance genre." —*Romancing Rakes*

For more Gwyn Cready, visit:
www.sourcebooks.com

Timeless Desire

by Gwyn Cready

—— ❦ ——

Two years after losing her husband, librarian Panna Kennedy
is reluctantly reentering the terrifying world of dating—but
she accidentally enters a portal through time instead.

Flung back in time to 1705 Scotland, she finds herself in
the massive library of her hero, Colonel John Bridgewater,
and meets his brother Jamie, currently accused of being a
Scots spy. Torn between loyalty to her hero from history,
her feelings for her late husband, and her blossoming love
for Jamie, Panna faces a choice that may alter the course of
time forever.

—— ❦ ——

"Romantic and wickedly witty." —Rachel
Gibson, *New York Times* bestselling author

For more Gwyn Cready, visit:
www.sourcebooks.com

A Sword for His Lady

by Mary Wine

A *Publishers Weekly* Top 10 Pick for Spring 2015

He'd defend her keep...

After proving himself on the field of battle, Ramon de Segrave is appointed to the Council of Barons by Richard the Lionheart. But instead of taking his most formidable warrior on his latest Crusade, the king assigns Ramon an even more dangerous task—woo and win the Lady of Thistle Keep.

If only she'd yield her heart

Isabel of Camoys has fought long and hard for her independence, and if the price is loneliness, then so be it. She will not yield...even if she does find the powerful knight's heated embrace impossible to ignore. But when her land is threatened, Isabel reluctantly agrees to allow Ramon to defend the keep—knowing that the price may very well be her heart.

Praise for Mary Wine:

"I always find the emotional and philosophical tugs of war interesting between Wine's characters. Her main characters are always admirable and there are always some true baddies to root against." —*For the Love of Books*

For more Mary Wine, visit:

www.sourcebooks.com

The Highlander's Bride

Highland Trouble
by Amanda Forester

Their attraction is forbidden

All Highland warrior Gavin Patrick wants is to get back to his native Scotland. But before he can leave the battlefield, he's given a final mission—escort Lady Marie Colette to her fiancé. Under no circumstances is he to lay hands on the beautiful, clever-tongued heiress…no matter how desperate the temptation.

Their desire, undeniable

Forced to pose as a married couple to make their escape from France, Gavin and Marie Colette find themselves thrown into peril…and each other's arms. As the danger mounts, so does their forbidden passion. But it isn't until Marie Colette is taken from him that Gavin is forced to decide—is he willing to lose the woman who stole his heart, or will he jeopardize his honor, defy his promise, and steal *her* in return?

For more Amanda Forester, visit:
www.sourcebooks.com

How to Seduce a Scot

Book 1 in the Broadswords and Ballrooms Series

by Christy English

———————— ❧ ————————

Determined to find a husband for his unruly sister, Highlander Alexander Waters strides into prim Regency ballrooms searching for a biddable English lord. To his surprise, his presence in the ton causes quite a stir, but in the process opens his eyes to the most beautiful woman he's ever seen.

Debutante Catherine Middleton is also on the prowl for a man to marry—a man with money, specifically. But when Alexander witnesses her preference in throwing knives over having tea, he knows the prim Catherine is as wild as the Highlands themselves…and needs a Highland man who can match her.

———————— ❧ ————————

Praise for *Much Ado About Jack*:

"Grace Burrowes and Amanda Quick fans will enjoy the strong ladies in the latest fun read from the ascending English." —*Booklist*

For more Christy English, visit:
www.sourcebooks.com

About the Author

Gwyn Cready writes contemporary, Scottish, and time travel romance. She's been called "the master of time travel romance" and is the winner of the RITA Award, the most prestigious award given in romance writing. Before becoming a novelist, she spent twenty-five years in brand management. She has two grown children and lives with her husband on a hill overlooking the magical kingdom of Pittsburgh.